Toward Her Passion

ALSO BY DANIELLE GRAINGER

THE DENTON HEIGHTS SERIES
Under Her Wing (Book 1)
The Shasti and Madison Story

In Her Cage (Book 2)
The Jaleesa and Tina Story

Within Her Grasp (Book 3)
The Marta and Shanice Story

By Her Command (Book 4)
The Rowena and Minjung Story

Toward Her Passion (Book 5)
The Rikki Carmichael Story

THE BERNADETTE SERIES
Wrecking Bernadette (Book One)

(S)mothering Bernadette (Book Two)

Becoming Bernadette (Book Three)

Desiring Bernadette (Book Four)

Loving Bernadette (Book Five)

Paperback ISBN   978-1-953734-41-9

First Edition 2025

9 8 7 6 5 4 3 2 1

Cover design by Sarah (Forcoverservice)

Published by:
Bibi Books Publishing Company, LLC

Dedication

This work is dedicated to all those strong people I've had in my life who have helped me navigate an often-scary world. I watched and learned from your actions—what you did and also what you did *not* do. Being strong in a world that continually tries to beat you down is exhausting, but having your shoulders to stand on has given me an advantage. I hope I am living up to your examples.

Acknowledgments

I need to acknowledge all those kind people who have encouraged me in my writing. Now that I'm retired, I thought I'd have oodles and oodles of time to work on my craft and become a book-writing machine. Ha! Now that I have time to explore, there are a lot of things to do in the world, I've discovered. I've met so many new and amazing people, seen incredible places, and experienced love and kindness despite the wave of hatred and ignorance that seems to be taking over parts of my personal world.

Breathe, everyone. This I tell myself on a regular basis. Thank you to all of you who help me breathe.

Thank you to my fabulous Beta reader, Jiske, for always saying, "Yes" when I ask her to read for me. She is a good friend, and I consider myself lucky to have her in my soul patrol. Olivia, as always, you're a godsend, and unfortunately, I'm giving up on understanding where commas go. I leave it up to you, my friend.

Table of Contents

Chapter 1

Rikki Carmichael gently released her client's chin and said, "You did well, Bob. Very well."

"Thank you, Mistress." Bob wiped at the tears in his eyes. "I—You—" He sighed. "Thank you."

"Always a pleasure." Rikki stood to her full height and, with a flick of her wrist, beckoned one of the ever-present dungeon masters to watch over her client. She handed Bob a small bottle of water, compliments of Dominique's Dungeon. "Drink all of this and then get another."

"Yes, Ma'am. I will."

And she knew that he would. Clients like Bob often came to her when they needed structure, guidance, and dominance. She tapped him on the shoulder, avoiding his red and pulsing back. Dominating submissives wasn't a full-time gig at Dominique's, just part-time, but she liked helping people release whatever it was that needed releasing. Bob's tension was palpable when she had walked over to him twenty minutes earlier. Apparently, he was stressed at work over something he didn't elaborate on. Rikki didn't want details, anyway. She only told him to forget about work and feel the physical pain of her flogger. That was all he'd wanted, nothing more than that, and Rikki was happy to oblige.

He took a swig of water, reached into the pocket of his neatly folded shirt on the bench, and handed her a twenty-dollar bill. "Thank you, Ma'am."

She took the folded bill and tucked it into her bustier. With the exception of private sessions in the back, it was customary to tip the Domme or Dom that serviced you, but clients didn't pay outright for services in the woodshed part of the club. They had an entry fee, and that was all. Dominique had to be careful and stay within the law, lest interactions like the one Rikki just had with Bob be considered paying for services. A tip, on the other hand, was different and within the law.

"Will you be here next weekend, too?" Bob asked as he took a swig of water, clearly trying to please his temporary mistress.

"Maybe I will, Bob. Maybe I won't." She grinned mischievously at him. "But if I am, I'll look for you."

"Thank you, thank you, thank you."

"Take care of yourself." Rikki nodded at the burly dungeon master who stepped in to take over Bob's aftercare.

Rikki headed to the break room in the back. Ever since Eileen left, she'd gotten out of shape. Doing short stints like this not only helped her get her impact groove back on, but it also helped pay the bills. Eileen, thank you very much, not only stole a boatload of cash from the coffee shop but also applied for credit cards in Rikki's name. So far, she'd charged thousands of dollars that those credit card companies were now demanding that she pay back. Her lawyer was working hard on her behalf with the companies, but it wasn't happening fast enough. And, to top it off, lawyers also cost money. With her figurative back against the wall, Rikki had called Dominique. The delight in Dominique's voice convinced Rikki she'd be welcomed at the dungeon, even as a part-timer. And she had been. The other Dommes beamed when she first showed up to work a few weeks ago. Their welcome was bittersweet, though, because they each gave her their condolences for her Aunt Matilda's passing in February, over ten months ago. Her aunt had been a beloved matriarch of the BDSM community, known by most, and their sympathy just widened the gaping hole in her chest from the loss. Not that Aunt Tilda had been her keeper, but Rikki wondered how different her life would be right now if her aunt hadn't had that damn stroke and died a few days later.

With a sigh and a vow to keep it together, Rikki plopped on the couch in the small breakroom. Starr, a late-forty-something career Domme, was sitting at one of the makeup stations, redoing her face. She must have just finished a private session. "Lace me tighter, doll?" She said to Rikki's reflection in the lighted mirror.

Rikki smiled. "If you'll return the favor." She'd felt her bustier top loosen up as she switched over to double flogging on Bob's back, buttocks, and thighs.

"Naturally," Starr said. "What's your stage name tonight, doll?"

"Robin," Rikki said. "Like Robin Redbreast." She smoothed a stray lock of her naturally red hair. She should redo her bun, too, apparently.

Starr chuckled. "Suits you."

Rikki grabbed the ends of the laces of Starr's corset and pulled. "Suck it in, girl."

Starr grunted but did as asked. Rikki made quick work and turned to receive treatment in kind. "Thanks, my friend."

"It's always good to see you here, Rikki. I mean Robin."

"It's good to get back in the groove." She rubbed her tired shoulders one at a time, stretched her neck, and then headed back to resume her rest on the couch. She'd go back out to the common woodshed area in another five, maybe ten minutes. She took a sip from the water bottle in her hand, hoping Bob was also hydrating after their session. The session seemed cathartic for him. She hoped so.

Years ago, her aunt introduced her to the BDSM lifestyle, and it had turned out to be just what Rikki needed to ground herself. Now at age thirty-four, well, fine, tomorrow she would be thirty-five, but now at age thirty-four, she knew the BDSM lifestyle to be more than, much more than, a way to get off sexually. Like Bob, for instance. There was nothing sexual about the impact session they'd just had in the public room. He needed physical pain to get those endorphins flying so he could get out of his own head. There was a delicate balance, though. And as a Domme for the last ten years or so, Rikki had learned to know and suss out that line between healing and hurting.

She took a breath and let it out in a sigh as she closed her eyes to regroup, hoping to calm her own inner turmoil. It lasted three seconds.

"You look so peaceful, Rikki," Dominique said softly.

Rikki looked up to see the matronly Dominique standing over her. "A bit out of practice, I think."

"Not for long," Dominique said, looking as always like the Domme in charge with her dark pants and tight leather vest pushing her ample bosom up enticingly. "You have a request for a one-hour private session."

Rikki sighed. She wasn't sure she was up for an entire hour.

"A woman," Dominique added.

Rikki's eyes lit up. "What does she want?"

Dominique handed her the small electronic tablet.

"Newbie, huh?"

"Yup," Dominique said. "Have a good time." And with that, she turned and strode over to Starr, handed her a similar-looking tablet, and said, "One of your regulars."

"Ooh," Starr said as she looked over the tablet. "He's an easy one. Basic humiliation."

Dominique chuckled and headed out the break room door.

Starr turned, grimaced, and said, "No rest for the weary, Rikki."

Rikki grunted as she stood up. "Guess not." Before leaving the break room, she turned and said, "Enjoy humiliating the male species."

"Always," Starr said with a chuckle.

Humiliation wasn't Rikki's favorite thing to do, but if it helped a client, then she would do it. Luckily, this new client only wanted a small amount. Beginner-level humiliation.

She opened the door to Private Room #3. The woman turned as Rikki entered. She was of average height but seemed fit and toned. Her button-down shirt was tight across her chest, revealing a small but enticing muffin top. Her loose chinos fit her well. Lesbian? Probably. Her short hair was a bit of a clue, but not foolproof. She didn't look scared, but she didn't look comfortable either. One arm hung stiffly by her side, with the other crossed over her chest, holding onto her bicep, effectively guarding herself.

Defensive, Rikki thought. *Apprehensive.*

Rikki wanted the woman to see her at her full five-foot-ten-inch height, amplified by five-inch heels, the red-laced bustier, and black miniskirt. Her naturally red hair was pulled back into a tight bun. Damn, she'd never fixed it. Oh, well. Madison called it her power bun. Funny kid. No, not a kid. Madison was a twenty-four-year-old young woman who was a *little*, so basically a grown-up kid.

Rikki's heels would come off once the flogging began. Flogging was athletic, and she wanted to focus on that rather than teetering on her shoes in front of a client. But first, the seduction.

"Why are you here, Caitlyn?" Rikki asked evenly.

"What?" The woman sounded surprised at the question.

Rikki took a couple of steps toward the woman. "Why. Are. You. Here?"

"I don't know," Caitlyn said. "I've never done anything like this before."

Rikki narrowed her eyes. The first statement was a lie. The second was not. Rikki made a mental note and continued. "It's okay to be nervous."

Rikki walked past the woman to a small table. She laid down the tablet with Caitlyn's requests face up, so she could refer to them if necessary. She wouldn't need it, though. She had a good idea what this woman needed.

"Some ground rules," Rikki said. "You will address me as Ma'am, Madam, Mistress, or Miss Robin. Failure to do so will have consequences. Do you understand?"

"Okay."

Rikki was in her face instantly.

"Yes, Miss Robin." The woman winced as she amended.

Rikki took one step back. "You catch on quickly. That's good. Maybe we can accomplish something today." She then went over safety ground rules, asking Caitlyn to acknowledge them, and, much to Rikki's satisfaction, Caitlyn addressed Rikki/Robin appropriately each time.

"Clothing is optional, of course," Rikki said. "I recommend we lose the shirt. That will be better for impact play. Lose the pants as well, staying in just your fundamentals."

Caitlyn chuckled lightly. "Fundamentals, Miss Robin? Sounds so old-fashioned."

Rikki grinned back. There was intelligence and a sense of humor in her client. Exactly what she wanted in a life partner. But…she was not shopping for one right now.

Caitlyn agreed to take off her shirt, and Rikki moved quickly. Caitlyn took a surprised step back and put her arms up in a defensive stance. Rikki took note of the posture and reached around the upright hands, unbuttoning the top button. Caitlyn lowered her hands, her face tingeing red.

Rikki smiled at her client and continued to invade the woman's personal space until the shirt was completely off. Rikki lifted her client's chin with one finger and said, "You have a beautiful body, Caitlyn. Toned. It's obvious you take care of yourself."

"Yes, Ma'am, I do." Caitlyn stood taller and unfolded her arms.

Interesting. The compliment had hit home. This was a woman who wanted to be noticed. And Rikki had noticed. She wished it had only been in a professional manner, but it hadn't been. It had been a while since she'd had a lover, and her body was taking notice.

Rikki instructed Caitlyn to remove her pants and fold both items of clothing neatly. Once the pants had been removed, Caitlyn didn't turn her back on Rikki; instead, she walked backward toward the chair where she'd been instructed to place her clothes. That was also interesting. There was something off here, and Rikki's gut told her to stay alert.

Rikki showed her the St. Andrew's cross, the large human-sized X mounted on one wall. She explained how the flogging would go and where she would and wouldn't strike Caitlyn's body. She explained the stoplight safeword system.

"Color, Caitlyn?"

Caitlyn looked confused for a moment, then seemed to realize what Rikki wanted. "Green, I guess."

Rikki pounced, pinning Caitlyn's back against the cross. "Forget something?" Rikki wished she could feel the woman's skin against hers, but Rikki didn't do that kind of thing at Dominique's. In fact, out and out sex was not allowed with the hired staff. Sex for money was illegal in most states, but clients could partake all they wanted to at Dominique's. And, besides, Rikki wasn't the kind of person who had sex with strangers, preferring to get to know someone first. Her body, though? It didn't care a flip about Rikki's or Dominique's stupid rules.

"Ma'am?"

Rikki backed off. "Always respect the dominant in the room, Caitlyn."

"Sorry, I forgot for a second, Ma'am."

"I'm the one who is going to tie you to this cross. I'm the one about to flog your skin. Best remember this."

Rikki pulled the wheeled table closer and grabbed two silk scarves. She tied one silk scarf to each upper branch of the X. These would serve as restraints. Newbies often said they wanted full-on leather cuffs, but Rikki was a seasoned Domme and knew when to break someone in slowly.

"Stoplight system," Rikki reminded. "Red means we stop instantly. Yellow means I stop while you decide what happens next. Green means you are effectively saying, 'Keep going, Ma'am.'"

"Green, Ma'am," Caitlyn said, a little smirk creeping up her mouth.

Rikki spun Caitlyn around, so she faced the cross. Rikki reached her hand around Caitlyn's body and splayed her fingers over tight abs. The feel of the woman's skin sent a surge of desire through her. Damn, she wished this were real. She pressed her front against Caitlyn's back, all in the name of the sensual package Caitlyn had requested. Still pressing her body tightly against the woman, Rikki pulled one of Caitlyn's wrists up and tied the silk around it. When there was no resistance, she quickly secured the other wrist.

The silk binding her client's wrists to the St. Andrew's cross was soft yet strong enough to keep her fastened tight even if she struggled. Rikki wanted the woman in her care to feel the helplessness of submission, and hopefully, she'd get there eventually. Rikki would make sure of it.

After securing both of Caitlyn's ankles to the cross with soft Velcro straps, Rikki maneuvered so she could see Caitlyn's face. Rikki grabbed the woman's chin and looked her directly in the eyes. "I don't think you know your place, Caitlyn." She flung the face away as if disgusted. She wasn't. It was all part of the game. Clients came to Dominique's Dungeon to feel something, whether it was humiliation, helplessness, or whatever. Being under someone else's dominance, if only for a little while, was liberating for many people.

Rikki still wasn't sure what to think about the middle-aged dark-haired woman who had requested Rikki specifically for this private session. She definitely wasn't like Rikki's usual female clients. Rikki typically serviced straight married women urged on by their husbands while the husbands watched. Caitlyn, however, had come in alone and had a definite sapphic vibe. Rikki couldn't know all the BDSM enthusiasts in the Cincinnati area, so maybe she was a newcomer or was traveling for business. Didn't matter to Rikki, though. She had work to do. Good work. Cleansing work, hopefully for both of them.

According to the list the woman had filled out, she wanted dominance, female dominance. She was okay with light bondage, light humiliation, and a beginner-level flogging. And what was also interesting was that she'd requested the sensual package on top of all of that. It sounded like she wasn't exactly sure what she wanted, but regardless, Rikki could and would deliver all of those things. Dominique's managers knew not to assign big-time humiliation seekers to Rikki, and as a guest Domme in the dungeon, they tried to accommodate her wishes.

Ah, yes, there it was, the slight pull on the restraints. Rikki caught the flashing look of defiance on the woman's face. Rikki was on her instantly, nose to nose. Her stern expression and one raised eyebrow told the woman that she'd seen the look and was not having it.

"Not used to being restrained, are you?" Rikki asked calmly. "It's time you learned what true submission is, Caitlyn."

Rikki backed off a little and watched as Caitlyn's shoulders relaxed. Slightly.

"You need to feel the leather of my flogger on your skin," Rikki said. "Oh, you'll resist at first. You'll want to call red and safeword out. They all do." Rikki's gaze remained locked on the woman's face, checking for signs of fear or panic. Every Domme worth her salt did this. So far, there were none. Even the defiant look had lessened, but not fully. Was she regretting her choices?

"But maybe, just maybe, Caitlyn is stronger than most," Rikki continued, referring to her client in the third person. Some clients relaxed more if it felt like Rikki was referring to someone else. "Maybe Caitlyn will absorb the pain, let it flow through her body, and release all that tension she's built up. Her skin will turn red and pulse with pain, but as Caitlyn works through it, she'll feel the shift." Rikki paused for a moment, assessing. "Caitlyn will eventually stop resisting. She'll know that Mistress Robin has her best interests at heart and will keep her safe. She'll realize that she can focus on her pain and use it. Maybe she'll even feel pleasure. Many do. I don't think Caitlyn understands that pain-to-pleasure connection just yet, does she?" Rikki didn't expect an answer and didn't get one. "Will she beg for more?" Rikki narrowed her eyes and then answered the spoken question, "Unknown at this time." She paused for a beat and added, "Trust takes time."

She caressed Caitlyn's cheek with the backs of her fingers. Caitlyn stiffened. Letting a stranger into your personal space like this wasn't easy. Rikki turned her hand over and gently cradled the bound woman's chin. Caitlyn had requested a sensual package, after all, so it was Rikki's job to make her feel it.

Rikki could be sadistic, but only if it benefited a client or girlfriend. But, alas, there was no girlfriend. Not anymore. The bitch took off with her money, leaving her scrambling to keep the coffee shop afloat and make ends meet.

Let it go, Rikki counseled herself silently. Caitlyn was new to the game, so it was best not to unleash too much of that sadistic part of herself.

As Rikki backed away, the woman's eyes strayed to Rikki's bosom, accentuated by the tight bustier. A slight sigh told Rikki the woman liked what she saw. There was a nervousness to the sigh as well. This was obviously a new experience.

Caitlyn looked up, her eyes searching Rikki's for something. Reassurance maybe?

Rikki leaned in close and whispered in her ear, "You're mine. To do with what I want." She paused to let that information sink in. "Within your limits, of course." There. Hopefully, that was the reassurance the woman needed for now.

Rikki wheeled the goodies tray closer so Caitlyn could see what was on it. There were blindfolds, gags, leather restraints, and handcuffs. There was even a black hood without eye cutouts, but none of these things would be used on Caitlyn this evening. They were props, plain and simple, to get her client's mind working. The flogger would definitely be used, as would the crop.

Rikki made a show of waggling her fingers over the delights on the tray as if picking out a favorite pastry at the bakery. She picked up the crop and whacked her own hand with it. The woosh and resounding slap made Caitlyn jump. Perfect.

Rikki gently tapped the business end of the crop on Caitlyn's shoulder blades, back, buttocks, and down to the back of her legs. "This is where my flogger will go. Never here." Rikki touched the crop head to Caitlyn's kidneys, then to the backs of her knees and below. "And never here." She touched Caitlyn's neck and head. She moved the crop between Caitlyn's thighs and tapped each side gently. "This crop will most definitely find its way here again." She pulled the crop back and whacked it in her hand again. Caitlyn flinched.

"Safeword?" Rikki moved so she could look Caitlyn in the eye.

"Yellow," Caitlyn said. "Red, maybe."

Rikki grabbed Caitlyn by the throat with one hand. "What was that?" Getting no response besides a panicked, wide-eyed look, Rikki tightened her grip. It wasn't enough to close Caitlyn's windpipe, not even close, but it was just enough to get the woman's attention.

"Ma'am. Madam. Mistress," Caitlyn stammered, clearly understanding the hierarchy in the room. "Red or yellow, Mistress."

"Color now?" Rikki moved behind her client.

"Umm," Caitlyn said and swallowed hard. "Yel—. Umm, green. Yes, green, Ma'am. I'm okay. I'm okay." The last she seemed to say to herself.

"Excellent." Rikki swapped the crop for the flogger and draped the tails over one of Caitlyn's shoulders. "Let us begin then."

Rikki stepped back and gently flicked the leather tails against Caitlyn's back. Caitlyn gasped. Rikki continued to be gentle, assessing at every step. She ran the ladder down Caitlyn's back, buttocks, and upper thighs. She came back up again. "Color?"

"Green, Ma'am," came the immediate answer.

Rikki's strokes increased in intensity. She stayed on the back for a while. "Ahh, yes, you're pinking up nicely. Very nice."

Caitlyn squirmed at the praise.

Rikki swished the flogger back and forth over Caitlyn's back, increasing the intensity as she got lower. Caitlyn's ass was round and fleshy, not fat, just…perfect. Rikki corrected her thinking. This was a client, not a potential lover.

"Mmm," Caitlyn moaned. "Good, Ma'am. So good."

"I'm enjoying myself, as well." Rikki stopped flogging, grabbed the crop, and tapped the insides of Caitlyn's legs. "Open." Caitlyn obliged and spread her legs wider. This she seemed to do quite willingly. Rikki almost laughed. Yes, she had an eager client. She tapped a little harder on the inner thighs, not enough to bruise, but enough to sting.

Caitlyn yipped at one particular stinging hit. Rikki smiled behind her. This was fun. Three more stinging hits on the inner thighs would give Caitlyn something to remember her by. She tossed the crop and snatched the flogger back up. She put more strength into each hit. Caitlyn squirmed. Her skin was fiery red and must be pulsing like mad. Back and forth, Rikki's flogger went. Yes, this felt so good. She'd missed this. She went up Caitlyn's body and back down, getting into an almost Zen rhythm. She went over the buttocks and thighs and back around again.

"Color?"

"Ungh," Caitlyn groaned. "Yes."

"Not a color," Rikki said, trying not to laugh. Caitlyn was reaching sub space, that delectable euphoric flying sensation that every sub craved, especially Eileen.

Caitlyn yelped. Rikki froze. She'd gone too far. Thinking about her ex had interfered with her professionalism. Damn it. Caitlyn's restraints were the only things holding her up as she drooped against the cross, obviously flying high. Rikki tossed the flogger, grabbed a silk cloth, and gently, oh so slowly, rubbed her client's red shoulder blades. The most contented sigh Rikki had heard in a long time escaped her client's body.

"Mmm, yes," Rikki said as she rubbed. "Let go, Caitlyn. You're okay here with me. Fly, fly, fly."

Rikki continued rubbing with the silk, then switched to faux rabbit fur. Caitlyn's moan was practically a purr.

It was time. Rikki moved in behind her client again and whispered, "It's okay to feel good." Her hand reached around and rested on Caitlyn's stomach. She pulled the restrained woman toward her, knowing the woman would feel the coarseness of Rikki's bustier and skirt against her inflamed skin. Craving flashed through Rikki. That spark of desire made her moan into Caitlyn's ear. Caitlyn's answering moan brought Rikki back to the present. Caitlyn was a client, not a lover.

Caitlyn strained to turn her head around, but Rikki leaned out of reach. "Color?"

"Green, Ma'am," Caitlyn purred, still a bit out of breath. "Will you kiss me, Ma'am? Please?"

"Oh, such urgency," Rikki teased. "Her first flogging and she becomes a needy little thing." Rikki released her client, whose obvious groan of displeasure made Rikki laugh out loud. "I'm not sure Caitlyn understands who's in charge, though."

"Please, Ma'am." It was a whimper.

Rikki ignored the plea and reached down to release the ankle restraints. Satisfied that Caitlyn could stand solidly on her own, Rikki put an arm around her again and undid a wrist restraint with one hand, a trick of the trade she'd learned early on. Caitlyn spun into Rikki's arms, her bra-covered breasts smashing against Rikki's clothed front. The look in her eyes was pure lust. "Please, Ma'am," she whimpered again.

Rikki didn't look at her directly when she undid the other wrist restraint. As expected, Caitlyn fell into Rikki, her balance not quite yet recovered.

"Come," Rikki said, helping Caitlyn walk over to a faux-leather couch. Rikki lay down first, pulling Caitlyn to her side. She reached behind the couch, found the sheet she knew would be there, and draped it over her client. Caitlyn snuggled up against Rikki, one leg draped over both of Rikki's in a possessive move.

"Ma'am?" Caitlyn said. "Will you kiss me?"

"Lay your head here," Rikki deflected and pulled Caitlyn's head to her chest. Rikki wrapped an arm around her client. "How do you feel?"

"Good, Ma'am," Caitlyn said. "I didn't know it would feel like that. I thought…"

Rikki waited an extra beat before asking, "You thought that BDSM was all about whips and chains and abuse?"

"Mmm," Caitlyn moaned. "Yes, Ma'am. I did, but I wanted to see." She cleared her throat and said, "I think I understand that pain-to-pleasure thing you mentioned before."

"Oh?" Rikki said succinctly.

"Umm," Caitlyn hemmed. "I just, I didn't know if you…Could we, you know, the sensual package?"

"The sensual package is just this, Caitlyn." Rikki stroked Caitlyn's arm and pulled a little tighter. "Closeness. Touch. Physical contact, but not *that* kind of physical contact. But it is perfectly acceptable for you to touch yourself, but I won't be holding or touching you when you do it. That is your choice. I can also leave the room if you need to take care of your needs."

Caitlyn grunted softly. Obviously, it wasn't the answer she wanted to hear. "Can we, like, maybe take this somewhere else? Can we have some fun later? When does your shift end? Can I meet you somewhere?"

Rikki stiffened. Damn it. She knew something was off with this client. She knew exactly what this was. Son of a—

Rikki needed to diffuse the situation and attempted to turn the conversation in another direction. "What did you forget, Caitlyn?"

"I can make it worth your time," Caitlyn said.

Dammit! It definitely was what she thought. Why can't anything be pure and come without some kind of price?

Caitlyn didn't out and out say she would pay for sex, but it was implied. She only needed Rikki to name the price, and Caitlyn would be able to arrest her and shut down Dominique's indefinitely. Rikki never accepted money for sex. Shit, she had to handle this right.

"You had a good session, Caitlyn, but it's time to end it." She nudged the nearly naked Caitlyn into a sitting position. "You have a much better understanding of what we do here at Dominique's, don't you?" She slid her way out of Caitlyn's embrace and stood up.

"Yes, Ma'am." Caitlyn took Rikki's offered hand and stood up, wrapping the sheet around her own body, clearly feeling shy.

Rikki pointed to Caitlyn's clothes and gestured for her to get dressed. Wordlessly, Caitlyn complied. Rikki, meanwhile, put the crop, flogger, and soothing cloths into the bins marked for cleaning.

"And you also, hopefully, understand, Caitlyn, that we do not cross the line here at Dominique's. This is not a brothel, cathouse, or a house of ill repute. Yes, BDSM can be sexual in nature, but it can also be transformative. I love helping clients like Bob, and maybe even you, Caitlyn. I help them find tension release from life's stressors. Stressors build up in the body, and it's like a cleansing. My clients have their boundaries pushed, and they discover strengths they never knew they had. Others find relief by letting go of control and being submissive to a safe and trusted Dominant. Control is tough to give up, Caitlyn, isn't it?"

Caitlyn nodded as she did up the last button on her shirt.

Rikki raised an eyebrow.

"I mean, 'Yes, Ma'am,'" Caitlyn amended, squelching a small smile.

"It's okay to give up control sometimes," Rikki said again. "And I'm sorry I have to do this, but I do." She walked past her client and pushed a red button on the wall near the door.

In less than ten seconds, Mel, one of the new female dungeon masters, burst through the door. Her broad shoulders and bulging muscles made her a formidable sight.

"You okay, Ma'am?" She looked toward Caitlyn and back at Rikki.

"Five-oh," Rikki said, nodding toward Caitlyn, who, by her body language and expression, knew she'd been outed.

Caitlyn merely nodded and headed toward Mel.

"You'll have to leave now, miss," Mel said gently. "As you recall from your waiver, Dominique's has the right to escort anyone off the premises at any time."

"I understand," Caitlyn said. "Just doing my job."

"As am I," Mel said and gestured toward the open door.

"May I have just one moment, please?" Caitlyn asked Rikki.

"Yes," Rikki said. "But Mel will be a witness to whatever it is you say."

Caitlyn nodded. "Figured as much." She took a breath and let it out as a sigh. "What you said about this being transformative? I get that. I do. I—" She paused momentarily as if trying to find the words. "Thank you for taking the time with me, even though I was here for other," she giggled and looked up shyly, "for other nefarious reasons. I understand better what it is you all do here. Thank you." She chuckled and added, "Ma'am."

Rikki's smile was genuine. "One question before you go."

Caitlyn raised her eyebrows in surprise but nodded.

"Why me? Did you think I'd be easy pickings?"

Caitlyn's cheeks flushed bright red. "No, Ma'am." She hesitated before adding, "Truthfully, I find you attractive. Your dominance with Bob was so gentle. I—" Emotion choked off her words, and she reached over to pat Rikki on one arm. "Thank you." And with that, she turned and walked out the door.

Mel shrugged and then followed the undercover cop into the hallway.

"Hmm," Rikki said as she wiped down the St. Andrew's cross. She tossed the restraints into the bin and headed back to the break room. She shook her head as she plopped on the couch. What a strange turn of events. But what did she expect? Her whole life seemed to be constantly turning. Her mother's death all those years ago led her to live with Aunt Tilda. And Aunt Tilda taught her about BDSM and loving dominance. That dominance and take-no-shit demeanor she'd learned from her aunt helped her find the courage to open her own business. It had just begun to succeed when Eileen entered her life and toppled everything. She thought she'd mattered to Eileen. Obviously not.

Rikki looked heavenward, "Give me strength, Mom, Aunt Tilda. I just…I just want to matter to someone."

Chapter 2

Rikki twisted her body to see the laces in the back of her over-bust corset in the full-length mirror. It was so much easier when a submissive laced them up for you. She pulled each strand systematically to tighten them, but gave up. Once she got to Dominique's, she'd ask one of the other Dommes to pull the laces tighter, but for now, everything was covered and secure. She loved how the dark green complemented her copper-toned hair. That's why Eileen had gotten it for her, at least that's what she'd said at the time. But that was back when they were together.

Yeah, that was back when Rikki thought she'd finally found the perfect submissive to her style of dominance. They'd been together for a year and two months or so when Eileen decided to take the money and split. She'd stolen Rikki's identity, run up credit cards, and taken out loans in Rikki's name. And that shit was still going on. She'd even poured salt in the wound by stealing some of Aunt Tilda's jewelry mere days after Rikki's aunt's passing. Rikki always thought she was a good judge of character. Apparently not in this case. Aunt Tilda had even warned her, saying Eileen would bring her nothing but heartache. She'd been right. The only saving grace was that Aunt Tilda had passed before Eileen's true colors were revealed.

Rikki closed her eyes and took a deep breath. Eileen had been out of her life for over nine months by this point, and Rikki still had trouble letting her go. She didn't know what hurt more, the thefts or the sham of their year and two months relationship. Had Eileen ever really loved her? Cared for her at all?

She groaned. "Stop," she said out loud to her empty studio apartment. The relationship was over and done with, and no matter how Rikki felt about that, she had to let it go. She let her breath out slowly, as Shasti had shown her, trying to keep her emotions in check. Eileen was the reason she had to moonlight as a Dominatrix down at Dominique's. Eileen was the reason she was in debt up to and beyond her eyeballs. But no, no, no, dammit. She couldn't let Eileen get into her head like this. What was done was done, right?

Rikki smoothed out her miniskirt, not too mini, of course, and checked her hair. Her long, wavy tresses were pulled back behind her head, instead of pulled back into her signature forehead-pulling bun. The thirsty men down at Dominique's would have to take her as she was. She sent a quick plea to the universe for at least one female client, one who wasn't a cop, of course. Maybe the universe could serve up a woman who wanted a flogging on a St. Andrew's cross or, better yet, a simple spanking over her knee. Oh, yes, that she could go for.

Despite being part of an undercover sting at Dominique's, Caitlyn the cop had been intriguing. Apparently, she and two male undercover officers found absolutely nothing to charge Dominique with, thank goodness. Rikki was glad Dominique's had dodged that bullet, but Rikki couldn't help noting that Caitlyn had been attractive. Desirable, even. Rikki had found herself responding to her client last night, and not just with her body. Caitlyn had been responding well to Rikki's dominance, fueling Rikki's dominant core.

Was it time to look for a new submissive? Should she scout out a prospective sub at Dominique's this evening? Maybe a play partner? She wasn't at all ready for a girlfriend. She wasn't ready for anything serious. Her best friend, Victoria, had a host of women at her beck and call, and maybe Rikki could do the same. Get one of those little black books with names and numbers of women she could call when she got a certain itch.

No. That wasn't her. She wasn't a player like her friend. A regular play partner, though, that might be just what she needed. It was her birthday after all. Shouldn't she get something, anything, on her birthday? Finding a willing play partner with no strings attached would be the best thirty-fifth birthday present ever.

Rikki laughed at the absurdity of her thoughts as she stuffed her keys and wallet in her overcoat pocket. She hated having to cover her outfit with the heavy coat, but winter was upon them, and December could be frigid in her chosen hometown of Denton Heights, Ohio.

She headed for the door to her apartment above the coffee shop, but stopped when the phone in her hand dinged with an incoming text. Shoot, did Lydia need something down in the shop? She looked at her phone. It wasn't Lydia. It was her other bestie, Shasti Balakrishnan.

> SHASTI: Madison and I are here. Come downstairs for
> a minute.

Rikki growled, not at her friend, but at the fact that a visit would delay her drive to the dungeon.

> RIKKI: Come up. Cut through my office. Lydia can let
> you in.

> SHASTI: Madison wants to show you something. Come
> on down. Just for a bit.

Rikki frowned. How long is a 'bit'? She couldn't show up in the coffee shop in her Domme regalia. It wouldn't be good for business if the owner showed up in fetish gear, would it? And why were they at the shop so late? It was pretty much closing time. She muttered under her breath as she took off her heavy coat, put leggings underneath her miniskirt, and threw a loose sweater over her corset. Satisfied that she wouldn't raise eyebrows, she headed out the door and down the stairs into her office. Thank God the shop should be fairly empty of customers at that point.

She checked her watch as she stepped into her office. She was okay. She could spare a few minutes. Shasti and Madison were good friends. Besties, even.

She opened the door to the shop.

"Surprise!" came the onslaught of voices. This was followed by the Happy Birthday song. Madison flew into Rikki's arms for a hug.

"I hope you're having a good day on your born day, Miss Rikki," the twenty-four-year-old Madison gushed. Her typically fly-away hair had been neatly pulled back into two pigtails, the obvious work from Shasti, her Mommy Domme.

Rikki tapped Madison on the nose and whispered, "I am now." To that, Madison leaped in the air and did several pirouettes while announcing that they had a cookie cake her Mistress let her pick out from the Queen City Bakery.

"I can't wait," Rikki said to Shasti's *little*.

Shasti sidled up to her side. She gestured toward their gathered friends eagerly waiting to greet the birthday girl and said, "We all wanted to do this for you, Rikki. We know this has been a tough year for you."

"It has." Rikki tried not to let the angst show on her face. "What an amazing support system I have in my life." And she did. She just had to remember that. No one except a small handful, which included Shasti, knew about her financial troubles and the fact that she had to work a full day in the coffee shop and then moonlight at the dungeon on the outskirts of Cincinnati to make ends meet.

"Enjoy the moment, Rikki," Shasti said, not quite scolding, but definitely advising. Shasti was a Mommy Domme and sometimes included Rikki in that mothering, even though Shasti was a year and a half younger at thirty-three.

"I will. I will, but I have to, uh, call Dominique to tell her I'll be late."

"Ahh," Shasti said knowingly. "I was wondering about the—" She gestured to the miniskirt.

"Mm hmm," Rikki said, tight-lipped. "Gotta try to keep this place afloat."

Shasti moved out of the way so Rikki could dive into the office to make her call.

"She'll be right back, everybody," Shasti called out to the gathering of friends. "How about some music?"

Rikki smiled. That would be Madison's cue, no doubt. The young woman was full of talent in so many ways. And to think she grew up in a family that didn't value or encourage her in anything. "But she has us now," Rikki murmured as she closed the door to her office.

She made quick work of her call. Dominique said she'd be okay if Rikki didn't want to come in at all, seeing as it was her birthday. Rikki assured her she'd be there, but maybe an hour or so later than planned.

Once Rikki stepped back out of the office, she was bombarded with well-wishers.

Lydia, her assistant manager and very first hire over three years ago, stepped up. "Got the customers out in a timely fashion, Boss."

Rikki rubbed Lydia's upper arm. "Thank you. You run a good ship."

Lydia just laughed and said, "It's your ship, Captain. I just do as I'm told." She laughed again, took three steps back, then turned to coordinate the coffee shop crew as they cleaned up and prepared for the morning.

"You finally caught up to me," Victoria said, referring to Rikki's age. She clapped Rikki on the back. "Happy birthday, my friend."

"Thanks, Vic," Rikki said. "No date?"

"Nah." Victoria was a well-sought-after Domme in the Denton Heights and Cincinnati BDSM scenes. She, Shasti, and Rikki had been molded under Aunt Tilda's guidance. Aunt Tilda called them her three treasures. "Sometimes I need a break from all those women throwing themselves at me."

Rikki burst out laughing, even though Victoria's words were very true. She shook her head and said, "What would we do without our resident sub-slayer?"

Victoria's perpetual single status made Rikki wonder if that might be the way to go. Forget trying to find true love. Just go for the temporary high of dominating women you didn't have to take care of for long. She scoffed. That wasn't her.

"You okay?" Vic asked quietly.

"Yeah, yeah," Rikki said, knowing she didn't sound convincing. In an attempt to deflect Victoria's concern, she gestured toward the table where there was some kind of punch in a bowl and the cookie cake. "Thanks for coming this evening."

"I've got your back, friend," Vic said, punched Rikki lightly in the arm, and moved away. "Whatever you need."

Rikki nodded as her friend walked away.

A non-alcoholic punch was delivered to her by one of the resident *littles*, and then a stream of friends wished her well and congratulated her on completing another year on the planet. A candle was thrust into the center of the cookie cake, the birthday song was sung again, and Rikki was obliged to make a silent wish as she blew out the lone candle.

She could have wished for a thousand things, but what she was really missing was someone to hold, someone who was hers. So that's what she wished for—companionship in whatever form the universe could provide. Whether it was one session, a night, or a lifetime, she'd leave it up to the powers that be. She had to. She didn't seem to have any control over much of her life at the moment.

"I hope it was a good wish, Miss Rikki," Madison said. Her hopeful look momentarily pulled Rikki out of her doldrums.

"You made it special, Madison," Rikki said and pulled the *little* into a quick hug. "Thank you."

"Course," Madison said, wiggling from side to side. "Can I ask you something, Miss Rikki?"

"Of course." Rikki desperately wanted to check her watch, but she didn't. Right now, her priorities were with the young woman by her side.

"It's kind of private, though." Madison glanced toward an empty table away from the group.

"Sounds serious." Rikki gestured for Madison to lead the way. Behind Madison's back, she shrugged at Shasti, who had raised her head and furrowed her brow in obvious question.

"What do you do, umm…" Madison said as she sat with her back to the rest of their friends. She often did that so her ADHD wouldn't distract her from whatever task was at hand.

"Go on."

"Well," Madison sighed and bit her lower lip. "Okay, so sometimes when we play, it gets kind of weird, and then I pretend that I don't notice or whatever, but change the situation if I can. But it's…I don't like it."

Rikki had no idea what Madison was referring to. "Have you talked to Miss Shasti about your concerns? If she's doing something that's uncomfortable for you, you absolutely must speak up. You understand that every submissive has a voice and a right to be heard. Miss Shasti takes care of you, but you have to be responsible for yourself."

"Huh?" Madison said. Her expression almost made Rikki laugh. The young woman seemed as perplexed as Rikki was. Madison looked off into space for a moment. "Oh. No, Miss Rikki," she said and leaned in closer. "I'm talking about Billy. Not Mistress."

"Oh, oh, oh. What's happening with Billy?"

Rikki's heart almost broke as Madison whispered what had been happening. Apparently, Billy, another *little* in the community and Madison's bestie, had recently become sexually aroused around Madison.

"When we wrestle," Madison added, "I can feel his thing, his hard thing." Madison swallowed, trying to hold back tears. "It's like he wants me to feel it. I don't like boys in that way. He knows that. And Mistress is my person." She looked up, almost pleading, "Miss Rikki, I don't…"

"Come here." Rikki stood up and pulled Madison into a hug. The poor kid had been sexually abused in high school by both girls and boys. She was currently in therapy, working on dealing with not only that part of her past but also her family's indifference to her. Poor kid.

"Did he hurt you? Or try to force himself on you? Be honest."

"No," Madison said, tears filling her eyes. "No," she said again. "But I thought he was a good one." She took a deep breath and let it out in an exasperated sigh. Rikki held on. "Boys are stupid."

"I'm sorry this is happening, little one." Rikki squeezed the *little* in her arms. "You will tell Miss Shasti as soon as you get home. Okay?"

Madison pulled back and nodded. She wiped tears from her face.

"And you will not be alone with Billy until Miss Shasti has a chance to speak with Billy's Daddy Dom."

"Mr. Seamus is going to be so mad at me."

"Not at all," Rikki said. "Remember how I told you how this community looks out for each other?"

"Mm hmm."

"Billy just needs to know that you don't want this. He needs to understand boundaries. And his actions have—"

"Consequences," Madison finished.

"Exactly right," Rikki said. "And your Mistress is person number one you need to talk to."

"What if she doesn't believe me?"

Rikki felt for the kid. Madison had been unsure where to turn and had turned to Rikki. "She'll believe you. I did. C'mon," Rikki said, "there's a party happening right here before our very eyes."

Madison's face brightened. "Maybe Mistress will let me have more cake." She waved a silly little wave and then broke out in a run toward Shasti.

Rikki chuckled and checked her watch. She had time to mingle.

"What was that all about, Boss?" Lydia said, rag in hand, clearly still working.

"*Littles*," was all Rikki said.

Lydia nodded knowingly. She started to say something, but then took one step back.

Rikki said, "Stop," before her assistant manager could take another step. As a submissive, Lydia had been trained in high protocol by one of her past Doms, and taking three steps back before turning your back on a Dominant was expected of her. Rikki was about to tell her that she didn't have to follow such high protocol because Rikki wasn't her Domme and had never required it of any sub she'd ever had. In a flash, she realized that Lydia needed the submissive gesture to stay grounded.

"Yes, Ma'am?" Lydia asked. Her cheeks reddened as if she thought she was about to be reprimanded for something.

"I'm going to make time for you tomorrow. After the morning rush, I'd like us to have a sit-down in the office." She put a hand up, sensing Lydia's apprehension. "Nothing bad. No worries. We haven't connected in a while, and it's probably time for that."

"Yes, Ma'am," Lydia said, her fear clearly evaporating from her expression. "Yes, Ma'am, I'd like that."

"Go on now," Rikki said with a slight head nod. "Make sure you get some cake. Enjoy yourself, too."

"I will. Thank you, Ma'am." And with that, she took three steps back and turned to walk away.

Lydia's long blonde braid looked as if it had just worked a full closing shift. And it had. Rikki made a mental note to start off tomorrow's sit-down by telling Lydia how grateful she was for her exemplary work at the shop. The real reason Rikki wanted the meeting, though, was that although Lydia hid it well, she was hurting. Tom, her most recent Dom, had released her without warning mere days after Aunt Tilda's funeral. And that was right around the time Rikki discovered Eileen's betrayal and her subsequent disappearance. Rikki had been so wound up in her own stuff that she didn't realize how fragile Lydia was. Lydia was also grieving. It was time for Rikki to get out of her own head and help.

Rikki made the rounds, thanking everyone for coming, then headed toward Shasti near the office door.

"I figured it was about time for you to head out," Shasti said.

Rikki knew Shasti had more to say. "Go on."

Shasti chuckled. "You know me very well, don't you?"

Rikki nodded and threw her hands up in a helpless gesture as if getting advice from Shasti was inevitable, and she wasn't going to fight it.

"Madison?" Shasti said, clearly worried.

"She's okay, but I've asked her to talk to you once you get home."

"Okay, good. I knew there was something, but she said everything was 'hunky dorey.'"

With a laugh, Rikki asked, "She used those words?"

"Mm hmm."

"What else?" Rikki crossed her arms and stood to her full 5' 10" height. It wasn't that she towered over Shasti, who was only three inches or so shorter, but she needed to steel herself for whatever it was that Shasti was going to say next.

"I know you feel alone," Shasti said. "But you're surrounded by people who not only love you, but need you, too. Your presence binds all of us, Rikki. We're here for you. This party was our gesture to let you know that."

"Thank you. I appreciate that."

"I understand that watching most of your friends in happy D/s relationships while you're suddenly not in one has to hurt, so I offer this advice, Rikki."

Rikki felt as if she was about to get schooled.

"Make room for her," Shasti said.

"Who?"

"We don't know yet," Shasti said with a laugh. "Unless you're hiding someone upstairs."

Rikki scoffed. "As if."

"That apartment up there is home right now. It's small, but there's room for another. Make room. Buy an extra toothbrush and hang it next to yours. Keep those extra pillows on the far side of the bed. She'll be sleeping next to you one day. Be ready. Make room in your closet for her things. Extra towels and—"

"Okay, okay," Rikki interrupted. "I get it. It's that whole manifesting thing, isn't it?"

"Mm hmm. I'm a firm believer that what you project to the universe will happen."

"I'm not doing a vision board," Rikki joked.

Shasti cackled. "Okay, okay. No vision board required, but you should seriously see Madison's college vision board. It's quite ambitious."

"I'll be sure to ask her about it," Rikki said. Sensing that the advice-giving session was ending, Rikki excused herself and left her friends celebrating without her. She dashed into her office and up the stairs to fix her Domme attire and get her coat. She headed out, knowing Shasti and Lydia would take care of the shop without her.

Chapter 3

With the morning rush over, Rikki dove into her office to sort through the mail before Lydia came in for a talk. Lydia was still out there supervising the morning crew and restocking for the inevitable afternoon crowd. Rikki picked up the stack of unopened mail. She didn't trust many people these days, but she trusted Lydia and Mark to pick up the mail from the carrier and bring it directly to her, unopened. Both had done admirably as assistant managers, and she needed to thank them more often. She'd start with Lydia.

The mail, as expected, was basically bills, bills, bills with some junk, advertisements, and crap thrown in. Wait, there was a letter from her lawyer. Why don't they just call? Why the formality? She dug her finger under an exposed flap and tore open the envelope. A bill. Naturally. There was nothing to indicate their progress with the credit card companies or that bank Eileen had used to take a loan in her name. She needed guidance from them about which bills to pay first, not another bill from them. Her father used to say, "Pay your mortgage first, so you always have a roof over your head." She pulled out the mortgage notice buried under a stack of stuff on her desk and then dug for the electric bill. She'd pay these, but she wasn't going to pay a dime on anything else until she got professional guidance—guidance she thought she was paying for, thank you very much.

"Fuck this," Rikki said and tossed the bills aside. She had to call them and find out what to do.

Like a blessing, there was a knock on her thick office door. Since she'd had the door and entire room soundproofed, she couldn't just yell, "Come in," so she got up, opened the door, and let Lydia in.

"Is this a good time, Boss?"

"Yeah, yeah, come in," Rikki said and gestured toward the couch. "Have a seat." Rikki shut the door and sat in her executive chair. She spun it to face her assistant manager. "Busy morning."

"No kidding, Ma'am," Lydia said. "Even Brittany held her own."

"Huh," Rikki said, surprised. "Come to think of it, I didn't have to redo any of the orders she made."

"She even remembered to put the drip tray back on Grumpy Gus."

Rikki laughed. "That espresso machine can definitely be grumpy." She chuckled again. "I'll have to get in touch with Brittany's Domme and give her a good report."

"When does Miss Patrice get back from assignment?" Lydia asked.

Rikki hesitated. It wasn't Lydia's place to ask about someone else's personal information.

"I was just wondering," Lydia added, "if Brittany was ever going to go on assignment with Miss Patrice. She's come so far, I'd hate to lose her."

Ahh, okay. That was her motivation, not mere curiosity for gossip. "I'd hate to lose her, too. Miss Patrice asked us to keep an eye on her and give her support. Is she listening to you more now?"

"Oh, most definitely," Lydia said with a nod. "Ever since you had that come-to-Jesus talk with her a while back."

"Good." Rikki felt herself relax a bit. "You've done such good work here at the shop, Lydia, and I want you to know that I see it and appreciate all you do." Rikki chuckled. "And all the other things you do that I don't see."

Lydia looked down. Her pink cheeks confirmed Rikki's suspicions. Lydia was a people-pleaser, which sometimes meant she did too much for others with little in return. Rikki needed to change that.

"Now, I need to bring something up that may be uncomfortable for you," Rikki said.

"Okay, Ma'am." Lydia's smile evaporated.

"That bruise I see on your shoulder near your neck." Rikki pointed to Lydia's left shoulder. "Self-inflicted?"

Although Lydia hesitated, she obviously knew not to lie. "Yes, Ma'am."

"You need relief, don't you?"

Hope gleamed in Lydia's eyes. "Oh, yes, Ma'am. Ever since…" She paused, clearly squelching whatever it was she was going to say.

"I know. I wasn't too fond of the way Master Tom released you."

"Without warning, Ma'am. I didn't see it coming. I thought he and I had something."

"You did have something, Lydia," Rikki said gently, "but it wasn't what you thought it was, unfortunately." Rikki steepled her fingers and tapped them together rhythmically. Thoughts were forming. She was having an idea.

"I haven't reached out to her yet, but I'd like to ask Miss Rowena if she'll take you in for a while."

"Oh, Ma'am," Lydia said, concern in her voice. "She's tried with me. I'm hopeless."

Anger and aggression were not the right approaches, so Rikki leaned in slightly and said gently, "You're not hopeless. On the contrary, you're looking for relief and a way to make sense of the world. Subbing for Miss Rowena is not a burden for her. She enjoys that kind of work."

"Thank you for the thought, Ma'am, but Miss Rowena has Minjung now. She doesn't need an extra burden."

"Just the same, would it be okay with you," Rikki said, "if I reach out and ask her? I won't do it if it's not something you want. But I do think you need some discipline and guidance to right your ship. It's always about consent. You know that, so I won't call if you don't want me to. And you know she won't take you on unless she wants to. She won't do it out of pity."

Lydia sighed and looked down at her hands. She rubbed them together as if hoping a spark of insight would burst out. "Yes, Ma'am. It will be okay to call. But I'll be fine if she doesn't want me."

Rikki's heart was breaking for her assistant manager. Lydia had voiced the one major thing she'd been feeling after Tom's rejection. She thought no one wanted her.

"Will do," Rikki said succinctly. "Like last time, she may ask you to stay in her home for a while."

Lydia nodded. "Yes, Ma'am. I understand. She has a mansion, so, uh, no hardship there." She chuckled.

Rikki chuckled along with her. "No, I guess not." She exchanged a smile with Lydia and said, "You know I can't give you impact, right? I can't be a temporary Domme to any of my employees. There's a line that we both have to toe. Protects us both, right?"

"Oh, Ma'am, yes, of course. I wasn't asking—"

"I know," Rikki interrupted. "I think I'm just reminding myself."

Lydia's relieved expression made Rikki fully understand how wound up her assistant manager was. "What do you need, Lydia? In the shop, I mean. I don't always notice everything, and I have a feeling that both you and Mark hide things from me. And I get that, but I need to know how to help."

Lydia hesitated again, clearly not wanting to overstep her role. At Rikki's urging, Lydia said, "Well, Marta seems to be settling in well back in the kitchen. I think she's more relaxed now about taking care of Shanice's needs, you know?"

"I've sensed that, too. Their domestic partner celebration last week was lovely, don't you think?"

As Lydia nodded, a wistful expression crossed her face. Rikki understood it. She'd felt it as well. She, like Lydia, also wanted the kind of love and affection Marta and Shanice had for each other.

Make room for her, Shasti had said. Rikki made a mental note to do just that upstairs in her apartment. The one right above where she sat.

Lydia knocked her out of her thoughts when she said, "Marta told me she wants to try some new recipes for the shop, but she's a little hesitant to ask you, I think."

"Noted," Rikki said. "Give her the go-ahead. One item as an add-on to the usual menu. We'll see how that goes, okay?"

"Okay."

"What else?"

"Brittany is doing better, but…"

"Not best. Go on. I won't throw you under the bus."

"Ma'am, she's just young, you know? Immature. I'm trying to get her to take some initiative instead of simply waiting for instructions."

"That would be nice," Rikki said and sighed. "At least she's doing better following the instructions we do give her, right? I have something positive to tell her Domme."

"I'm sure Miss Patrice will appreciate anything positive," Lydia said. "And you're right, Ma'am. Brittany has definitely made big improvements, that's for sure. She seems to be accepting the fact that her Domme travels and leaves her alone for long gaps."

"That's why Miss Patrice wanted her to work here, so she'd have a ready-made support network that understood the lifestyle." Rikki chuckled and added, "Well, you keep trying with her, but don't get frustrated. If you do, let me know, and I'll step in. Otherwise, she and the rest of the crew are in your and Mark's capable hands."

"Thank you, Ma'am." Lydia then brought up the rest of the staff one by one, and each seemed to be doing fine and pulling their weight. Working with Mark was also going well, so there was no need to worry.

Meeting concluded, Lydia went back to work, and Rikki picked up her phone. She should call her lawyer, but instead she texted Rowena.

RIKKI: Do you have time for a call? Regarding Lydia.

She reopened the lawyer's bill and was jotting down notes for her inevitable call to him when a return text came in.

ROWENA: You must be psychic. I've been worried about her. Yes, call now.

Rikki hit Rowena's number from her contact list.

"Hey, Rowena," Rikki said after her friend answered. "I think Lydia needs to feel her submission. She's feeling untethered after Tom's unceremonious dumping."

"He is such an ass for doing that," Rowena agreed. "The next shiny piece of candy came around, I guess."

Rikki scoffed. "Probably. Anyway, Lydia's a bit of a Domme here in the shop as an assistant manager, but that's not enough for her. She needs to feel her submissive side. Give in. Let go."

"What do you think?" Rowena asked. "One week with me or two?"

"Not sure. Tom didn't end it right, and I'm not sure what she needs."

"I always knew the man was a pompous, full-of-himself asshole."

Rikki laughed. "Don't hold back now." Rowena had little to no filter sometimes, but that was okay. She was being true to her own nature.

"Two weeks it is," Rowena said. "My sister and Minjung's mother are here now, but after New Year's, I can have her here. That's only a couple of days away, so we're okay there. Is she amenable, though? Does she know you're calling me to set this up?"

"She does, and I'm pretty sure she's fine with it. I'll leave it up to you to make arrangements with her, of course, but I have an idea."

"What's that?"

"She's a switch, as you know."

"Mm hmm," Rowena said.

"What if you help her feel submissive but then allow her some sessions dominating Minjung. Only if Minjung is okay with it. I think Lydia needs to feel her Domme side, but only with Minjung's permission, of course," Rikki reiterated.

"I'm liking this idea," Rowena said. "Lydia has been submissive to these user men for far too long. It's time she flexed her other side. At least explore it."

"Exploring boundaries is what we do, isn't it?" Rikki laughed and added, "She'll still need *your* dominance, though."

"And she'll get it. Can't turn it off." Rowena laughed into the phone. "All right. I'll send her a text to set up a phone appointment to discuss terms."

"Thanks, Rowena. Let's hope this helps. Personally, I think Lydia would be an amazing Mommy Domme."

"Interesting observation. Let me scheme with Minjung and see if she can be vulnerable with Lydia. Let Lydia guide her or something." Rowena laughed. "Minjung is a bit of a Mommy Domme to me, you know."

Rikki laughed. "She is, but she loves you and wants the best for you; that is clearly obvious."

"I know." This was said softly. A pang of something squeezed Rikki's heart. Even hard-nosed tough-ass, no-filter Rowena had found someone to love, someone who fit her perfectly. Minjung was a strong submissive. That's what Rikki wanted. Someone who understood who was in charge but could operate independently and wouldn't hide behind her Dominant. Someone like Eileen.

With a sour stomach, Rikki ended the call and then left a message with her lawyer's office, knowing it would be several days before she got a return call. Maybe it was time to fire him.

A wave of utter sadness hit her. She had no one. Even the lawyer who had been a connection to Aunt Tilda wasn't really there for her. There was no one to advise her. Aunt Tilda would have counseled her.

"But would I have listened?" Rikki said out loud and stood up from her desk. "I didn't listen when she warned me about Eileen, did I?"

Frustrated, she left her office and took a stroll around the shop. She talked to customers here and there, picked up wayward trash, and complimented employees. Her kitchen manager, Marta, was ecstatic to have the go-ahead to add cereal bars to her growing menu. She gushed about how if that worked out, she'd like to try other recipes. If that was okay with Rikki, of course. And it was. But see? This was the initiative Lydia had been talking about regarding Brittany.

Rikki sighed. She decided to tackle that another day and headed up to her apartment for some much-needed rest.

She let Lydia know she was going upstairs for a while. She'd had a late night at Dominique's. Apparently, word had gotten around that Rikki/Domme Robin had been the one who broke up the police sting, and her schedule was booked solid. She'd had no time to rest in between sessions. It was better for the paycheck, of course, but it was exhausting to be *on* all the time. And not to mention the physicality of impact sessions. She was both mentally and physically tired. She slogged up the steps in the back of her office to the studio apartment above the shop.

She stood in the doorway, surveying the mess. A submissive would have this place in shape, wouldn't she?

Rikki groaned. That was callous and downright disrespectful. Submissives weren't servants or housekeepers at her beck and call. A submissive was someone to cherish, guide, and lead. A submissive was someone to nurture and love. That's what had been missing in her relationship with Eileen. Love. They would have been better as occasional sex play partners instead of trying to make it more. But Eileen had been on the brink of homelessness, needed a place to stay, and despite Aunt Tilda's reservations, Rikki invited Eileen to move in with them. The sex had been good, really good, though. Eileen took her dominance well, but it hadn't been enough for either of them, had it?

Thoughts of her relationship with Eileen came flooding in. They'd been together over a year, one year and two months to be exact. There had been good times, hadn't there? Moving Eileen into the house had been a huge step, and one that Rikki thought meant some kind of permanency, even though they'd never talked about being life partners or anything like that.

"A year and two months," Rikki murmured out loud, finding herself drifting toward the St. Andrew's cross. It had been Aunt Tilda's, and she couldn't bear to part with it. Most of the dungeon equipment had been sold to Dominique or Victoria. She would have kept it all, but she needed the money to get herself out of the sudden debt she'd found herself in. Thank you, Eileen.

She stroked the solid wooden frame. Would anyone ever grace this cross again? Would there ever be someone she trusted? Would there ever be anyone who would trust her implicitly the way Eileen had? Or the way Rikki assumed she had.

Confused, Rikki dug out her favorite flogger. Well, okay, it was Eileen's favorite. She flicked the leather tails against the wood. Eileen's leather cuffs would have been fastened securely to those metal eye hooks. No breakaway Velcro or silk ties for Eileen. That was too vanilla for her. Another swish of the flogger against the wood had Rikki reliving their sessions in Aunt Tilda's basement dungeon.

In her mind, she heard herself say, "You can take more, can't you?" to the bound woman on the cross.

"Fuck me, Rikki," Eileen pleaded. Her short, light brown hair was ringed with sweat. She stood facing the cross, her wrists and ankles bound to it. Her legs spread wide. Her back, ass, and legs were deeply red from the flogging and caning she'd just taken. Oh, yes, Eileen could take more than most, but Rikki wasn't interested in being bossed around by her often vocal submissive.

Eileen's eyes grew wide when Rikki showed her the red ball gag. She knew enough not to protest, because she also knew that Rikki held all the power and her orgasm might get denied. That had happened on a regular basis during the early part of their relationship as the power dynamic worked itself out.

Ball gag in place, Rikki set to work. She smacked Eileen's sore ass. The resounding smack and subsequent screech were music to Rikki's sadistic ears. One by one, Rikki undid the restraints, and before Eileen understood what was happening, Rikki spun her around and bound one wrist to one branch of the upper X. Betrayal flashed in Eileen's eyes, but that was okay. She'd get her reward, eventually.

Eileen's suspicious gaze followed Rikki as her other wrist and both ankles were refastened to the cross, but this time Eileen's back was to it. She was now facing Rikki. Normally, Rikki would give a submissive in her care a kiss at this juncture. Rikki felt that a kiss helped a sub understand that the scene was moving on and helped to keep the Dominant and sub connected. It was a way for Rikki to show that she was looking out for her sub's best interests. The ball gag was obviously in the way at the moment, but that's not the main reason Rikki didn't kiss Eileen. In short, Eileen wouldn't have appreciated it. It had disappointed Rikki greatly when she discovered that Eileen didn't like kissing. She put up with it because kissing was one of Rikki's favorite ways to connect. Eileen never wanted that kind of reassurance from her Domme, though. Rikki was forced to find other ways to establish trust with Eileen. When Eileen visibly relaxed, Rikki knew the trust was there.

Eileen's expression became one of relief when Rikki held up nipple clips. And there it was, the signal that Rikki could be trusted, trusted to keep her safe, and trusted to give her what she wanted. The nipple clips had been a gift to Rikki from Eileen for some occasion Rikki couldn't remember in the present day. She did, however, remember what happened next. Rikki licked one of Eileen's nipples and then blew on it, hardening it sufficiently and then, without fanfare, snapped the clip onto it. Eileen blew out a groan around the gag. Ah, yes, such music to Rikki's ears. A sub's whimpering was the best kind of music. The second clip found its way onto the other nipple. The chain between them dangled against Eileen's naked body. One small fishing weight later, and Eileen was huffing around the gag as the pain coursed through her. Rikki flicked the weight. That whimper, yes, that's what she had been waiting to hear. She breathed into her core as she watched the weight swing slowly back and forth.

Rikki let the weight swing while she reached for the bag containing the surprise she had for her sub. She let the contents spill out on the goodies table. Eileen gasped behind the gag. Thirty or so clips lay at Rikki's beck and call.

"I wonder where these will go?" Rikki asked the dungeon. She certainly wasn't asking the now-whimpering Eileen. And Rikki wasn't moved to mercy by those whimpers. On the contrary, she was fueled by it, especially because Eileen lived for this. Craved it. And they both knew it.

The blindfold was a necessary accessory, Rikki decided. Better to let Eileen anticipate where the bite of each clip would be. The clips looked like ordinary clothespins but weren't. They had been designed and made for use in BDSM and didn't latch on as tightly as ordinary clothespins.

She had to make quick work of the pins because she never wanted to leave them on for too long. Hurting your submissive in the name of erotic pain was one thing. Damaging her was another thing entirely. Rikki attached pin after pin to her now blindfolded and writhing submissive's body. The first batch encircled a nipple. The second nipple was next. Each earlobe received one, but she was careful not to latch onto the cartilage.

"I really did have your best interests at heart, Eileen," Rikki said in the present, softening at the memory. A spike of sadness and something else, bitterness maybe, shot through her, but she waved them away to remember the scene from over a year ago.

Pins made a path down her submissive's toned belly and inner thighs. But it was when Rikki dug into Eileen's labia, spreading them wide open on each side, that Eileen stilled with anticipation. Rikki clipped both inner and outer lips wide open, effectively spreading her apart.

"Ahh, that's how she likes it," Rikki said. "Open for the taking." She stooped low and, without touching, let her exhaled breath land on Eileen's splayed open flesh.

Pleading moans made Rikki smile. She had to be careful. Eileen could ignite easily. In fact, she might blow without any direct touch from Rikki. Eileen had been single for a while before meeting Rikki and had been addicted to vibrators. When they first got together, Eileen couldn't get off without one, so Rikki set out to change that. She instituted clit-free days where Eileen had to cum without a vibrator or without any direct clitoral stimulation. It took many frustrating sessions and orders not to touch herself, but Eileen finally followed Rikki's lead. That was the moment when Rikki thought she and Eileen really had something. Well, they did have something, but it turned out not to be what Rikki thought it was. But at least Eileen, a fiercely independent submissive, had learned to trust her new Domme.

Eileen groaned as each pin came off her body, and blood rushed back to the pinched spot. Pleas behind the gag made Rikki's power centers soar. She moved into action. She pulled the last pin off Eileen's labia and smashed her body against her sub's. She ripped off the gag so she would be able to hear Eileen scream as she orgasmed. Rikki palmed her lover's sex. Her middle finger found the swollen clit and stroked twice. Eileen erupted. She screeched her release and bucked her hips, encouraging Rikki to continue stroking. Which she did. Rikki was sadistic, but a good orgasm was a good orgasm, and she wasn't about to renege on that promise. Eileen slumped in her restraints, spent. Rikki carefully undid the cuffs and lowered Eileen down to the mat, where they lay together basking in their session. Eileen didn't always like to be held afterward, but that time she didn't protest. It made Rikki think they were making progress in their intimacy. Unfortunately, hindsight told her differently.

A surge of arousal shot through Rikki at the memory. She blinked several times, bringing herself back to reality.

"Fuck," she muttered, tossed the flogger aside, and heard Shasti's words in her mind again. "Make room for her." She forgot about a nap. She made a concentrated effort to mentally picture a woman, someone other than Eileen, living in that apartment with her.

She got down to business and, as she cleaned, stopped every now and then to add to her physical list of items that would welcome another person into her life. She wanted to treasure this person, to desire her. She grabbed her list, took one last look at her small apartment, and headed down the stairs for a shopping spree she couldn't afford.

Chapter 4

New Year's Eve came and went quietly for Rikki. She declined all invitations, including the one from her dear friends Jaleesa and Tina. She'd felt bad about declining but desperately needed time to rest and regroup. She even turned down an offer for double pay from Dominique. She was just too tired. Shasti noted how pale Rikki looked one evening and recommended she find a way to recenter herself. Rikki wasn't sure how to do that, but staying away from the madness that was New Year's Eve sounded like a good starting place.

She closed the door to her office and sat at her desk. It was now the middle of January, cold and dreary, and creeping closer to the anniversary she dreaded. And now, it seemed she had yet another anniversary to dread. Two more, actually. Three in total. All in February. She'd often said that February sucked, but that was before. Back then, she'd been referring to the weather in Wilkes-Barre, Pennsylvania, where she grew up. But now? It wasn't the weather that weighed her down. People died in February. People left in February. Yeah, February sucked.

She leaned back in her chair, eyes closed, fingers pressing the bridge of her nose. The after-work rush was over with only one customer meltdown, but that had nothing to do with the shop. When she started her business almost four years ago, she had to learn that she couldn't fix every issue her customers and employees had. It was a lesson she was still learning, apparently.

Holidays felt very different now. Everything felt different. She truly wanted to give bonuses to her employees over the holidays, but keeping the lights and the heat on were her top priorities. Even the spring masquerade ball last May had been difficult for everyone without her Aunt Tilda there. She'd been the community's matriarch for so long that everyone was kind of at a loss, Rikki included. Everyone seemed to think she was the new de facto matriarch. She'd never thought of herself that way, but Seamus O'Neill and, oddly enough, Rowena Tate helped her accept the role and adjust to it. Rikki would have thought Rowena would have grabbed those reins, but when Rikki suggested it, Rowena had physically put both hands out in front of her and said it wasn't hers to take. Rikki thought that was odd, but didn't push. And with Seamus as co-host of both the May and December masquerade balls, she settled into the role. It proved to be easier to simply accept the role because the weight of the community's expectations was wearing her down.

After a deep breath, she vowed that once she got through those anniversaries in February, she'd get the Spring Masquerade Ball committee organized. It would be her second spring ball. Maybe it could be her last. She scoffed. No one was stepping up to take her place. Maybe she'd do the spring ball and then the December one and hand over everything to someone else. Maybe Jaleesa? Rowena? Shasti?

Rikki sighed. Whatever. The decision would keep for a while. She opened her eyes and leaned forward to work on payroll. She chuckled. The current cold of winter was definitely good for sales. She smirked. Shasti was always telling her to find the positive in things. Easier said than done, that was for sure.

After sending her employee hours to her payroll company, which included a reduced paycheck for herself, she felt strong enough to reread a recent email from one of the credit card companies she apparently owed money to. She was satisfied that the information was legit and sent them the final check that would pay off that debt. Yay. One down, how many more to go? Too many. Her lawyer had finally done something to help her. He had negotiated with the company to reduce the amount owed to the point of satisfying the debt. Well, the words they'd conveyed were writing it off as "bad debt." That hurt her heart a little, but whatever. The debt wasn't even hers.

She clicked the send button and, bam, done. Electronic check sent. Satisfied that at least one thing in the new year was going her way, she closed the laptop and tapped it twice. Of course, there were several other credit cards to take care of, those and that huge loan she'd never taken out.

The knock on the door was welcome.

"Everything okay?" Rikki asked when Lydia stood at the now-open door.

The grin on her assistant manager's face was priceless. "Everything is wonderful, Ma'am." She closed the door behind her. "Mistress Rowena thought it would be good if I told you about my 'progress.'" She made air quotes around the word *progress.* "At least that's what Mistress Rowena called it."

"Come in. Sit," Rikki said. "I'd love to hear about it."

Lydia sat on the couch.

"You've been at Miss Rowena's for two weeks now?"

"Yes, Ma'am," Lydia said. She smoothed her blonde work-disheveled hair off her face. She released me, though, and I'm going home after my shift. And don't worry, I'm okay."

"Good to hear," Rikki said, hopeful.

"So so so," Lydia gushed. "I'm way over Tom. *Master* Tom, I mean."

Rikki ignored the blatant disrespect. For now.

"We had something for a while," Lydia continued. She looked off to one side as if somewhere else. "When I met him, it was new and exciting, and he—" She waved her hands as if dismissing the thoughts about her former Dom. "Anyway, Miss Rowena is such a solid Domme." She turned her head to look directly at Rikki. "She's a real disciplinarian. She doesn't let me or Minjung get away with anything. Not a thing. She notices everything." This she said low as if telling tales out of school. "She helped me discover so much more about myself. She and Minjung both did."

Lydia rubbed her hands up and down her thighs repeatedly and then blurted, "Permission to speak freely, Ma'am?" She glanced at the closed door.

"Of course. Of course." Rikki gave her a go-ahead gesture.

"So, Miss Rowena sometimes had me and Minjung sit at her feet while she did her puzzles in the family room. Minjung lay her head against Miss Rowena's leg. She's so in love with her Domme. Don't worry. I wasn't jealous. I mean, the old me would have been, but I wasn't. And that surprised the heck out of me, you know?"

Rikki nodded.

"I remember how Miss Rowena had to let one of her subs go a while back, and she was alone for so long. Then she found Minjung. And look at them. Two happy love birds, so content with the life they have together." Lydia sighed. The sigh was so joyful that it almost seemed as if Lydia had been talking about her own relationship. "I know now that I can find someone. I just need to chill the frig out." She leaned closer and said, "Miss Rowena used a much stronger word when she told me that."

"Sounds like her," Rikki said with a chuckle.

"But then, but then—" Lydia swooned. "Now, Miss Rowena gave me wonderful impact sessions and very nice aftercare each time. After a few days, I was feeling better. Grounded even. She must have sensed it because she let me give Minjung impact. Minjung was a-ok with it, Miss Rikki. Her eyes lit up when Miss Rowena suggested it. At first, Miss Rowena supervised me with Minjung. Have you seen her dungeon? It's so cool. It looks like an exercise room or whatever. Everything has a double purpose. Anyway, after a while, she left me alone with Minjung. It was a little tiny bit awkward at first, but Minjung seemed so amenable. Maybe she liked having someone different give her impact."

"Consent is everything," Rikki said, not wanting to interfere with Lydia's monologue.

"It is. It is," Lydia agreed. "Did you know that Miss Rowena even gave me permission to, um, give Minjung special rewards during our private sessions?"

"Very generous." Rikki was surprised that Rowena would allow that. Maybe her friend was feeling so secure in her relationship with Minjung that she wasn't threatened by Lydia. Rikki wasn't opposed to sharing a partner, but she always wanted to be in the room. She was a little possessive that way.

"So," Lydia continued, "I bound Minjung over the spanking bench, obviously face down, bottom up." She hesitated momentarily as she smiled at the memory. "Miss Rikki, I like giving spankings, I've discovered. It's so personal. That may be my new favorite thing, you know?"

"It's lovely," Rikki said. "Flogging is personal, too, but also a bit detached. No skin on skin."

"Yass," Lydia gushed. "It's that skin-on-skin thing. With Master Tom, it always felt like a punishment." She frowned, but the expression was fleeting as she picked up the thread of her story. "I put a ball gag on Minjung and after the spanking and some light flogging on her back—" She interrupted herself to add, "I'm still working on my flogging techniques, but Miss Rowena says I had vast improvement in the short time I was there. Yay." She clapped her hands and tapped her feet in celebration.

Rikki grinned. She had never seen Lydia this happy before.

"So, anyway," Lydia said. "After the flogging, I was gently rubbing Minjung's red skin after the impact play. It was so warm that I put my cheek on her back to feel it. Minjung squirmed and snapped her fingers like I told her to. So, I carefully removed the gag. I thought maybe the gag was causing her distress. It wasn't. Do you know what she wanted?"

"No. What?" Although Rikki had a good idea of what Minjung wanted.

"She asked me. No, no, she *begged* me to put on a strap-on, told me where they were. I did it quickly because I could see she was in great need. I know all about that deep need. Master Tom used to—No, he gets no more air space from me. Anyway, I felt so damn powerful when I, at her request, mind you, when I slid the tip of the strappy into her mouth. I stroked the silicon thing dangling in front of my body, and whoa, a surge of power or something hit me everywhere, including my arousal centers. I mean, what the heck, Miss Rikki? It's just a prop."

Rikki raised her eyebrows and nodded knowingly. She didn't dare interrupt. Lydia was clearly in sub frenzy. No, actually, with the scene she was describing, it was more like Domme frenzy.

"So, then I moved behind her, when I felt like it, mind you." She looked directly at Rikki as her face grew intense. "I like that power, Miss Rikki. So, I rested the phallus on one of her ass cheeks as I grabbed her hips. Her moan of pure lust almost made me cum. OMG. You know, I could tell how wet she was. I didn't even have to check. I slid that phallus inside her and pushed until it bottomed out. She liked that and started to rock back and forth, but I was having none of it and smacked her once on the ass to get her to stop. And she did." She clamped her lips tight and shook her head in defiance. "Did I mention how much I loved the power, Miss Rikki?" Without waiting for an answer, Lydia continued, "I started thrusting, and it didn't take long. Her long moan of ecstasy came after maybe ten strokes. I was almost there, too, so I kept thrusting and then stroked myself a few times before I came. Minjung heard me cum and sighed the most satisfied sigh I've ever heard."

"Wow."

"I mean," Lydia gushed, "Minjung was super happy for me. Me!" She looked toward the floor, obviously confused.

"Minjung was happy that her body could give you pleasure," Rikki said.

"Yes, that was it, exactly it."

"It sounds like you needed those experiences. Eye-opening, weren't they?"

"Yes, very." She clamped her lips and then blurted, "I think I need to explore my D-side, Miss Rikki."

Rikki nodded knowingly. "Pushing boundaries, right? This time you're in charge of pushing your own." Although she should be ecstatic that Lydia seemed to have found some peace, she seemed a bit too manic for Rikki's liking. Rikki would quietly and informally keep an eye on her.

A knock on the office door brought their session to an end. Lydia thanked Rikki for listening and then practically skipped out the door back into the shop.

Madison burst into the office past Lydia, saying, "Hi, Miss Lydia. Bye, Miss Lydia."

"Hey, kiddo," Rikki said to the *little* who stopped just short of careening into Rikki's chair.

"Guess what, Miss Rikki? Guess what?" Madison held up an envelope, but the back was to Rikki, so she couldn't tell what had her so excited.

"Sorry, sorry," Shasti said as she came through the open office door a little out of breath. "She just couldn't wait to tell you." She shut the door behind her and then asked Madison, "Did you tell her?"

Madison shook her head, bounced on her feet a few times, and then blurted, "I got in. They took me. Me! They think I'm smart enough to go to college!"

Rikki gasped. "You got in? To Phillips College?"

"Yasssssss!" Madison said and did three pirouettes in a row. "Whoa," she said when she stopped spinning, obviously dizzy. She sat down hard on the couch and then handed Rikki the letter. "See?"

Shasti sat next to her *little* as Rikki opened the letter. As she read, she nodded a few times and then simply could not help the smile creeping up her face. She dared a glance at Shasti. As she expected, strong stoic Dr. Shasti Balakrishnan was tearing up.

"This is so wonderful, Madison," Rikki said. "See? You worked hard learning SAT words and writing your essay."

"Miss Tina helped me write it. She's so smart, being a banker and all."

"She *is* smart," Rikki agreed. "I'm glad she was able to help you out."

"Mistress," Madison said in alarm. "I have to call Miss Tina and Miss Jaleesa. They'll want to know." She pulled out her phone.

Shasti put a hand on her *little's* arm. "In a minute, love." She pulled out a twenty-dollar bill from her purse and handed it to Madison. "Go get our usual. Or, since we're celebrating, get that sugary concoction you like."

Madison shot up in an instant and took the cash. "Yes, Ma'am," she said, pulled open the heavy door, and ran out. The door reopened a microsecond later, and Madison said, "Sorry. Bye, Miss Rikki."

Rikki chuckled and said, "Bye, Madison. We'll be out in a few minutes."

"Bye," Madison said again and waved her silly little wave. She waved at Shasti and mouthed, "Bye" to her as well. And just like that, the blur was out the door.

"That one is a bundle of energy," Rikki said, her eyes widening.

"We should all have that much energy," Shasti said, and without wasting a beat, added, "Lydia looks happy. Rowena's special brand of therapy helping?"

Rikki loved her friend dearly, but she was always one to want all the deets on everyone else's business, although she often claimed to the contrary.

"Apparently," Rikki said succinctly. "How's the Madison/Billy issue?" Rikki wasn't prying. Madison had brought the concern to her, and Rikki felt justified in asking.

Shasti inhaled and let it out in a sigh. "I've made Seamus aware of the situation. He was surprised as hell. Just like I was when Madison finally told me."

"Wonder what's going on," Rikki said, letting her statement sit there. If Shasti wanted to discuss it further, Rikki would listen; otherwise, she would mind her own business. When Shasti didn't respond right away, Rikki busied herself at her desk by casually tucking her bills under some junk mail. Shasti knew about her financial issues, but at the moment, Rikki didn't want to have that discussion.

"Honestly," Shasti said at last, "I don't know what to think."

"I have to ask this," Rikki said, hoping her bestie would take the question for what it was and not an accusation of any sort, "but did Madison lead him on in any way?"

Shasti's head snapped in Rikki's direction, her eyes dark.

"Not insinuating anything," Rikki defended. "We both know, and maybe you're the one who told me this, but every story has three sides, right?"

Shasti's whole demeanor softened. She exhaled long and slow through her nose as if she'd been holding her breath. "There's his side, her side, and the truth somewhere in the middle."

"Exactly," Rikki said. "But she's clearly uncomfortable with the present situation, so how it started is kind of back burner stuff at the moment."

"I need to get to the bottom of this," Shasti said, her lips pursed together, brow furrowed.

"You can't force it," Rikki said. "Keep the dialog going with her. I don't know why I'm telling you this, because you know what you're doing. And hopefully, Seamus is doing the same with Billy." She flashed her friend a sympathetic smile, her lips pressed together. Rikki shrugged when her friend didn't respond and added, "Relationships do evolve. People grow, change, and move on. Maybe that's all that's happening with the two of them."

"You're right," Shasti said. She sighed again and added, "Well, maybe Seamus can offer us some insight, but for now, there will only be supervised visits. No more playing alone in her room, his room, or the backyard without someone with them."

"Does Madison know this?"

Shasti nodded. "She was the one who suggested it, but doesn't want Billy to know she was the one behind it."

"Understandable," Rikki said. "And how are *you* doing?"

"We're going to England."

"Wait, what?"

"I just—I think I'm having growing pains, too, Rikki. She's maturing, finding her footing, and maybe she won't need me as much anymore. Or at all." The tears came earnestly now.

Rikki moved to the couch and pulled her friend into a hug. "She'll always need you, Shasti." She paused before adding, "This is what you wanted for her, right? To grow? See her own worth? Go to college?"

Shasti pulled away, dabbed at her eyes with a tissue that Rikki hadn't seen her pull out, and then blew her nose. "Yes," she said succinctly.

"So maybe you're right. Maybe you and Billy are both afraid of how your relationships with Madison might change."

Shasti nodded.

"So, what's with this England thing?" Rikki asked with a laugh.

"I don't know. I want to show her things. Take her places she's never been, so that she'll always remember me as the person who opened up her world."

"There is no chance that Madison would ever forget who saved her."

"Saved her?"

Rikki nodded. "She loves you. Anyone—No, everyone can see that. You're just having a moment, Shasti."

"I know." Shasti sat up taller.

"Celebrate the win. The college acceptance. And," Rikki made a comical face, "go to England to celebrate. Have tea and scones with the royal family."

Shasti laughed. "I will. *We* will. Thanks for being my sounding board." She wiped the tears from her face one last time and tucked the tissue in her skirt pocket. "I'd best get out there. She might have devoured her entire drink before I get there."

Rikki nodded. She needed to get back out on the floor as well.

Shasti stood and headed for the door, but then turned and said, "Wait. How are you? Everything okay?"

"Fine. Fine. Everything's fine," Rikki lied. "In fact, I just paid off one of the credit cards and put it to rest." That part wasn't a lie.

"Excellent," Shasti said. "See you out there." Within a minute, she popped her head back into the office. "Guess who's out here?"

Rikki had no clue and simply shrugged.

"That woman who's been here every day for the past couple of weeks." Pretty. Blonde-ish. Early-forties. Tight sweaters? Probably single and ready to mingle."

"Get out," Rikki said with a laugh, pointing to the door.

And with that, Shasti was gone, and the office door closed again.

Rikki had indeed noticed the good-looking blonde, and Shasti had noticed her noticing. Ugh. Was nothing private? But, if she thought about it, it was damn time for her life to turn a corner, wasn't it? Feeling semi-good, Rikki tucked her bills and junk mail in the top desk drawer where lately those things went to die. She took a moment to find a genuine smile and wore it back into the shop.

Chapter 5

Rikki walked into the shop, ignored Shasti's gaze, and spotted the attractive middle-aged blonde woman by the front windows. Oh, Rikki had game, and she knew it, but the setting wasn't right for seduction. The woman was a customer, after all, so that made it seem kind of weird anyway. Rikki didn't know if the woman was part of the community, probably not, and it was always dangerous trying to bring someone in who knew nothing about Dominant/submissive relationships. One person could cause a lot of trouble if word got out about all the kinky people in Denton Heights, especially the owner of Rikki's Coffee Shop on Market Street, smack in the middle of downtown.

Now, at a BDSM event, sure, Rikki could corner and catch any cute young submissive easily. Just like she had done with Sarah at one of Aunt Tilda's many Sunday afternoon tea dances. That was almost three years ago. The party was a BDSM community event celebrating the one-year anniversary of the coffee shop's opening. Her aunt liked any excuse to have lifestyle parties, so why not celebrate Rikki's successful business? Rikki was the woman of the hour at that party, and dark-haired, cute-as-a-button Sarah was positively enamored by Rikki. At the time, Rikki was so charmed by Sarah's attention that the ten-year age gap didn't matter. It also helped that Sarah was the most eligible single female submissive in the community. Rikki pounced. They'd had a very fulfilling dating life for a few months. But the age gap proved to be a little too much for Rikki. She knew that Sarah would make someone a good partner—she was attractive and a strong submissive—but Rikki just wasn't feeling any long-term vibes, so she broke it off. Sarah didn't seem upset by it and, in fact, committed to a new Domme a few weeks later. That was about the same time Rikki started seeing Emily, an older submissive fresh out of a failed relationship. Emily was a creative writing instructor, and

Rikki always got the feeling that Emily was simply looking for a muse or something. In the short time they were together, Rikki didn't turn out to be that, so Emily broke it off and moved on.

Back then, unlike now, it seemed as if submissive women were falling out of the trees at her feet because cute, flexible Jessica came into her life just a short while later. It was at another one of Aunt Tilda's tea dances, this one in honor of Victoria's thirty-third birthday. Both she and Victoria had been ogling the new submissive on the scene, but Rikki was the one who got her. Victoria had been in a semi-serious relationship at the time, so Rikki knew she would have lost otherwise. Not that she competed with Victoria, but maybe she did a little. Talk about game. Victoria absolutely had the best game in town, maybe in all of Ohio and the Midwest. For Victoria, it was all about the conquest. For Rikki, it was partly that, but lately she'd begun to have thoughts about long-term relationships and life partners.

Her feet moved her toward the cute, mature blonde in the tight sweater sitting all alone in the coffee shop. The blonde seemed delighted when Rikki wandered by to say hello. She closed the paperback book she was reading when Rikki walked up. Putting the book down indicated that the woman was okay with the intrusion. And maybe she liked the attention? Rikki typically didn't flirt overtly with customers, but this woman seemed ultra sweet and appreciative of Rikki's attention.

"Can I get you anything else?" Rikki asked the forty-something blonde.

"You're sweet," the woman said, "but no, I have herbal tea, a delightful piece of lemon bundt cake, and a book, so I'm content."

Ahh, was that a cue that she wanted to be left alone?

"Well, if you need anything, just ask for me, Rikki." Rikki pointed to her name tag.

"Oh, I'm talking to the big boss," the woman teased. The slight blush and the way her hand went up to clutch imaginary pearls sent tiny tendrils of desire through Rikki. Was the game on?

Rikki chuckled. "I suppose so."

"I'm Esme." The woman stuck out her slender hand. "Short for Esmerelda."

Rikki shook the cold hand, and her mind instantly went to ways she could warm that hand.

"Enjoy your book," Rikki said, let go of the hand, and headed back to the front counter to help with the ever-growing line. She purposely avoided Shasti's gaze, because she knew beyond a doubt that Shasti had taken in the whole exchange.

Back when Rikki had broken up with Sarah, Shasti consoled her by saying, "Such is the nature of relationships. Some don't last. Better to get out of one that isn't working than to hang around and be miserable." Why Rikki was remembering that advice now was a mystery, maybe because Eileen's abrupt departure had been on her mind lately. Had Eileen been miserable with Rikki? Rikki scoffed at the thought, but it did seem like Shasti had been counseling Rikki about relationships ever since she'd moved to Denton Heights over two and a half years ago.

~~~

Three weeks later, Rikki found herself back at Dominique's. Rikki wasn't in her Domme regalia, nor was she brandishing a crop. In fact, she wasn't working at all. Tonight, she was a simple customer like any other. She'd paid her dues and walked in the front door. The coffee shop always closed earlier on Sundays to give her and her employees a break. Business was slow on Sunday evenings anyway, and now Rikki saw why. Everyone was at Dominique's. Maybe people were having one more thrill before the work week began. That, and the show scheduled to start in the theater in a few minutes, probably brought them in. The performers were from Akron, and Dominique said they were worth every penny. Hopefully, that was true for Dominique's sake.

For three weeks running, Esme had shown up every weeknight and stayed for about an hour. Rikki didn't always make contact; that would have seemed too forward, too thirsty, but she did slide by on occasion to say hello to the good-looking blonde. She'd been greeted with a warm and genuine smile every time. Rikki's interruptions never seemed to bother Esme, which was a good thing because Rikki certainly didn't want to become a pest. Monday through Friday, Rikki found herself anticipating Esme's punctual arrival. Of course, Rikki wondered what brought Esme to the coffee shop so regularly, but she couldn't figure out a way to ask without prying. That was the woman's personal business, right? Unfortunately, Rikki's body had also begun to anticipate Esme's arrival, and Rikki was having trouble finding a way to turn down her libido. Hence, this personal trip to Dominique's on a Sunday evening. Maybe she could find relief of some sort here.

She had a few minutes before the show started, so she hung out in the public woodshed area of the club. Several St. Andrew's crosses and spanking benches lined the walls. Most of these were occupied. To her immediate left, two young men were engaged in bondage. The younger one was gagged and strapped to a bench. The only article of clothing he wore was a loincloth. It was a stylish loincloth, though, with a pleasing dark turquoise-and-black pattern. Leave it to the guys to make bondage fashionable. Rikki chuckled and let a genuine, easy smile light her face.

She hadn't had many genuine smiles lately, especially now that February was there with only nine days left until the worst anniversary of her life. Yes, *that* anniversary. Just as the thought intruded, the gagged bottom let out a yelp. The red handprint on his back was clearly the reason. Rikki actually found herself smiling again when she realized the younger one was getting a fun-ishment. Apparently, the playful punishment was for some imagined wrongdoing, something about slamming a car door. It sounded like he was trying to apologize, but the ball gag in his mouth prohibited actual words from forming.

Rikki's smile faded as she left the loving bondage scene. Watching the cute couple made her wonder if she'd ever have another submissive in her life. Would she ever be in a real relationship? A forever one? Maybe not. Probably not. Eileen had burned her so thoroughly that she wondered if she'd ever trust anyone again. Time would tell, but for the moment, she was leery, despite all of Shasti's noise about "making room" for someone new in her life. To be honest, she wasn't sure what she was even doing down at Dominique's that evening. She wasn't looking. Was she?

Caitlyn, the undercover cop, had stirred something up in her. She had been attracted to the woman physically, that was for certain, but she'd been attracted to her intelligence, too, in their short session. That was, of course, before discovering that Caitlyn was trying to take down Dominique's club. But if honesty was still on the table, she was still attracted to the woman. Was that why she was at Dominique's that evening? To see if Caitlyn was there?

No. Not exactly. She'd never hook up with someone who had threatened to topple everything she held near and dear. Been there, done that. Cue Eileen. But maybe if someone else caught her eye? Dare she even wish for the attractive Esme to somehow manifest here at Dominique's on a random Sunday night?

Rikki blew out a sigh. She wasn't ready. And thoughts of Eileen kept invading her bubble, her very thin bubble. She checked her watch. It was the perfect time to sneak into the back of the theater.

She nodded to Mel at the door, received a smile in return, and an opened door. She was a stud, if ever there was one. The tall, dark-skinned, masculine woman was intimidating and the exact look Dominique wanted for her many dungeon masters. Mel's biceps bulged from her tight white shirt, showing off her buff physique. Dominique had done well hiring the burly woman. She was young, though. Too young for her. Not that Mel was interested.

She entered the room just as the lights were dimming. A few people smiled at her as she walked in. Some worked at the club, and others were customers she'd dominated at one point or another. Their smiles and greetings made her feel like she belonged somewhere. Her breath hitched. Was that it? Did she feel like she didn't belong anywhere? Aunt Tilda was gone. Eileen, too. And then, of course, her—

No! she scolded herself. Not tonight. She would not go there now. In nine days, she could and would allow herself to fall apart and ask all those what-if questions, but not now. She hugged the back wall near the door. The theater and other private rooms were clothing optional, but Rikki wasn't into public nudity. She always said if that was someone else's thing, then have at it. By the looks of it, many were doing just that. Aunt Tilda taught that people had the right to express themselves however they wanted to. Before she came to live with her aunt, Rikki already had that instilled into her by her—.

Her breath faltered again. No, no, no! She wasn't going to think about *her* right now.

A middle-aged woman with chestnut-colored hair piled high on her head clomped comically across the stage in way-too-high platform shoes. The spotlight followed her path. She seemed completely oblivious to the audience, but that was obviously part of the act. She wore a black latex bodysuit with a deliciously plunging neckline, accentuating her breasts nicely. The stretched corset laces binding her torso added to the elegance. Her legs were long and, even though the outfit wasn't Rikki's style, the woman rocked it.

Catcalls and flattering whistles accompanied her walk toward the far side of the stage. She stopped, faced the audience as if noticing them for the first time, and put a hand on her chest as if startled. With the other hand, she gave a you-flatter-me gesture. She then curtsied, first to one side of the crowd and then to the other. She acted like she wanted to interact more, but then put up a finger as if to say she'd only be a minute.

"You, boy," she barked and pointed to a young man in the audience.

A second spotlight found the attractive young white man in his early twenties. He was wearing a pink sleeveless button-down shirt and baggy black shorts. "Me?" he said and pointed to himself.

"Yes, yes," the woman said. "I need you."

"Me?" he asked again, clearly not believing he'd been chosen.

She stood up to her full height, put her hands on her hips, and said to him, "Unless you'd like me to find another volunteer to have my way with."

"No, no, Ma'am," he stammered and bolted for the stairs on the side of the stage. Once on the stage, he sprang toward her and then slid on his knees, landing right at her feet. The audience burst into applause at the surprise of it. He leaned down and kissed her feet repeatedly.

"Now, that's a good boy," she said to the audience. "Isn't he?"

Applause and cheers of "Good boy" and "Obey your Mistress" were called up to the stage.

"Stop," she said to the young man. He stopped kissing, sat back on his haunches, and looked up at her expectantly. She leaned down to him and stage-whispered, "Did you sign the waiver?" The audience cracked up when he nodded enthusiastically.

The Mistress beckoned her female assistant to come over. She was holding a collar on a tray, and wore her dark hair pulled up off her neck under an oversized top hat, the kind President Lincoln might have worn. She wore fishnet stockings, a tasteful black thong, and a tailored tuxedo jacket with long tails. As far as Rikki could tell, there was no shirt underneath the buttoned jacket. A slight tingle of arousal hit Rikki square in the belly.

The Mistress took the collar and dismissed her assistant, who turned and exited off the far side of the stage. The Mistress held the collar in front of the still kneeling young man. When he nodded his consent, she leaned down and put the black leather collar on his neck. Looking satisfied, she asked him, "Why are you still dressed?"

The startled, wide-eyed look on his face made Rikki and the rest of the audience laugh.

"Up," she commanded. He complied. "Strip," she ordered, stepping back as campy striptease music filled the space. It was something out of the forties, evoking images of giant feathered fans at a burlesque show.

The young man began a sultry yet comical striptease of his sleeveless button-down shirt. It was quite sexy until he had trouble with one of the buttons and had to appeal to his Mistress. They turned away from the audience as she, too, "struggled" to undo the button. At this point, it was very clear that he was one of the actors in the stage show and hadn't really been picked out at random.

The shirt was finally removed and suitably tossed to the audience, who eagerly snatched it up. The strip-tease music was still playing as he began a slow gyration of his hips. He unbuttoned the top of his baggy shorts and turned to face away from the audience. He made a clear show of pulling down the zipper and twerking toward the audience.

The Mistress of the evening groaned, rolled her eyes, and then walked behind him unnoticed. She grabbed both sides of his shorts and yanked them down. He shrieked at the invasion and covered his ass cheeks, but to no avail. The audience had already seen his very white gluteus maximus shining down at them. The music stopped.

The Mistress stepped back and made a twirling motion with one finger. He shook his head. She folded her arms and tapped one very loud platform shoe on the wooden stage. He visibly shrank, shook his head, and purposely looked away from her. He mouthed, "Help me," to the twenty-something buxom assistant who had reappeared on the opposite side of the stage. She gave him a sympathetic smirk, but then shrugged as if to say she had no power to help him. He stuck out his lower lip and then stuck out his tongue at her playfully. She recoiled as if offended but then leaned toward him wordlessly and motioned with one finger for him to turn around. The shocked look on his face at her betrayal was priceless.

"Turn around," the Mistress said, this time out loud. She motioned at the audience to join her in her chant of, "Turn around. Turn around."

Rikki was amazed at how enthralled the audience was by the antics on the stage. The performers had clearly honed their schtick and were delivering it masterfully.

The young man started to turn, but then shyly shook his head and retreated, keeping his back to the audience.

The audience got louder, and that seemed to be what he wanted to hear. He looked to the sky and made the sign of the cross over his chest. He kicked off the bulky shorts that had remained pooled at his feet and spun around, arms wide.

Rikki burst out laughing. His private parts were covered with a penis sheath in the shape of a large rubber chicken. It stuck up and out toward the ceiling. He seemed proud of it and strutted on the stage like a rooster, making the appendage bounce comically.

The Mistress smacked her palm to her face and shook her head. She turned to the audience and gestured as if to say, "Do you see what I have to put up with?"

As the audience laughed, the Mistress pulled the young man to her by the D-ring on his collar and then had a few stern but quiet words with him. He hung his head and reached down to remove the rubber chicken. Rikki laughed when he removed the chicken because underneath it was a rainbow-covered tube. It wasn't just a tube; it was shaped like a rocket. Rikki got the reference. It was a rainbow rocket. The lights abruptly went out, and Rikki laughed when the rainbow colors glowed. His "rocket" was covered with glow-in-the-dark bracelets. Very clever. Someone's hand pulled them off the rocket and tossed them one by one into the eager audience.

The crowd cheered this turn of events, and then the lights came back on abruptly. The young man now stood in a sensible pink thong, the rainbow rocket gone. The Mistress gestured to him, and he bowed to enthusiastic applause. However, unseen by the Mistress on the other side of the stage, stood the female assistant, twirling two floggers ineptly. A St. Andrew's cross stood behind her. It had apparently been wheeled out when the lights dimmed. Her comical motions made it look as if she were mocking a Dominant's flogging technique.

The Mistress stomped her foot, and the dark-haired assistant froze. She looked up, startled. The scared expression on her face made the audience scared for her. A nervous twitter of laughter rippled through the audience. Without breaking eye contact with her Mistress, she put the floggers down gently on the side table. The Mistress crossed her arms. The assistant pressed her lips together and then looked around innocently as if she hadn't been doing anything wrong.

Rikki chuckled at the silliness, but it was clear that someone was about to get cuffed to that St. Andrew's cross.

The Mistress snapped her fingers, and the young man flew into action. He ran off stage and wheeled a throne back on. After helping his Mistress sit in it, she directed him to kneel on a pillow she threw down for him. She then lifted her chin, snapped her fingers, and gestured for the female assistant to come toward her. The assistant took one step, but the Mistress tsk-tsk-tsked and gestured to the floor. Rikki laughed as the assistant grudgingly went to her knees, but not before comically rolling her eyes and making a face like any middle school girl would when asked to clean the cat box. The female assistant then crawled toward her Mistress, ending up at her feet. The Mistress pulled the armrest up like it was a La-Z-Boy recliner and pulled out a black collar and leash. The collar and leash were presented to the assistant, who nodded her permission, and the collar was then placed on the female assistant's neck. The Mistress opened her legs wide. She waggled her eyebrows and pulled on the leash. The female assistant crawled closer and closer. An excited moan came from the audience, including Rikki.

The Mistress cried out in surprise when the assistant's tall Lincoln hat stopped the assistant from reaching the desired goal. She gestured for the assistant to take off the hat. The assistant tried and tried to get the hat off, but it seemed stuck.

Rikki chuckled at the comical way they both tried and tried to get the hat off, but to no avail. Clearly frustrated, the Mistress directed the female assistant to the cross, facing it, and then had her place her hands through the two loose rope loops. The Mistress picked up a short bull whip.

"Uh oh," someone from the crowd said, making everyone chuckle nervously.

The Mistress snapped the whip several times behind the assistant, making her jump every time. And then with one well-placed snap, the top hat tumbled off the assistant's head to the floor. Rikki laughed. Underneath the top hat was a blue wizard's hat accentuated with gold stars. The bull whip sent that one flying off as well. The next was a colorful court jester's hat, complete with jingling bells. The assistant shook her head, and the bells rang out. The Mistress looked to be at her wits' end, but after a few bull whip snaps, one directed at the young man who was trying to grab the wizard's hat, she flicked the court jester cap off, revealing the woman's dark hair piled on her head in a messy bun.

The Mistress snapped her fingers, and the woman released herself from the cross, and they both took a bow. Meanwhile, behind them, the young man had put on the court jester hat. Once the applause died down, the Mistress spied the young man's thievery, put both hands up as if appealing to God, and mouthed, "Why me?" to much laughter from the crowd.

The Mistress sidled up to her female assistant, whispered something in her ear, and stepped back. Several pirouettes later, the assistant was on center stage. The striptease music cued up again, and she flicked her flats into the audience, then began a sultry unbuttoning of her long tuxedo jacket. She was very good. Rikki wasn't sure if the woman had a shirt on or not. She never revealed her breasts underneath, and no one seemed to be able to tell. Audience members craned their necks to see. With one final flourish, she whipped open the jacket, but the lights went out before anyone could see underneath. A collective groan from the audience filled the space. Rikki just laughed along with the Mistress.

"Mine," she said to the audience, and the lights came back on. The female assistant was now strapped to the St. Andrew's cross. Her back was to them, but it was bare. Obviously, she had *not* been wearing a shirt underneath the jacket. She was almost entirely nude, with only the thin fabric from the thong showing.

The Mistress whispered something to the bound female assistant. The assistant nodded. The Mistress then gestured to the young man to strap the female assistant's ankles to the cross. He reached up and tightened the loops around the assistant's wrists. She was now bound to the cross and at her Mistress's mercy.

Rikki noticed that the assistant wasn't gagged. Maybe that was next.

The Mistress pointed, and the young man handed her what looked like an oversized hairbrush. She showed the audience the hard wooden side and then the nylon bristles on the other. She gestured as she showed them again, asking them to vote for which side her assistant would receive. Rikki would have bet the wooden paddle side would be chosen, but there were some very vocal females in the audience who wanted the bristles.

Rikki laughed when the Mistress took the bristles' side and began to lovingly stroke her assistant's back and legs. It didn't look like she was pressing very hard, and, in fact, the assistant was purring at the treatment. A soft-looking cloth came next, and the assistant was practically a puddle.

The Mistress waggled her eyebrows as she placed the cloth on the small table. The young man then handed her a flogger. A great cheer went up as she brandished it, ready to strike. But she didn't. Not right away. Instead, she draped the tails over the woman's shoulder simply to inform her what was coming next.

Rikki liked that move. It was very considerate to the submissive in her care. Rikki had tried that sort of thing with Eileen, but Eileen didn't want soft or considerate. Eileen wanted hard because Eileen was hard. She wanted fast, quick movements. She never wanted to be told what was coming next, even though Rikki did most of the time. After a while, a couple of months into their relationship, Rikki thought, maybe Eileen would settle and want to be held, cuddled, or perhaps even coddled. Most women like some form of tenderness. But that never happened. Eileen stayed hard and demanding. Part of Rikki knew that Eileen wasn't her forever partner, but most of Rikki denied it. She thought she could live without all that mushy stuff, especially because Eileen filled Rikki's power centers on a regular basis. The sex had been incredible. Wasn't that enough?

No. It wasn't. Not for either of them. Rikki wanted love. Eileen, apparently, wanted financial freedom and got it by stealing from Rikki and Rikki's aunt.

The action on stage caught her attention. The Mistress was flogging her assistant with a slow but steady rhythm. Eileen said that kind of flogging felt like a massage. The Mistress snapped her fingers, and the young man brought over a water bottle. Without missing a beat with her flogger, the woman took a sip from the water bottle the young man tipped into her mouth. He put the bottle away and brought over a cloth to wipe her brow as if she were in a marathon. All the while, she kept up her steady back and forth rhythm on her submissive's back, bare buttocks, and legs. She snapped her fingers again, and a second flogger appeared in her hand.

She smoothly went into a four-point Florentine pattern. When the music picked up a moment later, she transitioned into a six-point pattern. Rikki was impressed. It took stamina to do what she was doing. Rikki knew that first-hand. It also took stamina for the submissive cuffed to the cross to withstand this much. In fact, the assistant's small grunts grew louder. Maybe this was why she hadn't been gagged. The Mistress slowed her pace. The assistant slumped over as soon as the Mistress tossed the floggers to the young man, who caught them deftly and put them back on the table.

To the sounds of the audience applauding politely, the Mistress brought the soft cloth back out and soothed her assistant's red, pulsing skin. The Mistress then tossed the cloth high into the air, and the young man dove to catch it before it hit the floor. That brought a great cheer from the audience.

The Mistress wrapped her arms around her submissive assistant from behind. The assistant's head fell back onto the Mistress's shoulder. She was clearly recovering from the impact play, perhaps even in subspace. A head nod from the Mistress spurred the young man into action. He undid the ankle restraints, then each wrist restraint. The woman fell back into her Mistress, who held her up firmly.

Rikki couldn't hear the words but read her lips. "You did well."

"Thank you, Mistress," the assistant said out loud.

The Mistress kissed her submissive on the cheek and then stepped back. The assistant turned toward the audience, finally revealing her chest, and the Mistress burst out laughing along with the audience. The assistant's nipples were covered with pasties bearing the face of her Mistress.

Rikki could tell that the surprise and joy on the Mistress's face was absolutely genuine. It was quite clear that she hadn't known about the pasties. The surprise got rewarded when the Mistress gave her submissive a soulful kiss right on the lips to the oohing and awwing from the crowd. Three young women in the front row caught Rikki's attention. She could see herself Domming over any one of them. She groaned. Not going to happen. Not tonight. Not…ever.

Dismissed, the assistant bowed her way off the stage to much applause, and Rikki was pleased to see that someone threw a robe over her shoulders just off stage.

The young man, meanwhile, clapped in a mocking way as if jealous of the attention the assistant had gotten. The Mistress turned on him and pointed to the opposite side of the stage. Rikki hadn't seen it until now, but a spanking bench had appeared. The young man flew to his knees and kissed his Mistress's feet in apology. She simply shook her head and pointed to the bench again. With the biggest boo-boo face, he crawled across the stage toward it.

That was Rikki's cue. She needed to get home. She wasn't going to find a relationship this way. The show had been fun, but she felt kind of creepy scouring the faces for someone she could get to know better, someone she could dominate.

Despite Shasti's urgings, Rikki wasn't sure she was capable of making room for someone right now. Maybe she was better off alone. At least for a while. It was currently February, the dead of winter, and not a good time for romance. Spring. That's when she'd think about possibly making room for romance and relationships again. For now, she would try to keep her business afloat, make time with her friends, and somehow get through the week leading up to the unavoidable anniversary.

She slid out the theater door, said goodnight to Mel, and slunk out the employee door in the back.

Chapter 6

Nine long and anxious days later, the day dawned sunny and bright but frigidly cold. *Fitting*, Rikki thought as she hopped into her Subaru behind the shop. It was almost a relief that the dreaded anniversary had finally arrived. She could do it, get past it, and get on with her life. She started the car, grateful that it started in the cold, and waited for the engine to warm up. She shivered for a while before finally turning on the heater, preferring not to tax the engine and stall the car.

Lydia and Marta were in charge of the shop and knew to leave her alone on her day off. They knew what this anniversary was to Rikki. Everyone seemed to know, but Rikki didn't need consoling; she needed alone time. Lydia was basically the only one allowed to contact her on this day, with the understanding that it was only in the direst of emergencies. Rikki trusted her people. They'd passed muster many times, so she felt safe to compartmentalize coffee shop business and Esme sightings into one sealed-off part of her brain for a short while. And that was saying something, because she only did it once a year, on this very anniversary date.

She knew she should have eaten before she left, but she didn't think her stomach would accept anything into the knot it was currently in. When she finally stopped shivering, she put the car in drive, hoping the engine had warmed up enough in the sub-freezing temperature. It was seven in the morning, kind of late for Rikki's usual start of the day, but thankfully, the rush-hour traffic was light as she headed toward the highway. Her goal was the nature preserve just west of Cincinnati. It was open year-round, and hopefully she'd have the place to herself. Hopefully, no one else would think a cold hike in nature was a good idea on a weekday. Victoria turned her on to the preserve a few years ago, saying it was a great place to clear one's head. Victoria was always so calm and cool, so it was discomforting to think of her friend needing a space to 'clear her head.' Guess she was human after all.

Rikki chuckled when she thought of her bestie. She'd been a loyal and true friend over the years, and that particular evening over two years ago was no exception. Rikki's then-girlfriend Jessica broke up with Rikki right there at the winter Masquerade Ball in front of everybody. They'd only been together for about four months at that point, but at that party, it became crystal clear that Jessica had only been with Rikki to get closer to Victoria. Jessica completely embarrassed herself by not only breaking up with Rikki loudly and publicly but then professing her undying love for Victoria. All eyes were on Victoria. She was single. She'd been dumped recently in what she'd thought was becoming a serious relationship. To Victoria's credit and Rikki's relief, Victoria didn't bite at the easy pickings. Instead, she chose to stay by Rikki's side and support her jilted friend. Victoria politely told Jessica she wasn't interested.

"This blows," Victoria had said to Rikki that night as they watched Jessica leave the venue crying in the arms of her friends. "I thought you had a good 'un there." One of Jessica's friends shot Victoria a dirty look as if Victoria had been the one to cause her friend's misery.

"I guess I hammered the 'honesty' pillar too hard with her," Rikki said with a laugh. She had laughed that night but hadn't really felt the mirth. "Fuck," she added so only Victoria could hear. "Single again."

"Yep," Victoria commiserated. "Sucks." She turned away from the distraught younger woman leaving the venue and said to Rikki, "We're good catches, aren't we? What the fuck?"

Rikki pulled into the nature preserve's empty parking lot and smiled at the memory. She, Victoria, and even Jessica all moved on within a week or two of that disastrous winter ball, anyway. Of course, Rikki had moved on to Eileen, which turned out to be another kind of disaster altogether.

Rikki put the car in park, grateful that she'd left early enough. The preserve never closed and was a popular place for hikes and meditation retreats. It was the latter she was there for. Meditation, hard thinking, letting go. Where else to do such things than the middle of a secluded forest not too far from home? Dr. Becker, the therapist she'd gone to right after the incident, encouraged her to take stock of the good things in her life before delving into harder stuff. This way, she'd counseled, Rikki would have a solid and grounded foundation from which to explore those difficult things.

Rikki pulled out her thermos of coffee, adjusted the woolen cap on her head, and got out of the car. She pulled her winter coat tighter around her and headed down her usual trail. Not that she came out here often, maybe once a season, but she definitely went on this particular date every year— February 14, Valentine's Day. And Valentine's Day, ironically enough, was also the anniversary of the day they buried her dear Aunt Tilda last year.

Rikki walked briskly to get her blood moving, passed by the bench she would let loose on later, and walked all the way to the fire tower. She didn't climb the steep ladder to the top; the lock was on the gate anyway, so she turned around and headed back for her bench. The cold air felt good against her warm cheeks, and she was cozy warm in her jeans and down winter coat. She sat down on her usual bench and loosened her scarf – a recent birthday gift from Madison. After a few sips of coffee, she was ready to begin. She'd been disciplined. Her mind wanted to get going on forbidden topics as she walked. She wouldn't let it. There was a time for those things, those thoughts, and she would allow them after working through her gratitude grounding. Sometimes a Domme needed to be firm and strict with herself.

She methodically uncapped her coffee thermos She methodically uncapped her coffee thermos. She laid the cap carefully on the bench beside her and took a sip of the hot beverage. She exhaled watching the steam. She took a deep breath, and letting it out slowly, she said out loud, "I'm grateful for many things in my life." Damn it, the tightness in her chest had already started. That tightness was always so close to the surface, but she wasn't going to give in to it yet. She couldn't disintegrate before she'd even started her gratitude track. "Aunt Tilda, you brought me out here to Denton Heights to give me a new start after it happened. You became the maternal figure I needed. I'm grateful for your wisdom, guidance, and for introducing me to the lifestyle. Not that it's working out for me these days, but still, you helped me find confidence and a presence I didn't realize I had. I also got Victoria, Shasti, and a host of others from this lifestyle community, and for that I am eternally grateful."

She decided not to dwell on the fact that she'd used the word "eternally." Dr. Becker would have a field day with her for using that word, but she didn't see Dr. Becker anymore. Dr. Becker was back home in Wilkes-Barre,

Pennsylvania, where Rikki was *persona non grata*.

"Home," she said out loud. "Home is not in Pennsylvania anymore. Home is here in Ohio. Here," she said again. "I have a successful business, loyal, hardworking employees, amazing friends, even two besties." The tightness in her chest loosened a little as she thought of Victoria and Shasti and the many other people she could count as friends. She thought about the customers she interacted with every day. Not all, but for the most part, they seemed to like feeling seen and noticed. Maybe that's all it was with the cute blonde customer. The woman had felt seen and noticed. Well good. Rikki was glad she could brighten someone's day.

"I have my health," Rikki said to the nearby trees. She listed more good things in her life, knowing full well she was avoiding the inevitable. She looked up at a bird flying overhead. She smiled. Jaleesa would know what kind of bird it was. Jaleesa was new to the community, but she, too, was becoming a good friend.

The sky grew more brilliantly blue as she sat there stalling. She looked down at the wood chips on the path. For the most part, she enjoyed the life she had in Denton Heights. But things were off now. She felt alone.

She sighed. It was time. She couldn't hold it back anymore and let the tsunami of emotions pummel her. "Mom, I miss you." The tight feeling in her chest almost knocked her over. "I'm so grateful for Aunt Tilda, but I feel totally cheated out of having you in my life for the last eleven years. It's not fair. And, as Dad continually points out, it's my fault that you're not here anymore. It's so much my fault."

The forest became blurry behind her tears. She didn't care. "I'm the reason you died, Mom. Dad's right. I shouldn't have encouraged you to work at the women's health clinic. I never thought that one stupid ass ignorant fucking zealot would decide that bombing the clinic, on Valentine's Day no less, was a good idea. Who the fuck was he to decide that my mother had to die that day? Who?"

Rikki let out a few moaning groans, trying to loosen the grief squeezing her chest and throat. "What if I hadn't encouraged you to volunteer, Mom? And if you hadn't gone to work at the clinic that day, you'd still be alive. And I could call you and talk to you and—"

Grief gripped her throat. It burned. *Let it out*, her therapist had said all those years ago. Rikki's sobs came from somewhere deep in the earth, channeled through her body, and shredded her heart. She couldn't breathe, her inhales were sobs, her exhales were sobs, her entire existence was misery. "I'm sorry, Mom. I'm so sorry." She shook her head and tears fell on her jacket. "So sorry." With her head in her hands, she did what she wouldn't allow herself to do any other day of the year. She let herself cry and miss her mother.

After a while, she wasn't sure how long, she cried herself out and got her breath back.

"Mom?" More tears came. She was amazed she had any more to give. "What if you were still here? Would I still live in Wilkes-Barre? Would I live nearby? With a life partner in a house or something? It's not like I have anyone here. Would I have pets?" It's what she had always pictured for herself back then. "Mom, do you think I would have gone to law school like I was planning? I definitely wouldn't still be a paralegal at Benson and Benson Law Firm, would I?" She chuckled. "No, you're right. I never did like people telling me what to do."

Rikki laughed again. "And who'd I get that from, Mom? I'm as stubborn as Dad. And then there's Aunt Tilda. She has more than her fair share, I think." She paused. "*Had* more than her share." Incredibly, Rikki smiled instead of crying. "You're together, aren't you? You and Aunt Tilda, what a pair. And you're with Grandma and Grandpa, too, aren't you? You have your parents up there with you." This time, the tears were happy ones, if there was such a thing.

She bathed in the idea that four very influential people in her life were together. Maybe they collectively looked out for her. Maybe she wasn't so alone. But…it felt like it.

"Alone," she said out loud. "I am alone. I have no family. None that will claim me, anyway."

That's not true, said a calm and even voice in her mind. Rikki looked around as if the words had been spoken out loud. There was no one in sight. Her mind was playing tricks on her. Was she too headstrong to think clearly? Her father had said as much.

She whimpered. Out loud on a bench in the forest, she whimpered. "Buck up," her mother would tell her whenever Rikki's father was being an ass or unreasonable. "You'll have your time." Rikki wasn't ever sure what that meant and didn't have time to ponder it because other thoughts were creeping in. *I have Caroline. And Pete. Maybe.* Her older sister and brother still lived in Wilkes-Barre. But did she have them? They were in Dad's camp when it came to their mother's death. Even so, she had spoken to Caroline a handful of times in the eleven years since their mother died. Rikki was the one who typically initiated calls to her family, usually at Aunt Tilda's insistence, but Caroline was the only one who actually talked to her. But now that Aunt Tilda was gone, maybe she wouldn't grovel to them anymore. Maybe it was finally time to let her biological family go. Maybe they could all take a flying leap.

Even though she knew she was being a brat, loneliness overwhelmed her. And so did the cold. She stood up and headed back down the path toward her car, and none too soon. She heard voices, young children's voices, heading toward her.

"Morning," she said to the woman trying to keep up with two young children. "It's a beautiful day." But was it really?

"It is," the chipper woman said. "Thought I'd burn out some of this toddler energy first thing." She laughed, and Rikki smiled.

"Hope it works," Rikki said as they passed.

"Oh, me, too," the woman called after her.

A high-pitched squeal from one of the bundled-up offspring pierced Rikki's head, making it throb. Damn it! The beginnings of a migraine. It wasn't the child's fault; she knew that much, but it was still aggravating.

Throwing herself in the car, she disciplined herself to wait until the car had warmed up properly. The car was an asset she couldn't afford to replace, so she babied it.

Once back on Market Street, she pulled down the alley alongside the coffee shop and parked in her spot. The parking space behind the building had come with the purchase of the building and the empty, overgrown lot next door. She needed to do something with that lot, but that would take money.

As she let herself in the side door to her office and then up the stairs to her apartment, a glorified attic storage room, actually, she wondered how much she could get if she sold her business. Maybe she could rent the space and make an income that way, but let someone else worry about broken espresso machines and employee paychecks.

She didn't dare turn the thermostat up; the heating bills were crazy high as it was, so she swapped her winter coat for a fluffy robe. Well, it used to be fluffy. It was kind of threadbare these days, but it was still warm enough. One day, maybe she would get another, but not in the foreseeable future.

She made fresh coffee to sip as she tried to settle her mind and relax her muscles. These were the things that helped when a migraine came on. Shasti would tell her the migraine came from tension and stress, but she already knew that, so there was no need to call her friend.

The one thing she did, though, was text Lydia to let her know she was back, but unwell and resting upstairs.

Three hours later, after a somewhat refreshing nap and a cheese sandwich, she was feeling better. Not best but better. Rikki headed downstairs to the shop to make sure her livelihood was intact. Thank goodness, all seemed well. The tables looked wiped, the customers happy, and her staff suitably engaged.

"You okay, Miss Rikki?" Lydia asked from behind the counter.

Rikki ignored the look of concern on her assistant manager's face.

"I'm fine," Rikki said succinctly, but then remembered her manners. "Just a bit of a headache this morning. How's everything here?"

A look of frustration flitted across Lydia's face. She tried to hide it, but Rikki was a keen observer and simply asked, "Who?"

Lydia took a deep breath as if weighing her options. Rikki raised one eyebrow.

"Brittany," Lydia said in low tones. "Brittany just being Brittany."

Although most of Rikki didn't want to deal with troublesome employees, she had to. To let transgressions slide was to lose control. Aunt Tilda had taught her that. She looked toward the young woman finishing up a coffee order and took a breath to bark her name when Lydia blurted, "No, Ma'am."

"What?" Rikki was shocked that someone had told her 'no.' Especially when that someone was an employee.

"I've got it handled. I've developed a reward system for when she does well."

"Hmm," Rikki said. Now she was amused. "Go on."

"With your approval, of course," Lydia said, her cheeks tinging red.

Rikki nodded and, out of the corner of her eye, watched as Brittany took a customer's order. Nothing looked out of the ordinary so far.

"Well, Ma'am," Lydia continued, "you once told me that it's better to catch someone being good and reward them for that than to punish them for bad behavior."

"I sound wise," Rikki said with a grin.

Lydia beamed. "You are, Ma'am."

"Go on." Rikki had not been fishing for a compliment.

"Well, for every hour she doesn't make a mistake, get a return order, or get reprimanded, she gets fifteen minutes as an assistant manager. I thought I'd make her a sticker or something that says assistant manager that we can affix to her name badge."

"How's she doing so far?"

"Well," Lydia said and looked over her shoulder. Brittany threw her a thumbs-up. She must have known they were talking about her. "After this morning's coffee spill—Don't worry. The customer didn't get splashed and wasn't mad. Brittany made a new latte so fast, even I was impressed. But after that incident, we had a private meeting in the kitchen. Well, Marta was there, but she didn't comment or even look at us. She's so busy making those cute little cookie bars. Anyway, Brittany liked the rewards idea and has been on her best game so far." Lydia looked up at the wall clock. "It's been three hours so far."

Rikki nodded but paused. Pausing was a technique her aunt taught her. Sometimes submissives, or anyone really, would add more information if you just waited. Lydia was savvy to this Dominants' game, though, and stayed silent, waiting patiently for Rikki's response.

"And when will this new assistant manager be doing her shift?"

"We'll tally her time at the end of the week," Lydia said. "And then we'll schedule a day for her to be 'the boss' next week. That's how she put it, Ma'am. She's excited to be 'the boss.'"

"Hmm," Rikki said. Remnants of her headache were making themselves known again. She pressed three fingers to her temple and rubbed gently. "And she knows she won't get assistant manager pay, correct? You will not take money out of your own pocket for this, Lydia."

"I know, Ma'am. And, yes, she also knows that it's for the experience only. I told her it would be good for her to gain perspective on the challenges we face managing people. My hope is that she'll understand how her behavior affects everyone around her."

Rikki smiled. Lydia would make a great Mommy Domme. Perhaps she'd recognize that in herself one day. "I'm assuming Brittany will be supervised in her new role?"

"Of course, Ma'am. She'll be the boss when I'm on shift. And she knows that I am also still the boss of her."

"'The boss of her'," Rikki repeated and chuckled. "You like this Domme thing, don't you?"

Lydia blushed as she shrugged and said, "Maybe." She shrugged again and added, "Ma'am, I've got things handled here. Mark's coming in a little early, and I'm staying a little late so we can make sure we have a smooth transition between shifts."

"I can't pay overtime."

"We know that, Ma'am. We just want to help."

Rikki didn't know what to do with that statement. Rikki didn't need help. She never needed help. She was the one who helped. *She* was the Domme.

"It's okay, Ma'am," Lydia said softly. "I assure you. It's okay."

"Huh," Rikki said, not sure how to feel about Lydia telling her how to feel. Without a word, she turned and headed back into her office, locked it, and headed up the stairs for her second nap of the day.

An hour and a half later, Rikki was awake, not feeling refreshed at all, but sitting at her office desk. Working helped stop the thinking. She'd done enough for the day. For a lifetime.

"Right, Mom?" Rikki asked the framed picture of her mother on her desk. Her mother was facing the camera but looking down as she held Caroline's new puppy. Caroline had been newly married, and before having kids, she and her husband decided to try caring for a dog to see how that went. Rikki smiled as she sat in her office. That had been a good time in her life. Everyone was still alive. Although her mother wasn't looking directly at the camera, because her focus was on the golden retriever in her arms, you could still see the calm love in her eyes. Rikki knew Dr. Becker would have something to say about the fact that the one framed photo of her mother was one in which she wasn't looking directly into the camera. She wasn't looking at Rikki. Dr. Becker, as any therapist would, said that Rikki was having a hard time facing her mother.

Tears welled up unannounced. Rikki closed her eyes, tilted her face skyward, and mouthed, "I'm sorry, Mom."

A sharp rap on the office door broke her out of her reverie. She wiped the tears away and got up to open the door. Her heart swelled a thousand times over. "You came to visit me," Rikki gushed at the twenty-six-year-old *little* sitting in a wheelchair.

"Hi, Miss Riri," Shanice said. "May we come in, please?"

"We're not bothering you, are we?" Marta, Shanice's Mommy Domme, asked. "She wanted to see you right away."

"Not at all," Rikki said and backed into the office. "Ooh, nice gloves," Rikki gushed at Shanice's fingerless gloves. "Domestic partnership present, perhaps?"

"Last birthday," Shanice said and wheeled herself into the office. "Watch this, Miss Riri." She turned the wheelchair around and then flung her body back, causing the chair to pop a wheelie.

"Shanice!" Marta called and ran over to right the chair.

"Oh, Mama," Shanice said with a grin. "You worry way too much."

Marta blew out a relieved sigh. "I know, but still, you shouldn't do that."

"I'm sorry." Shanice hung her head, but Rikki could tell that Shanice wasn't one hundred percent sorry.

"You're excited," Marta said to her *little*. She sat down on the couch. She smoothed a lock of her short, wavy hair off her face. "We'll let it go. This time."

"Yes, Ma'am." Shanice pressed her lips together, and Rikki couldn't help her own grin. The pair had unexpectedly found each other last summer and were already living together and in a legal domestic partnership. How they met was so unusual that it gave Rikki hope that in some way the universe might be looking out for her, too. Maybe the universe would throw someone in her path. Please? Okay, maybe not as dramatic as a hospital setting, like the two women sitting in her office, but something. And there was Esme, the pretty blonde. Would she be here later? Was that the woman the universe had thrown in her path, daring her to do something about it?

"Go on," Marta encouraged Shanice.

"Okay." Shanice turned to Rikki and said, "Can Mama have a day off? Two weeks from today? February twenty-eighth?"

Rikki was amused. Marta could have asked for the day off herself, and Rikki certainly would have granted it, but something was up. She narrowed her eyes and asked, "Why?"

"Because," Shanice responded, clearly understanding the game.

"Good reason?"

"Yes."

"In your opinion," Rikki teased.

"Yes," Shanice said, sitting up tall and not breaking eye contact with Rikki. "In both our opinions."

Rikki shot a look at Marta, who was tearing up, as usual. Marta was such a softy. How she'd managed to be a soldier in the army all those years was a mystery.

"Three strikes?" Rikki asked.

Shanice nodded.

"Okay," Rikki said. "If you answer 'no' for three of my questions, then I have three strikes, and I'm out. Then you have to tell me."

Shanice nodded again. She understood the game. Marta was the one who'd brought that communication game to their group of friends. It was a good way to help someone find her voice.

"Okay," Rikki said. "Marta needs an entire day off. Hmm." She put her hand on her chin. The only time Marta took time off was if Shanice needed something. "Does she need time off for an appointment?"

"Yes."

"An appointment for herself?"

"No."

"Dang it," Rikki said and pounded a fist on her thigh. "Strike one for me."

"An appointment for little Miss Shanice, then?"

Shanice nodded repeatedly and grinned.

"Judging by your non-poker face grin, I'll ask this. Is the appointment for a good reason?"

"Yes, Ma'am."

"Going for ice cream?" Rikki asked just to get another strike and move the game along.

"Stee-rike two!" Shanice yelled and made an umpire's strike gesture. Those two watched a lot of Cincinnati Reds games at their house.

"Shoot," Rikki said. She glanced at Marta and grinned. "Oh, wait. Is it time for that Benji's concert?" She realized her mistake instantly. "No, wait! I take that one back. A concert isn't an appointment."

"It counts. It counts," Shanice taunted. "Strike three." Shanice laughed as she swung her arms out in front and pulled back one fisted hand. "Yerrrr out."

"First of all, you watch too much baseball, and second, I goofed that one up." Rikki looked at Marta sheepishly. She really had. "But I'm glad you taught that game to me. Oh, well. I lost, but it was fun. And since I lost, you have to tell me now."

"Okay," Shanice said and then swallowed hard. It was clear she was struggling with her emotions. Tears brimmed in her eyes.

Marta groaned softly in commiseration. "Go on, baby," she said to Shanice. "It's okay. It's a good thing."

Shanice nodded at her Domme and said quietly, "I'm getting fitted for prosthetics in two weeks."

"Holy shit," Rikki gushed and leaped up. She hugged Shanice first and then Marta. "This is fantastic, you two. Fantastic. Tell me more." Rikki sat back down and handed out tissues.

Rikki needed another tissue as Marta relayed that Shanice's primary doctor thought Shanice's stumps from the car accident the summer before had healed well enough. She gave them a referral to a certified prosthetist. They'd had a devil of a time getting her stumps to heal properly following the amputations eight and a half months before. And poor Shanice had been in a lot of pain that whole time. She still was. Rikki had never fully understood phantom limb pain until meeting Shanice.

"I'm so happy for you both," Rikki said again. "And, of course, you can have the day, Marta. Whatever you need." She turned toward Shanice. "And you, too! Whatever you need."

Shanice simply put her arms out, clearly needing another one of Miss Riri's hugs. Rikki gave it gladly.

"All right," Marta said as she stood up, "it's time to head out. Our neighbor, Mrs. Pulaski, is waiting for us out front." She pointed to the coffee shop. "We're going out to dinner to celebrate. Would you like to join us, Boss?"

"Thanks for the offer," Rikki said. "I've got a pile of fun to deal with here." She gestured to her messy desk. As much as she would have liked to celebrate with them, the truth was she couldn't afford it. "Oh, hey, those lemon bundt cakes seem to be selling well. Are we able to stay stocked?" Rikki knew the cake question seemed to come out randomly, but Mrs. Pulaski was the baker of said lemon cakes, so it was perfectly reasonable that Rikki would bring that up. It had nothing whatsoever to do with the fact that pretty blonde Esme seemed to favor lemon bundt cakes. Nothing at all.

"I'll make sure we stay stocked," Marta said. "Mrs. Pulaski wanted me to find out if you wanted to try a cream cheese bundt cake or maybe a marble vanilla and chocolate blend cake."

"Yes and yes," Rikki said enthusiastically. "Customers love having something sweet with their coffee." *Or tea*, she thought, thinking of Esme's nightly tea habit.

"You got it, Boss," Marta said. "I'll let her know." Marta opened the office door and held it open.

"Bye, Miss Riri," Shanice said as she rolled by. "Good luck with all that." She made a face and pointed to Rikki's overflowing desk. One day, that desk would get organized.

Rikki laughed and stood up to shut the door after them. Her heart was full. What a great thing to hear on the shittiest day of the year.

She sat down at her desk and looked at her mother's picture. "Mom, I should call Caroline, shouldn't I? We're overdue." She wasn't really up for it, so she decided that a coward's text would do. Nothing major, nothing heavy, just a quick text to touch base. If Caroline responded, great. If not, then whatever.

She picked up her phone, tapped open her text app, and before she could do anything more, the phone rang in her hand.

Rikki jumped, almost dropping her phone. She was so on edge today. She looked at the caller ID. It was Caroline.

Chapter 7

Rikki wanted to let her sister's call go to voicemail, but decided against it. Caroline made the effort to actually call, so Rikki would oblige.

"Hey, Caroline," Rikki said.

"Dad's getting married," her sister blurted without preamble.

"Again? What happened to new wife number two? Evelyn."

"Who knows," Caroline said. "But look, I don't have much time. He insisted I call you today on Mom's anniversary. It's a total dick move, and I'm sorry about this, Rikki, but he wanted me to tell you that you are not invited."

The stone heart Rikki had been developing for her father hardened a bit more. One day, it would be solid granite.

"I see."

"I'm really sorry," Caroline said again.

Rikki wanted to ask why *he* hadn't called her. Was he a chicken shit? Not man enough to be held accountable for his actions? Why make Rikki's sister call? Easy answer—because her sister would do it, and he knew it. They'd all grown up in that house together with Dad's moods and tirades and unfair discipline. And yet, Rikki's sister and brother chose to remain there. Stockholm Syndrome, maybe? It was their mother who always tried to smooth things over. She had been the peacekeeper, making life with him in *his* house somewhat bearable. A week didn't go by that he didn't remind his children that they were living in *his* house, the house that he provided for them.

He didn't deserve you, Mom, Rikki thought silently. Her mother had taken a lot of his anger. He was never physically abusive that she knew of, but he could definitely be an asshole. That was part of the reason Rikki had encouraged her mother to get out of the house and volunteer somewhere, anywhere. Rikki wanted her mother to get away from him. And he knew it, didn't he? Yes, he obviously knew it.

"I have to go," Caroline said.

"Take care," Rikki said succinctly and ended the call. She sat there stunned. After a moment, she muttered, "He's the gift that keeps on giving." She was tempted to block her sister's number and give up on her family altogether, but decided against it. Caroline and Pete were her mother's children, and for her mother's sake, she didn't want to lose contact with them.

She tossed the phone on the pile of papers on her desk and mumbled, "He's looking for a new servant, a new wife to be his verbal punching bag." She groaned in frustration. "You were a saint, Mom."

She let the numbness take over. She would not cry. Never again would she ever cry for him. There was no way she was going to give him the satisfaction.

~~~

A couple of weeks after her glorious meltdown at the nature preserve and the gut-wrenching phone call from her sister, Rikki busied herself at the front counter. At the moment, there was a lull, but the customers had come in a relentless, steady stream, so she was helping Lydia's crew wherever she could. She had one eye on what she was doing and the other on Esme's profile. The attractive woman sat near the windows, just like she had every weeknight for the past two months. She had a beautiful ski-slope nose and full lips. During the brief moments they talked, Esme's light gray eyes had been bright and sparkling. She typically wore her hair up in a messy bun or, like today, let it hang free with a few strands pulled behind her head.

Rikki had vowed to wait until spring to even think about romance, but Esme was here again at the same table, and spring was right around the corner, officially only two weeks away. Rikki would deny it if anyone asked, but she had been waiting for Esme's arrival. The woman was quite punctual, arriving around 6:10 every weekday evening. And on this particular evening, Rikki personally delivered a carafe of hot water, a selection of teas including Esme's go-to chamomile, and a generous slice of lemon bundt cake. She didn't linger, though, and excused herself to let Esme read her book. She didn't want to be a pest.

And even though Rikki had sworn off relationships, she could still be friendly with a customer, right? Esme was a customer. She was intelligent and could carry on an interesting conversation without monopolizing it or making Rikki do all the talking. None of their conversations over the past two months had been long, but they'd been easy and never felt forced.

Shasti wasn't there this evening, thank goodness. Rikki could relax without Shasti's gaze boring a hole in Rikki's head to go talk to Esme, to make a move, to do…something. Rikki tried to tell Shasti that all she wanted from Esme was a casual, easy friendship and nothing more, but Shasti would raise that doubtful eyebrow, and Rikki would turn away. And the only reason Shasti wasn't there that evening was that she and Madison were at home scouring over the Phillips University course catalog, picking out two summer courses. Apparently, the deadline was approaching, and things were going to get very real for Madison soon. And for Shasti. Tomorrow, they were taking the day off for some fun at the zoo before school started. So tomorrow, on the first day of March, they would brave the cold at Madison's favorite place in the world, the Cincinnati Zoo. Unbeknownst to Madison, Shasti had arranged a private insiders' tour of the winter snow leopard habitat. Rikki was excited for them and couldn't wait to hear all about it. Madison tended to brighten rooms when she entered, and Rikki needed that.

Esme kind of did that, too. Thinking about Esme made Rikki close to forgetting she'd gotten another collections notice and, once again, had to pick between paying the electric bill or eating.

"Miss Rikki," Brittany said with a laugh, "I think it's clean now."

Rikki looked down. She blew out an amused scoff. She'd been so lost in thought that she'd been wiping the same spot on the counter for a while.

"Shut up," Rikki said good-naturedly to her employee.

"Go talk to her," Brittany said.

Rikki shot her an aggravated look, but Brittany simply shrugged and then grinned. Rikki groaned. *Does everyone know I like her?* She turned her back on Brittany and rinsed out the rag in the sink behind the counter. After drying her hands, she took a breath to calm her nerves. She took one step toward Esme, but then, like a coward, dove into her office. She needed a moment to regroup.

She took a breath, checked her hair, and headed back toward the door to the shop. Her brain made a snap decision, kind of without her permission, and she stopped in her tracks. "No, no, you're right. I need to do this. I'm going to do this." Screw just being friends, she wanted more. She was going to go out there and ask Esme out. If Esme turned her down, fine. Friendship would be okay, too. But at least she'd tried. 'Nothing ventured, nothing gained,' Madison always said. And bonus, asking out Esme would appease Shasti.

Her hand remained frozen in its reach toward the doorknob, though. It was winter. They couldn't go to the park to walk the path by the river and get to know each other that way. And she most certainly would not ask her out on a coffee date. Rikki's hand dropped down to her side. Maybe they could go to a movie. Unfortunately, that would mean minimal talking, but they could hold hands, right? What if Esme hated the movie Rikki picked? Well, she could let Esme pick it. Or maybe they could go to the Denton Heights Art Center. Harriet, one of Jaleesa's submissives, worked there part-time and said it had high-quality art shows. Was Esme into art? Rikki wasn't an aficionado or anything and no longer had any art pieces to speak of. Thanks to Eileen, everything had to be sold off to pay bills that weren't hers. But the Arts Center might be a good way to find out more about Esme.

She took one last look at herself and decided to toss the apron, even though it was relatively unstained.

"Wait!" Rikki pulled her hand off the doorknob. "What am I doing? What if she rejects me? What if she's only being polite to me? I haven't let her read that book of hers. She's still reading the same one after two months. A book about Amelia Earhart or something." Rikki groaned. "What if she's straight? Or vanilla?" *And what if I keep talking to myself?* She scoffed at her waffling. She wasn't normally this wishy washy.

"Stop," Rikki said to her office. "If she says, 'no,' then that's it. You will have taken your shot and move on. Spring is somewhere around the bend." Thinking about spring reminded her that at the next Denton Heights BDSM Women's Collective Board meeting, they needed to pin down a theme for the spring masquerade ball scheduled for May.

"Stop avoiding this," she scolded herself, stood up tall, and headed back into the shop. She meandered her way toward Esme's table, greeting other customers along the way. Esme immediately put her book down when Rikki said hello. It was as if she'd been waiting for Rikki to visit.

"How are you this evening?" Rikki asked. Good that came out calm and steady as if she wasn't petrified about asking this woman out.

"I'm well, thank you," Esme said and moved a lock of hair off her face. Rikki recognized it as the calming gesture that it was. "How's your day going? It doesn't seem to be too busy right now."

"It's been busy today, but we have a nice lull at the moment." Rikki stood on the other side of the table, both hands on the back of the empty chair. "Other than the morning rush and weekends, it's sometimes hard to predict when it will quiet down like this."

"People are unpredictable, I suppose," Esme said. "Do you have time to sit for a minute? This book isn't holding my attention."

A shot of excitement ran through Rikki. She made a show of looking toward the front counter, but yes, of course, she had time. "Sure." She pulled out the chair, sat down, and sighed. "Feels good to get off my feet."

"How long have you had the shop?"

And from there, the conversation moved from the shop to Denton Heights in particular, and then to Ohio in general. It seemed that Esme had recently moved to Denton Heights from Vermont and was still getting to know the area. Rikki suggested the usual Cincinnati sights like the American Sign Museum, the Hard Rock Casino, and the Cincinnati Zoo. When Esme seemed interested in the zoo, Rikki also mentioned the Newport Aquarium just over the river in Kentucky.

"It's so strange being in a city so close to another state," Esme said. She asked about the weather and hoped the summers would be like the ones she'd experienced growing up in Vermont. Rikki told her they were probably similar and mentioned growing up in rural Pennsylvania.

"So, is no one actually from Ohio?" Esme asked with a laugh. It was the best sound in the world.

Rikki laughed with her and felt warmth spread in her chest. She was just about to mention the art museums in the area and then segue into a possible date to the Arts Center, but Esme said with a laugh, "I have to ask, but is there a requirement to become a Bengals fan if one lives here?" She pointed to the oversized Bengals banner hanging proudly on the wall near the new dartboards.

Rikki burst out laughing. "No. Having said that, however, your character may come into question depending on what team you do root for." She laughed again, letting Esme know she was teasing.

"The Pats." Esme said succinctly.

"Nooooo," Rikki said. "Don't say that too loudly around here." She made a show of looking to see if they'd been overheard. "I'd keep that on the down low. I'll never hear the end of it if they find out I let a New England Patriots fan in here."

Esme laughed and added, "I don't think there's much of a problem remaining a Red Sox fan, is there?" She pointed toward the Cincinnati Reds banner. "The Reds are in the National League and the Sox are in the American."

"As long as you don't disparage our team, then you'll be fine." And Rikki was impressed that Esme knew and seemed to like sports.

The conversation then moved to the college banners on the wall. "Is Phillips University a good school?"

Rikki wondered why she was asking, but simply answered, "A very good school. From what I hear, Phillips is one of the best academically. Not quite the Ivy League of the Midwest, but very respectable." She went on to say that a very good friend of hers had gotten in and was starting her freshman year in May. "Madison's getting a bit of a late start, college-wise, but we're all so proud of her."

"That's wonderful," Esme gushed. She seemed genuinely happy for someone she'd never met. "I love stories like that. Go for what you want." A fleeting look crossed Esme's face, but Rikki wasn't sure what it meant.

Rikki paused, but when Esme didn't elaborate, Rikki pointed to another banner and said, "Blackwell College is down in Cincinnati. It's an all-women's school. I have two good friends who went there, and they both have amazing careers now."

Rikki stayed well beyond her usual five minutes, and Esme didn't seem to mind. In fact, they talked so easily it was as if Esme had been a friend for a long time.

"So, I design and make jewelry to sell on all the online platforms," Esme was saying after Rikki asked what she did with her days. Esme picked up her phone, swiped around on the screen for a moment, and then showed Rikki one of the online platforms.

"Jewelry by Esmerelda," Rikki read the title of the seller's page. "Hand-designed and custom-made one-of-a-kind jewelry." Rikki looked up to see that Esme was blushing furiously. "These are intriguing," Rikki said. And the pieces *were* intriguing. "Do you do the metal work yourself?"

Esme nodded.

"Impressive," Rikki said. "May I scroll down the page?"

"Sure," Esme said and let out a nervous sigh.

"These are so intricate," Rikki said without looking up. "Wedding rings? You make wedding rings."

"Yes, custom, of course," Esme said. "I typically sell online only but have been known to set up a booth at a craft fair or festival." She gestured for her phone, scrolled, and showed Rikki a different set of jewelry. "I also do gothic and mystical pieces for Renaissance Faires and the like."

"This really is remarkable, Esme," Rikki said and handed back the phone. "In the summer, we have Denton Heights days. It's a town festival with food trucks and a parade. All the businesses have some kind of sale or giveaway. The craft fair usually sets up down by the Queen City Subs shop. Great sub shop by the way. The festival seems to be getting bigger every year and attracts people from all over. You could look into getting a seller's booth or, better yet, a demonstration booth."

Esme's eyebrows shot up high. "Demonstrations? I never thought of that." She looked up, not at Rikki, and said, "Hmm."

Rikki loved helping people like that. It was in her Domme makeup to help someone grow. Not that Esme was her submissive or anyone's submissive, but Rikki couldn't help helping. They looked at each other for a moment without speaking. Unspoken questions seemed to pass between them. Rikki took in the small creases on either side of Esme's eyes. Character lines Aunt Tilda had called them. Her cute nose and light gray eyes were very pleasing.

"Rikki?" Esme said, breaking the silence, her shy smile threatening to melt Rikki.

"Yes?" Rikki said, giving Esme her full attention.

"Do you think—" Esme swallowed nervously.

Rikki wanted to blurt out, "Yes" to whatever Esme was about to ask, but a high-pitched screech made both of them jump. Rikki shot to her feet.

"Miss Rikki, Miss Rikki," came the frantic call from behind the counter. Brittany had her hands on her head and was watching Lydia attempt to undo something Brittany had obviously done.

"Gotta go. Duty calls." Rikki's feet were already moving.

Brittany shrieked again as a hot funnel of steam rocketed high in the air.

Lydia had everything under control by the time Rikki got behind the counter. Thankfully, no one had gotten hurt. Brittany had a scare, though.

"Grumpy Gus," Brittany said with a growl, pointing to the troublesome espresso machine. "I think he just unalived himself."

Rikki couldn't help but laugh. Brittany was not a *little,* but she was still very young psychologically, despite being in her early twenties.

"What do *you* think?" Rikki asked Lydia. "Did Grumpy Gus just breathe his last espresso?"

Lydia took a deep breath and let it out slowly. "We've been milking him along for a long time, Boss." She seemed quite sad, like she had just watched a sick old friend die. "I've repaired him so many times, but obviously, he just couldn't take the pressure anymore."

"Literally!" Brittany screeched. "Did you see all that steam? I wish Madison had seen it. OMG."

"Should we have a funeral?" Rikki asked, clearly amused by her employees.

Lydia chuckled, but Rikki could see the wheels turning in Brittany's mind. "No," Rikki said quickly. "It was just a joke."

"Aww," Brittany moaned, clearly dejected. "I was going to get Madison to help me plan it."

"Madison has enough on her mind these days," Rikki said.

"I know," Brittany gushed. To Rikki's amazement, Brittany picked up a rag and wiped up the water seeping onto the counter without being asked. "She got into that fancy college. I'm so jelly. I tried community college. Not for me."

"Not everyone has to go to college," Rikki said. She hated it when people thought less of a person because they didn't attend college. "Going or not going to college is definitely not a measure of a person's worth."

"Yeah, I guess," Brittany said, a definite tone of disbelief in her voice. Rikki patted her arm twice to let her know she understood her anxiety about it.

Lydia broke in, said she'd take care of the machine, and advised that Grumpy Gus wasn't a viable candidate for resale on the second-hand market. Rikki trusted Lydia and said she'd find a replacement ASAP.

"I'll leave all this up to you two," Rikki said and turned to look for Esme. Disappointment hit her viscerally, and she groaned. Esme was gone. Was she in the restroom? No, her coat and book were gone, too. And, apparently, she'd even bused her own tray. Rikki got a clean rag, walked over to the table, and wiped it down. Was she figuratively wiping Esme out of her hopes? Mixed feelings warred inside her. She hadn't even gotten a chance to ask her out. It was an opportunity lost.

As she cleaned a few tables on her way back to hide in her office, Shasti's wise but unbidden words came to mind. "Stop fixating on one moment," Shasti had told her once. "There's a bigger picture out there." If Shasti were there at that moment, she would tell Rikki to chill out and simply wait for Esme to show up again tomorrow evening.

Rikki felt one part exhilarated by the thought of seeing Esme the next evening, but two parts dejected by her sudden disappearance. Rikki hid her disappointment as she ducked into her office. Esme could have at least said goodbye. Oh, well.

"Didn't even get her phone number," she murmured as she sat at her desk. "My lack of game is astounding." She shook her head at her ineptness but also smiled. They'd had a moment, she and Esme. Hadn't they? No worries, she pepped herself up. There was always tomorrow night.

Rikki opened the laptop lid. It was time to prowl around her favorite pro coffee gear websites, anyway. But first, a quick search of the *Jewelry by Esmerelda* website wouldn't hurt, would it? And the Art Center website, too. She had to find out what kind of art shows were going on there. It was better to be informed when you ask an attractive woman out. And then after those two quests, she would search for a used espresso machine to order. Guess she wouldn't be eating this week. Or next. And, even though they desperately needed another morning-shift worker, she couldn't afford that either.

She had barely gotten her new favorite website loaded when there was a knock on the office door. She knew that knock. Hopefully, it was good news. She got up and let Marta in. Shanice was nowhere to be seen.

"It didn't go well," Marta blurted without greeting.

"Oh, no," Rikki said. Marta wasn't one for hugs, except when they came from her *little*, so she didn't offer. "What happened?" She gestured to the couch, but Marta decided that pacing was the better move.

"She wanted me to come tell you in person," Marta said, wiping at her eyes. "She's home with the cats. I asked Mrs. Pulaski to come over and stay with her."

"Wise move," Rikki said.

Marta stopped pacing and sat on the couch. She placed her hands in her lap and looked so vulnerable that Rikki's heart ached for her. They remained silent for a few moments until Marta said, "The stump wounds were healed, but the prosthetic guy said the bones underneath weren't quite strong enough." She looked up at Rikki. "They think it stems from a lack of good bone density. They did these tests."

Marta usually called her 'Boss' when she addressed her, but she didn't when she said, "Rikki, they think it has something to do with her lack of nutrition growing up. She didn't thrive in the foster system. She's told me some of what she went through, but there's a lot more she isn't saying."

"Oh, Marta," Rikki said. "Poor kid."

"Rikki, I hate this world. I hate people. No one took care of her. The woman who birthed her was disabled and lived in a facility her whole life, so she clearly couldn't take care of a baby. And I don't even want to know how she got pregnant in the first place. But the foster system?" Marta swayed from side to side as her face contorted in frustrated sadness and anger intermingled. "It's not enough. Rikki, why can't we take care of each other? Why the fuck is anyone starving in this country? Or homeless? Why do people feel unsafe? This is the goddamn United States of America. I fought a war to protect our way of life over here. Personally, I think—"

She clamped her lips together and exhaled loudly through her nose. She took a moment to get herself together and then said, "Rikki, there's like this basic lack of empathy running rampant in the world. The *as-long-as-I-have-mine* assholes disregard everyone and anyone who needs help. And do *not* get me started on those people who prey on the weak and vulnerable. There is a special place in hell for them."

Marta breathed out her anger for a moment, and Rikki let her. She had never seen Marta so steamed before. She was a combination of anger, frustration, and just plain exasperation.

Sensing that Marta had run out of energy for more ranting, Rikki asked, "Can the bone density issue be remedied?"

"They said to go back to her primary in a few months and get another bone density test, and after getting those results, we'd go from there."

"Ahh," Rikki said.

"But you know my girl," Marta said, sporting a slight grin. "She googled it on the way home, and we basically have to step up what we've already been doing. Good nutritious food, including calcium and vitamin D, exercise, and good sleep. I'm not sure how we're going to do the weight-bearing stuff—maybe we'll get the doctor's advice on that. Rikki, we can't afford a gym membership or a physical therapist. Even Shanice's good insurance doesn't cover that. I'm not sure how much physical therapy costs, but…" She trailed off, looking absolutely exhausted.

"We'll find a way," Rikki said. She wasn't sure how, but it was obvious that Rikki wasn't the only one with financial hardships.

"Yes, we will," Marta said. She took a cleansing breath, let it out, and added, "We can't count on that lawsuit from her accident coming through. Companies always get out of shit like this." She growled, took another breath, and said, "In the meanwhile, I want to get her a wheelchair-accessible van with hand controls so she can drive herself places. I want her to have some independence. Because God forbid something happens to me."

"It won't, but if it does, she'll have us," Rikki said. "Listen, we'll figure something out. If we have to start having bake sales and car washes, then we will."

Marta scoffed, but then nodded and said, "Thank you, Rikki."

"We take care of each other in this community, Marta. You know that."

"I do," Marta said. "And I didn't mean to lay all this on you. She just wanted me to tell you in person. I think she understood that I needed to melt down in private." She chuckled. "Knowing my girl, in the time I've been here, she's probably researched everything and has a plan mapped out."

Rikki smiled. "She's a smart one. That's for sure."

Marta stood up, turned toward the closed office door, but then turned for a rare hug. "Thank you."

"We won't give up, Marta. And, as always, if you need time off, say the word. Maybe Brittany can fill in for you."

Marta's eyebrows hit the ceiling. "Uhh, Boss? Let's discuss that particular employee another time, okay?"

Rikki only laughed. "Give Shanice a hug from Miss Riri."

"I will," Marta said. "Thanks."

Once the door closed behind her, Rikki let herself deflate. She groaned. "Poor kid. She can't catch a break. And poor Marta." Trying to be strong when all you want to do is give up and give in was excruciatingly difficult. She knew a thing or two about that, didn't she?

She spun in her chair and was just about to stalk a certain blonde jewelry maker when her phone dinged an incoming text.

> JALEESA: Can I come by sometime? I want to discuss something with you. To see if you're amenable, maybe.

It was kind of a weird text, but Rikki had just told Marta that the Denton Heights community looked out for and took care of each other, so Rikki replied right away.

> RIKKI: Sure. Maybe after Rocco's group brunch this Saturday?

> JALEESA: That will work, but it's not for public consumption. Maybe we can stay a bit longer or talk in my truck.

This sounded like secret undercover stuff, making Rikki curious about what Jaleesa was up to, but Rikki texted back and told her it sounded fine. She would see her in four days. Other than a "see you then" return text from Jaleesa, there was no further exchange.

Rikki tucked the phone in her pocket, trying not to be too curious about Jaleesa's obscure message.

Something had stirred in her, though. She needed to get some energy out. She pulled her phone back out of her pocket and punched in the familiar number.

"Dominique? It's Rikki."

"Hey, girl. Coming in?" the dungeon owner said, her voice cheery. "We could use you."

"Be there in forty-five minutes."

Exhilaration fueled her spring up the stairs. Changing into Domme gear made her feel powerful. Getting her Domme on made her feel in control—something that had been seriously lacking lately.

Chapter 8

"Thanks, Marlene," Rikki said to their usual waitress at Rocco's Diner as she lifted her refilled coffee cup in salute. Diner coffee puts hair on your chest, somebody in this group had said once, probably Jaleesa, and she'd been right. It wasn't Rikki's Coffee Shop coffee, but that was okay. Rikki wasn't too much of a coffee snob when she couldn't do much about it.

The diner was right off the highway and frequented by many travelers, including truckers. Rikki liked the comfort food the place offered, along with the private room they booked for their brunches. An absolute bonus was the fact that their usual waitress, Marlene, didn't seem to blink an eye about some of the discussions she must have overheard. She was a discreet server, and everyone felt comfortable with her. And because of that, despite popular lore, the women currently seated together in the private room tipped her well, very well.

Shasti leaned closer and asked quietly. "Are you going to eat anything?"

"I'll eat later," Rikki said. She hated to evade the truth, but it was easier than telling everyone her current budget didn't include a brunch buffet. Just coffee.

"Who's minding the shop?" Jaleesa asked, pointing first to Rikki, then to Lydia, and back again.

"Mark," Rikki said with a laugh, "Marta's there, too, of course. And I think Shanice was spending the day there, too, to keep Marta company." Rikki shot Lydia a smile, which was returned. Rikki had insisted that Lydia join them for the brunch because she wanted her to feel more part of the community. This was Lydia's first brunch since they'd started over seven months ago. She looked cute in her blonde braids, almost like a German fraulein serving tankards of ale at Oktoberfest. Now, if she'd actually worn a tight-bodiced dirndl, it would have completed the look.

"So, who's minding your salon?" Rikki countered.

"Harriet volunteered to manage, so Dana and I could have our date today."

"Yay," Dana put her hands up excitedly. The two made a cute but contradictory pair. Jaleesa was tall, over six feet, while Dana just tipped over an even five feet. There was an age gap between them, too, with Jaleesa at least twelve years Dana's senior.

"Is Miss Tina working at the bank today, Miss Jaleesa?" Madison asked. "Being an important bank manager?" Tina seemed to be Madison's latest crush, and everyone, including Tina, knew it.

"Yes, yes," Jaleesa said with a sigh. "She says it's easier to just go in than to expect everyone to do everything properly." She looked up at Rikki pointedly, but Rikki wasn't sure what the look meant. Maybe the chat she was going to have with Jaleesa later was about Tina.

Jaleesa broke eye contact, tousled Dana's overgrown afro, and said, "You need a haircut."

"I know," Dana said succinctly. "I have ideas."

"You do, eh?" Jaleesa bopped her submissive on the nose and said, "I'll see if Tina can give you a haircut in the kitchen. I have a bowl that will fit nicely over your—"

Dana nudged her Domme with her shoulder and stuck out her lower lip.

"Fine, fine," Jaleesa said. "I'll cut it, but we'll discuss your ideas? Okay?"

"Yes, Ma'am," Dana said, a gleam of mischief in her eyes. Dana was only one of Jaleesa's four subs, and Rikki had no idea how she managed that many.

Jaleesa looked back toward the assembled group and said, "Our second stop will be at Forbidden Treasures—"

"Adult Superstore," Madison finished. The table got quiet. Their community had fairly strict, agreed-upon protocols, one of which was that submissives never interrupted Dominants. Madison frequently forgot this rule. She looked around. "Oh, sorry, Miss Jaleesa. I'll wear a disrespect ribbon if you have one."

"No worries, bucko," Jaleesa said graciously. "Just be mindful in the future, okay?"

"Yes, Ma'am."

Jaleesa nodded at Madison and said, "Dana is getting rewarded this afternoon. She's going to pick out a few new toys at Forbidden Treasures."

The group oohed at this lovely thought, and Dana said to Jaleesa, "I have ideas." The blissful grin on her face was priceless.

"I bet you do, my love." Jaleesa kissed the back of Dana's hand. She looked back at the group and said, "Obviously, however, our first stop was here for the monthly, oh-so-casual, come-if-you-can, no worries-if-you-can't, brunch at Rocco's with the illustrious Denton Heights Women's BDSM Collective."

"Go us," Madison said and started a round of soft cheering. She wiggled in her chair and then knocked over her empty water glass.

Victoria reached across the table with her long arms and righted the glass. "You're such a wiggle butt," she said to Madison.

"I know *you* are, but what am I?" Madison shot back playfully.

Victoria pointed toward Madison but said directly to Shasti, "How do you handle this wiggle butt?"

"It's a challenge, and somebody whose name rhymes with Madison Kim had better learn to keep wiggling to a minimum soon. Sitting still in classes is a requirement at Phillips University."

Madison froze. Her eyes widened. She was clearly nervous about starting college in a couple of months.

"Congrats, kid," Victoria said. "We're so proud of you for getting into that hoity toity college." She pushed a perpetual lock of her short, sandy-brown hair off her forehead, then raised her coffee cup in salute, and the others did the same. "What did you sign up for?"

"English Composition," Madison said. "That's required for freshmen. Well, they call us 'first-year students' now because fresh *men* is kind of sexist."

"Yeah, it is," Victoria said, a frown on her face. "We take so much of that sexist shit for granted."

Madison inhaled sharply.

"Oh, shit," Victoria said again, probably on purpose. "I'll wear one of those 'I swore in front of a *little*' ribbons if you have one, Jaleesa."

Jaleesa burst out laughing, and everyone else joined in. "I'm fresh out, Vic. Sorry."

"I'll be mindful next time," Victoria said to Madison. "We don't want your brain melting before you even start college."

"What else are you taking, Madison?" Lydia said from her seat on the far side of Madison.

"Psychology," Madison said directly to Lydia. "I wanted to take philosophy, but Mistress and I went to see a guidance counselor or whatever they're called in college, and she said a great intro course would be Psychology. She said that taking only two courses was a good test to see if college was a good fit for me. What did she mean by that, Miss Lydia?"

"Well, for one thing, she was *not* implying that you aren't smart enough, so get that out of your head, please."

"Okay," Madison said reluctantly.

"She probably just meant that you'll have to juggle classes and work and life and a bunch of other things."

"And," Victoria interjected, "the most challenging part of all is juggling your strict and demanding Mistress." Victoria waggled her eyebrows at Shasti, who simply smirked and shook her head at Vic. Meanwhile, Madison was trying hard, oh so hard, not to burst out laughing. Her face was getting redder and redder.

"It's okay to laugh, honey," Shasti said, and Madison did just that. "Breathe, baby. Breathe."

Lydia chuckled as she rubbed Madison's back affectionately while Madison tried to catch her breath.

Yep, Rikki thought, Lydia was definitely a Mommy Domme in the making. Rikki loved the playful banter among her friends. None of the teasing was passive-aggressive or held hidden meanings. They were a group of like-minded people who simply enjoyed each other's company. The fact that they'd made it a priority to schedule and attend these monthly first Saturday gatherings was a testament to their collective friendship.

Once the laughter died down, Rikki said, "The spring masquerade ball in May is getting closer. We need to schedule our board meeting and plan the thing."

"Seamus's men's group, too?" Shasti asked.

"No, just the women's group, I think," Rikki said. "Once we settle in on our goals, then we'll get the ball committee rolling with the guys. So, before we start the arduous process of picking a date for the meeting—" She had to wait while the group at the table laughed and agreed how difficult it was to find a common time in their busy schedules for their quarterly meetings. "I think it's time we give back."

"What do you mean?" Jaleesa asked.

"We throw these extravagant parties for our own benefit, but there are people in our community who are barely getting by." Rikki was in no way talking about herself, so she quickly added, "You've all heard by now that Marta wants Shanice to have more independence. A hand-controlled van would be perfect for that. And Shanice needs more physical therapy—"

"And a nutritionist, I think," Shasti added.

"Yes, probably," Rikki agreed. "But they can't afford any of those things. Can we find a way to do some fund-raising for them?" Ideas about bake sales, donation boxes, and fifty-fifty raffles were thrown around until Rikki said, "These are all great ideas. How about we muse on this topic and present formal ideas at the board meeting."

"What about the lawsuit?" Victoria asked.

"They can't count on that," Rikki said. "And I think it's a long way from getting resolved."

"Marta won't like us doing this," Shasti said. "She's very prideful."

"She is, but too bad," Rikki said. "They need help, and we can give it, right?"

A resounding chorus of agreement sounded at the table.

"And if anyone hears about other folks in need, let the group know."

"I'll reach out to Seamus about this," Jaleesa said. "We're buds now."

"Oh, yeah?" Rikki asked, a little surprised, since Jaleesa had recently taken over the contract for one of his subs.

"He asked me to be on his darts team for the new league Rikki's Coffee Shop will be hosting in the summer."

"No shit," Vic said, causing an almost near meltdown from Madison. Lydia rested her hand on Madison's back to soothe Madison's shock. "Good for you," Vic said to Jaleesa.

"Join?" Jaleesa asked Vic.

"Nah," Vic said. "Not my thing."

"Can't get in the way of potential date nights, Victoria?" Shasti teased.

"Bingo," Vic said with a lecherous laugh.

"Okay, on to the schedule," Rikki said. "Obviously, I have to check in with Marta and Rowena to see their availability, but let's go weekend by weekend. Next weekend's out, because two somebodies will be in England." After the excited chatter about their trip died down, Rikki suggested the weekend following.

"Benjie's concert in Columbus," Jaleesa said matter-of-factly and then smirked at Dana.

"Wait, what?" Dana asked.

"You didn't think toy shopping was your only reward, did you?"

"No way. No way." Dana stomped her feet. "Really, Ma'am?"

"Yes. It's kind of your twenty-seventh birthday present from the family, and we'll be hanging with Shanice and Marta. Staying overnight in Columbus."

"Oh, wow," Dana said. "Wow." The young woman looked positively stunned. "And we can help Miss Marta with Shanice. And Miss Marta doesn't like crowds, so we'll be helping her, too. Right?"

Jaleesa nodded and bopped Dana on the nose again.

A pang of something hit Rikki square in the chest. She wanted a sub to please like that. To reward. To help grow. She held back the feeling and took a sip of her now-cold diner coffee. Yeah, the coffee wasn't good.

Jaleesa kissed the back of Dana's hand again and asked, "When is that dance performance for dancers of all abilities? You know, the tickets Rowena and Minjung got for Shanice?" Everyone shrugged until Madison raised her hand high in the air.

"Um, okay," Rikki said. "Yes, Madison?"

"It's called Dancing Wheels, Miss Rikki. And the concert is on June seventeenth in Cleveland, Ohio."

"That's our college kid right there," Vic teased. "Smart one."

"Tanks, Daddy Vic." Madison beamed.

Rikki smiled at their banter. "So that performance is not in the way. Good."

They ultimately settled on two dates, one at the end of March and one on the first day of April.

"I'll firm up the date with Rowena and Marta and let you all know on our group chat," Rikki said. "Oh, wait. Where are we having this meeting?"

Shasti volunteered her home, and Rikki was satisfied that she'd taken care of important things before the group disbanded. They settled their bills with Marlene, and then the group stood up to leave. Hugs were given all around. Rikki told Lydia to steer clear of the coffee shop and get some much-needed rest. Lydia seemed relieved and headed toward the exit.

Jaleesa handed Dana some cash and said, "Go play some arcade games while I talk with Miss Rikki."

Dana knew not to question her Domme and simply said, "Yes, Ma'am. I'll wait for you in the arcade."

"Perfect."

Shasti leaned in to Rikki and said, "Call me later."

"Will do," Rikki said. Of course, Shasti wanted Rikki to call her later. Naturally, she'd want the details on Rikki's talk with Jaleesa, but Rikki doubted highly that she would share those details, and Shasti would just have to wonder.

"Mistress," Madison said urgently, "can I go to the arcade, too?"

"Not at all," Shasti said evenly. "We're going school clothes shopping."

Madison clutched her stomach as if wounded. She groaned and squeaked, "My favorite," even though it clearly wasn't.

Once their friends were completely out the door to the private room, Jaleesa said, "I'm worried about Tina. Thanks for taking some time with me, Rikki."

"No worries. What's up? Oh, and by the way. This convo will be confidential."

"I appreciate that." Jaleesa sighed and said, "Tina gets wound up so tight that it's hard to get her to relax. It's her promotion to bank manager. She's trying to be perfect at it. Granted, she got thrust into the role without much preparation and is trying to learn everything she can in a short time, but dang, she needs some release. You know?"

"Yeah, I get that," Rikki said.

"You know she's asexual, so that's not really an avenue I can use to help her let go. Although I did recently get her a clit vibrator so she could give herself an orgasm occasionally. It's cleansing. It helps release tension."

"How's that going?"

"Not great, but I'm not pushing. I've asked her to find something that might relax her enough to let the physical vibrations take effect. But," Jaleesa hesitated before adding, "I've got to find something else. We've done some impact sessions, but I think because they're coming from me, she's trying to please me too much and isn't relaxing into it."

"That's tough," Rikki said, sensing where the conversation was going. She'd learned long ago to let someone actually ask before interjecting. When she'd opened the coffee shop almost four years ago, she'd turned into a 'rescue manager,' jumping in to do the employees' jobs if they messed up instead of letting them learn from their mistakes. She almost burned out in the first month until her Aunt Tilda helped her see a better way to manage. *Let them make mistakes and learn in their own way*, she counseled.

Jaleesa looked down at the table, "I know she won't, but addiction is a harsh mistress and…"

Rikki waited.

"And I don't want her using again. The littlest thing could spark it. A chance meeting with her old dealer. Something at work or home could trigger her need to use."

"I—" Rikki wasn't sure what to say. "Yeah, that is worrisome." She sounded like her aunt, but she truly didn't know how to help.

Jaleesa looked up, a pleading look in her eyes. "I want Tina to feel vulnerable but in a completely safe space. Do you get that?"

"I do."

"I want her to feel someone else's hand or flogger on her body. I want her to be fully present in the moment. You know we're a polyamorous family, right?"

"Mm hmm."

"Although I seem to be the only one doing the poly thing." Jaleesa shook her head as if this was the first time she realized that fact. "Anyway, Tina doesn't have other outlets, like I do. I have Dana. Dana has me and her horticulture projects. Harriet has art and our impact sessions when she needs them. DeShawn has woodworking and my discipline, which he craves. He is such a great fit for our family. I cannot wait for Lock-tober," she said with a gleam in her eye. She smiled and then said, "I mean, Tina goes to these monthly 'stitch-and-bitch' gatherings. Do you know the Crochet Corner? In town near the library?"

"Yes, yes," Rikki said. She did know it. "But what's a 'stitch-and-bitch?'"

"The yarn shop offers a place where people can hang out to work on knitting, crocheting, or whatever. They bring their current projects—Tina is currently knitting DeShawn leather-palmed work gloves for when he has jobs out in the cold."

"Nice."

"It is. Anyway, he doesn't know about them yet. But at these monthly things, they can get help with their projects or just sit and socialize."

"Ahh," Rikki said. "The 'bitching' part of it."

"Yeah," Jaleesa said with a laugh. "But it's not enough for her. I try to get her to exercise, but she's too tired. Once the weather gets better, we'll go on family hikes. You are more than welcome to join, by the way."

"Thank you," Rikki said. "I just might."

"Okay, let me get to the point. Tina is willing to let me find someone to give her an impact session, but she said it has to be at our house, where she'll feel safe. And she wants me in the house, but not necessarily in the room while it's going on. I mentioned your name, and she was quite amenable to that. As long as there were no whips involved." The last she said with a laugh. "Your whip demonstrations at masquerade balls scare all of us, Rikki."

Rikki chuckled. "Whips are not for the faint of heart." She took a breath and thought about Jaleesa's proposal. "I'd like a sit-down with her before I show up in my Domme regalia all scary-like."

Jaleesa smiled, but the tension was clear and present on her face.

"I have to give aftercare," Rikki added. "You can help with that, of course, but for my own sake, I need to give it."

"Done," Jaleesa said, but then wavered. "As long as Tina's okay with that."

Rikki nodded. "I'd love to see what you've done with your dungeon down there."

Jaleesa's eyes grew wide. "It's just a basement," she said in a tight voice. She relaxed and said, "We have strict rules *not* to call it a dungeon in case one of us slips up in front of Tina's, Dana's, or my parents."

"Good thinking," Rikki said. "All right, back to scheduling. She pulled out her phone and opened her calendar app again.

Once tentative dates were set for a pre-talk with Tina and the actual impact session, they stood and hugged. "I hope this helps," Rikki said.

Jaleesa groaned. "Me, too."

They parted ways in the parking lot, and as Rikki drove back to the coffee shop, she recognized that Jaleesa's soft yet authoritative dominance style was similar to her own. When Jaleesa and her family, as they called themselves, showed up in Denton Heights, it was like a puzzle piece that fit perfectly into their community.

Now, if Rikki could only find other pieces that fit into her personal life, then maybe she could reclaim a modicum of joy she'd once had. It was Saturday. Esme would not be at the shop that evening, and she hadn't been for the last three evenings, ever since Grumpy Gus exploded. Getting her phone number sure would have helped. Rikki was certain there had been some kind of connection between them, some kind of unspoken spark. Maybe Monday evening would find Esme at her usual table.

Chapter 9

Somehow, over the next four days, Rikki managed to evade Shasti's subtle and not-so-subtle prying about her talk with Jaleesa. It was a testament to how strongly Rikki honored privacy and boundaries. Shasti would live without knowing everybody else's business. But now Rikki was about to spend the whole day with her friend. Hopefully, she'd be strong enough to keep her promise of privacy to Jaleesa.

Rikki pulled her Subaru along the curb of Shasti and Madison's house. It was a lovely two-story executive home in a gated community, perfectly suited to Shasti's role as a general practitioner in town. Her medical practice was thriving, and somehow, she seemed able to balance her work and personal life with ease. This shopping trip that Shasti had forced on Rikki was probably part of Shasti's plan to help workaholic Rikki find some kind of balance. That and it was another opportunity to get in on the gossip.

Victoria's pickup was in the driveway, but she wasn't going shopping with them. Apparently, she and Madison were attempting to fix the failing washing machine in the basement. Rikki loved that her one bestie was helping out her other. See? Community. This is what it was all about.

Rikki got out of her car and headed up the walkway to the front door. It opened before she had a chance to ring the bell.

"Hi, Miss Rikki," Madison said and smashed herself against Rikki for a hug. Rikki had no choice but to put her arms around the shorter young woman and hug back.

"Good to see you, Madison," Rikki said as Madison pulled back. "Oh, my. I love the outfit."

"Thank you." Madison backed up so Rikki could enter the house. Madison's outfit was priceless. She wore jeans and a flannel shirt. A pocket protector was tucked into the flannel shirt, along with various pens and pencils. She typically wore contacts, but the glasses she had on didn't look like prescription glasses. Ahh, they were safety glasses. Rikki tried not to laugh when Madison adjusted the heavy tool belt around her waist. It was filled with tools, including a hammer dangling off one side. The huge leather gloves she wore were the kicker, though. They must be Victoria's.

"You're ready to fix that washing machine, aren't you?"

"Daddy Vic is going to teach me."

"That's awesome." Rikki let Madison lead her into the house.

"Mistress," Madison called up the stairs, "Miss Rikki is here."

"I'll be down in a few," Shasti said. "Show Miss Rikki the broken washer."

"Okay, Ma'am," Madison called up. She reached for Rikki's hand and pulled her toward the basement stairs. "Daddy Vic promised to wait for me before she does any more investigating."

"Hey, Vic," Rikki said to her friend once they reached the bottom of the stairs.

"Hey," Victoria said. She wasn't as decked out as Madison, but she did have on one of her old work shirts from her construction days with her father back in Indiana. A patch with her name, "Vic," donned one side, and "Addison Construction" donned the other. She, too, wore safety glasses, probably as an example for the very impressionable *little* in her care.

"Any progress?" Rikki asked. She snuck a peek at the stacks of boxes stored in one corner of the basement. Shasti graciously offered to house Rikki's boxes when it became clear that Rikki had to sell her Aunt Tilda's house and move out last year.

"It's getting off balance with every load," Vic said. "Lots of things to check. The levelling feet, suspension rods, shock absorbers, counterweights."

"We might even have to go to the DIY store, Miss Rikki."

"Oh, my goodness. That sounds exciting."

"Maybe I can get one of those flashlights that wraps around your head," Madison said excitedly and pointed to Victoria's tool bag. She must have seen one in Vic's bag.

"Exciting," Rikki repeated.

"Madison?" Shasti called down the basement stairs. "Come up here a minute, please."

"Gotta go," Madison said. "Be right back." She sprinted up the stairs, taking them two at a time, the hammer bouncing off the side of her leg as she went.

"That kid is a hoot," Victoria said. She put her wrench down and said, "You know Josey, right?"

"Sure." Josey was Victoria's latest girl-a-whirl.

"She's amenable to a threesome any time."

Rikki almost choked. She hadn't expected that to come out of Victoria's mouth. Other than sharing Aunt Tilda's boy toys for impact practice, they had never had a threesome. "I'm good."

"I can set you up with someone. In fact, Josey is a very compliant sub, and I can loan her out to you any time."

"Thanks, but no, Vic," Rikki said. "I appreciate what you're trying to do, but I'm okay. The shop has most of my attention right now, and I don't know if I have the emotional energy for much else."

"I'm your go-to if you change your mind," Victoria said.

"I appreciate that."

The blur that was Madison pounded back down the basement stairs.

"Guess what, chicken butt?" Victoria said to Madison. "I think I've found the problem, but I need you to verify it with me."

"Far out, Brussel Sprout," Madison responded and then added, "Ma'am," obviously thinking she had botched protocol. She must have really thought she messed up because then she added, "Sir."

Vic laughed. "Any of those will do."

"Really?" Madison asked, a devilish gleam in her eye. "I can call you Brussel Sprout?"

"No," Victoria said. "You're a dork."

Shasti came partway down the stairs and said to Rikki, "I'm ready if you are."

"Yep," Rikki said. She turned toward Victoria and Madison. "I need you two to come over and fix my washing machine."

"Nope," Victoria said. "I've already told you. It's rusted through and needs to be hauled out of there."

"Yeah, you did say that. Didn't you?"

"Get a new one. I bet those trips to the laundromat suck."

"They do." Rikki waved off that annoying reminder and said, "Okay, we're off. Be safe, you two, and I hope you get that thing fixed."

"We will," Vic said. There it was. Victoria's ever-present confidence. "Hey, Shasti, permission to take the kid to DIY?"

"Sure. She has a credit card. Make sure she brings it with her."

Madison beamed at the important responsibility she had been assigned.

"And is lunch out okay ?" Victoria asked.

"Sure, sure. Just no fast food or junk."

"You got it," Victoria said. "Solve the world's problems while you're out there, okay?" She flicked her head to get a stray lock of hair off her forehead.

"We'll try," Shasti said. "We'll try." She looked at Rikki. "Ready?"

"Yep." Rikki headed back up the stairs but paused when she heard Madison say in low tones, "Daddy Vic, I made the biggest turd this morning. Want to see?"

Victoria burst out laughing. "Tell me you do not have that thing in a box or something."

"I took a picture."

Rikki slowed her pace as she went up the stairs. She just had to hear more.

"Holy shit, squirt," Victoria gushed. "That's got to be a world record. That came out of you?"

"Mm hmm."

How Shasti heard the conversation going on in the basement, Rikki will never know, but Shasti yelled, "Do not post that online, Madison. Or text it to anyone."

"I won't, Mistress," Madison called. "Want to see, Miss Rikki?"

Rikki hustled up the stairs and, without looking back, said, "No, no, no. Gotta go."

Once in Rikki's car and heading toward their first stop, Rikki said, "Are you sure we can leave those two unsupervised?"

"Victoria is like a big sister to Madison," Shasti said. "Or a fun aunt. Or maybe even an uncle."

"A fun uncle," Rikki amended and then laughed. "A 'funcle.'"

Shasti chuckled. "It's good for Madison to interact with other people. And Victoria brings…" She hesitated for a moment before saying, "Well, to be totally sexist, Victoria brings masculine energy into Madison's life.

Madison needs a strong masc to help shape her."

"The whole world is sexist, Shasti," Rikki said. "And masculine doesn't mean 'male.' It just means a way of acting that *society* defines as male. That changes all the time. We all have masculine and feminine traits, right? Vic leans more on the masc side."

"Do you think she considers herself non-binary?" Shasti said as if the thought had just now occurred to her.

"She hasn't said anything," Rikki said. "I don't get the feeling that she's questioning her gender. Except—" She laughed.

"What?"

"Well, there is the whole 'Daddy Vic' thing now."

"You're right," Shasti said. "She knows that she can confide in us if she needs to."

"I'll make sure she knows that."

"She knows." Shasti pointed to the Linen Works store in the strip mall Rikki pulled into.

"First stop here we come."

Once inside the linens and bath store, they meandered together, using one cart between them. Rikki was finally trying to get started on making her apartment ready for someone. 'Getting you ready to receive,' Shasti reminded her as they walked in. Shasti was scouting out items for their big trip to England in two days. One of those things was robes. Apparently, Madison didn't have a decent robe to take on vacation.

"These are nice," Shasti said and pulled out a plush robe. "Too bulky for our trip, though. But there's a nice assortment of colors. What do you think? You said you needed a new robe."

Rikki was never one to spend copious amounts of time shopping. She saw what she liked and got it. Except lately. She couldn't afford—

"Buy one, get the second fifty percent off," Shasti said, reading the sign.

Rikki checked out the price. "Sold. And it's so soft."

Shasti pulled out a deep green robe and draped it across Rikki's front. "Yes, green for you. What color for *her*?"

"I don't have a 'her,' Shasti. And, before you ask, Esme hasn't been back to the shop since that evening we exchanged meaningful eye contact."

"I'm sorry to hear that. Did you push too hard?"

"I didn't push at all," Rikki said, stroking the soft fabric of the robe with her thumb.

"Maybe that was the problem," Shasti suggested knowingly.

"Oh, hush," Rikki said and rolled her eyes. Her smile let her friend know she wasn't upset. "And, anyway, I don't know what color Esme or any other *she* would like."

Shasti scowled. "Imagine it."

"Imagine it," Rikki mumbled and looked through the colors. Off-white wasn't very imaginative. The various shades of blue didn't quite work against her forest green. Red? Big, no. And then she saw it. "Purple. Deep purple."

Shasti inhaled sharply. "Perfect."

Rikki grabbed it off the rack and put it in their communal cart.

"Look," Shasti said. "They have towels and wash cloths and loofah sponges all in those same colors."

"And 'fifty percent off select items,'" Rikki read. "Hopefully, that will be the items I select."

"We've got this," Shasti said and dove in joyfully.

Rikki, caught up in Shasti's fervor, spent more than she wanted to, but took to heart Shasti's reassurance that Rikki was investing in the future. She'd needed that new robe, anyway, right? Rikki was hard-pressed to argue against that logic.

Shasti bought a cute pink robe for Madison, with matching slippers featuring the silhouette of a black cat on each.

One discount clothing store later, where Rikki bought nothing, but Shasti bought a few cute things for Madison, they agreed on lunch at The Indigo Café.

"Mission accomplished," Rikki said as she took a sip of her chamomile tea. Esme drank chamomile. Rikki wanted to see if she would like it, too.

"Yes, yes," Shasti said "We were both very productive. Of course, we haven't solved the world's problems like Victoria asked us to."

"There's always tomorrow," Rikki said with a laugh.

"By the way." Shasti's tone took a serious shift. "Lunch is one me. You will have more than tea this afternoon."

"No, you don't have to—" Rikki didn't get to finish.

"Don't blow smoke up my—" She shook her head at Rikki and waggled her finger. "You have to eat. If you're going to get through all this, you have to take care of yourself, and I can tell that you're not."

Shasti was right. Rikki looked at her friend, weighing what to say next. "Only you and Aunt Tilda can get away with talking to me like that."

"Are you having gastro troubles?"

Rikki shook her head.

"So, you're just not eating because you think you can't afford it or you're trying to save a dime or two?"

Rikki inhaled slowly while keeping eye contact with her friend. She had no words.

"I thought as much," Shasti said.

Shasti didn't have time to add to her response because the server came by to take their orders. Rikki ordered an inexpensive club sandwich, fully intending to take half of it home to eat later.

"Put a house salad on that order, too," Shasti told the server.

The server looked at Rikki for permission. "Fine. With your house-made vinaigrette, please."

After Shasti ordered and the server walked away, Shasti said, "Thank you for indulging me. I know I'm not your keeper, but you're looking a bit gaunt for my liking."

"I have been cutting corners," Rikki admitted. "So, tell me about this week-long trip to England."

"It's okay to change the subject," Shasti said knowingly, "but just know that I care about you and your well-being."

"Thanks." Rikki took another sip of tea, suddenly not knowing what to do with her hands.

Shasti then switched, with great enthusiasm, to describing the tour package she had booked for her and Madison. Stops included London, the famous Tower Bridge, and dinner at a family-friendly pub. There would be Stonehenge, of course, Oxford University, and a place called the Cotswolds. And apparently, they were also going to tour Edinburgh Castle and Loch Lomond in Scotland.

"You two are going to need a month to recover," Rikki said, half meaning it.

Their salads came, and Rikki dove in. She hadn't realized how hungry she was. "Love the food here," she said when she came up for air.

"Me, too. It's a nice homey place," Shasti agreed.

Rikki looked down at her salad, mixing it needlessly. "Shasti?"

"Mm hmm?"

"Aunt Tilda always said that sometimes you have to make your own family. Thank you for being part of mine."

Shasti's genuine look of sympathy brought tears to Rikki's eyes. Shasti followed suit and then handed Rikki a tissue from out of nowhere. "And I'm glad you're part of mine, too."

Rikki wiped her eyes, then turned away from her friend to softly dab at her nose. She put the tissue in her pocket and reached up to pull the wooden hair clasp out of her messy bun. She showed Shasti. "This was my mother's," Rikki said. "It was the only thing I could grab before my father kicked me out of the house after blaming me for her death."

"Oh, honey." Shasti squeezed Rikki's hand.

"I wanted something tangible of hers."

"Understandable," Shasti said, lunch on both sides abandoned.

"I'm toying with the idea of taking a trip back home. No," Rikki amended. "Wilkes-Barre is not my home anymore. It's just a place where I was born and lived for a while."

"Pennsylvania?"

"Yes. My father claims to have disowned me and yet gets my sister to send me messages from him."

Shasti clucked her disapproval.

"I've given it a lot of thought, too much probably, but I don't think there is such a thing as closure. There's only a…" She paused for a moment, searching for the right words to convey her meaning. "There's only a lessening or a coming to terms with whatever it is." She looked at her friend as a plan formed. "I think I want to visit my mother's grave. Maybe drive past the clinic if it's still there, you know? See what's become of that space?"

"I think you're absolutely right about closure. There's no such thing. I think we work hard to come to terms with the crap in our lives, some of it self-inflicted, a lot of it not. Madison is still working through a lot from her past. She's developing good reactionary methods when stuff bubbles up for her."

"That is so good to hear," Rikki said.

"It is. But it's not one and done, right? So, you're going to Pennsylvania to visit those places, but it might not seal the deal on your pain. You know that, right?"

"I do."

"But it might help you get perspective now that some time has passed. How long?"

"Eleven years."

"And you haven't been back since then?" Shasti asked. Her words were gentle.

"No. Not since the funeral. But I'm hoping I've progressed enough to get a better understanding about what happened and my role in it."

"You had no role in it, Rikki," Shasti said. "Please pardon me saying this, and I hope I'm not overstepping, but your father sounds like a bully or a master manipulator who is simply deflecting his role in what happened. You were an easy target, Rikki. And he also sounds like a narcissist. One can never reason with a narcissist." She scoffed her disgust.

"All of that sounds about right," Rikki said, meaning it. "I'm not welcome in his home, anyway. Although I may drive by to see what it looks like after eleven years."

"Sounds like you've made up your mind."

"I most certainly have not," Rikki said with a laugh. "I just wanted to say it out loud. See how it sounded. But if I leave for a few days, whenever that might be, Lydia, Mark, and Marta should be able to handle things, right?"

"You've trained them well, as far as I've witnessed," Shasti said. "And they can call on any one of us to come help."

"I wouldn't want—"

"It won't come to that," Shasti said gently. "I think you should plan to go. You just have to figure out the timing. And Rikki, you made good progress today. You're enthusiastically making room for someone to come into your life, whether it's that blonde bombshell at the coffee shop or someone else. You've kick-started a message to the universe that you're ready to receive."

"A while back, I actually went out to do what we did today. I couldn't find anything. I couldn't figure it out. Buying stuff to welcome no one specific was weird."

"You weren't ready," Shasti said. "Your happiness will come."

"I'm okay."

"I know you're not," Shasti said. "It'll come when you're not looking so hard for it."

"Do I seem desperate?"

Shasti shrugged and then said, "You have so much on your plate right now."

Rikki wasn't sure why; maybe Shasti's comment was the catalyst, but she launched into the details of her sister's phone call on the anniversary of her mother's death. She relayed her father's subsequent, pointed uninvitation to his latest wedding.

"Let him have that, Rikki. It's none of your concern. You're not responsible for him."

"I know."

She hesitated before saying, "Showing up at his wedding is a bad idea, Rikki."

Rikki scoffed. "As if. I'm a sadist, Shasti, not a masochist."

~~~

Two days after her shopping and lunch trip with Shasti, Rikki took advantage of a lull in the shop to survey her apartment. Shasti made her promise to keep working on the 'making room for *her*' plan. It was Friday afternoon, and she still wasn't sure what had happened between her and Esme. It felt like they had been connecting. No, they *had* been connecting, but then Esme got cold feet or something and disappeared. Oh, shit. Maybe something had happened to her. Should she call the hospitals?

"Stop," Rikki said out loud. She wasn't responsible for someone she barely knew. In fact, she didn't even know Esme's last name. But Rikki couldn't help feeling the bond that had begun to form over the two months since Esme had first come into the shop. Rikki had seen deeper into the talented blonde woman who made jewelry for a living. She wanted a chance to explore that bond further.

Rikki sighed and then laughed out loud when she found herself cleaning her coffee system in the kitchenette. "You can take the barista out of the coffee shop, but you can't take the coffee shop out of her." She finished her task, wondering if she had said or done something to scare Esme off. She replayed their conversations and couldn't find anything overt. "It was the overlong eye contact," Rikki said as she slid the portafilter back into place. "Maybe Shasti was right. Maybe that eye contact was sending messages that Esme didn't want to receive. I pushed too hard." Maybe Esme wasn't looking for a relationship or simply wasn't into women and had kind of panicked.

The drip tray got put back next, which reminded her that her replacement espresso machine should be arriving that afternoon or evening. If it did, Mark was downstairs to receive it. She checked her phone for the projected delivery time and texted Mark a reminder. It would be nice to get that second machine up and running. They were severely handicapped without it. Rikki let herself soften when she wondered what Lydia would name this one. Hopefully, something along the lines of Super-efficient Sally. One could only hope.

Rikki laughed out loud, disturbing the quiet. "I am not the one to name things." She sighed and then set about dusting her window blinds and sills with a damp cloth. "I should get curtains." She turned to survey the living room section. "And having only one chair isn't really welcoming, now is it? There's no room for *you*." As she said that, not a single image of the 'you' she was supposedly getting ready for came to mind. "*You* are still a mystery, aren't you?" As she dusted, she tried to force an image of Esme in the space. It gave her an uncomfortable feeling. It was like trying to fit a square peg into a round hole, or whatever that saying was. Esme was an independent woman and probably didn't need a Dominant type like Rikki. Maybe that's what felt off. But maybe they could be friends somehow. She found the woman interesting and intelligent.

Her phone dinged an incoming text. Rikki tapped her phone screen.

VICTORIA: I'm at the side door. Let me in.

Rikki glanced at the time on her phone. Ahh, school was out, which meant Victoria was free to roam the weekend. She worked security at a local elementary school and took her job very seriously. She wasn't a Mommy Domme by any means, but she liked taking care of young people. That's why she was so good with Madison and Shanice, the *littles* in their community. Rikki was sure it had something to do with Victoria's crazy upbringing on the outskirts of Indianapolis.

RIKKI: Be right down.

She hadn't been expecting Victoria, but she couldn't help thinking Victoria was coming by for some bestie time now that Shasti was on a plane with Madison, heading toward the United Kingdom and away for an entire week.

Rikki hustled down the stairs and unlocked the door for her friend. Victoria always dressed to impress. Today's ensemble included dark chinos, her signature boots, an untucked white shirt, and a gold-flecked black vest over it. "It's a nice sunny spring day out there," Rikki said. "Why aren't you out wooing some woman?"

"I'm meeting Josie later." Victoria took off her light leather jacket. She took in the overburdened coat hooks and gave Rikki a chastising look. She threw her jacket on the couch and was about to sit down when Rikki stopped her.

"Come upstairs," Rikki said. "I could use your opinion on something."

Once upstairs, Rikki asked, "Shasti's been after me to make room for another person in my life." She gestured to the spacious room. "What do I need in here?"

"Curtains for one," Victoria said. "And some freakin' furniture, Rik. What the hell? I haven't been up here since I declared that washing machine DOA, and you still have nothing." She walked toward Rikki's made bed. "A new comforter, please, but the whole king-sized bed on a platform near the oh-so-tempting Saint Andrew's Cross is perfect. Delectable. Enticing." She grinned back at Rikki. "You got this part right."

"That's reassuring," Rikki said.

Victoria whipped around and took in the kitchenette. "You have one coffee cup out. Put out a second. And not one that says 'Rikki's Coffee Shop' on it. Although that might be a good marketing ploy for you." She laughed and added, "Get two cups that complement each other."

As she headed toward the bathroom slash laundry room, she repeated,

"Furniture, Rik." She waggled her eyebrows. "Furniture isn't just for sitting, you know. I have to share a story about my date with Josey last night and how it relates to my brand-new ottoman."

Rikki scoffed. They always spoke freely with each other, most of their group did, but she wasn't sure if she wanted to hear about Victoria's latest sexual escapades. She didn't have a choice, that at least she knew.

"This," Victoria said with a frown as she entered the bathroom. "No. Just no." She pointed to the mounds of dirty clothes piled high on the far side of the bathroom. "You can't even get to your linen closet." She groaned but then added, "These, however, are perfect. All of this." She gestured to the matching towels, robes, and other bath products Rikki had purchased with Shasti. "Yes, yes, yes." Victoria squeezed past Rikki in the bathroom doorway to escape the madness. "There is hope for you yet, my friend."

"Thanks?" Rikki said sarcastically.

"Come by the condo tomorrow morning," Victoria said. "Bring those piles. We'll make a day of doing your laundry."

"I don't know, Vic."

"Shut up," Victoria said. "I'm helping you. It's okay to take help."

Rikki gave in. "Okay, fine. Thanks."

"The machines take credit cards if you can believe that," Victoria said. "If that's a problem, I can spot you." Victoria was only one of a tiny handful of people who knew about her financial woes.

"I think I'll be okay, but I appreciate the offer." Rikki hated charity. She was the one who helped other people. She was the one who saw the need, made the plan, and implemented it. She was *not* the one who asked for help. She had to change the subject. "So, Don Juan, tell me your story. Tell me about your ottoman escapade."

Chapter 10

"So," Victoria said and sat in the lone chair in Rikki's apartment. "Let me tell you the tale of 'Josey and the Ottoman.'"

"It sounds like a fairy tale," Rikki teased and sat on the edge of her bed, the only other seating option. Yeah, she needed some furniture.

"It does. Just wait 'til you hear what she did. So, I let Josey in the condo last night, and before I could order her to strip and present her body for my usual inspection, she blurts out that she wants to do something for me first."

"Really."

"I know, right? Apparently, this new sub of mine is a bit of an exhibitionist, so I give her the go-ahead. She slowly walks over to my new ottoman. It's big, Rik. Square, four feet on each side."

"That *is* big."

"Yeah, so anyway, she strips as she's walking, dropping her clothes on the floor as she goes. I don't say a word because, well, it was so damn sexy."

"It's not like you to give up power like that," Rikki said. She leaned back on her elbows, trying to get comfortable.

"I know, but it was exciting, so I let it go on. You probably do this, too, but I usually have some kind of script in my head for the evening, so it was refreshing not to be running things." Victoria threw both hands in the air as if she were ready to get to the good parts. "She pushes me down in my usual chair in the living room, grabs a condom from the bowl, and throws it at me. I lean forward, thinking she wanted me to, you know, take her right then, but she didn't. She puts a hand on my chest and pushes me back. Do you know that little imp wagged her finger back and forth in my face?"

Rikki laughed. "Living a dangerous life, that one."

"Normally, that would not fly with Daddy Vic," Victoria said, referring to herself in the third person. "I surprised myself by letting it go. She's completely naked now. She turns back to the ottoman, lifts the cover slightly, and says, "You'll need to wash this after."

Victoria blew out a sigh. "Rikki, I gotta tell you, I was aroused. No, what's a stronger word than that?"

"Awakened?" Rikki offered.

"Fuck, yes," Victoria said wide-eyed. "My entire body was awake."

"Good chemistry between the two of you, hmm?"

"Sexual chemistry, sure," Victoria offered, but didn't elaborate. "Anyway, she sits on the ottoman and scoots back a bit so she can sit criss-cross applesauce, which she does for a moment, but then she moves her legs apart and puts the bottoms of her feet together, effectively spreading herself wide open for me. She's looking at me the entire time, and it took all my strength not to leap up and whip out my strappy."

"Which you conveniently had on under your pants," Rikki said matter-of-factly.

"Duh, date night." Victoria laughed. "So, Josey licks her lips and then bites her bottom lip. Both hands slowly caress her inner thighs. I lean forward. She wags her finger at me again. I sit back. She pops one index finger in her mouth and rhythmically moves it in and out. In and out. Oh, God, I was dying. She pops two, then three, fingers into her mouth. Same motion. Meanwhile, her other hand has moved up to fondle her own breasts. She tweaks a nipple. Her head lolls back as she moans. The hand with the now-wet fingers moves slowly down to her center. She circles her sex, Rikki. I lean forward. She doesn't correct me this time, but I know enough not to leave the chair. I may or may not have pulled my strappy out of my pants."

Rikki laughed. "Yeah, I can bet which way that went."

"I can see that her breathing is deeper now. Her circling fingers move to encompass her clit. It's peeking out of its hood. That image is seared into my brain, Rik. Seared!" She moans at the memory. "I think she'll insert those fingers inside, but she doesn't. She pulls them back to her mouth and sucks on her own essence. My audible moan made her smile around the fingers. Then she plunges those two fingers inside and starts to pump. Her pelvis tilts. Her other hand reaches down and spreads her labia apart so I can see more clearly. She widens her legs and lies back on the ottoman. Her hips lift even more, giving me a front-row, orchestra-seat view of all the action. I am riveted. The hand holding open her labia moves to her clit. Her hips buck. Her familiar moans tell me she's getting close. God, I want in on this action, but I'm rooted to my spot. I don't have the condom on my strappy yet, but my right hand is stroking. Stroking to her rhythm. Her hips buck. My hand strokes faster. I press the strappy back so it bumps against my own sex. It hits just right each time, but I'll wait for my own release once I take her, which will happen as soon as she lets me."

"'Lets you,'" Rikki repeated.

"She raises her hips high off the ottoman. She's pushing up with her toes. If she could levitate, she would have. Rik, it got quiet. She strokes herself, but that's the only thing moving now. The guttural moan, I swear, starts somewhere in her toes and shoots through her body. She bucks her hips and moans her release. What a fuckin' sight. She slows her hand. She lowers her hips to the ottoman. Her eyes are closed, but she takes a breath and opens them. Damn if she didn't lick her bottom lip and give me this come-hither look. She scoots further back on the ottoman, opens her legs wide, and curls her finger just like this." Victoria mimicked the beckoning motion with her index finger. "I wanted to leap on her, but had to get back some of my power first."

"No kidding."

"I stand, put the condom wrapper on the side table, and roll the condom on." Victoria looked sheepish before blurting, "And then, I was on her like white on rice."

Rikki laughed. "Too funny."

"I came so hard, Rik. Holy shit. She came again, too. It was incredible." Victoria looked like she needed a cigarette after telling the story. "Mind you, we still hit up my dungeon afterward, and I got to practice my bull whip on her. And, best of all, she's softening to the idea of anal."

"Consent is everything," Rikki said.

"Consent makes it sexy. Meaningful. Powerful." Victoria moaned and looked toward the ceiling. "I cannot wait."

"Sounds like you've got a good one there, Vic," Rikki said and sat up.

"Oh, I have to tell you about—I'll send you a link, but I found this new kind of strappy. It's got a slit in the base for an egg vibrator. I haven't tried it yet, but I'll let you know."

"Because I have all these women lining up outside my door," Rikki said. She hadn't meant the bitterness to come through, but there it was, right at the surface.

"Aww, shit," Victoria said and pulled out her phone. "I didn't mean anything by that. And I have a number of eligible and sexy women I can hook you up with. Got my little black phone right here." She waggled it and added, "Just say the word."

"No, thanks," Rikki said. "Not ready. Not financially able nor emotionally stable."

"What do you need?"

Rikki scoffed. "A new washing machine for one." Rikki laughed and stood up. She should get back to the shop.

Victoria's phone dinged. "Dinner's here," she said cryptically. "C'mon, let's eat."

"What are you talking about?"

"Minjung and Rowena are downstairs. Jaleesa and her family, too, I think. Marta and Shanice. Lydia came in. Minjung wanted to treat all of us and thought the coffee shop might be the best central place." Victoria headed for the door. "It's Korean barbecue or something. C'mon, don't disappoint her."

Rikki took a breath and scowled at Victoria. Her friends were up to something.

"Rik, it's okay. C'mon." Victoria opened the apartment door. "We all want to help. Don't be stubborn."

Rikki crossed her arms and didn't move. Her father was right. She could be stubborn. As stubborn as he was.

"Look, there's something I don't think you know. Do you remember your surprise birthday party last December?"

"Yeah?"

"Minjung was the force behind it."

"Minjung?" Rikki repeated. "I hardly know her."

Victoria gave her a soft, knowing smile but didn't say anything.

"She's a service sub, among other things," Rikki mused. "She likes to help."

"Oh, you are so dense," Victoria said.

Rikki found her feet moving toward Victoria's retreating form. What was she so dense about?

Once in her office, she said, "Wait, Vic. What am I missing?" Did Minjung have a secret crush on her? Was Rowena wanting something from Rikki?

"These people love you, idiot. We see your struggles. You're not fucking eating, you jerk." They weren't normally touchy touchy friends, but Victoria latched her hands onto both of Rikki's arms as if to shake some sense into her. She said, "Let. Us. Help. You."

Sadness, so deeply seated and stuffed down, almost broke out. Rikki blinked back burning tears. Victoria let go.

"You should give me a warning about shit like this," Rikki said and stood to her full height.

Victoria scoffed. "So you can skip town? Not a chance. This was Shasti's idea, by the way."

Rikki groaned. Her friends needed to stop overstepping. They needed to stop meddling in her life. "This is the last time you all will do something like this for me, Vic. Make that known." Her voice was stern, and she meant every harsh tone of it. She flung open the door to the coffee shop and came face to face with a room full of her friends. Yeah, this had to stop.

"Hey, what smells so good?" Rikki said, putting on her best fake smile. Her smile froze. Esme was sitting at her usual table. She was relieved to see that Esme was okay and not in a hospital, but then anger bubbled up. Why had she disappeared for over a week? Rikki recognized the absurdity of her thoughts. She and Esme weren't a couple. She and Esme weren't even friends. Esme owed her absolutely nothing.

All of those thoughts rocketed through her brain, but she tucked them aside. She found Rowena on the far side of the shop, where her friends were setting up their feast. "What's going on?" Rikki said. She knew Rowena heard the accusatory tone.

"Impromptu meal," Rowena said cooly from where she sat in one of the cushiony chairs in their group's usual gathering spot. She was a stoic old-school Dominant, stout and strong. She reminded Rikki of a dark-haired Valkyrie. One you did not mess with unless you wanted to die a slow, painful death. One scowl from her could wither even the strongest of Dominants in her presence. Rikki wasn't sure what this meant, but Shanice always said that Rowena was an A-plus typical Scorpio with her deeply guarded and mysterious presence.

Rowena stood and pulled her submissive into a side hug. "Minjung wanted to say thank you to our circle of friends, and I okayed this gesture." She waved her hand over the feast set up on several pushed-together tables.

Minjung had been Rowena's submissive for almost two years at this point, but they were so suited for each other that it seemed like they'd been together for a lifetime. Part of Rikki took hope in seeing Rowena and Minjung so happy, because maybe that meant she would find a perfect fit for herself one day. One day soon, she thought. Best not to dwell on that at the moment.

"How cool," Rikki said. "Thank you, Minjung." Minjung nodded deeply, it was kind of a bow, perhaps part of her Korean ancestry, Rikki wasn't sure. Minjung nervously pushed back a strand of her long, dark hair. She typically wore it in a tight bun, but tonight it was looser, in a ponytail behind her head. She was slightly shorter than her Domme, but together they were taller than average. Rikki, of course, looked down at both of them from her own five-foot-ten-inch height.

"That was so nice of you to think of everyone like this," Rikki added. She touched Minjung's forearm and smiled. This smile was genuine. "Tell everyone what you brought for us."

Minjung looked toward Rowena, who nodded her approval to speak. Rowena always did like her subs to be seen and not heard. She was rather old-school that way.

"Thank you, Miss Rikki," Minjung said and bowed slightly. She looked professional in her white shirt, covered by a black-and-white striped apron. She addressed their gathered friends and showed them the various plates of skewered chicken, pork, and beef. She pointed out the dipping sauces, which included the traditional ssam and salted sesame sauces. She demonstrated the usual method of placing the meat, rice, and dipping sauce on a lettuce leaf, then rolling it up to make easy finger food.

"Looks fantastic, Minjung," Rikki said. She nodded to everyone around her so they would join in on the praise and the food. "Help yourselves, everyone." Rikki stepped back to let the hungry hordes move in. She noticed a hesitation in their collective movement, and she knew why. But Rikki wasn't going to give in. She was not going to fill her plate while they all watched to make sure she ate something. That was way too humiliating and gave them way too much power. She was stubborn, like Victoria said, and was going to do this on her own terms.

"Let's eat then," Jaleesa finally said, and handed a sturdy paper plate to her partner, Tina. Jaleesa stood at the head of the table, handed out plates to everyone, and pointed out the utensils. See? Even Jaleesa sometimes felt the need to take charge. It was in every Dominant's blood.

Victoria stepped closer to Rikki and growled in her ear, "You're a pain in the ass."

Rikki just laughed and turned on her heels for Esme's table.

"Hey, Rikki," Esme said, putting her book down. It was the same one she'd been reading since she'd started coming to the shop in January, over two months ago. "Special event?"

"Not really," Rikki said. She didn't sit. She didn't even grab the back of the chair, because that would imply she was looking for an invitation to sit. "One of my friends is an amazing cook and wanted to treat us all to Korean barbecue. I came over to let you know that you are welcome to help yourself. There's no charge, of course."

"Oh, that's nice," Esme said. Her genuine smile tugged at Rikki's heart. Oh, this woman and her mixed signals. "I've just eaten and…"

When Esme didn't continue, Rikki said, "No worries. If the food smells get to you, come on over. Enjoy your book."

She didn't wait for a response and headed back to her friends. She moved over to Minjung, who lowered her gaze at Rikki's approach. Rowena might have trained her submissive too well, Rikki mused, despite all of Rowena's fussing that Minjung was not a slave. "May I borrow her?" Rikki asked Rowena.

"Of course," Rowena said from her seat. Somehow, Rowena managed to make every seat she sat in look like a throne. Rikki would never be able to pull that off. She never sat for long, anyway.

"Minjung," Rikki said, "would you do me the honor of preparing two of those for me? I might botch it up, and that wouldn't be respectful to your hard work." She fanned her hand over the spread.

"Yes, Ma'am," Minjung said. "It would be my pleasure." She hesitated because she obviously didn't want to turn her back on Rikki.

"You're fine, Minjung," Rikki reassured her. Rowena must have instilled the strict notion of never turning her back on a Dominant. Many submissives in Denton Heights were expected to adhere to that rule. As long as it wasn't abusive, Rikki was okay with it.

Minjung looked to Rowena, who waved her on to her task.

Rikki said to Rowena, "You threw this together quickly." It sounded like an accusation. And it was.

"You'll live," Rowena said and grinned. She knew exactly what Rikki was implying. "Enjoy the moment, Rikki. Your Aunt Tilda would have been first in line, you know."

Mentioning her Aunt Tilda smacked Rikki square in the gut. It was a low blow, hitting Rikki in a vulnerable place. And Rowena knew it.

"Hey, hey," Rowena said softly. Her expression had softened as well. "Rikki, I'm sorry. I just meant that it's okay to go with the flow. To be honest, we've all seen how haggard you look lately, and then Shasti called me for ideas. Minjung was the one who suggested this. Minjung, wisely, said she didn't think you would like us dropping off baskets of food on your doorstep. She thought this would help make it feel like a community event."

Rikki closed her eyes and shook her head. She turned away from Rowena. Asking for help was absolutely not in her nature. Being offered help without her permission was not only embarrassing but demoralizing. No, it was more than that. It was mortifying. These friends of hers had been talking about her behind her back and decided that she wasn't taking care of herself. They collectively decided to intervene. That's how it felt, like a goddamned intervention.

Rikki sensed someone approaching. She looked up. Minjung held a plate of food toward her. "Thank you, Minjung. This looks fantastic."

Minjung handed her the plate and then nodded. Yes, she was bowing. Rikki wasn't sure she deserved that respect. She had been a brat. Minjung had put in a lot of effort in an attempt to help.

"I've made a take-home package for you, if you wish to have some all to yourself." Minjung's smile was genuine. Rikki had seen that exact smile on many service submissives, including Jaleesa's service sub, Harriet, who was presently fussing with the food, cleaning, and tidying the space. You just can't take the service out of a service sub, can you? Minjung's smile was called a Duchenne smile. It came from the 'helper's high' Minjung must be feeling at the moment. There was no way Rikki was going to rain on that parade. Minjung was a truly giving person and an amazing submissive partner to Rowena.

"Your staff and the customers are welcome to sample, Miss Rikki. There's plenty."

"Thank you, Minjung," Rikki said, her heart softening. "You are truly a giving soul. You do honor to your Domme and to yourself. I'm pleased that you somehow found your way to Denton Heights and were able to join our community." That emotional stuff was moving around her chest again, but she willed it to stay buried as she said, "You're a real treasure, Minjung."

"Ma'am," Minjung gushed. "High praise. Thank you."

Rikki patted Minjung's arm and then took a small bite from the plate of food. "Mmm, this is good." And it truly was. Her appetite woke up, and she devoured the first wrap in seconds flat. She forced herself to slow down. She would eat the second one in a few minutes like a sane person.

"Come," Rowena said to her submissive. "Sit."

"Yes, Madam." Minjung was about to sit on the floor at Rowena's feet, but caught herself in time and sat on the couch next to her Domme's chair. They all had to be on their guard in public, especially in Rikki's shop. Everyone innately understood this, so she didn't have to set out ground rules or anything like that. For that, Rikki was grateful.

Lydia drifted over. She too wore a big smile. Rikki was so glad she could please so many people simply by eating. This, she thought sarcastically, but flicked the nuisance mood away and instead said to Lydia, "I know you're not working, but if you could quietly invite the staff and customers over to enjoy some of this food, I'd appreciate it."

"I'd be happy to," Lydia said. "I'll let Mark know, so he can keep the front counter staffed."

"Perfect." Rikki dug into her second wrap.

"Oh, and the new espresso machine arrived. It's tucked in the storage room for you to check out."

"Thank you."

Rikki socialized with her friends, the staff, and even a couple of customers who sampled Minjung's feast. She purposely kept her back to Esme. If Esme wanted to interact, she'd leave it up to her. Rikki was not going to throw herself at anyone. After Eileen, she needed to keep her guard up. Too bad her heart and body wanted other things. It was her head that had to stay in charge.

"She eats," Victoria said quietly as she sidled over.

"Shut up." Rikki smiled to let her know she was kidding.

"And it didn't kill you."

"Vic," Rikki said with that certain tone her friend would recognize as a warning to stop pushing buttons.

"I'm out of here, anyway," Victoria said. "Want to hear more Josey escapades tomorrow? Tune in for more stories from Daddy Vic's hassock."

"No," Rikki said with a laugh. "Go have fun."

"Bye-ee," Victoria said as she headed over to thank Rowena and Minjung.

"Hey, Rik," Jaleesa said as she and Tina came over. "This was a great surprise, wasn't it?"

"Sure was," Rikki said evenly and without mirth.

Jaleesa hesitated. Yeah, she had gotten the unspoken message that the surprise wasn't really a good one for Rikki. And, as a Dominant, she would understand the turmoil Rikki was going through.

"I hear we're going to have a session soon?" Tina said. There was an excited lilt to her voice, and Rikki was glad to hear it. She wanted to talk to Tina about the planned impact session personally because sometimes Dominants overstep, trying to do the right things for the submissive in their care. Tina was not a shy submissive like Minjung or Lydia. As a switch, Tina could play both roles, but she did thrive with Jaleesa at the helm. Rikki often thought they made an interesting couple. Jaleesa was a tall black woman and quite imposing when she wanted to be. Tina, on the other hand, was a petite, short white woman. She was almost waif-like with her pale skin and delicate bone structure.

"We're on for a pre-session meet and greet next Wednesday evening, yes?" Rikki asked.

"Yes," Tina answered. "I'll text you a reminder earlier in the day if that works for you."

"Sure. Sounds good." Rikki smiled at Tina and said, "Maybe you can come with some goals or, in the least, be able to tell me what impact means for you. What does it do for you? How does it help or hinder you?"

"What great questions," Tina said. "I have a week to think about them." She looked at Rikki like she'd just had a revelation and said, "Thank you for narrowing my focus like that. I look forward to our chat."

"Me as well," Rikki said.

"Babe," Tina said and smacked her Domme in the chest with the back of her hand, "we need to head out. Dana has to finish that design tonight for Mrs. Rogers." She turned back to Rikki. "Oh, did you see?" She reached right into Jaleesa's personal space and lifted the necklace out from under her long-sleeve Henley. "We finally got DeShawn's initial. It was a bear trying to match his charm with ours."

Rikki looked at the T, H, D, and the new extra D charms hanging off Jaleesa's gold chain. "One for each of you. Tina, Harriet, Dana, and now DeShawn."

"He's walking on sunshine now that he's hanging around my neck," Jaleesa said. She leaned into Rikki and said quietly, "Please excuse me for what I'm about to do next."

Rikki had no clue, but didn't have long to wait.

In the big booming voice that was unique to Jaleesa, she announced, "My family! We're heading out. Last one in the truck has to wash it." Dana and DeShawn leaped off the couch they had commandeered and said quick goodbyes to their friends and a thank you to Minjung. Harriet hurriedly tied up the bag she had been filling, hugged Minjung, and bolted after her housemates toward the front door. Jaleesa's big belly laugh filled the space, making everyone, including Rikki, smile.

Tina simply smacked Jaleesa lightly on the chest again. "What?" Jaleesa said. They all knew that Jaleesa would be the last one in the truck, and she would indeed stay true to her word and wash the truck by herself. Knowing her family, they would probably set up lawn chairs, have snacks, and watch her do it, too.

"Bye, my friend," Jaleesa said and came in for a hug. Tina did the same but without words.

Jaleesa started singing a made-up country song about loving her truck as they headed out the coffee shop door.

One by one, Rikki's friends trickled out to head home. Rikki thanked Minjung and Rowena again and almost lost her mind when Minjung placed three huge bags on the table as Rikki's "take-home package." She didn't protest or suggest that Minjung and Rowena take some home with them, which is what she really wanted to do. She even considered bringing the bags to the local homeless shelter, but then decided to graciously accept the gift and split it with Marta. Marta was also having financial struggles and could use the boost as well. There. Rikki found a great workaround for the charity she had not wanted in the first place. Pay it forward, right?

She set two of the three bags in the shop's walk-in fridge, with a note for Marta to see the next morning. She'd fill her in during the morning shift. The third and smallest bag would end up in her empty fridge upstairs.

She was just about to duck into her office when she noticed motion by the front door. Esme was leaving. Without a glance or a goodbye. Well, sure. That was it then. The connection Rikki thought they'd had apparently wasn't. Rikki slid into her office. Her heart protested the fact that Rikki had simply let Esme walk out the door without a fight or even a conversation. But Rikki's mind was in charge now, and she shut the door on her heart as soundly as she shut the door to her office.

Chapter 11

The following Wednesday evening, Rikki stepped out of her office in time to hear Brittany say, "Have you ever thought of thinking?" to one of the younger employees, a high school student who worked part-time in the shop.

Rikki took one step toward them, but Lydia got there first.

"What mistake did Mia make, Brittany?" Lydia asked as she insinuated herself between the two young women.

"You don't freakin' reheat the same milk. That's disgusting. Fresh milk," Brittany said, clearly still agitated. She reached down to the under-counter refrigerator, pulled out a fresh container of milk, and slammed it on the counter." Lydia calmly said to Brittany, "Marta needs help with something in the kitchen."

Brittany glared at Lydia, knowing full well it was simply a ploy to get her out of the way. After too long a beat, she said, "Fine," and stormed her way past both women and into the kitchen.

"Let's breathe, Mia," Lydia said and initiated a cleansing breath. Rikki was pleased to see that Mia also took a breath. "We've all made this mistake. Even Miss Rikki has done this." She leaned in closer, but Rikki still heard her say, "Early on that is. Just go ahead and clean the steam wand while I get you a fresh pitcher."

"Thanks, Lydia," Mia said. "I didn't realize."

"Learning from oopsies helps us grow." Lydia plunked the new stainless steel pitcher on the counter and said, "But making mistakes does suck, even if the lesson turns out to be a good one."

"No kidding," Mia said and set about her work.

Rikki caught Lydia's eye and pointed to Lydia, herself, and the kitchen door. Lydia understood. They would take on Brittany together.

Before they opened the kitchen door, Rikki said, "I'm proud of the way you handled that just now. Calm and cool."

"She tries my patience, Miss Rikki." Lydia was shaking her head as she said this. "Do you mind if I handle this? You can come in, but I think I need to see this through."

"All right," Rikki said. "I'll pretend I need something from Marta."

Brittany was hard at work, glaring at the dirty dishes she was rinsing out in the oversized sink. She jammed the rinsed coffee and tea cups into the dishwashing rack that, once full, would be moved into the industrial dishwasher via a conveyor belt.

Brittany turned her head and seethed, "I'm quitting. But after my shift, so I get full pay."

"You're not quitting," Lydia said quietly. It wasn't said in a condescending or demeaning manner, and Rikki couldn't have done it better. "You're just heated right now. Let's figure out what happened, okay?"

"Whatever," Brittany said, but Rikki watched as the younger woman visibly relaxed a notch.

"Hey, Marta," Rikki said as she made her presence known, "I have a question about that last order from Monument Circle Roasters." She headed to the storage room.

"You got it, Boss," Marta said and wiped her hands on a clean towel. She followed Rikki into the small space. Once inside and out of earshot, Marta asked, "What's going on with that one?" She pointed over her shoulder toward Brittany.

"Not sure," Rikki said. "I just need to supervise them for a moment."

"Figured," Marta said.

Rikki moved closer to the open storage room door so she could hear better.

"It's too much pressure, Miss Lydia," Brittany was saying. "I'm not manager material."

"Maybe not yet," Lydia said as she took the now-full tray and turned on the conveyor belt. "But you do have more experience than Mia and some of the others. That means you can teach them."

"I guess," Brittany said and got to work filling the next dishwasher rack with sprayed-down dishes and saucers. "I kind of don't want that responsibility, though. You, Mark, and Miss Rikki know how to get people to do stuff. I'm more of a just let me do my job and stay out of my way kind of person."

Lydia laughed, making Brittany laugh as well, diffusing some of the tension. Lydia turned on the washing cycle, and their conversation got drowned out by the machine.

"So, how long do we hang in here?" Marta asked with a laugh.

"I don't know," Rikki said. "How'd you like that feast Minjung prepared?"

"Fucking fantastic," Marta gushed. "Aww, shit. Damn it." She scoffed at herself and said, "I really do have a potty mouth. Now I owe three dollars into the swear jar."

"That little one has you trained, doesn't she? How is she doing with the setback? And how are *you* doing?"

"Dealing with it the best we can," Marta said evenly. "What else can we do but implement the nutritional plan she's set up for herself. Looks very sound and good to me. Boss, honestly, I was stoked when I saw those two bags with my name on them. We had the barbecue for dinner that night and the night after. We even treated Mrs. Pulaski."

"I'm so glad to hear that." Rikki had even managed to make her own take-home bag last for several days, although she had run out and was now back to cheese sandwiches and ramen noodles.

Rikki snuck a peek out the door. It looked like they were wrapping things up by the way they were laughing with each other. Rikki loudly announced her and Marta's reappearance from the storage room, "I miscalculated, I guess."

"No worries," Marta said. "We'll make that adjustment, and all will be well." Marta smirked at her to indicate that she could play this weird game with the best of them.

Rikki pressed her lips together to hold in a laugh.

"Miss Rikki," Lydia said at their approach, "it's time for me to clock out. I heard Mark out front, so is it okay if I head out?"

Normally, Lydia wouldn't ask that; she'd simply tell Rikki she was clocking out. Brittany hadn't turned around, so Lydia gestured with a slight nod of her head and widened eyes that she didn't think things were finished with Brittany.

Rikki nodded. She'd take round two of Brittany care.

Brittany whirled around and said to Marta, "Got 'em all through the machine." She took off her kitchen apron, hung it up on an empty hook, and announced, "I'm on a break." And with that stormed out of the kitchen, slamming the door against the outer wall. It swung back with so much momentum, Rikki thought it might come loose from its hinges.

"Well, there you go," Rikki said in Brittany's wake. To Lydia, she said, "Go home. I've got this."

"Thank you, Ma'am." Lydia took a few steps backward, turned, and headed out the same kitchen door.

Rikki followed her out the door and saw Brittany sitting on one of the customer couches, her phone in hand. She had her back to everyone and was clearly in a self-imposed time-out.

Mark approached her, but she said loudly, "I'm on a break. An official break."

Mark said something Rikki couldn't hear, but she answered him with one word, a curt, "Fine."

Mark turned and raised his eyebrows high toward Rikki, who simply nodded and ducked back into her office. She sent a brief text and was rewarded within seconds with a video call from Brittany's own Domme, Patrice Southland, a political journalist currently on location in Austin, TX. Although her home was in Denton Heights, OH, she travelled all over the world for assignments for the up-and-coming *Politics Explained* online news source.

"Do you have a minute, Patrice?" Rikki asked. "You look like you're about to tape a segment or go on the air."

"Just finished, dahling," Patrice said with a happy lilt. She was in her late twenties but had the presence and demeanor of someone much older, someone who had lived long and hard and had seen things. Maybe she had. Her bleached blonde hair was pulled back behind her head with not a single lock out of place. Her makeup was clearly done up for filming, but still tasteful. And her suit looked quite expensive. "So tell me what trouble she's gotten into now."

Rikki laughed. "How did you know?"

"It's the only time you text me without warning, my friend." Patrice turned from her phone and said something to someone nearby. "Sorry about that," she said when she got back. "We just got a break in the gerrymandering bullshit they're trying to pull here in Texas. Bunch of cheaters, my God."

"You don't say that on air, do you?" Rikki asked.

"Not in so many words," Patrice said and then laughed.

"Listen," Rikki continued, "I'm not sure what's going on with Brittany, but she's been acting up and, to be honest, we are almost at our wits' end trying to help her."

"That may be my fault," Patrice said. "I need to get home. She needs some discipline, and not the kind you can give her."

"Subs do get angsty when they don't get their Dommes' attention," Rikki said. "Been there. Done that."

"Please continue to hold her accountable for her stuff, Rikki," Patrice said. Her tone had turned serious. "I had planned to get back for the May ball, but that's too long for her to wait, isn't it?" She tapped her phone a few times and then said, "Shit, that's over two months from now. No, I have to get home for a bit, but I will be back for the ball. I'll just have to rearrange some things. She's important to me."

"I know she is," Rikki said. "She's important to us, too. And you know that I can't give her impact or discipline her beyond the basics here at the shop."

"You've done so much for me already, Rikki. I do appreciate it." Patrice coughed, and Rikki wasn't sure whether she was coughing back emotions. Probably. "Hey, can you get the rugrat on the phone with you?"

"I will." Rikki stood up and opened her office door. There were relatively few customers, so she called, "Brittany, can you come into my office, please?"

"On a break," came the answer from the couch.

Rikki looked at the woman on the phone who, judging by the displeased expression on her face, had heard the exchange. Rikki walked over and sat down next to her bratty employee. She held the phone out so Brittany could see her Domme.

"Miss Patrice?" Brittany gasped and grabbed for the phone. Rikki held on to it. Brittany didn't try again. "What are you doing here?"

"I am not pleased, young lady," Patrice said. Even Rikki blanched at the tone.

"What? I'm on a break."

"I was going to come home this weekend for a few days, but if your behavior continues to be what I just witnessed on Miss Rikki's phone, then I won't bother."

Brittany tried to say something, but her Mistress interrupted by saying, "This grown-up is talking, and *you* should not be."

"Sorry, Ma'am."

"Better."

Patrice then asked Brittany for the best ways to make amends to all those she'd been rude to that day, and together they worked out something that even Rikki found acceptable. Brittany would sincerely apologize to all involved. Miss Rikki would verify to Brittany's Domme that all the transgressions had been satisfied, and then, and only then, would the disrespectful behavior be forgiven and forgotten.

Patrice then discussed with Brittany ways to ensure these behaviors didn't recur and ruin other people's days. Rikki almost laughed when Patrice phrased it that way, but she held her composure. One of the demands Patrice made was that Brittany be more honest about how she was feeling while her Domme was away. Clear and honest communication was important in any relationship, but it was vital in intense D/s relationships like theirs, Patrice counseled.

"Now, once I get off the phone, you will instantly talk to and apologize to Miss Rikki," Patrice said, looking unamused. "Is that understood?"

"Yes, Ma'am," Brittany said, sitting up a little taller on the couch.

"And then go apologize to Mia and Mark. Tomorrow, the same when you see Lydia."

"Yes, Ma'am."

"And, you understand, of course, that I've asked Miss Rikki to watch over you while I'm working. I have to know that you're safe and that you're behaving well, Brittany."

"I understand, Ma'am." Brittany hesitated for a moment before blurting, "Can I talk to you tonight? I don't know what time it is in Texas, Ma'am, but…"

"Yes," came the succinct answer.

In a Madison-esque way, Brittany said, "Yaaaaay," and pumped her feet with joy.

Patrice got called away from the phone and had to hang up. The moment Rikki closed her app, Brittany burst into tears. Rikki pulled her close and rocked her gently.

"She's coming home, Britt," Rikki said, rubbing her back.

"I know." Brittany sat up. She swiped the tears off her face and stood up. "I'm sorry I'm such an ass sometimes. I get cranky."

"Like Patrice said, you have to examine what's making you cranky."

"I guess, but even if I did know why," Brittany said and let out a big sigh, "I wouldn't know how to be un-cranky."

Rikki chuckled. "You'll be all right. You just need to connect with your Domme."

"Yeah." Brittany swallowed hard as emotion hit her again, but then made good on her promise and apologized to Rikki for her 'butthead behavior', as she called it. She mentioned several specific things she'd said and done that weren't cool, making Rikki understand that Brittany knew exactly what behavior wasn't acceptable.

"And with your permission," Rikki said, "may I call you out on your behavior when you do something that isn't 'cool.'"

"I guess you should," Brittany said. "Ma'am, may I go apologize to Mia and Mark now?"

"Off you go," Rikki said and stood up. The call to Patrice had been productive. The handful that was Brittany was still going to be a challenge, that was clear, but Rikki felt Patrice's intervention made a big difference. Now, if the woman could only be home more. Rikki grunted. That was unfair. Patrice was a good Domme.

Rikki didn't resent watching over Brittany; it was in her nature to nurture those new to the *life*, just like Aunt Tilda had done for her and Victoria all those years ago. Aunt Tilda sat them down on many occasions to make course corrections, but she also demonstrated loving BDSM in every action and every word she spoke. Rikki was currently thirty-five years old and had nowhere near the life experience her aunt had. Just like Brittany, Rikki had a lot more learning and growing to do.

A few hours later, Jaleesa and Tina appeared at the shop. Rikki insisted they have beverages on the house, and within minutes, Tina had her flavored coffee and Jaleesa had a small cup of black.

"Sit, sit," Rikki said, gesturing to the couch in her office.

"Oh, that's right, you have a side door," Tina gushed, pointing to the door leading to the side alley. "I remember now from when we moved you in here. Are you all settled and unpacked in your apartment up there?" Tina pointed to the stairwell. "It was such a nice space."

"I still have a lot of things stored at Shasti and Madison's," Rikki said. "One day I'll figure out where to put it."

"I'd love to see what you've done with that space," Tina said, looking back at Jaleesa as if needing a second vote on the idea.

"Not much going on up there, but sure," Rikki said. "I'll give you the two-second tour once we're done talking."

"Great," Tina said. "So, I was thinking about those questions you asked me last week. What do I get out of impact? For starters, I love the closeness I feel with Jaleesa. It takes a lot of trust to let someone flog you. Harriet likes a caning, too. Yeesh, I'm kind of a nascent pain enthusiast in that regard," Tina said with a laugh.

"You don't have to prove anything to anyone," Jaleesa said quietly.

"I was just about to say that," Rikki said. She exchanged a glance with Jaleesa.

"I know. I know." Tina said, then sat back slightly, leaning into Jaleesa. Their way with each other was endearing.

"Hurting someone when they're not getting enjoyment from it is abuse. Plain and simple." Rikki fixed her gaze on Tina. "How do you prepare for an impact session?"

"When I'm getting ready, I'm one part nervous, but that goes away quickly, and one part anticipating the relief I will feel."

"Tell me more about the relief," Rikki asked. She sat back in her office chair.

"It's that letting go, you know?" Tina said, glancing at the woman sitting next to her. "Jaleesa says that everyone, even Harriet, resists at first. I mean, it's not natural to want your body hit with objects. But, done right—" She paused to run the back of her hand gently down Jaleesa's cheeks. The beaming smile that crept up Jaleesa's face made Rikki smile in turn. These two truly loved each other. Although Rikki's mind wanted to go to dark places and inquire why she didn't have anyone in her life to make her smile like that, she forced her mind to stay in the present.

"So, when done right," Tina continued, "there is this sweet spot when I just have to stop tensing up and relax."

"You let your guard down."

"Yes. I trust she won't injure me. Physically, I trust that my body will react to the strikes by sending blood to my skin and that endorphins will explode all around." She looked down for a moment with closed eyes. "Honestly, just talking about it calms me."

Rikki nodded. "I understand that. Eileen used to talk about that calm she would get before an impact or bondage session.

"Yes." Tina nodded. "But then, because I am the worrier they all know and love, I worry that this might become another form of addiction." She looked to Jaleesa.

"We talk about this in our at-home twelve-step meetings," Jaleesa said. "We're ever mindful of the cravings associated with everything we enjoy. Impact, sex, food."

"And, babe," Tina said, "we spend time talking about ways to combat anxiety and fear." Tina looked at Rikki, "We give each other space to share our fears in our meetings. No judging, no belittling. We just throw out ideas." She turned to Jaleesa again, "DeShawn is starting to share more, isn't he?"

"He is. He's settling in nicely," Jaleesa said.

"So," Rikki steered the ship back to their potential impact session, "trust is important to you, of course. What makes you think you can trust me?"

Tina's entire body relaxed. "Rikki, I've known you long enough now. I've seen you in action, disciplining your employees, interacting with customers, and with us. What does Shanice always say? Something about the people she'd want on her zombie apocalypse team? Rikki, I'd want you on my team. I already consider you on my team. Or maybe I'm on your team. I'm not sure how to think about that."

Jaleesa stepped in. "I think maybe we're all on each other's."

"I'm proud to have you on my team, Tina," Rikki said and felt her face get warm.

Rikki steered the conversation back to tactical, tangible details about the impact session. When she asked if Tina wanted to talk to her alone, Tina declined but suggested that during the impact session itself, she might want it to be one-on-one. Jaleesa agreed that her presence might influence things and graciously said she'd leave the two of them alone for the session.

Rikki made good on her promise to show them the apartment. Thank goodness she'd made her bed before heading down that morning, although there were piles of folded clothes on one side of her bed she had yet to put away.

Tina gushed at the St. Andrew's cross on the far side of the space near the bed.

"Don't mind the clothes," Rikki said. "I did laundry at Victoria's, and then she helped me move the piles up here. And there you go." She gestured toward the stacks.

"Wait," Jaleesa said, "I saw a washer and dryer in here when we moved you in."

"Broken," Rikki said succinctly.

Jaleesa shot Tina a look, but Rikki wasn't sure what it meant.

"Do you need help moving your furniture up here?" Jaleesa asked, taking in the empty space.

"I don't have any to move."

Another look passed between Jaleesa and Tina.

"Babe?" Tina said and shrugged.

"Yes, for sure," Jaleesa said cryptically.

Rikki wasn't sure what to think, but said, "You two have that telepathy thing going on, don't you?"

"Mm hmm," Jaleesa said. "Have you seen our basement?"

"No," Rikki said. "Just the backyard and main floor."

"We have a basement full of stuff from the previous owner," Jaleesa explained. "Tina's been after me to do something with all the excess furniture," she gestured to the empty space.

"And, Miss Rikki," Tina added, "we have the old washer and dryer we need to move out, too."

"Her parents gifted us with a brand new washer and dryer set when we moved in," Jaleesa said.

"That was a nice gift," Rikki agreed. The truth was, she couldn't afford the financial cost or the charity cost. "I don't need—"

"Just think about it," Jaleesa interrupted.

"You can look at the stuff when you come over," Tina said with a perky tone. "The stuff down there may not be your style, anyway."

Rikki swallowed the frustrated sigh she wanted to blow out and said, "You two are very generous. Sure, I'll look when I come over."

"Two Sundays from now," Tina firmed up.

"Yep," Rikki said.

They headed back toward the door and then down the stairs.

So, inquiring minds want to know," Rikki said and chuckled. "Who ended up washing the truck?"

Jaleesa burst out laughing while Tina pointed at Jaleesa, a shit-eating grin on her face. "Harriet made popcorn for the event."

"And," Jaleesa said, pulling Tina into a side hug, "how long did it take before you all joined in?"

"Three minutes," Tina said with a laugh.

Jaleesa opened the side door after they hugged their goodbyes, and Rikki heard Tina say to Jaleesa, "Those two chairs and side tables for sure."

"Yes, yes," Jaleesa agrees. "And that coffee table."

Rikki closed the door quietly and locked it.

Chapter 12

The afternoon on the day before the scheduled impact session with Tina, Rikki surveyed her staff. Everyone seemed happy and engaged in their tasks.

"Miss Rikki," Mark said after handing a beverage to a customer. "The Spronater is working like a charm. Gus was a beast, but this thing is pure delight."

"Who named it?" Rikki asked with a laugh. This was the first time she'd heard the new-to-them espresso machine had a name.

"Who else?" Mark said with a shrug.

"Lydia."

Mark affirmed her answer with a head nod.

"Bye, all," came a farewell from behind the counter. Brittany, as she did every day, was announcing her departure.

"Drive carefully," Rikki said.

"Always do," Brittany said and practically skipped out the front door. Apparently, she and her Domme were working things out, and Brittany had been floating these past two weeks. Of course, Patrice's brief trip home probably had a lot to do with Brittany's new outlook on life.

Mark leaned in and said low, "She's rushing home for phone sex."

Rikki laughed and smacked him square in the chest. "Don't gossip."

Mark scoffed. "It's not gossip. She told anyone who would listen." He cleaned the drip tray of the new Spronater and said, "Brittany's really doing well these days."

Rikki put a hand up to stop him. "Thank you, Mark," she said, trying not to let her irritation show. "I appreciate all the hard work you do around here. I see it. Both you and Lydia. You two were the best hires I've ever made."

His cheeks tinged red. "Thank you, Ma'am." He stepped back, then turned and retreated into the kitchen. He and Marta had probably been scheming ways to reassure Rikki that all was well and that they could handle things. Rikki groaned as the door to the kitchen shut after him. She would not be coddled.

When Mark's shift was done, and Lydia came in, Rikki took that time to check in on Marta in the kitchen. "Looking good in here, as always."

"Thanks, Boss," Marta said. "I'm going to hang around another hour to finish this new recipe." She pointed to the time clock on the wall. "I've already clocked out."

"Why do you do that?" Rikki went over and punched Marta's time card back in.

"It didn't seem fair," Marta said weakly.

"It's fine, Marta. You're working for the shop."

"But I didn't get your approval," Marta countered.

"Like I said. It's fine. So, what are you making here?" Rikki asked, but then remembered. "Ahh, the gluten-free offering."

"I hope it sells," Marta said. "Mrs. Polaski and Shanice scoured the internet for recipes, and they assure me that this one recipe with this particular gluten-free flour will make the best pound cake."

"Not cookies?" Rikki asked. "I thought cookies were going to be the first gluten-free offering."

"They were," Marta said. "We sold out already."

"How did I not see that?"

"I made a small batch," Marta said. "I don't want to throw your money into something that won't work. But now I know that it will. For the cookies anyway."

"Excellent. I just told Mark that he and Lydia were my two best hires. I need to amend that and include *you* in my list of three best hires."

"Thanks, Boss," Marta said, her cheeks pinking up. "I enjoy this. This part of the job is creative, and you're so understanding about my need to have flexible hours for Shanice."

"Family looks out for each other," Rikki said.

"And speaking of family, I know Brittany is doing better, but she does not belong back here with me. She does a decent job, but…"

"But she's a people person," Rikki suggested.

"Exactly," Marta said. "She thrives interacting with the customers and the rest of the staff."

"And you would rather not be saddled with her anymore."

"Your words, not mine," Marta said with a laugh.

"I'll see what I can do on that front," Rikki said. "But now I have some potentially anxiety-provoking news."

"Out with it," Marta said. "Boss," she added quickly. Rikki never required her to use any honorific, but Marta felt it was warranted, so Rikki eventually stopped protesting.

"First things first, do you remember the health department's inspection a few weeks ago?"

"Shit, did we fail?" Marta looked ready to fight.

"No, no, no," Rikki said. "We passed with flying colors."

"So, what's the problem?"

"The inspector said she was going to recommend our shop as a place for interns to get hands-on training. They can get a feel for what to look for. And, apparently, she thought our shop would be a good example of how things should be."

"What?" Marta looked stunned. "This is crazy."

"I know, so we all have to keep looking and doing our best."

"And we won't know when they're coming." It was a statement.

"We won't."

"Blah," Marta said as if her sails had just lost all their wind.

"But I wanted to tell you that our high marks have a lot to do with you, Marta. You three are keeping this shop afloat."

Marta's expression softened. After too long, she finally said, "We're glad to do it."

Rikki realized her mistake. She'd just implied that she needed help keeping the shop afloat. She hated looking vulnerable in front of an employee. But Marta was more than an employee. She was a friend, so even though Rikki had practically announced that the shop was drowning in debt, it would be okay, especially since Marta was aware of the financial troubles.

Rikki turned toward the kitchen door. "Sounds like it's getting busy out there."

"And you need to get out of my kitchen," Marta said playfully.

"I'm going. I'm going." Rikki headed back into the shop, determined to ignore the back of Esme's head, although she snuck peeks at Esme's reflection in the front window from time to time. Esme was just a customer. The woman had made that perfectly clear.

Later that night, after the shop was closed and the customers and employees were gone, Rikki locked up and headed up the stairs to her apartment. One hot shower later, she lay in her king-size bed, the piles of laundry still in residence on the far side. She was comfy under the covers, enjoying a moment when no one wanted anything from her. Rikki tried to recall something Lydia had said during that evening's cleanup. It was something about understanding both sides of drop. Sub drop *and* Domme drop.

"I lived in sub drop after Master Tom broke our contract," Lydia had said. "And then after domming Minjung and then mentoring Brittany, I swung too far to the other side—the Domme side. Brittany didn't respond to my guidance, and it made me question my effectiveness as a leader, my methods, everything." She had looked up at Rikki as if having an epiphany. "Having power makes you hungry for more, Miss Rikki."

"It does," Rikki had said succinctly.

"And when I lost the power, I became irrelevant. You know, like when Brittany didn't respond to my assistant manager's plan for her? It came crashing down on my head. Who was I kidding? I don't have power. Who was I to think I could lead? But then I realized that I just made a mistake with Brittany, and that I am an effective leader most of the time."

As they talked, Lydia shared that she and Rowena had apparently been having deep conversations about submission and dominance, and that she seemed to be finding a balance with Rowena's help. Rikki asked pointed questions and was satisfied that Lydia was addressing her struggles in a healthy way. Who knew Rowena could be that nurturing?

Rikki reflected on Lydia's statements. *Having power makes you hungry for more.* But it was the other one that had hit Rikki right in the gut. *When I lost the power, I was irrelevant.*

"Irrelevant," Rikki said out loud. She rolled onto her side, her face landing inches from a pile of folded towels. "Am I irrelevant? Am I powerless?

Is that why I'm acting a fool when my friends try to help me? Am I giving them reasons to send in the cavalry?" *And is this impact session tomorrow more charity?* "Fuck." Victoria was right. "I am dense. I got played."

She rolled onto her back and scoffed. "I got played by well-meaning friends. And I didn't even see it." She couldn't exactly back out of the impact session with Tina the next day, so she'd go along with it and let them be smug about pulling one over on Rikki Carmichael. After that, she'd never accept another invitation to 'guest' Domme from anyone ever again, and that included whip demonstrations at masquerade balls. She didn't need nor did she want that kind of charity. "Who the fuck do these people think they are?" She sat up. "I am Rikki Carmichael, damn it."

She heard the words come out of her mouth and then groaned. "Hey, everybody, Rikki Carmichael here, having a God complex and quietly losing my mind." She lay back down and pushed the blanket off, suddenly warm.

An image of Eileen popped into her head. Eileen was bound to their bed upstairs in their room at Aunt Tilda's house. "I wasn't powerless with you, was I, Eileen? Not at first, anyway."

It was early in their relationship, and Rikki had been trying to wean Eileen off the vibrators. Meaningless orgasms, Rikki had said to her. She wanted Eileen to feel what *she*, Rikki Carmichael, could do for her. Not some plastic-and-silicone electronic thing.

Rikki wiggled into a comfortable position and closed her eyes as the memories resurfaced.

"You don't like being helpless, do you?" Rikki asked her face-down submissive whose arms were tied behind her back with a diamond weave arm binder. Rikki wasn't a rope expert by any means, but she could hold her own for basic ties. She wanted Eileen to understand that Rikki had all the power at the moment. But any good Dominant knew that they never had all the power. Ever. It was the permission the submissive gave that let the Dominant feel in control. Nothing would happen if that permission, that consent, had not been given in the first place.

Rikki remembered, as if it had happened yesterday, that Eileen had not been happy being bound and helpless. But she wasn't helpless. She wasn't gagged. She could use her safewords. They could pause. She could ask for the bindings to be loosened or removed. Rikki continually checked the bindings to make sure they were tight enough to hold but not so tight as to injure.

"Mmm," Rikki had moaned sincerely as she ran one light hand down Eileen's back, up and over the rope bindings, and then over one smooth ass cheek. Eileen had a lovely full ass. Rikki brought the other hand into play and caressed the second cheek. Eileen lifted up in an attempt to get more pressure and to invite Rikki to explore the notch between her legs. It was difficult for Eileen to scoot up on her knees because her bound arms gave her no leverage, but she managed to do just that. Rikki wanted to swat the woman she was seducing, but that wasn't the right approach at the moment. Quiet. Still. Methodical. That's what Eileen needed.

For who knew how long, Eileen had gone straight for a vibrator to get off fast. Past Dommes had indulged this method. Rikki understood that vibrators got the job done but ultimately caused more harm than good. Sure, orgasms were good things, but the sensuality was muted with a vibrator, and the closeness between the Domme and sub diminished. And Rikki wanted more for Eileen. She wanted more for the woman who seemed to be responding to her brand of dominance. Eileen wasn't a newbie. Rikki had her fill of newbies because they only seemed to want that immediate thrill. None of them had been willing to put in the work for bigger gains.

Hopefully, Rikki could move Eileen out of that instant orgasm mentality. The woman was stubborn. But Rikki, even more so.

"Ahh," Rikki said and took advantage of Eileen, now on her knees, her ass in the air, her legs spread. Her head and one shoulder were pressed down on the pillow, but she seemed comfortable enough. Eileen was ready to be taken.

"What a lovely presentation," Rikki said and ran both hands down Eileen's ass cheeks to her inner thighs. She was wet, as expected.

This was not going to be a pain-to-pleasure experience for Eileen. But Eileen already knew that. They'd been doing this no-impact and no-vibrators training for two weeks so far, and Eileen had been fighting it the entire way. Rikki wasn't going to break first and was determined to somehow get Eileen to loosen up, to let her body ease into the sensations. Impact would be back on the table at some point, of course, but vibrators would not. It would undo everything.

Eileen started bucking her hips like an addict needing release. Again, Rikki didn't swat her ass and tell her to stop. Rikki simply removed her hands and waited. When Eileen got the hint and stilled herself, Rikki returned to caressing her body. Her fingers ran through the slickness around the outer labia. The hips gyrated. Eileen clearly wanted Rikki to get to the goal.

"Actions have consequences, Eileen," Rikki warned softly as she broke contact again.

Eileen groaned. Rikki was not going to remind her again what the goal was. They'd discussed it. Rikki had reiterated the goal every day for two weeks. Eileen had to let go, let the sensations come to her, rather than force them.

Eileen stopped gyrating. There was a soft sigh, not one meant to send a message to Rikki's ears, like she'd done in previous sessions. This one was different. It was a slight giving in. Rikki was hopeful.

Rikki caressed Eileen's inner thighs on her way to her slick center. This time, her fingers parted Eileen's folds and caressed the sensitive flesh there. Although she'd told Eileen they were staying away from direct clitoris contact, that wasn't exactly true. She would stay away from the exposed clit, but there was the entire clitoral network that could and would be explored. And that's what Eileen and her former Dommes had been ignoring.

Rikki slid one finger, then two, inside and caressed the inner walls. Eileen started moving back and forth to get more sensation. Rikki pulled out.

Eileen's frustrated groan was muffled by the waterproof "love sheet" Rikki had thrown on the bed before their session. It had been a gift from Victoria when Eileen moved in. Leave it to Victoria to be on top of the latest trends in sex toys and accoutrements.

Eileen stayed still. Rikki moved to the top of the bed. Eileen turned her head to look at Rikki, but didn't say a word. Rikki nodded her praise at this quiet acquiescence and coated Eileen's lips with the essence on her fingertips. Eileen licked it off and looked at Rikki again. Rikki smiled, raised a teasing eyebrow, and moved back to continue her work. In essence, she was making love to Eileen. Eileen had come to her as a woman who wanted sex, not love. Rikki was hoping to change that.

Rikki thrust her fingers in again and gently caressed. Every time she stroked the G-spot, Eileen exhaled noticeably. Excellent. They could get there.

Rikki knelt behind Eileen and, although she didn't have a strap on, maneuvered her body between Eileen's legs, spreading them apart even further. Rikki's hand continued caressing. She kept most of her body weight on her stiff-armed hand on the bed and draped her body over Eileen's. Another soft exhale. This was working. Rikki's caresses progressed as she added a gentle in-and-out motion, followed by the familiar swirls.

A longer exhale. Good.

Eileen's hips started gyrating. "Fuck me, Rikki."

"Gentle movements," Rikki corrected as she stopped all motions.

The gyrations didn't stop. Rikki pulled out.

A frustrated groan filled the room.

Rikki said nothing. She was just about to reinsert her fingers when Eileen said, "Can I at least have nipple clamps or something? Jeez-us."

Rikki sat up, taking her weight off Eileen's back. She removed all physical contact. Rikki wasn't exactly denying Eileen an orgasm; she truly wanted her submissive to have one, but she wanted her to feel it differently. And, with every session they had, Rikki had been denying herself as well. She wondered if Eileen even noticed that. Rikki, her voice husky from need that would not be satisfied that evening, said, "You are to be facedown on this bed when I get home from the shop tomorrow evening."

When no response came, Rikki said calmly, "Is that understood?"

"Sure," came the short answer. There was no honorific, which was also something they had been working on. As a career bottom, Eileen was trying to get rewards without working for them. Rikki wanted rewards, too. She wanted her attentions and ministrations to be acknowledged and respected. Saying, "Ma'am," a few times wasn't too much to ask, was it?

Rikki moved off the bed to sit in the lone chair near the closet. She rested her elbows on the chair arms and steepled her fingers. She didn't mind waiting. She was a Capricorn, and Capricorns were known for their self-discipline and self-control. She would simply ignore Eileen and mentally plan her tasks for the following day at the shop.

Before long, a weak "Ma'am?" came from the tied woman on the bed.

"Yes?"

"Are you gonna untie me anytime soon?" The disrespect was almost tangible.

"No."

"Why not?"

"We're not done."

Eileen turned her head, trying to see Rikki, to no avail. "What do you want from me, Ma'am?"

"I want you to let go, give in," Rikki said softly. To show anger or frustration would be to undo that evening's progress, and there had been some. "Feel the sensations, Eileen. Release your tensions, not just the ones gathering where you feel you need it most. Let your entire body feel the release." Rikki stood up. "Let your guard down, Eileen." She caressed one of Eileen's calves. "You're safe here. Drift in the sensations. Your body is in good hands with me. I'll take care of her."

"Which will in turn take care of *me*."

Rikki smiled. She knew Eileen couldn't see the smile but would hear it in her voice. "Yes, yes. I have you. All of you. Give in, Eileen." She got back on the bed. Both hands slid their way back up to Eileen's open center. Rikki knelt between Eileen's legs again and draped her body over Eileen's back. She wanted Eileen to feel Rikki's possession of her. Rikki's right hand made its way back inside. Eileen was as wet as ever, which made Rikki's movements smooth and easy. She made the patented "come-hither" motion over Eileen's G-spot, eliciting a soft moan.

"Let go, Eileen. Let me in." Rikki worked her fingers in and out, swirled them around, spent time stimulating the G-spot, and finally, after what seemed like forever, Eileen started moaning deep and long moans. Rikki did not stop her motions. Eileen did not buck her hips, gyrate, or make demands.

Eileen's moans were low and intense. They increased in pitch until her entire body convulsed in orgasm. Rikki's fingers were squeezed by the pulsing contractions, but she kept them moving. She stopped once Eileen collapsed on the bed, letting out the longest, most satisfied sigh Rikki had ever heard from a submissive.

Rikki pulled her fingers out slowly and then moved up on the bed to kiss her submissive on the lips. Eileen eagerly returned the kisses.

"I'm going to untie you now," Rikki said and made quick work of undoing the Shibari ropes. She massaged the red spots and helped Eileen lower her arms to her sides.

"I…" Eileen started, ending her non-sentence with a sigh. "Thank you, Rikki. Ma'am. Mistress. Miss Rikki." She chuckled and asked, "Did I do it right?"

"You did everything right," Rikki said.

"That was hard," Eileen said and found the strength to roll over on her back.

"I know," Rikki said. "I'm proud of you."

"Proud?" Eileen scoffed.

"Truly. Letting go is difficult."

"I'm bullheaded," Eileen admitted in a rare moment of vulnerability. She rolled over to face Rikki. "I didn't know it could be like that." She closed her eyes and stretched all her limbs, shaking out the tension. "Thank you."

Rikki leaned in for a kiss and received a sincere one in return.

Back in the present day, Rikki blew out a sigh at the memories. See? She wasn't powerless. She wasn't irrelevant. She knew how to help people. She had knowledge and experience. So why did it feel like she was powerless over everything in her life? She couldn't even muster up the courage to talk to Esme again. Esme, whom she thought she had connected with. Esme, who had acted as if nothing had happened. Maybe it hadn't.

It didn't matter, anyway. Rikki didn't have the strength for games or for a new relationship.

And even though she had gotten aroused by the memory of Eileen, she refused to satisfy her physical need. She hadn't been satisfied with Eileen back then, and she wouldn't now. Eileen, the ultimate betrayer, did not deserve that reward.

Rikki rolled over, smacked her face into the towels, and shoved them off the bed onto the floor.

Chapter 13

Rikki pulled up to Jaleesa and Tina's home and parked in the empty driveway. Were they home? Was anyone home? Five people lived in this house. She pulled out her phone and double-checked the date and time. Right date. Right time. Maybe something had come up, but she'd go up to the front door and ring the bell to find out.

It was late March, and Ohio was still pretty damned cold. She didn't wear her full Domme regalia; instead, she chose an all-black, form-fitting ensemble of leggings and a tight, low-cut cotton blouse that she could move in. Her hair was pulled back into a tight yet functional bun. She'd dressed for herself that morning. Tina would get Rikki's best, but Rikki was also going to be comfortable while doing it. She'd play nice and let them think this impact session was just what she'd needed. Thank you so much. "Blah, blah, blah," Rikki muttered as she reached forward to ring the bell.

Within seconds, the door opened, and Jaleesa invited her in.

"Still friggin' cold out there," Jaleesa said. "It's officially spring, you know," she called out the door to the universe.

Rikki chuckled. "Mother Nature will do what she will."

"Fickle bee-otch." Jaleesa pointed to the coat rack, and Rikki hung up her Fleece hooded jacket. It was black, like the rest of her outfit. Jaleesa gestured to one of the comfy recliners in the living room. "Have a seat. I'll go find Tina. Water?"

"Sure."

Jaleesa turned and headed toward the kitchen. She bellowed down the hall that led to the primary bedroom, the one she shared with Tina, "Babe, Rikki's here."

"Oh, excellent," came Tina's excited response. "Be right out."

While Rikki waited, she noticed mats and bean bag chairs lined up against the far wall. She was perplexed by it, but then remembered that four submissives lived in this house. Well, three submissives and one switch, and they had regular twelve-step meetings as a family. Rikki softened her posture. Other people were going through a lot, too. She needed to remember that.

Jaleesa came back in with an unopened bottle of water and handed it to Rikki. "Plenty more where that came from." She nervously looked toward the hallway. "She's in there working, you know. She just cannot take a day off."

"Does she usually go in on Saturdays?" Rikki uncapped the water. She took a small sip.

"She does," Jaleesa said. "Convincing her to take a day off for this was…difficult."

Rikki simply nodded. Maybe there was some truth to the workaholic aspect of Tina's life. Maybe Rikki could do some good here. She held onto that small kernel of hope when Tina came in and sat down.

"Hi, Miss Rikki," Tina said. "Thanks for coming today." She plopped into a smaller recliner next to the bigger Jaleesa-sized one. She blew out a sigh. "I swear, I leave them alone for one day, and it falls apart."

"Hopefully, you've trained your employees well," Rikki said, knowing that Tina most likely had.

Tina nodded. "Corporate warned me about trying to do everything for everyone else. She said to guide but not *do*." She widened her eyes and then shrugged. "Easier said than done."

"See the Domme side in her?" Jaleesa said to Rikki.

Rikki nodded.

"Oh, hush," Tina said and waved off her life partner.

Rikki scoffed knowingly and said, "There's that Domme side that needs some relief, methinks."

Jaleesa and Tina shot a glance at each other. Tina motioned for Jaleesa to speak, "'The lady doth protest too much, methinks.'"

Rikki burst out laughing. "*Hamlet*. Perfect. I didn't even realize I'd set you up for that, Jaleesa." She took a look around and said, "You all are settling in nicely into this house."

"We are," Tina said. She gestured to a small area just off the front door, lined with stacked boxes. "We want to put a piano there, once we can figure out what to do with our collective stuff."

"Do you play?" Rikki asked.

Jaleesa laughed. "No one in this house plays. I just think it would fit that space."

"And," Tina said, leaning toward her life partner, "she's hoping she can convince Dana to take lessons."

"Dana's having none of it, though," Jaleesa said and shrugged. "But anyway, we should set up your session." This she said directly to Tina.

"Sure, sure," Tina said. She purposefully powered down her phone and handed it to Jaleesa. That must be protocol in their household. Tina turned to Rikki and said, "People always ask how we make our setup work. Basically, we respect each other. We communicate well. After our weekly twelve-step meetings, Jaleesa asks everyone to voice whatever's on their mind. We clear up a lot of things this way."

"It clears the air," Jaleesa said. "It took DeShawn a hot minute to learn how to share. He didn't have a voice over there." By 'over there' she meant with Seamus and his household. Apparently, communication and the sharing of feelings weren't top priorities.

Rikki made a mental note to check in with Shasti about Madison's issue with Seamus's *little*, Billy.

"DeShawn's a great fit here," Tina said.

"Now," Jaleesa started while looking at Tina. Apparently, she was going to say something tough. "Tina has difficulty, and she acknowledges this, but she has difficulty asking for what she wants. And, don't get me wrong, I like subs that do what I ask them to, but not if it's a detriment to their own well-being. We all fall into that trap of thinking we can do it all, and as long as everyone else is happy, our own needs don't matter."

"And that happiness is valid," Rikki said, "but I understand what you mean. My mother was a people pleaser, and she didn't do much for her own enjoyment. She was a great mom, but it wasn't until I was basically out of college that I took my blinders off and realized how much she'd lost herself." If Rikki hadn't encouraged her mother to...Rikki stopped her thoughts. To go on would be to rip open those still-raw wounds.

"You okay, Rikki?" Jaleesa asked.

"Yes." Rikki put on a smile, hoping it would become genuine. "I just miss her."

"Yeah," Jaleesa said. "It's tough to lose people. But we keep them in our hearts and in our memories."

"Not the same, we know," Tina said and reached for Jaleesa's hand.

Rikki cleared her throat and changed the subject. "So, what do you want to get out of this session downstairs?"

Tina looked lost for a moment and then said, "Honestly, I just want to get out of my head."

"And feel something physical?" Rikki suggested.

"Yes, and now that the weather's turning nicer, or should be, we'll go on more of those family hikes Jaleesa likes so much."

"At some point," Jaleesa interjected. "I want her to play in a rec softball league. But we've agreed that this summer's too soon. Her job is overwhelming enough."

"And I'm way too out of shape for competitive softball, Babe."

"So, we'll get you into shape," Jaleesa said and scrunched her face teasingly. "We have over a year."

"I'd actually love that," Tina said. "Not the whole working out thing, but playing again. I still have my glove from high school."

"That's impressive," Rikki said. Tina was thirty-two years old, so fourteen or fifteen years out of high school. "I think it's an admirable goal and one you have a bit of time to get ready for." She stood up.

Tina also stood, but she was stiff. Ahh, nerves. Rikki wondered when they would show.

"Can I see the setup?" Rikki reached down for her water bottle.

Once down in the basement area, Rikki's eyes grew wide at the size. It ran the whole length of the house and was filled with furniture, boxes, and stuff she couldn't identify.

"We can look at all that furniture after your session," Jaleesa said to Rikki.

"And the washer and dryer," Tina added. "But you don't have to if you're not interested. Absolutely no pressure from us."

"I'll take a look after." Rikki wished her other friends would adopt that no-pressure rule. Ever since Shasti and Madison had returned home from their overseas trip, they had both been subtly and not-so-subtly prodding her to ask Esme out. As far as Rikki was concerned, even though Esme still showed up at the shop every weeknight, that ship had sailed.

Rikki slid a privacy screen aside to reveal a hidden floor-to-ceiling set of doors. "DeShawn's handiwork," Jaleesa said. She moved two rolling carts out of the way and then unlocked the padlock with a key she'd taken from her pocket. She opened both doors wide to reveal a gorgeous St. Andrew's cross bolted to the wall.

Rikki ran her hand over the oak wood. "This is gorgeous," Rikki said, thinking about her old, worn-out cross in the apartment.

"DeShawn wishes he'd made it," Jaleesa said, "but he's apparently come up with an improved design of his own. He wants to add leather padding."

Tina sounded like a proud mom when she added, "Harriet said she can work the leather padding and teach him how to do it."

"Sounds like the two of them are kindred spirits," Rikki said.

"They seem to be hitting it off really well. It's more than I could have hoped for." Jaleesa kissed Tina on the forehead and said, "I'll be upstairs if you need me."

"Thanks for this, Babe," Tina said. "I think I need this."

Jaleesa, to her credit, simply smiled and headed up the stairs.

Rikki hadn't been sure whether Jaleesa would stay and observe, which would have been fine, but maybe her absence was better. Once the door shut, Rikki got into Domme mode. She sat on the couch and directed Tina to sit next to her. "We'll take it slow so I can judge how much you can take or want to take."

"Yes, Ma'am."

"Tell me your safewords."

"Red and yellow, Ma'am."

"And green if all is going well?"

"Oh, yes, of course," Tina said with a nervous giggle.

Rikki revisited Tina's hard and soft limits. They'd already discussed them, but she wanted to reassure Tina that she was mindful of her wishes and her safety.

"And right here on this couch is where I'd like to hold you afterward. Did Jaleesa explain that I need to give aftercare?"

"She did," Tina said. "She does, too. It helps her avoid Domme drop. It'll be fine, Miss Rikki. I'll need the help catching my breath, I think."

"Perfect," Rikki said and stood. "Up you go." She pointed to the cross. "Can you remove your over shirt? I see your racerback tank underneath. And those compression shorts are fine."

Tina took off the button-down shirt and stepped up to face the cross. Rikki stood behind Tina and said, "I'm going to touch you, but not in a sexual way. I just want to get a feel for what I've got here in front of me."

"That's fine," Tina said. Rikki could hear the nerves in her voice. They would shake out soon enough. There were two sets of cuffs attached to the cross. One was leather and the other velcro. Rikki pulled the softer velcro cuffs out and attached them to Tina's ankles and wrists, in turn. Interesting. Jaleesa must have tailored the height for Tina's short stature. Nice.

Rikki pulled out a paddle and both floggers, making sure Tina saw them. Tina's slight nod said green. Rikki also pulled out a few soft cloths she would use later to soothe the burning skin and nerves. She smiled devilishly at the rough burlap, gags, and other instruments of impact play stored in the closet. Jaleesa must use these on Harriet or Dana. Maybe even DeShawn. Definitely not with Tina.

Rikki put the supplies on a side table so Tina could see them. Rikki stood behind for a moment and then laid one hand on Tina's shoulder. Tina jumped.

"You're okay," Rikki said. "I'll walk you through everything I'm doing."

"Thank you, Ma'am."

"That reminds me," Rikki said as she placed her other hand on Tina's bicep. "Many subs forget honorifics during impact. And that is fine. Don't worry about any of that, please. I just want you to let go."

"That's a relief," Tina said. She breathed out some nerves. Good. Time to get going.

Rikki moved her hands methodically over the areas that were in bounds for striking and told Tina as she went. Once she felt Tina exhale another set of nerves, Rikki picked up the flogger. It was too soon for the paddle, and she wasn't even sure Tina would make it to the paddle.

Rikki draped the flogger tails over Tina's shoulders.

"The back first and then down to the buttocks and the back of the legs," Rikki said and got to work. She swished the single flogger back and forth on Tina's body as gently as she could. Back and forth, the tails went in a figure-eight pattern, finding resistance as they hit Tina's clothes. Rikki understood Tina's need to stay covered, but impact was so much better on bare skin. But these were Tina's boundaries, and Rikki would honor them.

The flogger travelled down Tina's body as promised and back up again. She was simply warming up Tina's muscles, just like an athlete before a competition.

"Increasing intensity," Rikki said and put a little more speed and a little more flick into her strikes. She stayed on Tina's buttocks a bit longer. Subs can get used to a pattern and get bored. Rikki didn't want that. Boredom might lead to dissatisfaction. Can't have that for the one and only time Rikki would be a guest Domme in this house.

After several minutes, the back of Tina's legs and the only part of her back that showed above the tank top were turning a lovely shade of pink. It was time. Without losing her rhythm, Rikki grabbed the second flogger and began a two-point together-same pattern.

"This feels great," Rikki said.

"Mmm," Tina said. There was no stress in her voice, so all was well.

Rikki hadn't been to Dominique's in a while, but muscle memory was kicking in. She really did love the physicality of flogging. Rikki announced her switch to a two-point alternating pattern.

Tina adjusted her body. That was a good sign that she was feeling the strikes. She hadn't guarded or tried to move away; that would come, probably soon, but it wasn't there yet.

And Rikki was just getting warmed up, anyway. Her rhythm and pace were steady, but she didn't want to get tired, so she changed it up again.

"Three-beat weave," she announced.

Tina moved her hips. She was trying to guard.

"Color?" Rikki checked in, keeping up her pattern.

"Green."

"Color?" Rikki asked again, a bit louder.

"Green!" Tina barked back, a hint of irritation in her voice.

Rikki smiled behind Tina's back. She was getting feisty. That was a good sign. People pleasers like Tina often put others ahead of themselves, and that would never do, given the situation they were in at the moment.

"Let go, Tina," Rikki said. She needed to change her strokes. She decreased the speed of the floggers, stopped momentarily, and restarted with a two-point together-same pattern, but this time she hit Tina's buttocks on the upswing.

Tina moaned. Rikki knew better than to interpret the moan as sexual. For Tina, it wasn't, but it did sound satisfying. She changed to an alternating pattern on the buttocks and then continued up Tina's back and down to the thighs, skipping the buttocks that must be pulsing hot.

When Tina grunted every so often, Rikki knew it was time to regroup.

"Countdown to change," Rikki said. "Five." She waited a beat between each number. "Four. Three. Two. One." Rikki pulled the floggers back and listened to Tina's breathing. It was slightly labored, but not overly so. Rikki placed a hand on Tina's back over the t-shirt.

"Mmm," Tina moaned at the touch. It was giving her relief. She pressed Tina's back and legs repeatedly with the palm of her hands.

"Buttocks now," Rikki warned. She didn't wait for a response and pressed both hands on Tina's butt cheeks. She didn't squeeze or roll the cheeks. She simply applied slight pressure to help relieve the pulsing that must be there.

Rikki moved closer, knowing she was in Tina's personal space, and whispered into her ear, "How are you feeling?"

A soft moan was the only response. It was a good moan.

"Color?"

"Green."

Rikki heard the anxiety in Tina's one quick word. She knew the woman wanted more. They always did.

Rikki moved to Tina's side, bent down, and lengthened the strap on Tina's ankle cuffs. She needed Tina to be able to back away from the cross a bit. There was a spanking bench, but she didn't want to release Tina from the cross yet.

"Back your feet up," Rikki requested. She tried to keep her command tone out of her voice. Tina wasn't her submissive. This was all in the name of impact and not necessarily overt dominance. Rikki picked up the paddle and checked its weight. It had a nice feel but was a bit heavier than she preferred. Oh, well. When in Rome and all that.

"Lean forward," Rikki said, and then ran her hand down Tina's now-bent form. "Perfect."

She stood behind Tina off to one side and swung the paddle like a tennis racket, but gently. She let the paddle come to rest on Tina's left buttock for a moment. Would Esme like something like this? Was Esme adventurous? She flung the thoughts aside; now was not the time. The time for thoughts of Esme was basically never. Rikki pulled the paddle back and tapped lightly. The taps increased in intensity until Tina groaned. Rikki changed to the right cheek. The groan came sooner. She alternated left, then right, then left. She switched to backhand swings when her arms and shoulders got tired.

Tina squirmed at every new strike. It was time, time to wind it down. Rikki slowed the paddle and the intensity. She stepped back and let Tina catch her breath. Her body weight hung from her wrist cuffs, suspended from the cross.

After a long moment, Rikki asked, "Color?"

"Yellow," Tina said. But Rikki already knew.

Rikki moved so she could see her play partner's face. Red, but not overly so. Breathing was good, like she'd just done a nice cardio workout. Rikki desperately wanted to rub her own sore shoulders, but would do no such thing in front of a submissive. *One does not show weakness*, she reminded herself. It wasn't something she learned from Aunt Tilda; it was something she'd honed on her own over the years.

Rikki reached for one of the soft cloths and wiped the sweat off Tina's face. "You did well."

"Mmm," was all Tina could manage at first. Rikki used the cloth to soothe Tina's exposed skin. She pressed lightly against Tina's tank top and shorts in an attempt to give her some relief.

Rikki grabbed a fresh cloth and wiped Tina's face one last time. "I'm going to walk you over to the couch in a moment, but only when you're ready."

"Thank you," Tina said with a nod.

Rikki grabbed some bottled waters and a small chocolate bar from the mini-fridge near the basement door, then placed them on the end table next to the couch. She opened the water bottles so she wouldn't have to fuss with the caps when she had Tina in her arms.

"Ready?" Rikki asked.

"Mm hmm," Tina said. Oh, yes, she was in sub space. Rikki had seen that dreamy, sleepy look on many subs' faces over the years.

Rikki unclipped the ankle cuffs. "Wrists next," Rikki said as she positioned herself to take Tina's body weight if necessary. "One cuff," Rikki said, and gently lowered Tina's arm around her neck so she could hold on to Rikki, which she did without being told. Rikki reached up and undid the Velcro on the other wrist. "Two cuffs."

"Red cuff, blue cuff," Tina added with a laugh.

Rikki didn't get it at first, but then chuckled when it hit. "One cuff, two cuff, red cuff, blue cuff. Funny."

"You got it," Tina said and let Rikki walk her to the couch.

The landing wasn't smooth, but Rikki managed to spin them around, so Tina landed in a seated position in Rikki's arms.

"Mmm," Tina said as she snuggled back against her temporary Domme. "Thank you, Ma'am."

Rikki handed Tina a bottle of water. Tina took it but just held it close to her torso. And that was okay. She was letting herself feel the sensations flying around her body. Rikki took the bottle from her, and Tina mumbled something, but Rikki couldn't make out what it was. Probably just a thank you.

Rikki sat on the couch, trying not to move. Tina's back was pressed against Rikki's front, recovering from their session, and she didn't want to disturb her bliss. Aunt Tilda had drilled into their heads that sub drop was a real thing. It was a temporary imbalance as the body tried to compensate for the flooding of chemicals it received during play. Dopamine is the pleasure drug that gives a euphoric feeling, typically when someone anticipates a pleasurable experience. During the scene, endorphins flood the body, bolstering that feeling of euphoria. Enkephalins, a natural type of opioid, appear when pain is present. And on top of all that, epinephrine, or basic adrenaline, helps the body deal with pain. The combination of those chemicals gives people the feeling they're after. The combination can also contribute to sub drop if the Domme does not provide adequate aftercare.

After quite some time, longer than most, Tina moaned a good cleansing exhale and stretched her arms up high. She arched her back and moved her body around. "So good." She blew out another sigh and sat up. "Thank you,

Rikki." She took the offered water bottle back. "That was so good. Cleansing."

"Good, good," Rikki said. She'd initially had her doubts about her friends' motivations for the session, but at this juncture, it didn't matter. She'd helped Tina.

Tina sighed again and took a long swig. "Miss Rikki?" She adjusted so she could look at Rikki directly.

"Yes?"

"What do you get out of this?"

"I like giving pain that turns to pleasure," Rikki said. "For you, the pleasure is the endorphin and chemical releases that get you out of your mind and into your body. That nice floaty feeling you have right now?"

"Mm hmm," Tina said. " S'nice."

"Your whole body is relaxing into bliss. No worries. No cares." Rikki rubbed Tina's arm gently. As an afterthought, she added, "Topping like this makes me feel in control. You, on the other hand, let go of your control. It was a beautiful surrender." Rikki cleared her throat and said, "That's what I get out of it. Knowing that I helped someone."

"Mmm," Tina sighed. "So good."

"That and I get a physical workout," Rikki said with a laugh, and Tina chuckled as well.

Rikki reached for the small chocolate square and handed it to Tina, whose eyes lit up. "Ooh," she said, "I forgot about this part." She eagerly bit off a small piece from one of the corners.

"Chocolate helps replace those receding chemicals temporarily until you can right your own ship. We don't want you dropping too fast."

"That's how Jaleesa and I met, you know," Tina said, her eyes brightening.

"Tell me more."

"I'm not a fan of public speaking," Tina said, "but my sponsor and I felt it was time for me to tell my story again at an NA meeting. It was a joint NA/AA meeting, and Jaleesa was there. I didn't even know her. After my talk, I sat down and got really disoriented and dizzy. No one else saw, but she did. She put her arm around me, held both of my hands in one of hers, and told me what was happening to me. She told me she 'had me' or something like that and she would take care of me."

"Looks like she still 'has you.'" Rikki said softly, a warm feeling spreading through her chest.

"She does," Tina said.

"I'm so happy for you both," Rikki said.

Tina adjusted again, creating more distance between them. The move felt natural, and Rikki wasn't put out by it. On the contrary, it meant that Tina was recovering and they were falling back into their usual roles as friends.

"Miss Rikki, I hope whoever you meet next is wonderful. I hope you can be yourself around her."

Rikki was a little startled by the abrupt statement, but covered it with, "Me, too. Thank you." Was that what all her friends talked about behind her back? That she needed a partner? That shit was getting old. And tiring. It was time to move things along. "I'll call your Domme back down."

Rikki opened the basement door and called for Jaleesa, who arrived within seconds. She must have been hovering. The expectant look on her face almost made Rikki laugh.

"Babe," Tina said and opened her arms, but stayed on the couch. "It was great. Thank you for this."

Rikki looked away while they started kissing. Jaleesa, with Tina's permission, of course, had told Rikki that Tina was a *romantic* asexual. She liked all the trappings of romance, like affection, attention, kissing, hugging, and caressing, but that's as far as it ever went. But still, it felt intrusive to watch them kissing.

Instead, she meandered toward the furniture they had pointed out before the session. "What's for sale over here?" Rikki asked, deciding to interrupt the lovebirds.

"Nothing," Jaleesa called. "It's free to you. Pick out whatever you want."

"I will, thank you." The words were out of her mouth before she could stop them. What the hell? Maybe endorphins were messing with her brain, too. As she looked, Jaleesa started selling her on a few things. The woman was like a used-car salesman, pointing out the advantages of each piece and ultimately "selling" Rikki on a couch, two overstuffed chairs, two end tables, and a low coffee table. The pieces matched in style, and they all agreed the ensemble would fit nicely in her apartment. By then, Tina had recovered enough to stand and show her their old washer and dryer. Rikki surprised herself again by accepting. It was a huge act of charity on their part, but Rikki vowed to pay them back at some point. She vowed this silently to herself, of course, and was going to let them think they'd done their good deeds for the day, the week, the year. Whatever. But, yes, she would truly pay them back. Once she got back to the shop, she would look up the going market prices on each and every piece and pay them back once she got out from under Eileen.

They worked out a date for Jaleesa's family to deliver the items to Rikki using Jaleesa's big pickup truck. Rikki then took her leave. This was, of course, after turning down their offer of lunch.

The charity ends here, Rikki thought as she headed out. Although she'd had water before and after the session, Rikki recognized the signs of her own drop. That was okay. She'd grab one of Marta's sweet treats as she checked on the shop and then head upstairs to lie down for a bit. If she napped, great. If not, that was okay, too. She'd mentally arrange the new furniture in her apartment if it came to that.

Once back on Market Street, her radar went up. There were several cars parked in the alleyway next to the shop. The alley was not a parking area. She couldn't even get to her designated parking spot and had to park on the street.

Flaming mad, she walked up the alleyway after parking and flamed even hotter when she saw someone parked in her spot. She unlocked the side door to her office, locked it behind her, and then entered the shop. Lydia's petrified yet relieved expression greeted her first. A young man in a white coat and a clipboard emerged from the kitchen. Shit, they were being inspected. Two more inspectors came out of the kitchen, followed by the head inspector who'd given them those good marks recently.

Rikki sighed in relief. These were the interns, learning their craft. She'd forgotten to tell Lydia. She quickly pulled her assistant manager aside and filled her in. She also apologized for forgetting to tell the one person who should know. Rikki figured she'd be at the shop when the interns came for professional development.

"Just be natural," Rikki told Lydia. "And, again, I goofed."

"No worries, Ma'am," Lydia said. "Just shows that you're human."

Rikki chuckled, but didn't feel the mirth. Jeez, she was tired. Why, on that day of all days, did they decide to come back? This was the one day she'd granted herself to help a friend and maybe get some relief for herself.

Apparently, the universe wasn't having it.

She stuffed her Domme drop deep inside; there was no time for it now, and plastered her best smile on to greet the head inspector.

Chapter 14

Rikki checked the time on her watch. She was going to be late. Couldn't be helped. Yes, it could, but she had the *don't cares* and *can't help its* ever since the impact scene with Tina back in March. Not that the scene itself had set her off, it was just the fact that all of her friends seemed to be trying to manipulate her. That was not cool, and she didn't appreciate it. And, unfortunately, she chose the *"if you don't know what you did, I'm not going to tell you"* approach to handling it. Juvenile, for sure. Satisfying, not so much. She was supposedly a brat tamer, and yet here she was, the biggest brat of them all.

It was now the last weekend in May, a little over two months since the impact scene and Jaleesa's family hauling all that unpaid furniture up into her apartment. Rikki was grateful for the furniture, washer, and dryer, but not for the charity that had come with them. They would be paid back as soon as she could afford it. But that was not her worry at the moment. The spring Masquerade Ball was set to begin in twenty minutes.

She checked herself in the mirror. She wore the barest makeup. Why bother? There was no one to impress. It didn't matter what she did, anyway. She checked her look one last time. She loved the new *little black tux* that Victoria had convinced her to order. It was a suit made for a woman's body. Kudos to the folks who came up with that idea. When the suit arrived, Victoria insisted on having it tailored at Robert's shop on Kirkland, but Rikki wasn't interested. Robert was pricey, and he was handsy. Instead, she hired Harriet, one of Jaleesa's service subs, to alter the fit. Best of all, Harriet had come to the apartment, so Rikki didn't have to go out. Harriet had done an amazing job and seemed genuinely happy to help.

Rikki loved the tight fit of the black pants and the long lapels of the tuxedo jacket. Her white blouse could have and probably should have been opened to reveal a bit more cleavage, but she wasn't looking for that kind of attention.

Heading to the venue, she ignored yet another incoming text from Shasti. She'd see Shasti soon enough. The parking lot at the former IGA grocery store, where their party was being held, was filling up fast as people arrived. Some were in full fetish gear, and others in more vanilla garb. The latter would probably change once inside. The windows were blacked out, and the space looked completely abandoned, which was just what they wanted for their very private semi-annual masquerade balls.

Once inside, Rikki was surprised to see Mel, one of the dungeon masters from Dominique's, working security at the door.

"Miss Robin," Mel said with a nod, using Rikki's stage name at Dominique's. She opened the velvet rope to let her pass.

"Thanks, Mel." Rikki handed her ticket to a handsome young man taking tickets just beyond the rope barrier. She didn't get more than five more feet when a blur of sage green ran up and stopped just before smacking into her.

"Hi, Miss Rikki," Madison said.

Rikki motioned for Madison to twirl. As she did so, Rikki said, "Now don't you look adorable in this suit. Suspenders to match. And this," she reached down and adjusted the bow tie, "positively makes the outfit."

"Thanks, Miss Rikki. Mistress and I are going for springy-ish colors this year." Madison said. "You know, for the *Spring is Here* theme."

"That makes sense."

Madison reached for Rikki's hand.

How do you *not* take the offered hand from a *little*? Rikki clasped Madison's hand and let herself be led to the table of their friends.

"We were worried," Shasti said as she stood for a hug. She wore a long, flowing skirt in the same sage green as Madison's with a similar off-white blouse.

Before she could respond, Madison maneuvered in for a hug. Rikki hugged her back, and when she let go, Madison was still hanging on. Rikki patted Madison on the back and said, "I need to breathe, young one."

"Sorry," Madison said and let go.

"You two look so nice. Matchy, matchy," Rikki said, totally deflecting

Shasti's statement. Shasti's slight eyebrow raise let Rikki know that Shasti was fully aware of this deflection.

Rikki greeted Marta and Shanice and then excused herself to find Seamus. As she passed by Jaleesa's family's table, then by Rowena, Minjung, and Lydia's table, she nodded to her friends but didn't stop for hugs or conversation. She had business to attend to; they'd understand. And besides, they'd gang up on her later, that was certain.

She found the older man standing alone next to the makeshift stage. It was basically a raised platform, but it would suit the needs of that evening's festivities. He smiled when he saw her approach, smoothed down his snow-white hair, and fixed the collar of his pink button-down shirt. His white pants, white coat jacket, and bow tie made him look like he was headed to an Easter egg hunt or something. But she had to admit, he was pulling it off well. And no doubt his three submissives were dressed similarly, but with a lot more skin on display.

"Find it," Seamus said to Rikki.

"Find what?" she asked.

"A better attitude."

"What the fuck, Seamus?" She wasn't one of his submissives.

"Your mood sucks," he said. "I can feel it coming off you in waves." He looked at her with concern. "And they'll feel it, too." He flicked his hand toward the throng of excited people milling about.

She sighed.

He moved into her personal space, turned her away from the crowd, and said, "Relax your jaw."

A flash of something hot went through her, and she glared at him.

He nodded. "I know, hun. I know. Life simply sucks sometimes, and you're going through something, but the show must go on. We're the emcees, and we need to get these folks pumped up for a good time."

Rikki took a breath and let it out slowly. She lifted her head and looked down her nose at the shorter man. It was a power move, and they both knew it.

"Have they all been talking?" It was her turn to gesture to the crowd.

"Of course," he said with a laugh. "It's when they stop gossiping that we become irrelevant."

She chuckled. It was kind of true.

"There's Tilda's girl," he said.

In that moment, she realized Seamus had known Aunt Tilda for over thirty years and was also still grieving her death. Aunt Tilda used to be the emcee and host at parties like this. When she died, the honor passed onto Seamus and Rikki. For years, Aunt Tilda's had been the lone voice welcoming their unique community to these balls, and now it just felt like something was missing.

Other people are going through stuff, too, Rikki, she reminded herself. She had to get out of her own head. Easier said than done.

"Now," he said again, "relax your jaw."

"I bet you say that to all the boys," Rikki quipped.

Seamus burst out laughing, which made Rikki smile in turn.

"Okay, jaw relaxing," she said.

"Relax your shoulders and then take a nice breath in, hold for a second, and let it out slowly." He encouraged her to take another breath. Funny how she felt better after that.

"Sorry to interrupt, Master Seamus," a young woman Rikki had never seen before said. "Can we get a mic check on you and Miss Rikki?"

"Of course, of course," Seamus said.

It was interesting how the young, twenty-something woman knew who Rikki was, but Rikki could swear she'd never seen the woman before. The woman's cheeks pinked up as she handed Rikki the other microphone. "You turn it on here," the woman directed.

Although Rikki graciously acknowledged the instruction, she was seething. How inept did this woman think Rikki was? If she were Rikki's submissive, she'd be punished for sure.

"Find it," Seamus said softly.

Rikki rolled her neck while relaxing her shoulders and jaw.

He turned his microphone on and spoke into it. "Check, check. One, two, ten. Oh, how great is BDSM?" A chuckle ran through the assembled crowd.

Rikki turned her microphone on. Thank goodness she'd been shown how, she thought sarcastically. She said into the mic, "Check. Check. One cuff, two cuff, red cuff, blue cuff."

Tina screeched with laughter from her family's table to their bewildered looks. Rikki smiled at her. Okay, fine. It wouldn't hurt to have a little fun that evening. It might make the event go by more quickly.

The young woman gave them both a thumbs-up and moved behind the DJ platform. Oh, she was that evening's entertainment. Good to know.

"C'mon," Seamus said and stepped onto the platform.

She ignored his outstretched hand and stepped up without help. *Do they all think I'm an invalid or something?*

"And, we're finding it," Seamus said quietly.

"Shut up." She smiled to let him know she was teasing.

The DJ announced that people should find their seats because the emcees would welcome them in five minutes. People gave quick hugs and hustled to find their spots. A few people, like Victoria, stood on the outskirts. She was obviously on the prowl ever since she and Josie amicably broke off their relationship, but Victoria also didn't like being told what to do, so she stayed right where she was.

Rikki grinned. Was she becoming a bit like Victoria? One part 'get off my lawn' and one part 'don't tell me what to do?' Maybe she and Victoria had absorbed this from Aunt Tilda, the matriarch herself. No, Aunt Tilda wasn't as standoffish as Rikki was becoming.

Seamus handed her the script, and she read it over. She'd play her part adequately, but she couldn't promise to put in as much enthusiasm as Seamus was sure to. That wasn't her style, and she wasn't about to change it for anyone or any reason.

"Finding it," Seamus whispered.

How does he know? Rikki wondered. *Maybe that's what makes him a good Dom; he has that sixth sense.*

The DJ gave them a nod, and the show was on.

Seamus took the helm in his booming voice. "Good evening, Dominants, submissives, and everyone in between." He leaned over to Rikki as if whispering, "We call those in-betweens switches." The audience chuckled. Seamus was turning on the charm; that was clear.

He continued, "We've got your hets, gays, lesbos, bi's, enbies, asexuals, intersexuals, trans folks, and queers." He paused to take a deep breath before continuing. "We've got cross-dressers, pets, sadists, masochists, Mommy

Dommes, Daddy Doms, *littles*, service subs, poly folks, monogamous folks, tops, and bottoms." He took another huge intake of breath before continuing, "Masters, Mistresses, Doms, Dommes, subs, and slaves with consent."

"Always with consent," Rikki interrupted. It was in the script, but she would have said it anyway. "You're forgetting a few more, Master Seamus." Unfortunately, she had to read from the notes he'd given her because she hadn't prepared beforehand. He gestured for her to continue, "Rope tops, riggers, rope bottoms, rope bunnies, wax players, brats, leather folk, latex folk, kinksters, and fetishists." It was her turn to take a comical breath.

"Mistress Rikki," Seamus said into the microphone as he turned to her, "I think we could be at this all night, and these folks want to eat, get their dance on, and check out the exhibits."

"Fair point, Master Seamus."

He turned toward the assembled crowd. "Welcome to the spring masquerade ball, where masks are optional but—"

"Clothing is not," Rikki finished. "To be very, very clear on this point, clothing is mandatory in this rented venue, and all your dangling bits must remain covered." Rikki received good-natured boos, but she took them with grace and dignity. "I know. I know. And, as I'm sure you also know, there will be no sexual liaisons happening anywhere in this space this evening."

"How about the bathrooms?" someone heckled.

"Nope," she said, expecting and getting some good-natured pushback. "And definitely not in your car in the parking lot."

"Oh, now you've gone too far," someone yelled from the back, getting a big laugh.

"Save it for home," Rikki called back to him. She turned back to her co-host. "There's also that important matter, Master Seamus."

"Yes, of course," he said. "We're going to turn serious for a minute. Some of you have already donated generously, and we thank you for that. Our community is one in which we not only monitor each other to keep us safe, but also help each other in times of need. And one of our family members needs some help. Please give what you can." He looked up to see Hayley and Hayley's submissive, Ashley, holding up a decorated cardboard box. "Mistress Hayley has the donation box and would appreciate seeing you at some point this evening. And I think she has candy for you as a thank you?"

"Sure do," Hayley called from across the room. She reached down and held up a big bowl of candy.

Rikki knew that Marta was deeply embarrassed by this public ask for charity to help fund Shanice's medical needs, but it needed to be done. She'd take the brunt of Marta's displeasure later. What was done was done.

"Was there anything else, Master Seamus?" Rikki asked.

"Only that this crowd looks fab-u-lous." He snapped his fingers on each syllable, much to the crowd's delight. "Everyone looks so springy." He turned and looked her up and down. "Everyone except maybe this goth emo in all black next to me." He pointed to her black outfit. He put his flattened hand by his mouth as if excluding Rikki from what he was about to say. "Somebody, get this one a girlfriend."

Rikki scowled at him while some people groaned and others chuckled politely. He slowly turned toward her, and she raised one Domme eyebrow in displeasure. That little comment of his had been unscripted.

"Uh, oh," he said into the microphone. "I think I'm in trouble."

"Yeah, I'm not finding it at the moment." This she said with her microphone turned off.

Seamus turned away from her, his eyes wide and his face grim, which made the crowd warn him that he was toast.

"Uh, Mistress Rikki?" he said sheepishly as he turned back around.

She turned her mic back on. "Yes?" she said coldly.

"I was hoping to ask you a question."

She nodded for him to go ahead.

"I have this burning—"

"You should get that looked at," Rikki interrupted him on cue. She laughed. The crowd laughed with her. The awkwardness had been diffused, and they were back on script.

"Mistress Rikki, you are hilarious. But seriously, I have this burning," he looked to the crowd, "*question*." A few chuckles greeted him. "Together you and I have listed all kinds of BDSM roles, but is there anything else striking about BDSM?"

Rikki looked as if she were thinking, then said, "Beats me."

The crowd burst into laughter, and then Madison yelled, "Not *you*, Miss Rikki. You have a whip!"

"Oh, yeah," Rikki said. "You're right." Rikki smiled at Madison. Her gaze then caught Shasti's, and Rikki nodded to her bestie. It was Rikki's way of letting her friend know that she was okay despite her frosty arrival.

Shasti patted her chest. She was saying, "I love you" back.

Rikki couldn't let the emotion of that exchange get her and almost missed her entry into the next joke. "Master Seamus," she said, "I have this submissive friend. He's a biologist into BDSM and humiliation. How would you classify someone like that?"

Seamus waggled his caterpillar eyebrows and said, "It's obvious, Mistress Rikki. He's bio-degradable." Another enthusiastic chuckle rippled through the crowd. Even stoic Victoria laughed. She gave Rikki a thumbs up, which Rikki acknowledged with a smile.

"You know," Rikki adlibbed, "you're right about me being single, so let me ask you some advice. What do you think about BDSM and one-night stands?" This was not on script. Yes, this was her passive-aggressive way of getting back at him.

Seamus narrowed his eyes at her, thinking. You could almost see smoke coming out of his head as he worked the joke. Delight hit his eyes, and he said, "Never a good idea, Mistress Rikki."

"Why not?" she asked, wondering what he'd come up with.

"They always rope you into a second date."

She practically snorted her laughter. "Good one," she said, impressed with his response. "I figured there would be strings attached, but I think we'd better move this along. They look hungry."

"Ahh, yes. I see that the lesbians are starting to eat each other."

Rikki grimaced, and the grimace was real. She backhanded him in the chest. "Here are the rules," she said to the crowd, and outlined that the servers would call tables up one at a time for the buffet line. She also reminded them that there was plenty of food and to take only what they could reasonably eat. The leftover food would go to the "Cincinnati Feeds" organization that very night.

Seamus then listed the various demonstrations that would be open after dinner, and they were welcome to participate, but only if consent was given.

"Consent always," Rikki echoed.

"Consent always," Seamus said again. "Especially for the

electrostimulation demonstration."

"I hear that's a charged display," Rikki said, trying not to grimace at Seamus's bad pun she'd been forced to read. "But if anyone interferes, they can be the bottom in Mistress Dominique's flogging workshop."

"Too many people would sign up for that, I'm afraid."

Seamus added a few more housekeeping items and then gestured to the head waitperson, a volunteer from the Cincinnati BDSM group, to take over.

As the first couple of tables were called to get food, the din of conversations increased.

"That was a low shot, Seamus," she said as she handed the powered-off microphone to the DJ. "Even for you."

"It was too soon," he said. "I realized that when I saw your face. I'm sorry, Rikki. I know you're struggling."

She wanted to ask him what exactly he thought she was struggling with, but held it in.

He continued, "I knew something was up when you weren't doing a whipping demo. Mark was so disappointed."

"He won't be," Rikki said. "Madam Magdalene came highly recommended from Dominique. Mark will be fine."

"If you need to talk or vent," Seamus said, "I'm your guy. I'll be seeing you every Monday evening for darts night, anyway."

"Thanks, Seamus," Rikki said. "I appreciate your offer." She sincerely did appreciate it, but there was no chance she'd ever take him up on it. She turned toward the tables and said, "I have to go make amends."

He simply smiled and nodded as she left.

Rikki took her time getting to the table she would share with Shasti, Madison, Marta, and Shanice. She stopped to talk with Rowena and also made sure to acknowledge Minjung and thank her for participating in one of the rope demonstrations later. Rikki wasn't sure she'd still be there to see it. That was to be determined. Her flight mode had been tweaked since her arrival. She also thanked Hayley and Ashley for collecting for Marta and Shanice and then made her way to Jaleesa's family's table.

"That was so funny, Miss Rikki," Tina said, leaping up to give Rikki a hug.

"Not everyone got it," Rikki said.

"Young pups." Tina shook her head. "Does no one read Dr. Seuss anymore?"

Jaleesa pulled Rikki into her long arms and patted her on the back several times. "Good to see you."

"And you," Rikki said. She smiled at DeShawn and Dana, and then gestured to her suit and said, "Thank you," to Harriet.

"You're welcome, Ma'am," Harriet said, a shy grin creeping up her face.

She chatted with the group for a while and deflected questions about why she wasn't giving a whipping demo later that evening. Truth was, she just wasn't feeling it. She wasn't feeling the community at the moment. Spring wasn't exactly the time to hibernate from life, but there she was doing just that. Her mother had always tried to knock her out of her deep downs. That's what her mother called it, 'deep downs.' Rikki knew it for what it was—depression. Apparently, she didn't want young Rikki saddled with the label of depression, but here it was waving its flags in all its glory.

Rikki complimented Jaleesa and her family on their complementary outfits. Each of the submissives wore a different pastel color. DeShawn was in baby blue, Dana in pink, Harriet in soft green, and Tina in yellow. "And this," Rikki said, pointing to Jaleesa's suit jacket, consisting of the four colors that each of her family members wore. "This is exceptional."

"Tina and Harriet's creation," Jaleesa said, pulling Tina into a side hug. The look of pure adoration on Tina's face made something in Rikki shift. She wanted that. She wanted someone to look at her like that. Her flight mode ratcheted up. She excused herself with a promise to come back and talk more, but wasn't sure if she'd live up to that promise. Her plans were to stay at the ball long enough, so Shasti didn't give her grief, but she needed to get out of there soon. It was too 'peopley,' as Madison would say.

Rikki had barely five seconds to compose herself. Madison was bouncing on her toes, not-so-patiently waiting for Rikki's arrival. Rikki opened her arms, and Madison flew into them.

"Hi, Miss Rikki," Madison said, her voice muffled in Rikki's suit jacket.

"Hi, Madison."

"You did good." Madison let go.

"Why, thank you, young one." Rikki stood tall, looking proud of herself. She was only putting it on for Madison, and it worked. Madison was bouncing on her feet again.

"Not fair," a voice said behind Rikki.

Rikki knew that voice. She could have teased and looked around as if not seeing the owner of the voice, but decided to go right in. She spun around, reached into the wheelchair, and hoisted Shanice into her arms. Shanice latched on with both arms and giggled as Rikki spun her around.

"Hi, Miss Riri," Shanice said in between giggles.

"I've missed you," Rikki said, giving her a sloppy kiss on the cheek, which made the young woman in her arms squirm. Shanice was suddenly heavy, so Rikki carefully swooped her back into the chair. "Don't you dare forget to say hello if you come to the shop to harass your mama. You hear?"

Shanice saluted and said, "Ma'am, yes, Ma'am."

Rikki chuckled and then shot Marta an inquisitive look.

"She's been fascinated by my stint in the army," Marta said, accepting a hug from Rikki. She leaned in close and said, "She's been calling me 'Corporal Mama.'"

"That's cute," Rikki said.

"It is, but it's weird, too."

"Stop talking about me," Shanice said and put on her best pout.

"Oh," Rikki said and lifted Shanice's chin, "I bet that look gets all the girls running."

"Running away," Marta quipped.

"Mama!" Shanice protested and crossed her arms.

"Someone's in trouble," Rikki teased Marta.

"Let's dance, baby girl," Marta said to Shanice in a playful attempt to make amends. "And you," she said to Rikki, her smile gone, "You were the one behind this, weren't you?" She pointed to Ashley, now taking donations near the buffet line.

"Partly, yes," Rikki said. "We'll talk about it later, okay?"

"Humph," Marta said.

"Mama," Shanice blurted. "Good song. The Benjies."

"Can't miss this," Marta said to the young woman and wheeled her onto the dance floor to dance with Dana and DeShawn, who were already out there cutting a rug.

"Mistress," Madison said, "can I dance with them?"

"Go, go," Shasti said.

Once their tablemates had vacated, probably on purpose to give Rikki and Shasti a few moments alone, Rikki sat down.

"Whoa," Shasti said, eyes wide as she noticed something on the dance floor.

Rikki turned. "Look at that. What an interesting development. Who knew?"

"Who is that?" Shasti asked, always needing to be in the know.

"That's Mel," Rikki said. "She works for Dominique."

"They seem very interested in each other," Shasti said.

"Lydia is exploring her horizons, I think," Rikki said. "She's not usually submissive to women. Except Rowena."

"And you."

"Fair point." Rikki smiled, but it wasn't genuine. It was more of a sad grimace.

"You okay?" Shasti asked, concern clearly etched on her face.

"Yes," Rikki lied.

One eyebrow raised up.

Rikki knew that eyebrow. "Okay, no," Rikki amended. "But I'm trying to find it."

"You sound like Seamus."

Rikki chuckled and rolled her eyes. "The whole time up there, he kept telling me to 'find it.'"

"And did you?" Shasti pressed her lips together. Two things were obvious. One, Shasti completely agreed with Seamus, and two, she was holding back and wanted to say so much more. If anyone else had given Rikki that expression, she would have ignored them and moved on either physically or in conversation.

But this was Shasti, one of her best friends that she'd known for over three years. Shasti was the one who helped her through Aunt Tilda's death. Shasti was the one who gave her advice about Eileen, even when Rikki didn't want to hear it.

Rikki nodded that yes, she had 'found it.' But then she sighed and said, "Spill it."

"I'm worried about you," came the quick answer. Shasti leaned closer. "I need you to find a way out of your 'deep downs.'" Shasti's expression softened at the phrase. Rikki had shared that part of her childhood with her friend. "Maybe go see someone?"

Rikki remained silent. Part of her, no, most of her, wanted to say, "Hell, no" or quip, "I'll take that under advisement," and then ignore the advice. But this was a woman who seemed to understand her and knew what she needed. She was the friend who knew that an impromptu Korean barbecue dinner would help.

Rikki's silence lasted so long that Shasti finally said, "I can make a recommendation. Someone who is BDSM friendly, so you won't have to stay guarded." When Rikki didn't speak, she added, "Or I can shut my trap and let you live your life."

"Shasti," Rikki said and put a hand on her wrist. "I need you to keep pushing me." Okay, that was hard to admit. "But it's hard for me. I can't seem to push the financial shit out of my way to focus on anything else. Even my own well-being." She had an epiphany. "These balls remind me of her."

"Eileen?"

"Yes," Rikki said as a hot wave of anger shot through her. "And Aunt Tilda, too." A cold wave of sadness replaced the anger. "I miss her," Rikki said, a tightness spreading through her chest.

Shasti's arms went around her as Rikki's tears fell.

Rikki vowed not to sob. She would not sob. She would…too late.

"Oh, honey." Shasti rubbed Rikki's back. "I know. I know. We all miss her, too."

Rikki didn't reply. She didn't trust her voice at the moment. She wiped the tears from her eyes and off her cheeks before sitting up. Shasti handed her one of her ubiquitous tissues.

"Thank you," Rikki said and dabbed at her face. "I know you think I meant Aunt Tilda. And, yes, I miss her like life itself, but I meant Eileen. I miss Eileen." Fresh tears fell. "It doesn't make any sense, Shasti. She ruined my life, but I keep flashing back to the good moments, the tender moments." Rikki scoffed. "As tender as one can get with Eileen."

A hand was on her back, not Shasti's.

"Hey," Victoria said. And that's all she said. She sat down on the other side of Rikki's chair. The hand still pressed against Rikki's back.

Rikki managed a smile. "Hey," she said. Victoria's hand on her back was grounding.

"You're feeling alone," Shasti said.

"Yes."

"We all do it," Victoria said. "Remember the good stuff, gloss over the crap." She rubbed Rikki's back a few times. "The mind and body want to feel good, so it finds ways to keep the good shit front and center.

"I'm not sure it's Eileen herself that you miss," Shasti said quietly. "Maybe it's just the intimacy. Not just the sex, but the other stuff, too."

"And the power," Victoria added in true Victoria fashion. "I'm sure you need some part of your Domme nature to be satisfied. Bossing around a bunch of twenty-somethings making coffee isn't doing it for you."

Rikki laughed. "No, it's not." Both of her friends had good points.

"Esme?" Shasti suggested.

"That ship sailed," Rikki said. "If she comes to the shop at all, she's kind of distant. So there's nothing there, I guess."

"Too bad," Victoria said. "She's hot."

"Shut up," Rikki said with a laugh. She gave Victoria a side glance. "Yeah, she is hot."

Victoria patted her back once and then rested her hand on the table. "Glad to hear that part of you hasn't withered away."

Rikki had the perfect retort on her lips, but heated voices interrupted them.

"Queerdo," Billy said to Madison, who was walking back to their table.

"Baby," Madison shot back.

Shasti was on her feet and moving fast.

"Dyke," Billy spat. This was not a friendly exchange. They were not teasing each other.

"Faggot," Madison said. Rikki had never seen her so angry.

"Stop right there," Shasti said. "Both of you." They did. Being *littles,* they were used to Dominants' commands.

Seamus bolted toward them and grabbed Billy by the elbow. He steered his *little* to the other side of the hall. "Not a word," he growled when Billy tried to defend himself.

"Mercury must be in retrograde," Shanice said seriously when she and

Marta came back to the table.

One of Shasti's tissues found its way into Madison's hand.

"I'd like to discuss this," Shasti said to Madison, "but perhaps we can table it for another time."

"Yes, Ma'am," Madison said. "Sorry I ruined everyone's party." She hitched back her tears. "I think I don't want him as a friend anymore."

"Oh, honey," Shasti said. She pulled Madison into her lap and rocked her gently. "I hope you didn't start it."

"I didn't."

"She didn't," Shanice corroborated.

Rikki waited a couple of beats and then said, "Hey, how about I order some pizzas tomorrow at the shop?" Shasti shot her a grateful look. "You can take an hour or so break from homework, right, Madison?"

Madison perked up. "Yes, Ma'am."

"I haven't seen the rest of the pictures from your trip to the United Kingdom."

Madison's eyes lit up. "I made a slideshow presentation." She pivoted in Shasti's lap so she could look directly at her. "May I bring my big tablet, Mistress?"

"Of course."

Madison started squirming, so Shasti nudged her off her lap.

"Daddy Vic, you can come, too."

"Oh, joy," Victoria said sarcastically, teasing Madison. "A ten-hour vacation slide show."

"Stop," Madison protested. "It's only nine and a half hours."

Everyone laughed, and then Madison invited Shanice and Marta to come by. They readily agreed.

Shasti mouthed to Rikki that she would buy the pizzas.

Rikki nodded her acquiescence. Here was another friend she owed.

Chapter 15

The very next day, Sunday after the Saturday night ball, Rikki found herself energized for the pizza party that afternoon. The night before, she'd seen how cozy Lydia and Mel seemed to be getting, so she told Lydia not to come in to work, and Rikki would handle everything. The grateful look in Lydia's eyes made it clear that neither she nor Mel would be getting much sleep that night.

It had been a slow morning, and that afternoon was no different. The Memorial Day weekend could be hit or miss in that regard, but she was glad she had time to pull out chairs and push a few tables together.

"Let me help, Miss Riri," Shanice said as she wheeled her chair from the kitchen doorway. She had come in early with Marta and spent much of the day working on her computer. The lovely *little* was a highly successful computer programmer and could basically work from anywhere.

"You got it, little one," Rikki said and pointed to the end of a small square table closest to Shanice.

Shanice pushed but ended up rolling backward. Both she and Rikki burst out laughing.

"What's so funny?" Marta said, coming out of the kitchen. She wiped her hands on a cloth towel and then draped it over her shoulder.

Rikki and Shanice looked at each other, wide-eyed, and broke out laughing again.

"Basic physics, Mama," Shanice said. She looked back at Rikki and said, "Let's try this again, shall we?" She wheeled herself forward to the table, locked her wheels this time, and pushed. It moved successfully.

"Yass," Rikki said and did a silly dance, one she'd see Madison do. "Problem solving at its best."

Together, they moved four tables into one large square. It was Shanice's design because she reasoned that if you put the tables in a long line, the people on one end couldn't really talk to those on the other. With the square, they could put the pizzas, plates, and other stuff in the middle and use the space efficiently.

"Smart, that one," Rikki said to Marta.

"Oh, no," Shanice said, panic in her voice. "Where's Riri?"

"Someone," Marta said cooly, "and I won't name names, but someone left her stuffie toy in the kitchen."

"Bye," Shanice said and tore off for the kitchen.

Once Shanice was out of the room, Marta said, "She's taking her setback well."

"The delay in getting prosthetics?"

"Yes," Marta said as they slid the chairs back under the tables. "She's eating well, exercising, and taking supplements. But she's also doing a lot of things she shouldn't be doing."

"Like?"

"I found her in the backyard a few days ago. Her wheelchair was abandoned on the back patio, and she had kneel-walked herself and the hose across the lawn to the new vegetable garden we just planted."

Rikki sighed, not sure what to say.

"She wants to show me that she isn't handicapped, that she isn't differently abled. But Rikki, she shouldn't be crawling around on her knees all the time like that. Her knees are crucial to holding her weight on prosthetics, but I can't get her to understand that."

"That's tough," Rikki said and patted Marta on the side of her arm. "She just wants to do things. Does she have knee pads?"

"Yeah, she has them, but doesn't put them on. We're saving up for an electric wheelchair, but the money Hayley handed us last night was specifically collected for a hand-controlled van, so…"

"Yeah, Rowena thought we'd get more donations if we collected for something specific and something big."

"I mean, yeah," Marta said. "I get it. And I'm a thousand percent grateful, although still a bit shamed for needing help."

"We all need help sometimes," Rikki said. When Marta started tearing up, Rikki added, "Hey, on the flip side, Shanice doesn't seem depressed. She's not lying on the couch watching daytime dramas."

"I know. I know. I just…" Marta sighed.

"You just worry."

"Yeah."

"You're okay," Rikki said. "You'll both be okay." She pulled back when a certain *little* came thundering back into the seating area.

"Did you say nice things about me, Mama?"

"Always," Marta said. She leaned down and kissed Shanice on the forehead. "I'll be back."

"Don't threaten us, Mama," Shanice said, and then laughed so big that Rikki started laughing. They caught each other's eye and laughed even harder.

"You're going to make me pee my pants, kid," Rikki said and wiped the tears of laughter off her face. As she exhaled, she let go of a lot of tension in the process. "Thanks, Shanice. I haven't laughed like that in a long time."

"You're fun, Miss Riri," Shanice said. But then her expression and tone turned serious. She squeezed her fox stuffie tight and said, "You'll find your happiness, Miss Riri. August and September are favorable for a Capricorn to find love. Still, I think the end of the year, December or January, is your better bet because Venus, the Goddess of love, will be transiting into your sign at that time."

"I have no idea what all that means, but I'll have my eyes peeled for hotties during then." Rikki gently touched Shanice's cheek. "Thank you for the pep talk."

Just then, the bell jangled on the front door to the shop. Madison and Shasti came in carrying five pizzas between them. Behind them, Victoria held a few grocery bags.

"Perfect," Shasti said, referring to the table arrangement. She and Madison placed the pizzas in the middle. Victoria took out paper plates, napkins, and plasticware from the bags.

"Hi, Miss Rikki," Madison said and hugged Rikki without waiting for an invitation, but that was okay. Rikki could use the love.

"Go set up," Shasti said to Madison, who let go of Rikki but then spun around and put her arms around Shasti's neck. "You're clingy today," Shasti said to her *little*. She turned to Rikki and added, "I've had little to no personal space today."

Madison didn't let go. Her googly eyes were full of love. "I'm addicted to your personal space, Mistress."

Rikki burst out laughing. "Go get set up for your slide show, little one."

"Okay, fine," Madison said and let go, but only after stealing a kiss from Shasti.

"Handful today," Shasti whispered.

"The whole Billy thing."

"Yes," Shasti said. "We'll talk later."

Rikki nodded.

Jaleesa, Tina, and Dana walked in at that moment, so Rikki's attention was diverted.

"We brought little ice cream cups for dessert," Tina said.

Rikki directed her to the kitchen where Marta was. "And tell Marta that whatever she's doing is not as important as vacation slides."

"Yes, Ma'am," Tina said enthusiastically.

Out of the corner of her eye, Rikki saw Jaleesa hand Shasti some cash. *They'll do what they'll do*, Rikki thought to herself. She wouldn't dwell on her friends' charity now. It was exhausting. Somehow, some way, she'd repay them all.

Once everyone was seated and the pizza slices distributed, Madison adjusted her tablet so everyone could see. Then she began her narration. "So back in March before school started—" She was interrupted by enthusiastic cheers and calls of "We're so proud of you, bucko," and "Our little scholar." She grinned comically and tried again. "Soooo…" She waited for more interruptions, but none came. "It was a long flight," Madison clicked on her tablet, and up popped a picture of the two of them on an airplane. "Mistress even had a drink of alcohol on the plane." The next pic showed Shasti's drink on the tray table, with Shasti's hand clearly holding it.

Polite chuckles ran through their friends.

"We got to London, like in the afternoon, and went directly to this fancy schmancy hotel for tourists. We got settled in our room, and I wanted shower sex, but Mistress said it was tea time. I thought we were going golfing, but she'd said, 'tea' as in, you know, the drink."

"Mm hmm," Rikki said with a nod when Madison looked right at her.

"We went downstairs and met our tour guide and the rest of the group.

They ushered us into this big room off the lobby. These serving people, like tea baristas or something, served the tea. Their accents were so cool. And even though they were speaking English, Mistress had to help me understand them sometimes." She smiled at Shasti. "I was allowed to have a sugar cube and some cream. It was so good." She raised her eyes skyward. The enthusiasm waned when she added, "And then they gave us scones. They were okay, but Miss Marta's bundt cakes are way better."

"See? See?" Marta said comically. "I'll tell Mrs. Pulaski the good news."

Madison beamed and then showed picture after picture of their trip. Thank goodness there had been some obvious culling of what could have been a thousand pictures. Victoria's prediction of ten hours of slides might not have been far off the mark. Shasti, bless her, nudged Madison back on track when her stories meandered too far off the path.

Apparently, according to Madison, Stonehenge in Wiltshire was kind of boring. It was "just a bunch of big old rocks." Clearly, the significance of the ancient structure had been lost on Madison.

"The University of Oxford was cool, though," Madison continued and showed several pictures of the oldest English-speaking university.

"The Cotswolds," Shasti said with reverence when Madison showed pictures of quaint cottages and spring flowers. "I'd love to spend the summer in a cottage there. It's a bucolic region northwest of London."

"We got to eat in a pub there. Pubs aren't just bars," Madison informed them. "You can also get food like bangers and mash and stuff." She went on to show pictures and describe how cool Liverpool was, "You know the Beatles and all."

Somewhere between the English towns of Birmingham, Manchester, and Leeds, Madison called an intermission so Miss Tina could "fetch" the ice cream for "everyone to enjoy."

When ice cream was in the hands of those who wanted it, Shasti said, "And then we got to Loch Lomond." There was a teasing grin on her face.

"Arrrgh," Madison groaned and flung her head back. "Fine." She showed pictures of their hotel, the loch during the day, and several of the loch at night. It was hard to discern anything in the dark photos. "Sooo," Madison began and started giggling. Shasti pressed her lips together, holding in her own laughter. "I stayed up all night looking for the Loch Ness monster."

Rikki bit her lower lip, suppressing a laugh.

"Mistress informed me the next morning at breakfast that if there really was a Loch Ness monster, it would be in Loch Ness. We were at Loch Lomond, a completely different lake."

The group laughed, and it was wonderful to see how Madison drank in the love their amused laughter expressed. Pictures of Edinburgh Castle were next, then one of Shasti's "alcohol drink" on the flight back home.

Applause burst in the shop to comments of "That was great, kid," and "I know a lot more about the UK now."

Victoria stood up and looked at her watch. "You were right, squirt. Nine and a half hours."

"It was not," Madison squealed and laughed when Victoria came by to snatch Madison into a side hug.

"No, seriously. That was great," Victoria said again, including Shasti in her praise. "Thanks for the party, but I have a date."

Victoria pulled a handful of nitril non-latex gloves out of her jacket pocket and waved them at Rikki. "Thanks for these."

"Victoria," Rikki said, vexed. They'd already discussed Victoria taking gloves from the shop to make dental dams.

"What? You cut out a square-ish shape, but leave the thumb part to house your tongue."

Rikki had only one word for her friend. "Go." She pointed toward the door. At least Victoria didn't sit in the shop and cut out the dams anymore. Maybe Rikki should be grateful for small favors.

Victoria waved her little black phone, taunting Rikki. Rikki simply shook her head and said, "No."

"Suit yourself," Victoria said. With a shrug, she turned and headed for the door.

"Off you go then," Rikki said quietly. She caught Shasti's eye and shrugged. "Always on the move, that one." Rikki stood up to begin the cleanup.

A customer walked up to Rikki and said, "Excuse me. Your cashier said you were the shop owner?"

"Yes," Rikki said. "How can I help you?"

"This looked like such a lovely gathering," the middle-aged woman said.

"Your shop runs so smoothly, so efficiently. It's almost military, but not really. It's something else."

Jaleesa moved closer and was now hovering. Did she think Rikki was in danger of some sort? Did she think Rikki needed protection?

"Do you rent out your space?" the customer asked. "My sister's turning fifty next week, and I want to do something different for her."

"We don't rent the space, no," Rikki said, leading the woman away from their gathered group. Jaleesa followed. "But you are welcome to bring in outside food and use this space as you wish. A heads up is always welcomed, and we would, of course, appreciate your group partaking in our wares." She gestured to the chalkboard menus hanging above the prep stations.

"So, we could bring a cake and sing happy birthday? That would be okay?"

"Absolutely," Rikki said. "Last week we had a gender reveal gathering here."

"How sweet," the woman said. "And children would be okay? I see you have dart boards."

Rikki chuckled. "*Supervised* children are always welcome."

The woman laughed. "Understood."

Rikki was facing the windows. A familiar face walked by. They locked eyes for several long seconds. Too long to be an accident. It was Esme. Was she coming in? No, she was walking in the other direction. Rikki said, "Please, excuse me. Jaleesa can help you from here."

As Rikki headed for the door, she heard Jaleesa take over as if she worked there. "Do you have the shop's number?" she asked the woman.

Rikki heard nothing more as she flung open the door. Esme was nowhere to be seen. Rikki forced herself to not look like an idiot as she searched the sidewalk and the parked cars lining Market Street. Maybe Esme was in the furniture shop? No, it was closed on Sundays. She took one step in the direction Esme had been heading and stopped. This was crazy. If the woman wanted to see Rikki, she would have come into the shop.

"Lost your puppy?" Rowena said as she approached. Minjung walked behind her.

"No," Rikki said. "Just thought I saw someone I knew." She held the door open for her friends to enter. "You just missed the slide show."

"By design," Rowena said.

Yep, Rikki thought, that was Rowena. Blunt as ever.

They headed back toward the gathered group. The middle-aged customer was leaving and said to Rikki, "Thank you. We'll be back next week."

"Looking forward to it. See you then." Rikki hung back, letting Rowena and Minjung join the group on their own.

Jaleesa came by with her phone in hand. "Details sent." She tapped her phone.

"Thanks," Rikki said.

"Who was out there?"

"No one."

"Esme," Jaleesa said. At Rikki's exasperated expression, Jaleesa said, "What? Shasti talks. Victoria talks. What can I say?"

"Yes, Esme," Rikki admitted. "But she was gone by the time I got out there."

"Don't give up."

"Pfft," Rikki scoffed.

Tina and Dana sidled up to Jaleesa, and Jaleesa said, "We're heading home. This one," she pointed at Dana, "has two separate projects to work on this evening. One of them is the design for the landscaping around the strip mall's signage."

"Love the new sign," Rikki said. Jaleesa owned an entire three-shop strip mall, her hair salon in one. Although Rikki hadn't seen the sign in person, she'd seen pictures.

"Trying to modernize the dump," Jaleesa said, earning a backhanded smack from Tina.

"Babe," Tina scolded. "Wrong attitude. Send good thoughts to the universe."

"Okay," Jaleesa said. "I hope date night is sizzling." She looked up as if appealing to the heavens.

"Babe," Tina scolded in protest.

"What? We're having a date night." She pulled Tina closer.

"Oh, lawd," Rikki said. "Go have fun." She headed back to the group, and Jaleesa and her family headed out the front door.

Rowena and Minjung each had a slice of pizza in front of them when Rikki walked up.

"Maybe there's a Loch Lomond monster, too," Rowena was saying. Madison must have told them the story.

Madison's eyes grew wide. "Imagine if I saw it, Miss Rowena. OMG."

"So," Rowena said as Madison put her tablet away, "I haven't heard about your college experiences. How are things going?"

Rikki sat at a table and grabbed one of the melting ice cream cups. She offered the box to Rowena and Minjung, but both declined.

"Well," Madison said, "For one thing, there's a lot of homework."

Shasti kissed the top of Madison's head as she sat down. "Sorry to interrupt." She turned to Rikki. "Marta wanted me to tell you she went back to work to 'earn her pay' as she put it. And Shanice is with her, working on a big programming project."

"Thanks," Rikki said. She nodded for Madison to continue.

"I just finished my third week of the twelve-week summer session. We have Memorial Day off. Yay."

"What are you taking?" Rowena asked, shifting in the plastic chair. Rowena was uncomfortable. That was unacceptable. Rikki stood and suggested they move to more relaxed seating.

Once resituated, Madison said, "I'm taking two courses. English Composition and Psychology, Ma'am."

"Before classes started," Shasti said, "she read practically the entire Psychology book, much of it while we were in England."

"Studious," Rowena said. Minjung nodded her agreement. Minjung didn't say much in public settings. Rowena seemed to prefer her submissives that way. To each her own, Rikki thought. She would never silence Esme that way.

Whoa, Esme was *not* her submissive. Esme wasn't in the picture at all. Okay, fine, Rikki had done some internet searching, and Esme's jewelry website was still bookmarked, but that didn't mean anything.

"So," Madison continued, "on the dance floor last night, Dana was asking me about my classes, so I was telling her about this narrative essay I wrote. It had to be a personal story, so I wrote about how that stupid manager at Petology in Columbus harassed me. You know, like, sexually, and how I ended up quitting. He told everyone he had fired me for incompetence, but he was the one who didn't know how to feed the birds, so I did, and then he cornered me because he thought—."

"Shh, shh, shh," Shasti said. "It's over."

"I know, but it still makes me mad," Madison said.

"Which is a good thing," Rowena said. "Don't accept shit like that."

"I got an A+ on that essay, Miss Rowena," Madison said. "How about that?"

"Nice. Nice." Rowena sounded like a proud aunt.

Rowena could be rough around the edges sometimes, but she had a good heart, especially for the people she let get close to her. An idea sprouted in Rikki's brain. She wasn't going to wait. She'd lay out her idea tonight before Rowena left. Funny how the weight on her shoulders suddenly seemed lighter.

"And then I started talking about the different essays I have to write for the class," Madison continued.

"All of this while on the dance floor?" Rowena asked with a chuckle.

"Yes, Ma'am."

Rowena motioned for her to continue her story.

"So, then," Madison said, "I was telling Dana that I would have to write a descriptive essay, an expository one, and an argumentative one. And it was then that Billy came up to us. He said, 'You think you're so smart, Madison. You're just a sheeple.'" Madison looked at Shasti, who nodded for her to go on. "Mistress had to explain to me last night that 'sheeple' means people who blindly follow others like sheep or something. I guess he was mad that I was going to college, like I was just copying those other people who went to college." Madison looked over at Rikki and then Rowena. "Honestly, I don't know why he was so mad. And at me. What did I do to him?"

Rowena nodded and said, "You're moving on without him. Leaving him behind."

"That's what Mistress told me last night," Madison said. She sighed so heavily that Rikki's heart almost broke. "And then he started calling me all those names. I didn't know what to do, so I called *him* names back. It was so stupid."

Rowena turned to Shasti. "Have you talked with Seamus yet?"

"Not yet," Shasti said. "I wanted us all to have a cooling-off period. I texted him that he and I would talk tomorrow sometime. He agreed."

"Wise," Rowena said.

"I'm done with him," Madison announced. "Billy."

"We'll see," Shasti said. "We're taking a minute to regroup, remember?"

"Yes, Ma'am," Madison said.

"We'd best be getting home," Shasti said. "You need a shower."

Madison narrowed her eyes. "Your shower or mine."

A devilish smile crept up Shasti's face. "Mine."

"Shower sex," Madison announced and bolted out of her seat. She said hasty goodbyes, grabbed her tablet, and practically dragged Shasti out the door.

"I'll call you tomorrow," Shasti called over her shoulder.

"You got it," Rikki called after her.

"Cute couple," Rowena said.

"You're softening on *littles,* Rowena."

"Hard for me to admit when I was wrong, but it just shows you have to get to know people before judging their whole category."

"Wow," Rikki said, surprised. "So philosophical." She cleared her throat. "I want to run something by you."

"Sure," Rowena said, then nudged Minjung. "Go help Marta."

"Yes, Madam," Minjung said and then bowed her head deeply to Rikki. Rikki nodded back.

"What's up?" Rowena asked once Minjung was out of earshot.

"This was my last masquerade ball," Rikki blurted. "I'm quitting the Women's Collective. I want you to take over because I can't—. I just—" Rikki sighed. "I have too much on my plate. I'm overwhelmed."

"You're overwhelmed because you're still grieving," Rowena said softly. "And that is exactly why you should *not* quit as head of our Women's Collective or chair of the masquerade balls. You need something like this to keep you focused, to keep you in the community. I know you have a lot going on in the shop, and your living situation isn't ideal, but if you don't have this extra obligation—" She grunted. "Not the right word. If you don't have this *outlet,* I'm afraid we would never see you again."

Rikki scoffed. Why would no one give her a break?

"Okay," Rowena said, "I think you should stay in these roles a bit longer. It will be good for you. You're not a quitter, Rikki. Neither am I, and as much as I'd love to grab the reins you're throwing at me, I won't take them. I would, however, like to propose this. Finish out this calendar year, at least. I think you'll regret not sticking it out for longer. You're a good and effective leader. You listen, weigh options, and make good decisions. And, seriously, I think that if you stay in these roles next year, too, you'll be proud of the things you can accomplish with this group." When Rikki stayed silent, absorbing Rowena's words, Rowena said again, "You can't give up. You're not a quitter."

"I'll take it under advisement," Rikki said mechanically.

"Fuck that, Rikki." Rowena leaned forward. "Your Aunt Tilda, do you know what she would do? She'd grab the universe by its fucking lapels and kick it in the nuts before giving up so easily. You have to show the world that you, Rikki Carmichael, will embrace its absurdity, but not its bullshit. And you quitting? No fucking way. Rikki Carmichael does not quit. Fuck, no. The Rikki Carmichael I know kicks ass and takes names."

Chapter 16

The woman bound to the bed beneath Rikki squirmed for Rikki's touch. Rikki's fingertips obliged as she caressed Emily's face and moved ever so slowly down in exploration. They were used to each other's bodies, so the exploration was precise, intimate. Rikki knew all the spots that made the bound woman writhe. Oh, yes, the feel of Emily's skin was divine.

"Lower, Rikki," Emily pleaded. "Please, Rikki."

Rikki said nothing and continued her slow exploration. Full breasts, peaking nipples needing soft kisses, a lifted pelvis asking for devotion.

"In time, love." Rikki's murmur was barely audible. She inhaled the smell of lavender. Lavender was Emily's smell. Emily. Lovely Emily.

The kisses followed the path of the hand. A cupped hip was followed by reverent kisses. Emily's was a woman's body waiting to be explored and brought to fruition.

Rikki knew how to please a woman while also getting her own needs met. Making love was all about mutual fulfillment. Emily—older, middle-aged, experienced—knew what she wanted, and Rikki was happy to deliver.

Emily arched her back. She tilted her pelvis. Rikki shimmied down her lover's body, worshipping the feel of skin on skin. Her kisses moved quickly toward their goal—toward it but not *to* it. Rikki shimmied lower and gave the writhing woman's inner thighs the attention they were due.

"Rikki, Rikki," Emily pleaded. "I need your touch. Please."

"Begging women," Rikki murmured, "always turn me on."

"I'll please you. You know I love your taste, hun," Emily said, her voice desperate. "Just untie me and let me use my hands this time."

"Soon," Rikki said, peppering the musky thighs with fingertip caresses. She had every intention of undoing Emily's bonds before receiving her own pleasure. Rikki loved sex for sex sake, but she also loved making love to a woman. Bondage and impact and dominance fed her power centers like nothing else, but she also got energized from tender touches and well-placed nuzzles.

Rikki repositioned herself. She was going to tease and build and then back off. Emily was alternately going to hate it and love it. But first, a souvenir. She kissed the mons in front of her and moved up a tiny bit further to Emily's sexy-as-hell middle-aged pooch. Rikki latched on with her lips and sucked. Satisfied that the creative writing teacher underneath her would have a suitable reminder of their lovemaking, Rikki moved back to the target.

Feathery light kisses hit the target, making Emily squirm. "C'mon, baby," Emily cried. "Harder. More direct." Rikki obliged and then backed off as the universe received a few four-letter words from the community college teacher in her clutches. Teachers always made good partners. Their ability to absorb a lot of information at once made them especially fun to play with and tease. Rikki always gave her lovers what they needed, which wasn't always what they wanted.

A shot of arousal hit Rikki. She abandoned the teasing and spread the flesh before her. Exposing the tender nub, she blew a gentle puff of air. Emily's legs tried to close around Rikki's body, but she couldn't get much purchase with bound ankles. Rikki dipped a finger in Emily's center, merely to wet it. She circled the sensitive bundle of nerves with one hand and pushed up the mons with the other, creating a beautiful display underneath her. Emily's moans of encouragement spurred Rikki on. Another waft of lavender somehow managed to pierce the musky scent of her lover. Rikki's own lust spiraled.

She wrapped her arms around Emily's legs. Her tongue circled the pearl. Emily was going to peak soon. Rikki's tongue enabled it. Rikki's moans encouraged it. Emily strained against the ropes as she raised her pelvis against Rikki's straining arms.

Emily bucked her hips and screeched her release. Rikki kept up the stimulation. Once Emily fell back spent, Rikki kissed her way back up Emily's body slowly. She'd give the woman a short, very short time to recover, then demand her own release.

Awareness crept in. This wasn't real. She was dreaming. Damn it. Didn't matter. Rikki's hands flew down to her own need and urged the fantasy to continue.

In her fantasy, Rikki straddled Emily's hips and rocked her sex against Emily's body. Their gazes locked as Rikki maneuvered higher and placed her sex over Emily's willing mouth and active tongue. Shit, she'd forgotten to take Emily's restraints off. Anything could be done in a fantasy, and just like that, Emily's restraints disappeared. Emily's hands grabbed Rikki's hips, which helped lock Rikki into position. It didn't take long. Emily's tongue hit its mark. Emily's lips finished the job.

In her bed, all alone, Rikki cried out in release and then lay still.

"Fuck," she said. She got another whiff of lavender. "What the hell?" It was then she realized Victoria had given her a sample of lavender laundry soap. The clean towels were still stacked on her bed. The smell had triggered the memory of Emily, a lovely lover, a lovely person, but both had agreed they weren't long-term material for each other.

Rikki sat up in bed. Maybe she needed to contact Emily and see if she was available. "For what?" Rikki asked herself. Early on in her BDSM explorations, she was okay with one-night stands and casual lovers, but not now. Now that she was thirty-five, she just wasn't looking for quick sex. Not like Victoria and her many conquests. Rikki wanted more from a relationship.

She got out of bed and headed for the shower even though she'd taken one the night before. Her phone alarm went off just as she put her pajama bottoms in the laundry basket. Mark was opening, so there really was no rush. She was going to head out for a hike and come back in for the lunch crowd. It was something she started doing after the spring masquerade ball. She'd needed something to change, and since Rowena convinced her to stay on as head of the Women's Collective, something else had to change. Her routine was the one thing she could vary, and for the last three and a half months, everything had gone well.

It was mid-September now, and Rikki had been fairly successful getting out to a hiking trail or a town walking path since the ball. For three and a half months, she had moved her body and broken a sweat practically every day. Shasti was pleased with this development and gave just the right encouragement. Funny how all that exercise not only made her feel better physically but mentally and emotionally, too.

She did the occasional stint at Dominique's, but those were few and far between lately. She didn't want her impact skills to atrophy. After a refreshing shower and a quick cup of coffee upstairs, she headed out to a trail that led to a secluded spot by a river. Victoria occasionally accompanied her on hikes and had turned Rikki on to this one. It was a short hike, but the reward at the end was soul-soothing.

She pulled into the county park and was grateful that Monday mornings were not a popular time for hikers or dog walkers. The lot was empty.

She slung the water bottle strap over her shoulder and tucked the water bottle into it. That had been a gift from Victoria, for no particular reason at all. All she said was that she was happy Rikki was getting out more. "New air is a good thing," Victoria had said to her on one of their hikes. Rikki was sure Victoria was implying something else, but Rikki was relieved when Victoria didn't elaborate.

Rikki breathed in the autumn air as she strode to the path. The mid-September leaves had begun to change colors and fall to the ground. That earthy smell, for whatever reason, seemed to calm and soothe her. She had been in a funk in the spring, that was for sure, but had powered through, and with help from her friends, she was hopefully on the other side.

The month of June had been quiet. Rowena and Minjung treated Marta and Shanice to a unique dance concert in Cleveland called Dancing Wheels. The four of them, Shanice especially, had been impressed by the able and differently abled dancers. So much so that Shanice now took dancing lessons from Minjung once a week or so. What an amazing connection her friends had made with each other. And also in June, Jaleesa finally got that piano she'd wanted for their living room, even though no one in their household played.

July brought Marta's thirty-seventh birthday with a small, intimate party thrown by her lovely *little* Shanice. Rikki always enjoyed gatherings with her friends, especially when they weren't in the coffee shop, where it felt like work. Which it kind of was. July also brought the weekend festival of Denton Heights Days, and with it came a boom in sales, which helped Rikki's disposition immensely. Her financial troubles were far from over, but at least she had been able to make payroll for the next few months. To her extreme credit, Rikki also resisted the urge to show up at the craft fair to see if Esme had a booth set up. The woman had been intriguing and lovely to talk to, and even though there had seemed to be a mutual attraction, it simply was not going to go anywhere.

August brought a few more birthday celebrations. Minjung's thirty-ninth birthday was celebrated at a Korean Restaurant in Cincinnati that no one had been to before. It was a definite do-over, for sure, they all agreed. Victoria's thirty-sixth birthday bash at Rowena's had been a party to remember. Victoria and two of Rowena's guests apparently didn't go home that night, all three making use of the room Victoria often crashed in at Rowena's mansion. Madison's summer term ended with the rascal earning A's in both courses. Of course, the fall term had already started, today in fact, and things were getting serious. The poor kid had four difficult-sounding courses. Biology, Chemistry, Intro to Anthropology, and the one that sounded ominous—Calculus 1. Shasti threw a Mexican fiesta-themed 'Back-to-School' party for Madison two nights ago, and Rikki had given the *little* an overlong hug. Madison would need their support. Even Shasti was a bit worried about the ambitious schedule. So much so that she was considering suggesting that Madison quit her job at Petology, the pet store where she worked part-time.

There was a slight chill in the air that morning, but she didn't mind. Her blood was pumping, and she felt alive. Madison would say it was from all the vitamin D she was getting while soaking up the sun. Of course, the endorphins from a decent workout also helped elevate her mood.

She heard the river before seeing it and increased her pace. She burst into the clearing and, once again, the sight of the flowing water and the far shoreline boosted her mood. One day, she'd like to bring someone special to this clearing so she, too, could feel what she felt. Emily had been someone special, even for a short while, but why had Emily featured in her dream this morning?

When they met, Emily had just gotten out of a stagnant relationship and was looking for some fun, which Rikki gladly provided. Rikki also had just gotten out of a short-term relationship with cute-as-a-button Sarah. Everyone loved Sarah, but she was too new to the *life*, and after a couple of months, the ten-year age gap proved too much of a barrier for Rikki. Emily showed up at one of Aunt Tilda's parties. She was a friend of one of Victoria's many short-term liaisons. So there she was, ripe for the picking, and Rikki picked. Less than two months later, Emily had apparently had her fill and broke it off. It was just as well. Again, Rikki wasn't feeling long-term vibes. The sex was good, really good, hence the sex dream that woke her up with its urgency. Rikki wasn't too bothered when Emily broke it off. Just as well not to spend time on something that wasn't really going anywhere.

Rikki slowed to a stop and uncapped her water bottle. She walked slowly around the open clearing, letting her breath and heart rate recover. She inhaled deeply. Nothing was like the mountain air back home in Pennsylvania, but right now, Denton Heights' air was doing the job.

She wasn't sure why thoughts of her exes kept popping up recently. Maybe she still needed to process the breakups and find the common cause. She sighed and physically flicked her hand to send the analyzing part of her thoughts elsewhere.

She looked up at the treetop and then at the blue, cloud-laden sky. Thoughts of her mother pushed to the forefront. And that was okay. Lately, she had been learning how to pull the thoughts in instead of brushing them away. Shasti had said something to her recently about Madison. Through therapy, Madison was learning that the only way to handle the hard stuff was to go through it. There was no way around it. It was hard, but Rikki was trying. She tried to let in the good memories, even if it made her emotional.

Her mother always told her to look up. Don't miss the good stuff, she'd told young Rikki. Her mother pointed out skyscrapers in Chicago, squirrels' nests in trees, and even constellations and slow-moving satellites in the night sky. In her early twenties, before her mother was killed, Rikki had been looking at the stars one evening and saw a shooting star. She made a quick wish, and even though the woman of her wish hadn't materialized, she'd felt like she was on top of the world then. When her mother died. Rikki had stopped looking up. Until recently.

The clouds were cirrus, wispy and fast-moving, indicating high-altitude winds. Down on the ground, Rikki felt none of that turbulent wind, only an occasional light autumn breeze.

"Autumn. September," she said out loud as she walked toward the water. Shanice predicted that August or September might be a favorable time to meet someone special. Ahh, well. August was long gone, September had only two weeks left, and so far, her prediction hadn't manifested. But that was okay. Despite the turbulent trip her mind wanted to go on, she resisted. She was going to stay grounded in her calm right where she was, thank you very much.

She squatted down and dunked her hand in the cold, fast-moving river. She swirled her hand in the water, feeling its force, and deliberately changed its flow. Obviously, she didn't have much influence on the entire river's path, but she was able to change this small part of it. Every one of her ex-girlfriends and play partners had had some influence on her, hadn't they? And there would be other lovers. She was sure of that now, but maybe she needed to sit in her newfound calm for a while. Maybe she needed to shift her focus and be the one to help her friends and influence others in positive ways. She could offer support, guidance, or whatever someone needed. A listening ear, perhaps. Helping other people had always been her passion, and if she could just remember to move toward her passion, then maybe she wouldn't feel so alone and stuck.

She groaned and sat back on her haunches. "That's what they've all been doing for me," she said out loud to the quiet line of trees. "No, scratch that. That's what they've been *trying* to do for me." She groaned again. "Victoria was right. I *am* dense."

She leaned forward and dipped both hands in the water. She patted her warm cheeks with the cool water and then decided it was time to head back. She needed to check in with Lydia, not about shop business, but about her ongoing relationship with Mel. Ahh, but she didn't want to be a nosy buttinsky. She'd wait for Lydia to approach her, if she ever did.

She took another drink from her water bottle and headed back up the trail. A chirping cardinal accompanied her all the way. She wasn't sure whether she believed that a cardinal represented a loved one who had passed, but either way, she was glad for the company.

Once freshly showered and back in the shop, she felt good as she guided her crew and pitched in where needed. She split a quick sandwich for dinner with Marta in her office, a new ritual she was coming to treasure. Marta was becoming a good friend. Sure, she was also an employee, but there was more to it than that. Rikki felt it in her heart.

Lydia knocked on the door. The crew schedule for the following week needed Rikki's approval. Marta excused herself and left to return to the kitchen.

Rikki took a quick look, signed the sheet, and handed it back to her assistant manager.

"Thank you," Lydia said.

When Lydia didn't immediately head for the door, Rikki asked, "Is there something else?"

"Do you have a minute?"

"Of course," Rikki said and closed the open door. "What's on your mind?"

"Mel," came the simple but quick answer. Lydia looked like she was about to swoon.

"Things going well then?" Rikki smiled at the obviously smitten woman now finding purchase on the arm of the couch.

"Yes, yes, yes." Lydia looked at Rikki with eyes filled with puppy love. "It's not long-term or anything like that. We're just play partners. She calls us 'fuck buddies,' but I find that to be a little crude."

Rikki shrugged but nodded her agreement.

"She's a top-class stud, Miss Rikki. She's dominant. Quietly dominant. And those muscles. Yum. But she's also showing me how to be dominant in the bedroom. I mean, she's showing me with what she does to me, of course, but then do you know what else?" Lydia's eyes grew wide, her eyes crinkling with excitement.

"No, what?"

"She lets me top her sometimes."

"Is she a switch then?"

"No, no, no," Lydia said. "That's what makes it special. I feel like I'm in the school for lesbian lovemaking, and I get to be in charge. I mean, sometimes. You can't take the stud out of the stud, right?"

"I guess not," Rikki said with a laugh. "It sounds like she's being really generous with you."

"She's so sweet," Lydia said. "I've always liked masculine energy and went to Doms like Master Tom, but maybe..." She shrugged as her face turned pink.

Rikki chuckled quietly. "I'm glad this is working for you, Lydia."

"You know what she said?"

"What?"

"Sometimes the foundation needs reinforcement."

"Meaning?"

"Sometimes the giver needs to receive. The top needs to bottom. The holder needs to be held."

"Wow," Rikki said. Mel was young but seemed very wise.

"She says that submissives are strong people. They have to be, she says, to let go and trust the way they do. As a sub, I get that whole trust thing." Lydia nodded her head emphatically. "When she bottoms for me, she teaches me how to read the subtle and not-so-subtle clues. Like when her breathing changes, what does it mean? Arousal, or maybe I've gone too far? Lydia leaned in closer and whispered, "She's not a fan of the flogger getting used on her body, but she lets me practice."

"That's impressive," Rikki said. "Maybe she wants to learn how it feels for a sub."

"Yes, that's exactly what she told me."

"But I'm starting to be able to tell when it's becoming too much for her, and I need to move spots or stop altogether."

"Relying on subtle clues is not always accurate," Rikki said. "Do you have safewords in place?"

"Oh, we do." Lydia brushed a wispy lock of blonde hair off her face. "Last week, we talked about people-pleasing subs who will go farther in impact or bondage than they should. She play-acted a sub she had once, and I missed some of her cues. She finally said her safeword, and then we talked about what I missed. She reminded me about sub frenzy and also the flip side, Domme frenzy."

"Yep, yep," Rikki agreed. "That pesky new relationship energy. It can cloud your judgment."

"I'm learning," Lydia said and stood up, crew sheet in hand. "But I wanted you to know what Mel and I are to each other. Just play partners."

"I appreciate you telling me," Rikki said. "I didn't want to meddle, but I was actually hoping you'd check in with me soon."

"Mel said I should."

"Mel is wise," Rikki said with a laugh.

"All right," Lydia said. "Back to work." She headed out to the shop and closed the door behind her.

Rikki had a warm feeling in her heart. She was glad Lydia had checked in with her. As Rikki bundled up the discarded trash from the Queen City Subs sandwich she'd split with Marta, she mumbled, "I should have checked in sooner." *Do better,* she heard Aunt Tilda say in her head. "I will," Rikki said to the universe. She headed back into the shop.

Rikki tossed her trash at one of the busing stations and heard Lydia greet a customer.

"Yes," Lydia was saying to a customer. "She's here."

Rikki turned and froze. It was Esme.

Chapter 17

"Hi, Rikki," Esme said softly. She stepped closer.

Rikki couldn't respond. She couldn't move. Her feet were positively cemented to the shop floor.

"Hi," Esme said again, more softly. She seemed nervous. "Do you have time to sit for a minute or two?"

Rikki opened her mouth as if to speak, but no words came out. Why had Esme suddenly reappeared? No answer came. Her heart led the way and swelled. Her soul softened at the attractive woman in front of her. Her mind, on the other hand, started waving red flags as if a parade was going by.

"Uh, sure," Rikki heard herself say. Okay, fine. She had committed. *Now stop drooling and act like a sane human being.* "Chamomile?"

"That would be lovely," Esme said. Her smile filled her whole face, even reaching her eyes. "I'll just—" She pointed to her usual table.

"I'll be back in a second."

When Rikki got to the counter, Lydia handed her a tray with a carafe of hot water, two teacups, an assortment of teas and sugars. There was even a small pouring pitcher of cream. Wordlessly, Lydia handed her the tray and then had the audacity to wink.

Rikki wanted to scowl or at least roll her eyes, but she was kind of numb. She nodded her thanks as she took the tray and headed back to Esme's table.

"Here we are," Rikki said, trying to sound like a good host. The numbness around her brain was thawing out, but a war was starting. "*You're going to get hurt,*" one part said while another said, "*But we like her, and she's so pretty.*" She focused on the tea service, which pushed her warring thoughts to the background, albeit temporarily.

"How've you been?" Esme asked.

"Doing well," Rikki said, and then thought what she desperately wanted to ask, '*Why are you here?*' She felt like a middle schooler. *Do you like me? If so, check the "Yes" box.* Rikki wanted to take a calming breath, but didn't dare. Her nerves would show. *Lead with love,* she heard her mother's words in her head. "Keeping sufficiently busy."

"That's good," Esme said and took a sip of tea. "Mmm, good. I don't know what your secret is, but everything is good here."

Rikki wanted to quip something about leaving a five-star review on Yelp, but didn't. She was at a loss, sitting in front of someone she was attracted to. Her stomach was all fluttery, not exactly in knots, but her body was definitely reacting. "We make it with care and dedicated attention to detail," Rikki offered. She hoped that was true.

"Sounds like a good branding tag line," Esme said with a laugh. "Can I steal it?"

"Go for it," Rikki said and took a sip of her own tea. "Mmm, this *is* good." *And why are you here, Esme?*

"Rikki," Esme said with a sigh. "I know I've been in and out, but I wanted to see you."

"Oh?" *Why?*

"I enjoy your company," Esme said. "You're intelligent, and we've had the best conversations."

"We have, and thank you. I think the same about you." *Will you go out with me?* What the hell, brain? She was losing her mind. Over a woman. Yeesh.

Esme's features softened. "I'd hoped."

Esme took another sip of her tea. She glanced at Rikki and then looked down again. She sighed, clearly unsure how to continue.

"Would you like to go to the Arts Center with me?" Rikki asked. *What if she says, 'no,'* her brain shouted in her head.

"Yes," Esme blurted. She moved her hand closer to Rikki's.

Rikki moved her own hand closer until their fingertips touched. "Good. Saturday?"

"I can find someone to cover," Esme said.

"Cover?"

"My older sister is autistic. I'm her legal guardian now. She is fairly high functioning," Esme said. "But at times she can be a handful. It's been a learning curve for me."

"And hence the career you can do from home," Rikki said.

"Yes, exactly."

"Tell me more."

From there, Esme became animated, telling stories about her older sister Margie. Apparently, autism was often associated with monotropism, a hyper focus on something. And, according to Esme, Margie was an expert on women's basketball on every level, domestic and international.

"She's a member of chat groups and forums on women's basketball," Esme said. "She has a game on in her room constantly. I had to get one of those sports packages for her. She qualified for SSI—"

"What is that?"

"Supplemental Security Income," Esme said. "It's not much, but she needs the support. She can't hold down a job, you know? And the federal government wants to cut benefits for disabled folks like her. It's unconscionable."

"A few people abuse the system, and everyone loses," Rikki said.

"See?" Esme said, lifting her hand toward Rikki. "You get it." The hand came down and landed on top of Rikki's.

Rikki's heart pumped extra loud. Oh, how she wanted to lift the hand and kiss the back of it. Her rational brain told her that was preposterous; she barely knew the woman.

Rikki turned her hand, squeezed once, and let go. Both women reached for their now-cooling tea. Rikki cleared her throat. "So, Saturday at eleven. Should I pick you up?"

"No, no," Esme said. "I'll run some errands beforehand and meet you there."

They exchanged phone numbers, and Rikki texted her the location. "Might we go to lunch afterward?"

"I'd like to say yes, but it depends on how things are going at home with the caregiver."

"Understood."

Esme looked at her watch and yelped. "I should go. Thank you for the lovely tea, but I need to go."

"Saturday?"

"Yes." Esme pushed her chair back and then looked at Rikki. She had that same searching look in her eye that Rikki had seen back in late February, almost seven months ago. "Bye, Rikki."

Rikki stood. "Bye, Esme." And with that, it was a matter of trying not to hold her breath until Saturday.

~~~

Throughout the week, Rikki wondered if going out with Esme was a wise idea. And even though Shasti had been the one to push Esme on her in February, she was rather cool about it now in September. During a phone conversation, Shasti asked Rikki about her motivation for going out with Esme.

"I like her?" Rikki answered, hearing the question mark at the end of her response.

"I'm sure you do," Shasti said. "But are you sure it's not just lust? Lust and loneliness?"

Rikki frowned. "It's one date, Shasti. Let me figure it out, okay?"

"Of course," Shasti said, her tone softening.

That was Wednesday's phone call, but now it was Thursday, two days before the big date, and Shasti and Madison were at the shop, eating takeout Chinese and visiting. And, of course, they had brought enough to share with Rikki.

"Thank you," Rikki said when she finished her vegetable lo mein. "That was so good."

"You're welcome," Shasti said. "I needed to get her out of the house for a minute. We're trying to find a balance between school, work, and personal life." She looked over at Madison, entertaining herself by throwing darts at the electronic dartboard.

"And?"

"I mean, we're barely a week into the semester, but she's trying to read ahead in every class." Shasti groaned. "She's going to burn out. So we're trying to create a schedule based on when her classes meet and when homework or labs are due. Do you know she has a Biology lab due tomorrow?"

"Already? Seems kind of quick," Rikki said and stacked their finished take-out plates. Naturally, Shasti had ordered too much and was positively one-hundred percent going to give Rikki the leftovers. Her friends were still trying to make sure she ate.

"Yes, already," Shasti said. "I think the professor is trying to show them how serious he is about his course."

"And the other courses?"

"Going fine. She likes Anthropology so far. It's a lot of reading and an online homework platform, so that's doable. Chemistry? The jury's still out on that one, but I think she'll like the labs. She has a Safety and Measurements Lab tomorrow morning. She should be fine."

"And Calculus?"

"I love Calculus, Miss Rikki," the blur that was Madison said as she plopped down on the couch and bounced once. "My teacher, Dr. Garneau, is really good. She makes sense but is no-nonsense. If she's in the *life*, she's a Domme for sure."

"Oh, is that so?" Rikki asked.

"Yes," Madison said. "She's cute and nice and—" Madison's sigh was ethereal.

"A crush already?" Rikki said to Shasti.

"Mm hmm," Shasti said with a head nod. "But I'm thinking the Calculus homework will get done well."

"Want to see a picture?" Madison asked and pulled out her phone. "No, a video. On the Mathematics Department's website, there are videos of all the professors teaching. It's not long, like twenty seconds, but it's who she is, like for real."

"Hit me with it," Rikki said.

Madison swiped and tapped her phone, then said, "Okay, here it is." She leaped to her feet and moved to stand next to Rikki's chair.

"Miss Rikki," Lydia screeched from behind her. "Come quick. OMG, you have to see this."

Rikki was on her feet and moving before she had time to think. Madison was right on her heels.

"Look at this masterpiece," Lydia said, pointing to a freshly made cup of coffee.

Rikki gasped. "This is incredible. Who?" She looked from Lydia to

Brittany and back again.

Lydia pointed to Brittany. "Fantastic, Brittany," Rikki said. She looked at the customer whose coffee they were all gawking at. "A swan," she said to the middle-aged woman, a regular at the shop.

"It's beautiful," the woman said, but didn't reach for her cup.

"That's so cool," Madison said and then laughed. "For hot coffee." Everyone ogling the coffee chuckled.

Rikki said to the customer, "No one in the four and a half years I've owned this coffee shop has managed a swan that actually looks like a swan."

"I'm honored," the middle-aged woman said. "Did you take a picture, dear?"

"May I, please?" Brittany asked.

"Of course, of course," the customer said. "I'm going to take one, too. I have to show my students. Third-graders."

Once the pictures were taken and the customer whisked the creation away, Rikki beamed at Brittany, then narrowed her eyes. "You've been practicing."

Brittany chuckled evilly. "I have."

"I'm impressed. Seriously."

"Thank you," Brittany said, stepping away to make the next order.

Rikki said to Lydia, "Go bring a slice to the teacher. Whatever Marta has fresh. On the house."

"Will do, Boss," Lydia said and scampered away.

"That was impressive," Shasti said. "You're making inroads with her."

"Seems that way," Rikki said, "but she's not going to like Patrice's latest request."

"Which is?"

"Rocco's, every first Saturday of the month, ten a.m."

"Ahh," Shasti said, eyebrows raised. "Our monthly gatherings. She'll live." She laughed. "We have to go, baby," she said to her *little*.

Madison groaned, "Aww, we just got here."

"We've been here for over an hour," Shasti said. "Someone has a Biology lab to write up."

"Oh, yeah," Madison said, her shoulders drooping.

"I bagged up the leftovers," Shasti said, pointing to a bag on the table where they had eaten. "We won't eat it, so you might as well keep it."

"Thank you," Rikki said. "I appreciate your kindness. Truly."

They said their goodbyes, and Rikki went back to calming the butterflies in her stomach about her date on Saturday with a certain blonde-haired, gray-eyed jewelry maker.

~~~

Rikki sat in her car in the Arts Center parking lot, preferring that to pacing the sidewalk in front of the doors. She arrived early, her nervous energy too much even for herself, so she left sooner than initially planned. If all went well, Rikki would invite Esme for lunch at the Indigo Café, her treat. But that's as far as she'd take it today. First date sex never used to faze her, but now she vowed to get to know someone a little better before bringing in that aspect of a relationship.

"And she may not even want to have sex with you, dork," Rikki said to her reflection in the rear-view mirror. She looked at herself sternly, "Do not get ahead of yourself."

Yes, Ma'am, she answered her reflection. "Good chat," she said, laughing. Hopefully, no one was watching her. Now, that would be embarrassing.

She looked toward the door, and adrenaline spiked through her. Esme was walking toward the entrance. She wore a gorgeous mid-calf overcoat with a buttonless shawl collar. The woman had style, that was for sure. Rikki bolted out of her car and headed toward the front doors.

"Hi, Esme," Rikki said. "Right on time."

"Phew," Esme said. "I'm still not sure how far things are from home." She reached up and touched Rikki's forearm.

Okay, that was fine. No greeting hug. No worries. "Shall we go in?" Rikki opened the door for Esme to pass through first.

Once inside, Rikki took the lead, paid the small fee for both of them, and then declined the greeter's offer of a tour guide. She wanted Esme all to herself. She did, however, take two brochures outlining the current exhibits.

"Oh, local artists," Esme said. "We'll definitely have to check out that section, but let's do that last, okay? I want to see this Tiffany lamp and the stained glass." She headed toward the glass exhibit off to the right. "Are we allowed to take photos, Rikki? I may get inspired."

"I'm not sure." Rikki scoured the brochure. "Yes, you can, but there are conditions. No flash, no tripods, no selfie-sticks, and no selling of the photos."

"Excellent." Esme stopped in front of an intricate stained glass window. "Rikki," she said, and reached for Rikki's hand. "Look at this."

Rikki could barely focus with Esme's warm hand in hers. "Beautiful," she said, partly meaning the window.

Esme smiled at her. "I've always wanted to get into stained glass. Not sure I can make money from it, though." She let go of Rikki's hand as if it were no big thing.

"Do it for the joy of it," Rikki said. She turned back to the window. "The colors are so vibrant. It's incredible."

"The backlighting helps bring out the brilliant luster."

Esme took over as tour guide from there, and that was just fine with Rikki. Esme didn't reach for her hand again, and Rikki didn't reach either. She wanted to, but time would tell. *Take it slow*, she told herself. *You don't know this woman at all.*

They spent an entire hour in the glass exhibits, including the incredible Tiffany Library Lamp made around 1900. Rikki read the words describing the lamp's structure, but Esme brought them to life, explaining what they meant. Words like spider medallion, leaded glass, and mosaic vase. Rikki was impressed with Esme's knowledge and easy way of explaining things.

"I've always loved art," Esme said. "I wanted to open an art studio, but you know, my sister. So, I found jewelry as an outlet." They headed for the local artists' section, and Esme said, "Sometimes I lose myself when I'm working and hours will go by without me noticing."

"You must find it rewarding," Rikki said.

"I do, and I've done quite well with it."

"I'm glad," Rikki said. "Oh, wow. They have a high school students' section." She pointed to the far side of the room. "And local artists here."

They meandered through the room in a counterclockwise direction, and Rikki was especially moved by some of the portraits on display by one particular artist. "Can you buy these?" she wondered out loud.

Esme leaned down to read the information about the artist. "It says here that you can contact the artist through the Arts Center website if interested in any of her work."

"What's the artist's name?"

"Harriet Monroe," Esme read. "It says she's a local Denton Heights artist."

"Harriet?" Rikki said, confused. She looked closely at the artist's signature. "Well, I'll be darned. She didn't tell us about this."

"You know her?"

"Yes," Rikki said. "Harriet. She's in our circle of friends. Wonderful woman. She even did some tailoring for me recently."

"She might be one of those people who doesn't want to make it seem all about her, you know? A quiet soul? I get that from her work. These portraits show relaxed people and," she paused for a moment and said, "and genuine."

"Yes, I get that, too," Rikki said. "Harriet is that. Genuine. A good soul."

"Do you know any of the people in these portraits, Rikki?"

"No, no one looks familiar."

"You should take pictures."

"Oh, good idea." Rikki got out her phone and took several pictures of each portrait and the sign about the artist. Leave it to Harriet to be quiet about her accomplishments. Rikki wondered if Jaleesa and the rest of their family knew about the exhibit. Either way, it didn't matter. Harriet needed to be celebrated. She'd get in touch with Jaleesa. Celebrating each other's wins was definitely something their group tried to do regularly.

Once they'd made their way around the exhibits, oohing and ahhing at the amazingly talented AP Arts students from Denton Heights High School, they found they had finished their tour and were standing together on the sidewalk.

"Can I interest you in lunch out?" Rikki asked. "The Indigo Café back in town has a wonderful selection of salads and sandwiches."

"I wish I could," Esme said. "I'm afraid my sister's caregiver—" She shrugged as if frustrated that she didn't have much freedom on her own.

"I understand," Rikki said. "Let me walk you to your car."

"That's sweet." They headed to the parking lot. "You're sweet."

"Thank you. You are, too." Rikki didn't want to waste a minute. "When will I see you again?"

"Monday evening," Esme said enthusiastically. "I have coverage for my sister every weeknight for a couple of hours."

"And you come to my shop." Rikki opened the now unlocked car door. "I'm honored."

"Well, I had my pick of coffee shops," Esme teased, "but I picked the one with the cutest barista." She sat in the driver's seat.

Yes, yes, yes. Esme was flirting. During their entire time at the gallery, Rikki simply could not read Esme. But now she knew.

"Excellent," Rikki said, hanging onto the still-open door. "Lemon or Cream Cheese bundt cake?"

"You are single-handedly going to make me fat."

"Gladly, if it gets you to come see me," Rikki said. Yes, she could flirt back.

Esme caught Rikki's gaze and bit her bottom lip.

Rikki held her breath. It could go either way, either way. She leaned closer.

Esme looked away, her smile sheepish.

Damn. Wrong way.

"Thank you for a lovely afternoon, Rikki. I enjoyed this immensely."

"Me, too." Rikki stepped back so Esme could shut her car door. "I'll see you on Monday then." She tapped the top of the car, turned, and walked back to her own car. Only two whole days to wait. Easy peasy, as Madison would say. Rikki's perma-smile led her all the way back to the shop.

~~~

Monday evening had been crazy with the darts league in-house, so Rikki moved Esme to a quieter corner away from the action. They talked for an hour, and then Esme left. Tuesday through Thursday were similar, except they were back at Esme's original table. Rikki now understood cloud nine. It was soft and comfortable, and she looked forward to remaining there for a long time. Every day from atop that cloud, she looked forward to her friend Esme's arrival.

But, of course, in true Rikki fashion, she worried that maybe that's all she and Esme would ever be—friends. They seemed to match well together, though. They were like-minded on many things. The taboo subjects of politics and religion had even come up, and they were on the same page. That was a relief. But Rikki wanted more. Okay, okay. Maybe she was rushing things, but on the flip side, she'd met the woman over nine months ago. Shouldn't she know more about her by now? When Rikki asked Esme why she moved away from Vermont, she got a vague "We needed a fresh start" answer in return and nothing more. Obviously, the "we" referred to Esme and her sister.

When asked, Rikki didn't give Shasti any details or share the niggling concern about the vague answers Esme often gave her. She just said, "We're getting to know each other." Shasti's working jaw and narrowed eyes didn't break Rikki's resolve. It was true, Rikki was getting to know Esme and vice versa. She didn't want to rush things, as she'd done in the past. Like she'd done with Eileen. Shasti respected her privacy and didn't push too much.

Rikki looked at the analog clock hanging behind the counter. It was half an hour before Esme was due to arrive. It was Friday, and Rikki hoped one or both of two things would happen. The first was that Esme would take her up on the offer to see the apartment, and then maybe Rikki could finally steal a kiss. The second was that Esme would let Rikki take her out to dinner or lunch or breakfast over the weekend. Rikki didn't care which. She just wanted more intimate time with Esme.

She wiped down Esme's favorite table and was heading back to rinse out her rag when an unexpected friend walked in.

"Harriet," Rikki said, "it's nice to see you here. Is your family in tow?"

Harriet smoothed down her short, windblown, slightly graying dark hair and said, "No, Ma'am. It's good to see you as well. Mistress Jaleesa suggested I stop by and see you."

"Oh?" Rikki looked up at the clock again. "I have a few minutes. Come back into the office with me."

"Thank you, Ma'am."

Harriet declined the offer of a beverage or snack cake, on the house, of course. That was one way Rikki was giving back to her friends. None of them had to pay for anything in her shop. They'd given her so much already, too much.

Once settled in the office, Rikki asked, "What's on your mind?"

"Ma'am, please bear with me while I meander through my thoughts." Harriet looked down at her hands in her lap.

Rikki settled back in her seat. She wondered what brought the former art teacher to her door, but gave Harriet the space she seemed to need.

"My soul needs to do art," Harriet said. "I need to plan a painting on a canvas, pick the medium, the colors, everything. But, as you know, I lost that privilege when I lost my job. My fault, of course. Addiction takes over, and nothing else matters. Addiction didn't care that I did a line of cocaine in front of a twelve-year-old student and her mother. Addiction only cared that I got the fix."

"I remember the media circus after that," Rikki said softly. The poor woman, a beloved middle school teacher, was made an example of by local and national news outlets.

"I'm not telling you this to get sympathy, Ma'am," Harriet said. Upon Rikki's head nod, Harriet continued. "Jaleesa saved me, Ma'am."

Rikki interrupted. "The way I hear it, you saved each other in a way."

A small smile crept onto Harriet's face. "In a way, I suppose that's true. I feel safe, secure, and taken care of in her household, Ma'am. We all take care of each other, and DeShawn is the brother we didn't know we needed." She paused for a quick breath for courage and continued, "Jaleesa and Tina encouraged me to continue my art. They made sure I had the biggest room to fit my easel and painting supplies. I've started to uncoil little by little. Believe me, I'm still coiled, but I'm loosening up some. Jaleesa encouraged me to get the job at the Arts Center. And my new friends there encouraged me to display some works in the gallery. That's what you saw when you went there last Saturday. They didn't know either. Jaleesa and the rest of the family, I mean. They didn't know. It was a tentative move. Jaleesa was happy for my bravery, but not pleased that I didn't tell her. She was even less pleased that she had to hear about it from someone else."

"From me," Rikki said. "At Monday night darts."

"Yes, and that was okay, Miss Rikki. I was used to being so independent before meeting Jaleesa," Harriet said. "And I guess I forgot that I wasn't on my own anymore. She wouldn't have forbidden me to show my pieces, but she said it would have been good to talk it over." Harriet looked up for the first time. "You know, to weigh the pros and cons. And also so Jaleesa would know how to help me if there was any backlash."

"Dommes do like to stay in the know," Rikki said with a slight chuckle.

"Jaleesa's taking the whole family to the Arts Center tomorrow to see my paintings on display." Harriet's expression of grateful love melted Rikki's heart. "That wouldn't be happening if you hadn't said something to my Domme."

"Wonderful," Rikki said. "You're a very talented artist, and they will be proud to see your work."

"Thank you, Ma'am," Harriet said and stood. "I should get back. I'll let Mistress Jaleesa know that we spoke and that I explained my hesitation about telling anyone about my art to you."

"As will I." Rikki also stood. Her chair rolled back and hit the edge of her desk.

"And Ma'am?" Harriet said, gaining eye contact again.

"Yes?"

"As a teacher, I had to read a room quickly and discern the various moods of my students. I hope I'm not being too forward by saying that it is relieving to see your energy and spirits improving lately."

"I—" Rikki didn't know how to respond to that. "Thank you," was all she could come up with.

"Earlier this year," Harriet continued, "when I came by to alter your suit, you were closed and, for lack of a better word, hiding. I knew you would be okay eventually, but you were very guarded."

Rikki lifted her chin.

"And, Ma'am," Harriet said, crossing her arms, "your new friend has that same energy. Guarded. I'm way overstepping, I know, Ma'am, but I hope we're able to learn from each other in this community. At fifty-five years old, I've seen a few things. Go slow with her. She may open up. Don't rush in. And beware of that dreaded new relationship frenzy." Harriet let out a nervous sigh. "I'll leave that with you, but just so you know, I don't usually meddle in other people's business like this. I just—" She groaned, obviously searching for the right words. "I just feel this need to mother you sometimes. Protect you. For some reason, I've always had this feeling when I'm near you." Harriet's face scrunched up as she fought back tears. "I'm sorry, Ma'am," she said in a high, tight voice. "I'll go now."

Rikki wiped at her own sudden tears. "Come here." She held her long arms out, and Harriet obliged, letting herself be hugged. "I value your counsel, Harriet. Thank you." She relaxed her arms, and Harriet stepped out of the hug.

"Thank you, Ma'am," Harriet said. "I'd best be going."

Rikki nodded and opened the door for her friend. Yes, "friend" seemed to be a good word to describe the nurturing submissive who found the courage to give Rikki advice.

Rikki poked her head out of the office door. Her heart swelled. Harriet was holding the front door open for Esme to enter.

Chapter 18

Friday evening's tea with Esme had been lovely; Rikki got brave and suggested a tour of her apartment. Esme gracefully declined. Rikki then suggested lunch out the next day, and Esme apologized for not being able to get away. What followed that Friday tea was another lonely weekend with no contact from Esme.

Rikki made it through the weekend and then saw Esme four evenings in a row. It was Thursday, and Esme had left over an hour ago, and Rikki was getting the Thursday night blues. If Esme turned her down again tomorrow night, then it would be yet another solo weekend for Rikki.

Rikki wanted to be respectful and not push. Harriet's advice about going slow played in her thoughts. Another frustrating thing was that Esme apparently didn't respond to texts. Rikki wanted to call, but remembered Esme's autistic sister and knew Esme had her hands full at home. So, coffee shop tea times were it for now.

The winter holidays were fast approaching, and Rikki wondered how she would spend them. Would Thanksgiving be at one of her friends' homes again? Or would she be at Esme's, meeting the sister and taking in Esme's new home? She'd gotten that much out of Esme. She lived in a house somewhere near the high school on the east side of town.

But she was getting ahead of herself. The holidays weren't there yet. It was only the first week of October, but thank goodness the workday was done, and there was only Mark to let out. She thanked him for a good day's work and relocked the shop door behind him. She turned off the lights and headed up to her apartment. Somehow, she needed to shake off this blue cloud. A shower, yes. That's what she needed. Maybe even a cold one.

She stepped into her apartment and felt her tension ease. It was amazing what a clean and show-ready apartment did to one's disposition. Her new gray and teal comforter, satin of course, really brightened up the bed. And somehow, she'd managed to keep her laundry done, folded, and put away just in case Esme ever took her up on that tour.

She placed her work clothes in the hamper and stepped into the shower. Her movements were automatic, and the decision to wash her hair was made without her consent. She laughed. She was so distracted these days. But even though she recognized that fact, it didn't stop her endless thinking.

"What if she's shy?" Rikki thought, lathering up. "What if she's never been with a woman before? Or maybe she just got out of a relationship and wasn't keen on getting into another so quickly? And why did she leave Vermont?" This last question was spoken into the soap in her hand, as if she were recording her thoughts. "All good questions."

And if Esme was new to sapphic relationships, Rikki would take it slow. Just like she'd done with her ex, Sarah, over three and a half years ago. Sarah had only been in one power exchange relationship before she'd met Rikki. After a few dinner dates where they discussed expectations and soft and hard limits, Rikki took her back home to Aunt Tilda's downstairs dungeon.

Silly Sarah thought she was going to direct the scene that evening when she asked, "You're going to fuck me, aren't you?"

Rikki was a bit taken aback by the question's bold, assumptive tone, but she hid it. Sarah was young, in her early twenties, and with newbies, sometimes nerves took over. Rikki would fix that. "Young women like you don't always get what they ask for," Rikki said as she took a step closer. Sarah stepped back. "They don't always get what they want. But they might, just might, get what they need."

"And what is that, Ma'am?" Sarah's grin was priceless.

"Let's find out together, shall we?" Rikki spun Sarah around and wrapped her arms around her. Sarah's back was now pressed against Rikki's front. Rikki moved the long chestnut brown hair out of the way and bit the neck in front of her.

Sarah's moan filled Rikki's power centers. She released the bite and repeatedly kissed the area. As she did so, she unbuttoned Sarah's blouse and slid it off her shoulders. Sarah took the hint and helped peel the silk garment off her arms. They both let it hit the mat. Rikki slid one bra strap off Sarah's shoulder and kissed the reddened and indented skin underneath. The other strap followed next. Rikki leaned back to unlatch the hooks. A small moan escaped Sarah's lips as Rikki snaked the straps down her lover's arms. Once free of the bra, Sarah reached behind her with both arms and pulled Rikki's hips to her. Her head fell back against Rikki's chest.

"Ma'am," Sarah murmured, obviously needing something.

Rikki spun her around. One hand went to the small of Sarah's back, the other behind her head in a total possessive power move. She kissed the woman in her arms until they both moaned. Rikki helped Sarah lie down on the daybed. Rikki crawled on top, still fully clothed, Sarah topless.

Their first session together would be rather vanilla. Rikki needed to suss out Sarah's needs. She'd entertain some of Sarah's wants, of course, but only if it suited Rikki. True dominance, Aunt Tilda taught them, was about showing up and being present. It was about leading and caring for a vulnerable submissive who was giving you the ultimate gift—their trust. Power exchange in a Dominant/submissive scene was not about the dominant selfishly getting what she wanted. It was about creating a sense of safety that allowed the submissive to surrender. And for Rikki, that surrender was what BDSM was all about. Helping her sub feel cradled, cherished, and loved. Helping her grow and become more than she was.

Rikki explored the body underneath her. She peppered it with kisses and playful nips. With one hand, she held both of Sarah's arms overhead and kept them there. With the other hand, she explored, moving lower, past the small breasts, beyond the tight stomach of youth, and tugged the bottom of the short skirt up, so she could explore further. She opened one of Sarah's closed fists and curled the fingers around the railing. Sarah grasped the idea and held onto the sturdy metal structure behind her head with both hands. Rikki moved the rest of the skirt out of the way and hooked two fingers on either side of Sarah's sexy lace panties. She pulled them down slowly. Sarah helped by raising her hips slightly.

Once the panties were discarded, Rikki yanked the legs apart. Sarah inhaled sharply. She squirmed as Rikki began her slow but methodical exploration. It was a privilege to be able to worship a woman's body, and the trust it took to allow this worship the very first time was both humbling and empowering.

Before dipping into the place Sarah wanted Rikki's fingers most, Rikki reached up and pulled Sarah's hands down. That night, there would be no bondage, definitely no impact play, and probably no oral. There would, however, be exploring and fast-moving fingers that would give the young woman what she so desperately wanted. Yes, Rikki would oblige. This time. Trust needed to be established. And then it was all about figuring out how far she would go the next time.

Rikki reached up and ran a finger over Sarah's lips. She poked one index finger in. Reflexively, Sarah's lips closed around the finger, and she sucked lightly. Rikki moved her finger in and out, wetting it sufficiently. "Open," Rikki whispered. Sarah complied. Rikki took the now-wet finger and swirled it around one of Sarah's nipples. She then used her thumb to repeatedly flick the nipple into hardness. The other nipple got the same treatment. Once both were sufficiently hard, she suggested that Sarah keep them that way. She was not to let them soften. Sarah clearly understood the assignment when she swirled her own wet fingers around both nipples, tugging at them, squeezing, and pinching.

Satisfied, Rikki turned her attention below the skirt line. Her fingers found Sarah ready and very willing. Sarah arched her back when Rikki entered. A soft moan greeted Rikki's movements. The moans increased in fervor, and it wasn't long before a full-throated cry ripped through the quiet dungeon. Sarah's bucking hips helped Rikki milk the orgasm out longer until Sarah collapsed on the bed, obviously spent.

"Miss Rikki, holy fucking—" She arched her pelvis as another pulse hit her. "Shit," Sarah finally managed to say when she caught her breath.

"We have a problem," Rikki said.

"Ma'am?" Sarah's eyelids were half-closed.

She tweaked one of Sarah's nipples. "These are no longer tight and pleasing to my gaze. They are no longer hard."

"Oh, shit," Sarah said. "I'm sorry, Ma'am. I'll do better next time."

"Mmm," Rikki said, allowing her feigned disappointment to show. "You will, because the next time we meet, you will have to make amends to me for this clear disobedience."

"Yes, Ma'am," Sarah said. "I'm sorry, Ma'am." The tone Sarah used told Rikki all she needed to know. Sarah understood the game that was afoot. During their next date, Rikki would introduce punishment. The sheepish grin creeping up Sarah's face told Rikki the young woman was very interested.

In the present, three and a half years later, the water ran cold over Rikki's skin. She did a quick check to make sure she had rinsed everything properly since she had no recollection of washing, and then turned off the water.

"And that's how I'll approach Esme," Rikki said as she toweled off. She threw on her new green plush robe. She glanced at the never-been-worn purple robe and wondered when Esme would first wear it. Even if Esme wasn't submissive, all women wanted to be noticed, needed, and nurtured. Rikki could provide that. Rikki would make sure that Esme got the attention and affection she wanted. In short, Rikki was all about making sure that Esme felt seen and appreciated.

"Aaack," Rikki groaned out loud. "Slow down, Carmichael. We're taking our time." A shot of adrenaline hit her when she realized that she'd see Esme in less than twenty-four hours.

~~~

Esme breezed into the coffee shop, her face lighting up when she saw Rikki. Rikki could neither confirm nor deny that she had been watching the door for a certain blonde's arrival. And she was sure her face mirrored Esme's. Esme's mid-length, deep-brown trench coat, cinched at the waist with an oversized belt, looked fantastic on her. Rikki could think of a few things she'd like to do with that belt, but she tossed that thought in her "to be explored later" bin in her brain. She desperately wanted to give Esme a hug in greeting, but they weren't at that stage yet. Another thing to be tossed in that bin.

"Happy Jeddi Taylor's birthday," Esme announced after hanging her coat on a hook near the front door. She chuckled.

"Jeddi who?"

Esme laughed again. Rikki signaled to Lydia to bring over their usual tea setup. And this time, she was going to surprise Esme with a new type of cake. Marta had been experimenting with variations on Mrs. Pulaski's recipes, so far with great success.

Esme sighed. "My sister. Apparently, it's some Australian basketball player's birthday today." Esme took off her coat and hung it on one of the hooks near the door. She headed toward their usual table.

Rikki pulled the chair out for her; it was a small gesture of affection and the only one she had allowed herself.

"And before you ask," Esme continued, "no, I don't know much else about Jeddi other than she was on the Australian Olympic team in the early 2000s."

Lydia brought over the tea service and greeted Esme warmly. Rikki gave Lydia a smile of gratitude not only for the tea and cake but also for being friendly to Esme. Lydia nodded and headed back to the counter.

Rikki sat down opposite Esme.

Esme leaned in closer. "Why does she always take, like, two or three steps backward before walking away?"

Rikki raised an eyebrow. She hadn't been expecting that question. "It's a sign of respect. She's not required to do that. She just does." Okay, that was vague enough, and hopefully Esme wouldn't press for further clarification. She didn't, thank goodness. Rikki was not one to lie but had learned how to skirt harmful truths. After pouring their tea, she raised her cup and said, "To Jeddi Taylor, Olympian extraordinaire."

"To Jeddi," Esme echoed, and they clinked their cups ever so gently. They both took a sip of their tea, and when Esme put hers down again, she said, "You're so sweet to go along with my nonsense."

Rikki simply chuckled. She was desperate to learn more about Esme, so even though she didn't really want to share their sacred hour with anyone else, she was willing to do so to get more information about the woman she was falling for, so she asked, "Hey, what do you think about bringing your sister here one evening?"

Esme's eyes grew wide. "That is a lovely gesture, Rikki, but Margie isn't big on things that are new and unfamiliar."

"The move from Vermont must have been difficult," Rikki said.

"It was," Esme said and looked down at her cup, and then pulled over the slice of cake they would share. "This looks yummy. Another new Marta creation?"

Rikki recognized the avoidance tactic but didn't call Esme on it. Instead, she went with the flow. "Lemon poppyseed. I had to hide a piece because it was very popular today."

"Maybe you should become part bakery." Esme laughed at Rikki's panicked expression. "I respectfully withdraw the suggestion."

Rikki laughed with Esme. It was so freeing. She liked feeling free and easy with someone like this, but she was realizing that Harriet might have been right about Esme being somewhat guarded. If only Esme would agree to a tour of the apartment. Nothing big had to happen. Rikki might simply press the curvy woman against the wall, place both hands on either side of her head, effectively pinning her there, and lean in slowly to—

"Rikki," Esme said, her breath a bit labored, "You're looking at me like you want to, uh, devour me or something."

Rikki gently slid her hand over Esme's. It was a small, possessive move, but desperate times called for desperate measures. "Why won't you come upstairs with me?"

"Rikki," Esme said, looking lost. "I want to." This was whispered. Esme looked down and pulled her hand back. Both hands were now in her lap. "I don't mean to pull away. I just need more time, I guess." She looked up. "I like you, Rikki. I think you know that. But my obligations…my sister…I have this short window every weeknight."

"We can make that work," Rikki said and pulled her hand back into her own lap.

Esme's lips parted, and it was so damned sexy that Rikki wanted to kick everyone out, including the staff, and lock the front doors. *You can't always get what you want,* flashed in Rikki's brain. She wasn't going to beg, even though she wanted to. "I understand," Rikki said with a sigh she hadn't meant to be so audible.

"You're frustrated," Esme said. "I'm sorry for that. You're sweet, and I really enjoy your company. More than you'll ever know."

No, no, Rikki would not beg. Nothing good ever came from coercion. "Let's enjoy the time we do get to share then," Rikki said, trying not to make the words sound too icy. She pulled the cake toward her and divided it into two roughly equal pieces. Was Esme pulling away? Was Esme letting her down gently?

Without looking up, Rikki pushed one of the plates toward Esme. A hand covered hers. Rikki looked up. There it was again, that soul-searching gaze. Esme's expression softened. "I can make it work, Rikki," she said softly. "You've been so patient with me. I must seem like the most wishy-washy woman on the planet. Here is this fabulously gorgeous woman wooing me patiently and respectfully, and I'm just seeming to be unaffected." She squeezed Rikki's hand and held on. "I am, though. I look forward to our tea parties. I look forward to seeing you, and I hate leaving. I hate the weekends because I can't see you."

Rikki swallowed hard. "What are you saying, Esme?"

"I'm saying that I want you to take me upstairs." She inhaled sharply, clearly nervous.

Not letting go of the hand holding hers, Rikki pushed her chair back.

"Mom!" The sharp word cut through the coffee shop.

Rikki whirled her head toward the sound.

A teenage girl, dressed in a white karategi with a blue belt, stormed toward their table, a coat draped over one arm. Her long blonde braid swung back and forth. Esme pulled her hand back. Rikki stood up.

"Mom," the teenager said to Esme, "you need to check your phone." She reached down and turned Esme's phone over. The screen was filled with texts and missed calls. "Dad said Aunt Margie is off the rails. He called the dojo when he couldn't reach you. I had to leave class to find you." The teenager looked at Rikki and said, "You're very pretty. I see why she comes here." Her focus went back to her mother. "We're not moving again," she growled. And with that, the teen turned and headed for the door. "Come on, Mom," the teenager spat, clearly agitated.

"Rikki," Esme said. "I'm sorry. I'm so sorry." Her tears were real as she got up calmly. "I wish things could be different." She walked to the coat hooks, grabbed her coat, and followed her daughter out the door.

Rikki stared at the now-closed front door. She was stunned. Daughter? Husband? With unfocused eyes, Rikki stumbled past her seat and somehow made it into her office. She closed the door gently behind her and then miraculously made it up the stairs to her apartment.

The moment the door to her apartment clicked shut, she stared at the back of it. "I should paint that," she said out loud.

And then she made a decision.

Without moving, she pulled out her phone and called Shasti. "Bring me my suitcase from my pile of shit in your basement. The small one. Please. I need to pack and don't want to lose any more time."

"I'll be over in twenty."

"Make it ten."

"Where are you going?" Shasti asked.

"Pennsylvania," Rikki said and added, "I have to pack." She hung up.

Shasti arrived in twelve with Victoria in tow.

Chapter 19

This one called in the cavalry. Me," Victoria said and pointed to Shasti. "What's happening, friend?"

"Thank you," Rikki said to Shasti. She was thanking Shasti for the suitcase, and most definitely *not* thanking either of them for the damned cavalry storming her castle. She plopped the suitcase on the bed and unzipped it. Yes, this was her way of stalling because she really didn't want an inquisition right now.

"Going on a trip," Rikki said and threw some clothes and toiletries in the suitcase. She made sure her mother's wooden hair clip was tucked in the inner mesh pocket inside the bag. She would need that for strength.

"Where?" Victoria asked and settled into one of the new overstuffed chairs. Okay, apparently, Victoria wasn't leaving anytime soon.

"Home," Rikki said, letting her annoyance show. "Why are you here?"

"We're just figuring out if you're okay."

"What prompted this sudden trip, Rikki?" Shasti asked gently.

Rikki sighed, ignored her friends, and mentally went over everything she'd put in the suitcase. She had no idea what she'd need for a four-day or more trip away. Once thing she did know for sure was that Lydia and Mark would have to cover.

Rikki snapped her fingers at the realization that she didn't have time to organize new duty schedules. She whirled to face Victoria. "Vic, can you go downstairs through the office into the shop and tell Lydia that she, Mark, and Marta will have to figure out the crew shifts. Tell her that I'll be gone for about four days, maybe more. Tell her she can call me, but that I need them to figure stuff out on their own." She turned away and realized she was barking out orders to one of her best friends. She turned back and said, "Thanks for helping, Vic. Sorry. I'm a bit frantic."

Victoria stood but hesitated.

"Is your family okay?" Shasti asked. "Did something happen?"

"Nothing happened to any of them," Rikki said.

"All right," Vic said. "But what should I tell Lydia about where you're going and why it's so sudden?"

"Tell her whatever you want." Rikki waved her hand in dismissal. She cringed. Her friends were going to disown her. "Again, sorry, Vic," Rikki said. "Can you just go take care of that for me? Please?"

"On it." Victoria headed out the apartment door, closing it softly behind her.

Rikki wheeled the suitcase to the door and shoved her wallet, keys, and phone in her pocket.

"A phone charger," Shasti said.

Rikki pointed at her and nodded. She grabbed the charger from her bedside stand and shoved it in the suitcase.

"Do you have cash?"

"Uh," Rikki pulled out her wallet. As expected, it was empty. "Let me, uh…" She headed to her dresser and rifled through the drawers. She sometimes stashed cash in her underwear drawer. She came up empty. "I'll get some at the ATM."

"No," Shasti said. She reached into her pocket and handed Rikki one hundred dollars in twenties. "Just take it," she said when Rikki tried to object.

"I'll pay you back."

"I'm not worried about that," Shasti said. "Can you just stop moving for a second and take a breath?"

Rikki knew better than to defy her other bestie. She stopped, breathed in, and then headed to the kitchenette to grab some power bars Shanice had given her to try.

"Try again," Shasti said, stepping up to Rikki in the kitchenette. "You're in panic mode. Fight, flight, or freeze. You're in flight mode. What sparked this?"

Rikki let out a breath and closed her eyes. She took the cleansing breath Shasti wanted her to take and let it out slowly. She relaxed her jaw and shoulders and took another breath. She opened her eyes and saw the deep concern etched in Shasti's face.

"Shasti, I can't remember the last thing I said to my mother. Or the last thing she said to me. Her last words ever were probably 'Thank you' when the deranged idiot handed her the bomb." Rikki would have cried at the imagined scene, but she was too numb. "I need to see her grave. I need to—I need…" Anger boiled up from somewhere deep, and she couldn't speak. Shasti led her to the couch and sat next to her, holding her hand.

Rikki searched Shasti's face and saw compassion. Tears were forming now. Sadness was overtaking the anger. "I need to see the clinic if it's still there. Did they rebuild? It's been over eleven years, and I don't know, Shasti. I need to see her headstone. Maybe I need to see my father and my sister, too. And my brother. All their kids. Maybe. I don't know. I'm not delusional. I know it won't be a happy reunion because my father blames me. I struggle with that. It may be my fault."

"No, no," Shasti said and rubbed the back of Rikki's hand.

"I know it wasn't directly my fault, but maybe it was indirectly. That's the logic I can't work out, but I can't help wanting to go back in time and never suggest that my mother work at the clinic. My father was against it, but I didn't care what he thought."

"Apparently, neither did your mother."

Rikki looked at Shasti. She'd never thought of it that way.

"I wish I could go with you, Rikki," Shasti said. "But why now? What sparked this?"

Rikki looked down. She pulled her hands away from Shasti's grasp. In her head, she relived the soul-crushing scene in the coffee shop but wasn't sure how to voice it. "Esme…" She hesitated.

"Go on," Shasti said, her voice gentle, not forceful.

"Well, apparently, Esme's married with kids." Rikki looked up. She couldn't bite back the tears any longer. Shasti pulled her into her arms and rocked her gently. "Shh, shh," Shasti murmured. After a few minutes, Rikki sat back up, wiped at her eyes, and said, "I knew something was off, Shasti. I wanted it so badly that I didn't listen to my intuition. I let myself get hooked in."

"Is there an angry husband or wife hot on your trail?"

Rikki chuckled. "No, no. Nothing like that. And it's a husband. I think she had a genuine attraction to me, and I did her, but she kept the family thing hidden."

"Ahh," Shasti said, "and you just found out tonight."

"Very publicly. Lydia is probably giving Victoria the daytime drama version of it. Esme's teenage daughter walked into the shop and spilled the beans. The hidden, covered-up, nondisclosed beans."

"Oh, hun, I'm so sorry." Shasti patted Rikki's thigh. "And what's the connection between that incident and rushing to Pennsylvania?"

"I'm panicking," Rikki admitted. "Remember a while back I said I wanted to go to PA?"

"Mm hmm."

"I don't want to waste any more time. Esme wasted so much of my time and energy. I need to go. Now."

"Let's think logically about this," Shasti said. "Tomorrow is the Rocco's brunch. Patrice is counting on you to take Brittany."

"I forgot," Rikki said. "Can you take her?"

"And you may have forgotten, but Madison is expecting your feedback on her anthropology paper. She's at home right now working on it, so 'Miss Rikki will be so proud of me.'" She used air quotes to indicate what Madison said.

"She is?" Rikki closed her eyes. "What's the topic?"

"She's arguing, with cited sources, mind you, that sexuality and gender are culturally constructed and not exclusively a result of biology."

"Heavy stuff," Rikki said. "Why me?"

Shasti's look of utter disbelief confused Rikki. Shasti shook her head slowly as if wanting to say the words, "You're so dense," but unlike Victoria, she was too polite to do so. "She treasures you, Rikki. I haven't even been asked to read it."

"No?"

Shasti shook her head. "Nope, she wants you, but I can tell her you had some kind of family emergency. She'll understand."

Rikki grunted. "Don't play me, Shasti. I've had enough of that for today."

"Will you stay for the brunch tomorrow at least?"

Rikki exhaled a long groan. "I'll be there."

"Excellent," Shasti said. "And, please, for my own sanity. No sneaking around. No changing your mind in the middle of the night. I'm not your keeper. But I care for you, Rikki. We're family to each other."

"Yes, Ma'am," Rikki said and smiled. She returned the cash Shasti had so generously loaned her and then pulled out her phone. She entered the passcode and handed it to her friend. "Here. Do that shared location thing on my phone like you have with Madison. This way you'll know where I am. I have no one to share that with, and since you're my family, I guess you're it."

Shasti tapped the phone a few times. "Done. And I'll do the same for my phone." After a moment, she said, "Done." Shasti took a minute to show Rikki how to use the app.

After a few more reassuring words in both directions, Shasti pointed to the suitcase and said, "You don't have to unpack that, but maybe you should tuck it somewhere out of sight."

"Good thinking." Rikki gave her friend one last hug. "Can you fill in Victoria?"

"Yes, of course. See you at Rocco's tomorrow."

Once she heard the shop door open and then close, she shut and locked her apartment door.

Why does it feel like I'm doing everything for everyone else? When do I get to do something for me?

And that something was a trip back to her hometown in Pennsylvania. She would stay true to her word to Shasti and not bolt in the middle of the night, so it was simply a matter of when.

~~~

Once her head cooled down and she wasn't in flight mode any longer, Rikki settled in to find a way to live without the anticipatory rush of seeing Esme. She'd toyed with the idea of assigning Lydia or Mark the evening shifts just so she wouldn't see Esme if she dared come into the shop again, but that was a coward's way out. Instead, she bucked up and spent weeks convincing her staff and friends that she was fine and that they did not have to walk on eggshells around her. And the upside? Esme never showed.

At Rowena's forty-first birthday party at her mansion on the last day of October, Shanice pulled Rikki aside. She reminded her that Venus would be flying over Denton Heights, dropping love bombs to all the Capricorns in

December and January. Well, that's not exactly how she'd phrased it, but that was the gist. Rikki planned to put up her strongest umbrella and dodge every single one of Venus's love bombs. She'd had enough of romance and pitty-pat heart feels. No, thank you, Venus. No one's home.

Early November brought a double-birthday party, with Tina turning thirty-three and Shanice, the old lady, turning twenty-seven. Mid-November brought a joint planning session with Lydia, Mark, and Marta to arrange schedules so the shop would be staffed while Rikki went home to Pennsylvania over Thanksgiving. Since the shop was closed on Thanksgiving Day, it made sense to go then. And that's all they needed to know. They didn't need to know that she'd had no invitation to Thanksgiving dinner from her father and his new wife or from her sister. Forget her clueless brother. She wasn't sure she'd even see them while she was in Wilkes-Barre. She was going for herself, not to seek closure, but to help her face what had happened. Back then, when her father kicked her out of the house, she bolted so quickly to Denton Heights and into the arms of her Aunt Tilda that she didn't really have time to process anything.

At three o'clock Thanksgiving morning, Rikki left Denton Heights. It would take nine to ten hours to drive there, barring weather or holiday traffic. As she passed Columbus at five in the morning, she waved to Madison's parents and grandparents per Madison's orders. Dana, upon hearing this request, asked if Rikki would also wave to her family. She did. At a little before seven, she saw the signs for Akron and thought of the BDSM club there. Clearly, this was not the trip nor the time for a visit, but according to Dominique, it was the club she'd modeled her own club after. Rikki saluted the exit sign but kept on going.

Once she crossed the border into Pennsylvania, the reality of what she was doing hit her. "It will be hard," Shasti had said to her, "but it sounds like something you've needed to do for a long time."

"It is," Rikki said to the interior of her car, somewhere on Interstate 80 in Pennsylvania. She took a couple of restroom breaks on the way and walked a bit to ease her stiffness, but she was determined to get there before two o'clock. That's when he had always demanded Thanksgiving dinner. The one time her mother miscalculated how long it would take the turkey to cook, it almost sent her father into a frenzy. No, not almost. He blew his top. Rikki hid in her room until he was on his third beer and settled in front of the football game with her brother. Then she snuck down and silently helped her mother expedite the meal prep.

She wasn't really sure she wanted to see him or lay eyes on his selfish, smug face. What she really wanted to ask was when he had stopped loving her? It was well before her mother's murder. Well before. She remembered feeling his hatred in high school. Maybe because she brought her girlfriends home and 'flaunted' her sexuality in front of him. He'd used the word flaunted, but she wasn't flaunting anything, she'd defended. She pointed out that she was merely doing what Caroline had done, bringing dates home. He'd made it uber-clear that her 'lifestyle' was not acceptable in his house. Caroline counseled her to keep the girls out of the house. "That's what cars are for, little sister," she'd told her back then. She even went so far as to mention a few isolated parking spots where Rikki could bring her dates.

He resented paying for part of her college tuition. She didn't know what he was going on about because, truth be told, she had paid most of her college tuition herself with work-study and several academic loans. With Aunt Tilda's help, she finally paid them all off and eventually paid back her aunt.

Rikki turned off the Wilkes-Barre exit that led to her childhood home. She'd made it by one o'clock. Perfect timing.

She hadn't been back to her hometown in eleven years, so she drove by her old high school since it was right by the highway. It looked the same. Weathered bricks, aging roof, but at least the sign out front was new and shiny. "Go Wolfpack," she said and pumped a fist as she drove by. The clinic was not on her way to the house. That would be later. But she was pleased she'd made it in time for dinner. Not that she was going to their dinner. No, she simply wanted to sit in her car and see if she could catch a glimpse of any of them.

She pulled onto the street. The houses looked so different. Dumpy and uncared for. Poverty had hit the area hard. She parked on the opposite side of the street, a bit down. They didn't know her car, so she felt safe to sit and watch.

It didn't take long. Her sister Caroline walked out the front door and unlocked a car with a key fob. She opened the trunk and reached in for something. Rikki's heart was in her throat. Her sister looked older, tired. And her hair shouldn't have that much gray. She was only in her early forties. *Oh, Caroline.* Rikki's hand went to the door handle. She stopped herself from flying out of the car and running up to hug her sister.

As if sensing something, Caroline shut the trunk and looked down the street in Rikki's direction. Not seeing anything, she looked the other way. She shook her head as if shaking off a weird thought. Rikki pulled her hand off the handle. Caroline's head shake reminded her that she wasn't welcome in or near her father's house. It would only set him off and ruin the day for everyone, including the poor woman who agreed to marry him.

Rikki sat outside the house for another half hour before moving on. She slowly drove by and took a look at the upstairs bedroom she shared with her sister when they were growing up. She could have taken a picture, but decided to let those memories sail away.

The cemetery was next on the list, but she deliberately took the route that led past the clinic. She had to see what had become of the space.

"Holy shit," she said out loud when she saw the building. The original clinic was gone, and in its place was a Planned Parenthood Clinic over twice the size of the original. Rikki parked in front of the closed building and took some pictures. She went up to the front door and peered in. There wasn't much to see in the foyered entryway, but there were a couple of plaques on the wall. She moved closer to read them. Her breath caught in her throat as she read the inscription on the largest one.

*This memorial plaque is a tribute
of remembrance, honoring four
innocents killed in the senseless
bombing of the Wilson-Solomon
clinic.*

There was a date, too. It was the date her mother died. Rikki couldn't breathe. Her mother's picture, along with pictures of the three other people who were killed that day, was displayed below the words. Their pictures had been etched into the bronze.

"No one told me," she said out loud. She pounded her leg. "Why did no one tell me?" Aunt Tilda must not have known either. "How fucking insidious of them." Outrage boiled deep inside her. "So cruel," she said, growing numb again. No, she would not grow numb. She wouldn't let them have the satisfaction.

She took a deep breath, stood to her full height, and took pictures. She zoomed in, tried different filters and angles, and once satisfied, sent one of the better pictures off to her friends back in Denton Heights. She made no comment about the picture in the group chat, but simply said, "I'm fine. I'll be back sometime late tomorrow."

She drove away bewildered. Even Caroline hadn't told her about the memorial plaque. Surely after ten years, they could have shown her some mercy. It was her father; it had to be. Caroline and Pete had partaken in their father's Kool-Aid, hadn't they? Were they that afraid of him that they couldn't show their younger sister common courtesy? Or did they truly believe his demented brand of truth that Rikki had something to do with their mother's death?

The cemetery was on her before she realized it. She pulled in, grateful that it wasn't closed on Thanksgiving Day. She made a short stop at the restroom near the entryway and then drove the narrow road to her family's row of plots, a row she would never be laid to rest in, not if he was in it. No thanks. She parked her car, pulled out the flowers she had purchased before the trip, and headed across the brown grass. She stopped for a few moments to pay her respects to her grandparents on her mother's side and then moved one plot over to her mother's. Emotion squeezed her chest, and she had to swallow hard.

"Hi, Mom," Rikki said. "Shanice told me that you're always with me. Other people have told me that, too, but she said that you have probably been with me on this entire trip and together we're looking at your marker." She brushed a leaf off the top of the headstone and then traced the letters of her mother's name. She was pleased to see that her mother's maiden name was included in the etching. "Good," Rikki said out loud. "He doesn't get to have complete control over you anymore." The headstone had been ordered but not placed when Rikki had been unceremoniously invited to leave. There was no picture. Just her name, the basic begin and end dates, and a generic sentence that read, "Forever in our hearts."

"Flowers for you, Mom." She laid the flowers at the base of the stone. A small part of her hoped that her father would come to the cemetery, see the flowers, and wonder who'd left them. Caroline would know.

Rikki took a deep breath and let it out as she pictured her father, sister, and brother on a paper sailboat gliding downstream away from her and her mother. It was a technique Shasti said Madison was trying. Once the fog obliterated her biological family from her mind's eye, she smiled at her mother's headstone.

"Aunt Tilda helped me navigate all of this, Mom," Rikki said. She squatted down, as if looking her mother directly in the eye. "I know you loved the clinic, and I'm sorry that it ended the way it did." A realization came to her. It seemed to come from outside herself. "Working at the clinic was a way for you to get away from him, wasn't it? You weren't happy with him. All of us kids were launched, well, except that I still lived at home while I worked at Benson and Benson." She chuckled. "But I was making noises about moving out. I remember not wanting you to live alone with him without me there. Were you afraid, Mom? Were you afraid he'd get worse? Had I picked up on that? Or were you hopeful that when I moved out, he'd mellow?"

Rikki knew she'd never get those answers, but it gave her something to muse on. She mentally thickened the fog hiding the sailboat, because her father kept interfering.

Rikki switched gears and told her mother all about the coffee shop, her friends, and how she'd enjoyed serving them and the community. "People need coffee, Mom," Rikki said with a laugh. She reached back and pulled the wooden hair clasp from her hair. "I kept this, Mom. I hope you don't mind. I use it to feel close to you, and I hope you don't think I'm an emotional sap, but I miss you so much."

The tears fell as she touched the headstone. Was that her way of trying to feel her mother? She wasn't sure, but it felt grounding. When she felt more in control of her emotions, she reminisced about her childhood years, including the time her mother had to untie Johnny Stewart from the swing set where Rikki had tied him. What? They were playing pirates, and Rikki was, as always, the captain of the pirate ship. Johnny was trying to organize a mutiny. She *had* to tie him up. But it was probably the fact that she left him out there while she went inside for a sandwich that upset her mother. Of course, that incident was never relayed to Rikki's father.

"We had some secrets, didn't we, Mom?" Rikki pulled her coat tighter around her. It was already getting too dark to see. She hated to leave, but she needed to go. "I'll stop by again tomorrow morning, Mom. Before I head home. I don't think I'll ever be back here, and Shanice says you'll be riding home with me anyway."

She headed to her hotel, checked in, and had a solo Thanksgiving dinner at the hotel restaurant. She sent a selfie of her profile and her plate of food to the friends' chat group and was delighted when a slew of Thanksgiving feast photos from her friends flooded her phone.

The next day, she kept her promise to visit her mother. The hotel manager was even kind enough to give her three potted mums to bring and place on her grandparents' and mother's graves. After her visit, she felt a little lighter. She didn't even need to invoke the paper sailboat this time. Maybe she was making progress.

She made a quick restroom stop near the front gates and then was on the road home. Home was Denton Heights, of that she was sure. Wilkes-Barre was where she had been born and lived for the first twenty-four years of her life. Closed chapter. No. Closed book.

As she eased onto the highway with its post-Thanksgiving Day traffic, she mused on her visit.

"Mom," Rikki said, glancing over at the passenger seat, hoping Shanice was right, "Part of me loves Dad. You know, like, my elementary school days. He was fun. He played with me. He helped me with homework. But something flipped somewhere. I think I didn't turn out to be what he thought I should be. I'm sure it wasn't all about me, but maybe it was because he was losing control of you and tried to control me." Rikki laughed out loud. "And we know how trying to control me goes, don't we?"

She sighed and said, "But it's really clear that I'm not loved by anyone there. Not anymore, for whatever reason. And if I'm not valued, then I have to just stay away. You know?" At this point, she knew she was reasoning things out loud to herself, but it felt good. It felt good to acknowledge how hurt she was by them. And her father still found ways to hurt her. Like making Caroline call Rikki on the anniversary of her mother's death. And Caroline? That was the one that really hurt. Caroline didn't have to do it. Somehow, he made her.

"Ass," Rikki said and sighed. "I don't know why I became his enemy, but he doesn't get to have any more of my energy."

It would take time, but she hoped she could reach a point where she could be indifferent toward him and her siblings. Well, mainly him. Someone, somewhere, once said that the opposite of love is not hate, but indifference. And that was now the goal, because keeping this hatred burning was not serving her at all.

As Rikki drove away from her former life, she also knew she would keep her mother's love in her heart forever.

Chapter 20

Upon returning home to Denton Heights, Rikki threw herself into prep for the Holiday Masquerade Ball. It was only three weeks away, and now that she was doing a decent job of freeing her mind from her father and Esme, she was free to guide and participate in her friends' lives. Best of all, she allowed them to participate in hers.

A few days before the ball, Harriet placed the pin in the hem of Rikki's dress and said, "Please don't find this forward, Ma'am, but I like you unguarded like this."

Rikki smirked as she looked down at the older woman squatting in front of her. "My Aunt Tilda would say it was about time I got out of my own way."

Harriet smiled, and it warmed Rikki's heart.

Rikki put her arm out to help the older woman stand and said, "I'm grateful you all were willing to help me on this project." She gestured to the dress.

"It's a miracle they've been able to keep this a secret," Harriet said and adjusted something on the top. "Well, let me rephrase. It's a miracle the college-going *little* has been able to keep the secret. Minjung and Shanice were never a problem."

Rikki laughed again. "Yeah, I think you're right about that."

"And this is a wonderful gesture, Ma'am," Harriet said and stepped back.

"I was hoping it would be," Rikki said, suddenly feeling vulnerable with Harriet's mothering tone.

"Let me hand stitch this hem, add the gorgeous red piping, and then I think you're ready for the ball."

Rikki thanked Harriet for not only designing the dress but also for making it to Rikki's very unique specifications. "Only a few days until the unveiling."

"You'll be the belle of the ball, Ma'am."

It was absolutely *not* her intention to be the belle of the ball; her intention was to let her friends know she loved and appreciated them.

A few days later, on the evening of the ball, Rikki held up the newly framed picture of her mother smiling directly into the camera. She'd dug the picture out of one of her boxes stored at Shasti and Madison's. The photo had been taken at Rikki's college graduation. "Love you, Mom," she said to the image. "Give me strength tonight. I have a lot of people to thank."

She put the photo down and freshened up her deep red lipstick. The color was Harriet-approved because it matched the dress's deep red piping. How Harriet found the exact color piping Rikki wanted was beyond her.

She turned in the full-length mirror and admired the fit. The off-shoulder three-quarter sleeves hit just right. And the delicate chain straps holding up the bodice were a perfect adornment. Her bust looked great, not that she was trying to catch anyone's eye, but the fit was, indeed, very flattering and made her feel good. The mid-length of the skirt was short enough to be interesting, but long enough to cover important areas.

She arrived early to the ball, much to Seamus's delight.

"You look like a dessert, my dear," he said and air kissed both of her cheeks.

"Thank you," she said. "And so do you and the boys." She gestured to Seamus's three subs, who wore candy-cane-striped shorts and matching suspenders. And that was it. Seamus's striped shirt and red shorts with white fur trim would look gaudy on anyone else, but not Seamus.

"Did Robert do the tailoring?" Seamus asked her.

"Nope," Rikki said. "Harriet."

"Ahh," Seamus said, "It fits you like a glove. I think Mistress Rikki is going to have to fight off the ladies with a stick tonight. Or a whip, even."

"Not looking," Rikki said.

"Understood. But I do know one thing. You seem to have found *it* tonight. You seem more grounded."

"Indeed." She knew he wanted her to elaborate, but she didn't. Instead, she excused herself to stand by the front door to personally greet incoming ball-goers.

Lydia came in wearing a delightful Mrs. Claus outfit in deep red. She was alone. Rikki raised her eyebrow in question but didn't ask.

"Mel's moved on," Lydia said, answering Rikki's unasked question. "It's fine. She met a really femmie femme and is hoping for sunsets and ever-afters. And before you ask, I'm fine with it. We ran our course."

Rikki nodded and patted Lydia's bare shoulder. "Enjoy the ball," she said.

"Oh, I will." And with that, Lydia skipped toward a table in the old IGA.

Rikki vowed that the next ball would most certainly *not* be held in the old grocery store space. She wanted something a little more unique for her community. Something that didn't say "left over space" but said, "a space designed to please." Yes, Rikki vowed to be more present from now on.

One by one, she greeted the arriving guests, including her close friends. Once all her friends arrived, she moved to the table she would share with Shasti, Madison, Marta, and Shanice.

When Rikki walked up, Madison placed both hands over her mouth so as not to spill the secret. Shasti looked at Rikki for an explanation of her *little's* odd behavior, but Rikki just made a dramatic shrug and shook her head, indicating that she had no idea.

"You two are up to something," Shasti accused from her seat.

Madison giggled behind her hands. Shanice wheeled over, and her grin was so big that Marta and Shasti simply looked at each other, puzzled.

Rowena, Minjung, and Lydia walked over and gave out hugs to everyone, which was totally out of character for Rowena. Maybe other people were evolving, too, Rikki thought and smiled. Rowena teased Madison and Shanice by saying, "You two are weird." It was then that Minjung started giggling. To her credit, Rowena simply grinned at her submissive but narrowed her eyes, trying to puzzle out what was going on.

Jaleesa, Tina, Dana, and DeShawn were attracted to their laughter and stepped up. Harriet's shit-eating grin sent the other three submissives into uncontrolled giggles. Even the usually composed Minjung was clutching her stomach with laughter.

"It's very well done," Minjung said to Harriet.

Harriet nodded. "Thank you."

"Just wonderful," Shanice said, sounding grown up.

"Indeed," Madison mimicked.

"What is going on?" Shasti asked again. When no one could or would answer, she threw her hands up, exasperated.

And then Victoria waltzed over with a red ombre button-down dress shirt.

Shasti gasped. She'd figured it out. "Rikki Carmichael," she said, awe in her voice. Tears welled up in her eyes, much to the bewilderment of their gathered friends, who still weren't in the know. "You did this?"

"Harriet made it," Rikki said. "Shanice, Madison, and Minjung were my spies."

Shasti reached over to touch the red ombre stripe of Rikki's dress.

Gasps of recognition circled the group.

"Well, damn," Jaleesa said. "We had a spy in our house." She pointed to the colored stripes representing the different colors her family was wearing: red, green, gold, silver, and Jaleesa's white.

"Sorry, Ma'am," Harriet said, a blush spreading on her face. "I was sworn to secrecy."

"And this," Rowena said, pointing to the red sequined stripe. "Thank you for including us in this." She pulled Minjung closer and whispered to her submissive, "You did good." Minjung nestled into her Domme. It made Rikki's heart swell. This was precisely what she'd wanted.

"Mama," Shanice said to Marta, "do you see us? Right there? The snow people print?"

"I see it, baby girl," Marta said. "I see it." She looked up at Rikki, tears in her eyes. "This is special, Boss. Thank you."

Rikki looked over at Lydia and pointed out the deep red piping all around her dress, and then pointed to Lydia's own Mrs. Claus dress.

A chorus of awws went through the assembled friends.

"Thank you, Miss Rikki," Lydia said, obviously grateful to be included. Shasti handed her a much-needed tissue.

"You sneak," Victoria said to Madison. Her gaze then playfully included the other spies. "All of you. How the hell did you know what shirt I was wearing?"

Silence fell over the group as all eyes looked at Madison.

"Sometimes you don't realize that *littles* have ears, Daddy Vic. At the coffee shop last week, you told your blind date what kind of shirt you'd be wearing."

"I did?"

"Yes," Madison said and started laughing. "You even bragged on the brand."

"Oh, geez," Victoria said and shook her head. "Women far and wide can't get the lowdown on me, but this one." She wagged her finger at Madison. "You really are a spy, aren't you?" Victoria snapped her fingers and pointed at Madison. "I knew it. Squirt is your code name."

Everyone laughed and teased Madison for a moment. After that, Rikki was overcome with gushy mushy sentiment from her friends. It was exactly what she needed. She had a quick window to tell them why she'd had a dress made out of all the colors and fabrics her friends would be wearing to the ball.

"I'm glad you're all here," Rikki said. There must have been something in the tone of her voice that forced Shasti to hand Rikki a tissue. "Each and every one of you, in your own way, has lifted me up. I'm coming to realize that leaning on people isn't a sign of weakness. And I've hurt some of you. For that, I'm sorry. You don't hurt the people that are trying to help you."

A few more tissues were distributed.

"When you asked, I often said, 'I'm okay,' but you all knew that I wasn't. I didn't want to seem weak in front of anyone. I thought I could handle all my sh—" She stopped, not wanting to offend the *littles*. "I thought I could handle my *stuff* on my own, and I ultimately had to do that, but I was doing that standing on your shoulders. I thought I was alone. I'm not. Far from it. I have people in my corner. And there's a lot of you." She chuckled, which eased some of the emotional tension. She put an arm around the nearly sobbing Marta, "You'll be okay, Marta."

"I know," Marta said with as much of a laugh as she could muster. "I know."

"Mama's a softy," Shanice said gently and reached for Marta's hand.

"I know," Rikki said, eliciting a soft chuckle from the assembled group. "I have to meet up with Seamus to go over our opening notes in a minute, but I wanted you all to know that I now understand I'm not alone. I was kind of sleepwalking after Aunt Tilda's death and Eileen's unceremonious departure. I'm still grieving my mother's death, too. I felt lonely. I felt that nobody had *me*, you know? But that was so far from the truth. All of you had me. And I realize it now. In my heart of hearts, I understand now that it's okay to get help and that I don't have to be the stoic dominant Domme in the room." She rolled her eyes. "I—" Emotion stopped her words as a wall of friends hugged her and offered words of encouragement.

Rikki, along with every single one of her friends, including the stoic Rowena and the always composed Victoria, had to wipe tears from their eyes. It took a good ten minutes for her friends to disperse, and apparently, Seamus knew enough not to interrupt the lovefest.

Rikki finally stepped away from the group and turned to head toward Seamus, who was waiting patiently near the stage. Madison tugged on her sleeve.

"Miss Rikki," Madison said, "Will you be at the next Rocco's brunch?"

"In January?"

Madison nodded.

"I plan to. Why? What's up?"

"I invited my Professor," Madison said and bounced on her toes. "Professor Bernadette Garneau, Department of Mathematics at Phillips University."

"You invited your teacher?" Rikki said, trying not to raise her eyebrows too high. "Is your professor in the *life*?"

"I don't know," Madison said. "If she is, she's a Domme because she doesn't let anyone get away with late homework or cheating on tests."

"I'll be there, little one," Rikki said. She pointed toward the stage. "I have to go. I have to try to keep up with Master Seamus now."

"You'll be great, Miss Rikki," Madison said as she turned and put her arms out to her sides like an airplane. She flew back into Shasti's open arms.

Rikki made a mental note to talk to Shasti about the potential disaster of having a person from outside the community attend their brunch. A plan was forming. She'd run it by Shasti later. For now, she had a community to uplift for another inspiring holiday ball.

~~~

Three weeks later, a new calendar year had started. In late December, Rikki had quietly turned thirty-six with no surprise parties or parades.

Although Rikki did acquiesce when Madison insisted on another cookie cake to celebrate. And in those three weeks, Shasti and Rikki successfully implemented their plan. Madison wasn't privy to the fact that they had gotten the word out that a vanilla might be attending the January brunch at Rocco's. The friends each sent their regrets about attending brunch on the group chat. Madison was very attentive to the group chat and understood why it would only be Shasti, Rikki, Brittany, and her at the brunch that morning. Madison was disappointed, of course, but hopefully none the wiser.

Rikki glanced over at Brittany in the passenger seat as they made their way to Rocco's. "We are vanilla. You can talk about Patrice, but please don't refer to her as mistress or anything like that."

"I can be vanilla, Miss Rikki," Brittany said. "But why do I have to go to the meet-the-teacher brunch? It's snowing." She gestured to the flurries. "And besides, everyone else got out of it."

"Miss Patrice wants you to experience more than your room at home and the coffee shop."

"Fine," Brittany said and crossed her arms. "Ma'am," she added.

Rikki wasn't in the mood for Brittany's brattiness and hoped beyond hope that Madison's teacher wouldn't show. After the brunch, Shasti planned to have a talk with Madison about inviting *non-lifers* into the fold. She clearly should have asked Shasti first, and Shasti would have made that clear.

Rikki hoped the brunch would be quick. She had to keep an eye on the storm. If the snow got too heavy, she'd need to hustle back to close the shop so her employees could get home safely. And then she could spend a lovely afternoon bundled up in a blanket watching *Roman Holiday*. Oh, yes, a dose of Audrey Hepburn was just the ticket for a snowy afternoon, any afternoon really.

Rikki pulled into the nearly empty parking lot and, before getting out, Brittany said, "You like helping people, don't you, Ma'am?"

Rikki chuckled. "I think I'm hardwired for it." She looked over at the young woman in the passenger seat. "Why do you ask?"

"We're out here going to a truck stop in the snow, which is kind of crazy, but you're doing it for Madison."

"Yeah," Rikki said. "I'll keep an eye on the storm if that'll make you feel better."

"It will." Brittany looked down at her gloved hands. "But you're also keeping your promise to Miss Patrice."

"Mm hmm." Rikki didn't want to open the car door and disrupt Brittany's thoughts. Brittany was important to her, too.

"And me," Brittany said. "You always say you want me to grow and learn and stuff."

"I do."

Brittany looked directly at Rikki. "Why? Why me? Why Madison? Why anyone?"

"Maybe selfishly, it helps me feel good."

"Really? I never thought about it that way." Brittany grinned. "So, helping other people helps you somehow."

"I guess."

Brittany put a closed fist up to her head and then exploded her fingers outward. "Mind blown."

"We have to get in there."

"I know, but Ma'am?"

"Yes?" Rikki said.

"I wish I had a passion like yours. Helping people, I mean."

Rikki smiled at her young charge, patted her leg twice, and said, "You'll find yours. Ready to go in?"

Brittany nodded and reached for the door handle.

"Best behavior," Rikki reminded.

"Yes, Ma'am." It sounded genuine. "I work at the coffee shop. I do vanilla all day long."

Rikki chuckled and stepped out of the car.

Shasti and Madison had just pulled into the parking lot, and the timing couldn't have been more perfect. They got out of their respective cars at the same time. Shasti looked to the sky. She, too, was worried about the snow, but when she gestured to the bouncing, pirouetting Madison, she shrugged. Disappointing a *little* was never high on anyone's list.

Madison ran to the front door, her pink Trolls scarf flying behind her, and then held the door open for everyone to enter first. Once inside, Madison craned her neck, looking.

"There she is. I told you she would come." Madison waved at a woman seated at one of the tables near the window. She ran over and greeted the woman. "Hi, Professor Garneau."

"Hi," the woman said softly. She had short disheveled blonde hair and wore a light blue flannel shirt, obviously designed for comfort. She was a soft butch, if ever there was one. She looked to be in her early thirties. The woman's movements were sure and confident. Teachers had to be sure and confident, Rikki mused, otherwise their students would eat them alive.

"I told them you would come," Madison said to her teacher. She pointed back to them near the front door, where they were undoing scarves and taking off jackets and hats in the warm diner.

The woman turned to face them. Her blue eyes pierced Rikki's brain. *Whoa.* Her feminine features softened the masculine demeanor.

Rikki blinked, breaking the spell. The woman looked familiar. *Do I know you?* It was an odd yet warm feeling. Maybe she'd come into the coffee shop at some point? Rikki's heart sped up. She was riveted by the woman's comportment, her very presence. The woman smiled, it was a nervous smile, and Rikki wanted to rush over to the booth and tell her everything was going to be okay and that she would protect her from the world. She also wanted to reach out and touch the woman's perfect dimples.

Rikki exhaled loudly. Too loudly. Rikki realized her mouth was hanging open, so she shut it. Shasti turned to look at her. A smile lit Shasti's eyes, but Rikki was too riveted by the blonde stranger to make sense of it.

"Please join us, Professor," Rikki heard Madison say.

Yes, Rikki thought, not taking her gaze off the teacher. *Please do.*

~~~ The End ~~~

About the Author

Danielle Grainger

Dani is a retired instructor who currently resides in the southeastern USA when she's not travelling the country and putting her newfound freedom to good use. She has always been an avid reader and ventured into writing after reading several novels she felt didn't accurately represent the BDSM lifestyle. With so many rampant misconceptions, she took a chance and crafted admittedly idealized versions of possible experiences. Ever the romantic, Dani hopes not only to entertain her readers but to enlighten and educate them as well.

Dani's Amazon Author Page:
www.amazon.com/stores/Danielle-Grainger

Dani's Facebook:
facebook.com/danielle.grainger.7777

Dani's Instagram:
DaniGrainger84

Dani's Goodreads Page:
www.goodreads.com/author/show/19699760.Danielle_Grainger

Books by Danielle Grainger

THE DENTON HEIGHTS SERIES

The Denton Heights Series is the series that comes BEFORE the Bernadette Series. This group of books tells the stories of the beloved characters who populate the Bernadette Series world and live the BDSM lifestyle. We learn more about the origin stories of Madison and Shasti; Jaleesa, Tina, Harriet, Dana, and DeShawn; Rowena and Minjung; and Rikki. Victoria (AKA Daddy Vic), Lydia, and Brittany also feature in this series. The Denton Heights Series is basically the "Prequel Series" to the Bernadette Series.

Under Her Wing (Denton Heights Book 1)
(The Shasti and Madison Story)
An age-gap lesbian erotic romance with consensual light BDSM aspects.
*** 2023 Finalist in the Golden Crown Literary Society Awards ***

Madison Kim finds herself on a bus bound for Denton Heights, Ohio, a Cincinnati suburb. Her mother sent her there without notice to care for an elderly Korean woman Madison had never met. Madison is twenty-two-and-three-quarters years old and has a high school diploma, but she isn't smart enough to go to college...so they tell her. Now, she spends her time caring for Mrs. Park, going to the beloved Cincinnati Zoo, and watching movies on her outdated phone. She's not really sure why she's there, but she's taking it day by day. Then, she meets strong, nurturing Miss Shasti at a tea dance.

Shasti Balakrishnan has been looking for someone to call hers for more years than she cares to count. She wants a woman to love and care for in a nurturing Mommy Domme/*little-girl* scenario. She's thirty-two and already a partner in a thriving medical clinic in Denton Heights, but truth be told – she's lonely. She thought she'd found a companion in Amber back in D.C., but that fizzled out once they realized they weren't what each other wanted—or needed. And then she meets adorably precocious Madison at a tea dance.

ISBN: 978-1-953734-10-5 (e-Book)
ISBN: 978-1-953734-13-6 (Paperback)

In Her Cage (Denton Heights Book 2)

(The Jaleesa and Tina Story)
A lesbian interracial erotic romance with consensual light BDSM aspects.

Jaleesa Whitmore is a lesbian Domme in and out of fast relationships fueled by sex. She didn't understand addiction. Not yet, anyway. Although she had been almost one full year sober, she was done with it. She was moments from heading down the familiar road of drinking that always made her feel good and filled that void. She was about to get her life back on its old track when a fateful encounter with a stranger, who would become a trusted friend, halted her downslide. She didn't know it then, but this encounter would not only lead her to a series of events and people that would change how she looked at life, but also how she approached it.

Tina Jenkins likes women but is asexual and afraid to try for another relationship. She does understand addiction. Just shy of eleven years clean of her opioid addiction following a dental procedure right out of high school, her parents carefully constructed and monitored everything in her world. It didn't matter that she was thirty-one years old and still living in the pink bedroom in her parents' house. It didn't matter that her mother now had to work from home and that her parents had to track her location and conduct routine searches of her bag, car, computer, phone, and room. None of it mattered because she was clean.

And then asexual Tina meets promiscuous Jaleesa. And everything changed for both of them.

ISBN: 978-1-953734-28-0 (e-Book)
ISBN: 978-1-953734-29-7 (Paperback)

Within Her Grasp (Denton Heights Book 3)
(The Marta and Shanice Story)
A lesbian age gap interracial erotic romance with consensual light BDSM aspects.

"Within Her Grasp" is an age-gap interracial lesbian romance that tells the tale of two women who had settled for unhappy lives. And then they meet.

White, thirty-something Marta Ingersoll was done with people. She just wanted to be left alone at work and at home, thank you. Her inside cat and the outside stray were all she needed. And her sister, Nora, too, of course. But that was it. And then, one fateful afternoon, her instincts to save a woman in obvious distress kicked in, and her life was shoved onto a strange new course.

Black, twenty-something Shanice Ward never got a break. Life had thrown challenge after challenge at the young woman, and this latest thing was too much, but it wouldn't stop. Woken up from a sound sleep by someone trying to remove her clothing, she shrieked for him to leave her alone. He didn't, but then, the most amazing thing happened. She discovered that superheroes were real, and one had just flown into her room to save her, and her life was shoved onto a strange new course.

ISBN: 978-1-953734-30-3 (e-Book)
ISBN: 978-1-953734-31-0 (Paperback)

By Her Command (Denton Heights Book 4)
(The Rowena and Minjung Story)
A lesbian interracial erotic romance with consensual BDSM aspects.

"By Her Command" is an erotic interracial lesbian romance containing consensual aspects of BDSM. It finds Rowena Tate in need of a submissive who can also manage her household. It's also the tale of Minjung Lee, who is desperate to find a Domme so she won't find herself homeless again. Trust does not come easily for either of them.

Rowena is a white Domme in her late thirties. Through experience, she has come to believe that most, if not all, submissives are selfish creatures who only want what she can provide without considering the person behind the flogger and the paycheck.

Minjung is an East Asian submissive in her mid-thirties. Through experience, she has come to believe that most, if not all, Dominants are selfish creatures who go well beyond contracted limits because there is no one to tell them not to.

Despite their reservations, both are told by members of the Denton Heights BDSM community that they are a good match and lucky to have found each other. Rowena isn't so sure. Neither is Minjung. Time will tell, won't it?

ISBN: 978-1-953734-32-7 (e-Book)
ISBN: 978-1-953734-33-4 (Paperback)

Toward Her Passion (Denton Heights Book 5)
(A Rikki Carmichael Story)
A lesbian erotic reminiscence with consensual BDSM aspects

Rikki Carmichael is strong, stoic, and in charge. She does *not* need help from anyone. She can navigate her own life, thank you very much, and resents her friends' efforts to give her charity. She doesn't take charity; she gives it. Financial troubles threaten to topple her coffee shop business, her livelihood, and her sense of self-worth. Abruptly single and oddly uninterested in finding a new relationship, be it a long-term life partner or a short-term lover, she finds herself reminiscing about past loves and relationships: Hard Eileen, fun Emily, newbie Sarah, and young Jessica.

The anniversary of her mother's death all those years ago sends her into another bout of 'deep downs,' the code words her mother used for Rikki's bouts with depression growing up. Her bestie, Shasti, advises her to make room for someone, a new lover, or a life partner. Shasti wants Rikki to send a message to the universe that she is ready to receive someone into her life. And, lo and behold, in walks Esme, a blonde bombshell customer at the coffee shop. Rikki's hopes are lifted...until they aren't. With no biological family left to lean on, Rikki has to find the strength to become vulnerable and ask for help. Easier said than done. It's much easier to counsel others than to ask for help for herself. She discovers, however, that asking for help is where real strength lies.

ISBN: 978-1-953734-40-2 (e-Book)
ISBN: 978-1-953734-41-9 (Paperback

THE BERNADETTE SERIES

Dr. Bernadette Garneau holds a Ph.D. in Mathematics and has just gotten out of a four-year relationship. Shortly after the breakup, she began an exploration of her repressed sexual desires. One message from a beautiful and powerful online Mistress and Bernadette leaps into the world of BDSM. The Mistress takes charge, and Bernadette reels in the heady power this stranger has over her. She has gotten a taste of the life, and she wants more. She needs more. Several online and in-person experiences with BDSM and Power Exchange have led to cravings she doesn't quite understand. A brief sexual exchange with an online Goddess unleashes an incredible pain-to-pleasure connection that she hadn't understood before. As she sifts through the posers and one-night stands, she homes in on what her submissive nature needs from a Domme. The Bernadette Series follows Bernadette's journey into the world of BDSM and her search for love and sexual satisfaction. As she said, "I want a monogamous partner who wants to not only love and nurture me but who also wants to drape me over her lovely couch and have her way with me."

Wrecking Bernadette
(Book One in the Bernadette Series)
A lesbian's exploration of her sexuality with consensual aspects of BDSM.

Dr. Bernadette Garneau holds a Ph.D. in Mathematics and has been out of a four-year relationship for four months. One good thing about breaking up is that Bernadette is free to explore her repressed sexual desires. One message from a beautiful and powerful online Mistress, and Bernadette leaps into the world of BDSM. Mistress Ciara takes charge, and Bernadette reels in the heady power this stranger has over her. She has gotten a taste of the *life*, and she wants more. She *needs* more.

ISBN: 978-1-953734-00-6 (e-Book)
ISBN: 978-1-953734-14-3 (Paperback)

(S)mothering Bernadette
(Book Two in the Bernadette Series)
A lesbian's continuing exploration of her sexuality with aspects of BDSM.

Dr. Bernadette Garneau's universe is pushing her toward change. Her initial experiences with BDSM and Power Exchange have led to cravings she doesn't quite understand. A brief sexual exchange with an online Goddess unleashes an incredible pain-to-pleasure connection she hadn't understood until that encounter. But after sleeping on it, she clearly understands that this Goddess would never be the long-term relationship she sought.

Disappointed, she wonders if she should just give up and move back to California to be closer to her family. That is, until she meets Mama_Luvs, an online Mommy Domme. The woman is nurturing yet stern from the start and is just … perfect. And then Mama_Luvs wants to meet. Starry-eyed Bernadette packs for a New Year's Eve weekend, hoping that this time she's found *the one* – the one who wants to love and nurture her but who also wants to drape her over a couch and have her way with her.

ISBN: 978-1-953734-01-3 (e-Book)
ISBN: 978-1-953734-15-0 (Paperback)

Becoming Bernadette
(Book Three in the Bernadette Series)
A lesbian erotic romance with light consensual BDSM aspects.

University professor Dr. Bernadette Garneau has fallen in love with the world of BDSM. She has a nascent interest in the pain-to-pleasure connection, but she has yet to find partners interested in nurturing the soul within her body that they play with. Admittedly, she's had incredible sexual encounters with experienced Dommes, but all of them left her feeling cold for whatever reason. Most of them simply wanted a sadistic roll in the hay. Bernadette wants a strong Domme who will love and nurture her before flogging her on a St. Andrew's cross and afterward when her body is spent.

One afternoon, she finally musters the courage to venture out and meet some new friends in the local BDSM community. In walks a tall, handsome butch woman with fantastic hair and a confident stride. When this woman asks Bernadette, "Are you collared?" Bernadette truthfully answers, "No," and accepts a dinner invitation for that very evening. She is walking on stars when she gets home at 2 a.m. after an ethereal sexual liaison. On the one hand, she wonders who she is becoming – she's never been this promiscuous. And on the other hand, she wonders if this strong butch woman could finally be the Domme of her dreams.

ISBN: 978-1-953734-02-0 (e-Book)
ISBN: 978-1-953734-12-9 (Paperback)

Desiring Bernadette
(Book Four in the Bernadette Series)
A lesbian erotic romance with light consensual BDSM aspects.

*** 2022 Finalist in the Golden Crown Literary Society Awards ***

Rikki Carmichael finally feels that deep D/s relationship she has been craving since her Aunt Tilda introduced her to *the life*. She embraced her dominant side early on, but finding a suitable submissive woman who wanted more than a quick roll in the dungeon proved elusive. That is, until Professor Bernadette Garneau arrived on the scene. Now collared and committed to Rikki, will Bernadette prove to be different, or will she turn out like all the others — fickle and full of lies and deception?

And will this perfect sub stay with her when she realizes Rikki's ship is sinking? She'd almost lost the coffee shop she owns when creditors came knocking down her door en masse, seeking payment for debts that weren't hers. Rikki managed to keep her staff and most of her friends in the dark about it, but she has not been able to get out from under it. With high stakes all around, Rikki looks for the peace she seeks within her relationship with Bernadette. If this one fails, it may be time to leave the *life* entirely and go live in a cabin somewhere isolated in the woods. But buying a cabin takes money – money she just doesn't have.

ISBN: 978-1-953734-03-7 (e-Book)
ISBN: 978-1-953734-09-9 (Paperback)

Loving Bernadette
(Book Five in the Bernadette Series)
A lesbian erotic romance with light consensual BDSM aspects.

Bernadette Garneau, a beloved professor of mathematics, is a natural submissive. She likes structure and rules, and finally found a way of life and a woman who would provide them. The BDSM community she stumbled upon in Denton Heights, Ohio, is where she found Rikki Carmichael, now her dominant partner and fiancée. Rikki is everything she's dreamed of. Yes, Bernadette found the captain of her ship. With Rikki's support and guidance, maybe other parts of her life can finally come together, too – like the respect she deserves but hasn't gotten at the university. Why won't anyone see that she deserves to teach those upper-level courses? And to move out of her closet of an office? What do they know that she does not?

Rikki Carmichael, the respected owner of Rikki's Coffee Shop in town, has finally found the woman of her dreams in super-smart and super-real Bernadette Garneau. Bernadette is a submissive who instinctively knows how to take care of Rikki and accepts Rikki's need to be in charge. Bernadette is the first submissive Rikki's ever had that wasn't solely out for her own gain. Once Rikki can climb out of the deep financial debt she's found herself in, she will finally make their engagement to be married public.

Miscommunication, faulty assumptions, and unmet expectations threaten this union seemingly made in heaven. When life comes at them hard and fast, they must rely on their bond and their loving, self-made family of friends.

ISBN: 978-1-953734-08-2 (e-Book)
ISBN: 978-1-953734-11-2 (Paperback)

www.ingramcontent.com/pod-product-compliance
Lightning Source LLC
Chambersburg PA
CBHW071140260626
47162CB00003B/857